P9-CLS-984

ILLUSIVE

EMILY LLOYD-JONES

LITTLE, BROWN AND COMPANY
New York • Boston

Little, Brown and Company

Hachette Book Group
237 Park Avenue, New York, NY 10017
Visit our website at www.lb-teens.com

Little, Brown and Company is a division of Hachette Book Group, Inc.
The Little, Brown name and logo are trademarks of Hachette Book Group, Inc.

The publisher is not responsible for websites (or their content) that are not owned by the publisher.

First Edition: July 2014

Library of Congress Cataloging-in-Publication Data

Lloyd-Jones, Emily.
Illusive / Emily Lloyd-Jones. — First edition.
pages cm
Summary: "After a vaccine accidentally creates super powers in a small percentage of the population, seventeen-year-old Ciere, an illusionist, teams up with a group of fellow high-class, super-powered thieves to steal the vaccine's formula while staying one step ahead of mobsters and deadly government agents" — Provided by publisher.
ISBN 978-0-316-25456-4 (hardcover) — ISBN 978-0-316-25458-8 (ebook) — ISBN 978-0-316-25457-1 (library edition ebook)
[1. Vaccines—Fiction. 2. Superheroes—Fiction. 3. Adventure and adventurers—Fiction. 4. Robbers and outlaws—Fiction. 5. Organized crime—Fiction. 6. Science fiction.] I. Title.
PZ7.L77877Ill 2014
[Fic]—dc23

2013025295

10 9 8 7 6 5 4 3 2

RRD-C

Printed in the United States of America

To my mother

PART ONE

For they would inherit a world so devastated by explosions and poison and fire that today we cannot even conceive of its horrors. So let us try to turn the world away from war. Let us make the most of this opportunity, and every opportunity, to reduce tension, to slow down the perilous nuclear arms race, and to check the world's slide toward final annihilation.

—President John F. Kennedy,
Radio and Television Address to the American People
on the Nuclear Test Ban Treaty, July 26, 1963

1

CIERE

Ciere Giba wakes to pounding on her hotel door. "This is the NYPD! We have a warrant to search this room."

Sitting up is more difficult than it should be—the sheets are tangled around her naked body. Clutching the duvet to her chest, she frantically takes stock of her surroundings. A teenage boy is facedown on the carpet, one arm thrown out, and a miniature bottle of tequila clutched in his fist. His shirt is missing, and there's a tattoo of a Celtic knot on his left shoulder, the black ink just visible on his dark skin. Ciere would know that tattoo anywhere—it belongs to her best friend, Devon Lyre.

The pounding starts again.

Ciere leaps from the bed. Any second now, NYPD will burst into the room. The first thing they'll do is trip over

Devon, and the second is that they'll see her pink backpack—the one currently holding hundreds in stolen cash.

Bracing herself, she heaves Devon under the bed. He goes with a soft mumble of protest. Good thing he's out—she can only hope he won't wake during an inopportune moment.

After kicking the backpack beneath the bed, Ciere leaps atop the mattress and crouches there, poised for action.

She draws in a long breath and brings a single memory to the forefront of her mind: the hotel room when she first entered it—the faded white carpet, the duvet stretched tight across the bed, and the floral artwork on the walls.

Holding that memory firmly in place, she reaches out and overlays the room's current reality with that image. The illusion is like throwing a sheet over a table—it covers everything. The room's appearance transforms from messy to pristine in a matter of seconds. It's her talent, her immunity.

The illusion flickers and vanishes.

Too bad she's not very talented.

A hard voice rings out. "We're opening the door!"

Ciere hears the click and whirr of the lock; the police must have retrieved a master key from the front desk.

She swallows a curse. Panic flares in her chest, and it gives her the motivation she needs to try again. Concentrating hard, she once more projects the image of the pristine hotel room from her mind and over her surroundings. The illusion slides over the bed, the walls, the table, the chairs. It even extends into the bathroom.

All at once, pressure builds behind her eyes and temples. She's pretty sure this is what divers feel when they go too deep underwater—like being squeezed from every angle. But the illusion is in place, and it's not a moment too soon.

The door is flung wide, and a cop's expansive girth appears framed in the doorway. He peers into every corner of the room before edging farther inside, his gun held at the ready.

"Clear," the cop says, and two more follow him inside.

"There's no one here," the first cop says as he stares into the bathroom. "Looks like the place hasn't even been slept in."

The second cop, a woman, mutters, "This better be the right room." She pushes a strand of hair out of her eyes, tucking it back into her messy ponytail. Louder, she adds, "What did the manager say?"

The third cop, a middle-aged man, strides to the window and throws the blinds aside. Morning sunlight spills through the window, making Ciere's eyes ache. The sour taste of old vodka and peanuts lingers on the back of her tongue. Of all the days to be hungover.

"This is the right room, I'm sure," the first cop answers, peering under the bed.

"No criminal is stupid enough to book a hotel room with

stolen cash." The female cop jerks several dresser drawers open and slams them shut. "This was a damn decoy."

Relief makes Ciere's muscles go limp. This is going to work. The cops will leave. She is about to relax when a loud *BEEEEP* reverberates through the room.

"What was that?" the first cop says, hand drifting to his belt.

Ciere goes cold. That beep is familiar; it's her text alert. *Crap*—she must have forgotten to silence her phone. She bites down hard on her lip, using the pain as a focal point to keep her concentration. She can hold an illusion around her own body for hours, but extending it into her surroundings is like trying to envelop the room with her skin. There's pain and stretching, and it *hurts.*

The woman cop zeroes back in on the room, eyes sharp and nostrils flared. She lifts her gun from its holster and slowly makes her way toward the bed. Her gun is still pointed at the floor, but Ciere knows how fast that barrel could swing up. A chilled breeze coming in through the air conditioner ghosts over her bare skin and she shivers. Despite the fact that the cops can't see her, Ciere finds herself drawing her arms protectively around her chest. It's a useless gesture; a single bullet would tear through her easily. She's had close calls before, but she's never been shot. How long would it take to die of a gunshot wound? She imagines how it would feel for a small ball of metal to slam into her—slam through her. Even so, a bullet would be better than discovery. As an illusionist, she would be taken into custody and given a choice between only two options: work for the government or head for confinement in Blanchard Penitentiary.

What's worse is that Devon will be considered her accomplice. He's been in trouble before, but nothing like this. Could his dad buy him out of a felony charge?

The cop steps closer to the bed. All she has to do is reach out and she'll touch Ciere. Illusion can fool many senses, but touch isn't one of them.

Ciere holds her breath. Her chest aches and her lungs burn, but an exhalation could give her away. She is close enough to the woman to see her pores and the way her hair curls around one ear. Too close. She's too close. Just a few more inches—

The cop turns and stalks away from the bed. "I think it came from the fire alarm."

The first cop snorts. "So we can't tell the manager if he's got criminals squatting in his hotel or not, but we can tell him that the fire alarm batteries need replacing. Great."

"We'll post Greg in the lobby," the other man replies. "If the thief is still here, we'll find him." He walks out the door, holstering his gun. The first cop follows. The last cop, the woman, pauses with her hand on the doorknob. Her gaze sweeps over the hotel room one last time.

The door clicks shut, and the illusion shatters.

Ciere falls back onto the bed, panting and trembling in reaction to the unspent adrenaline still humming through her blood. She sprawls there for a long moment, hyperaware of her surroundings—the crinkly material of the duvet, the rumble of the air conditioner, and the sunlight beaming down on her. Scrambling off the bed, she goes to the door and rises to her tiptoes, peering through the peephole. She can just make out three fuzzy figures strolling down the hall in the direction of the elevators. Ciere waits, heart still pounding, watching as the three cops vanish around a corner. What if this is a ruse? What if they come back?

When a full minute has passed, she relaxes. "Okay," she says aloud, "not the best hotel wake-up call I've ever had."

She retrieves one of the hotel's robes and slips it on. The terry cloth is soft and clean, and she belts it around her waist with a feeling of relief.

Crouching, she reaches under the bed and grabs her backpack. It's a faded pink, edged with glittering bits of plastic. The figurine of a tiny white cat with a pink bow on its head dangles from the main zipper. Her mother gave Ciere the backpack when she was ten, telling Ciere the cat's name was Hello Kitty. It was part of some foreign franchise, an export that made it out before Japan closed its borders.

Ciere digs into the front compartment, and her fingers

close on the hard plastic of a cell phone. The phone is a cheap, disposable number—one of the many that Ciere keeps shoved in her backpack.

The text reads: *You robbed a bank???* The area code is from Pennsylvania, so it can only be from Kit Copperfield.

She texts back. *How the hell did you know?*

> *Because someone walked out of a Newark bank with $40,000.*

Ciere grins. *And you immediately thought of me?*

> *The only other thing taken was a Hello Kitty bobblehead. The news is calling you "The Kitty Burglar."*

That makes Ciere laugh. The Hello Kitty bobblehead sits on the bedside table, a testament to her recent criminal success. She nabbed it from a clerk's desk, thinking it would match her backpack.

Why should you care? Ciere's fingers dart over the keypad and press Send.

> *I told you to keep a low profile. Come home. Now.*

Why?

Because I'm the closest thing you have to a parental authority.

A moment later, a new message appears.

Also, I have a new job for you.

What?

Not over the phone.

It's enough to intrigue Ciere; she texts him back, saying they'll meet later. She has other things to worry about at the moment.

As if on cue, Devon makes a choked noise. He sounds as if he's gagging on his own morning breath. A hand appears, groping along the carpet as he tries to pull himself out from under the bed. It appears to take great effort for him to roll onto his back. He grinds the heel of one hand into his eyes, trying to focus his bleary gaze.

"Did you shove me under the bed?" His words are overlaid with a light English accent.

"No," Ciere lies, straight-faced. "Why did I wake up naked?"

Devon rolls his shoulders and sits up. He tilts like a man who has stepped aboard a boat for the first time and is unsure how to keep his feet. "You were blathering on about how your clothes were a metaphor for how restrictive society is, and you needed to be free." He looks down at his naked chest, and adds, "I tried to do the same, for solidarity's sake, but I passed out before I could get to my trousers."

"Well"—Ciere rubs a hand over her eyes—"at least I'm a philosophical drunk."

She staggers into the bathroom, ready to wash the remnants of last night's makeup from her face and hair. Pushing the bathroom door open brings a surprise. There is something in the bathtub—something she doesn't remember from the night before.

She remembers robbing the bank and going to a private messaging service to send most of the money to one of her semi-illegal accounts. It's standard practice; there's no way the feds can touch an account in Switzerland, even if they trace it back to her. The downside is that Ciere can't touch it, either. But it'll be there if she ever decides to flee the country—in her line of work that is a definite possibility.

She remembers getting on a bus out of Newark and arriving in Manhattan. She remembers the rave—the shots of clear vodka, with drops of red thrown in, held suspended in the liquid like tiny gems. She can recall the burn of the drinks as they slid down her throat, reveling in the heat and weightlessness. She remembers the flashing lights, the pills she saw passed from hand to hand, the thrum of the music in her bones, and the swell of dancing bodies all around her. The crowd moved in waves, empty cups surfing a tide of hands. People screamed just to make noise—although it couldn't be heard above the blaring music. The crowd seemed to emanate joy and energy—laced with fear and desperation. She vaguely remembers Devon's arm around her waist and her hand on his shoulder as they steadied themselves enough to walk up the stairs into the hotel. She hit every button in the elevator because the lights were pretty.

But here's the thing—she doesn't remember how a dog got into the bathtub.

Ciere doesn't own a dog. She's never even seen this particular dog before. It's small and white, curled into a ball, and dead asleep in the middle of the bathtub. She reaches down and touches the soft fur. The pup's nose twitches, and it quivers in that way animals do when dreaming. Thankfully, her illusion reached into the bathroom. She unknowingly hid the dog from view when the cops were searching for her.

"Please tell me we didn't knock over a pet store," Ciere says.

Devon fumbles with the coffeemaker, his fingers trembling as they rip open a fresh filter. "I think you found him in an alley." Devon is an eidos, which means he has perfect recall. But just like a camera taking pictures with a dirty lens, things get fuzzy when he's inebriated.

The puppy twitches itself awake and rolls to its feet. Its eyes are big and black, the white fur stained brown around its face. It sees Ciere and begins wagging its tail frantically.

She holds out a hand for the pup to sniff. It knocks its head against her palm, all but begging aloud for a scratch. She obliges, rubbing its ears. The dog leans into her and its eyes droop almost shut. Ciere fights back a surge of warmth and protectiveness—she wants to pick up the puppy and snuggle it to her chest. Maybe feed it some strips of bacon and smooth out the tangles in its white fur. She swallows and tries to shove that reaction aside. Emotions wreak havoc when she's on the job. She learned that a long time ago. So instead of cuddling the dog, she picks it up and sets it on the bathroom floor. It can fend for itself. It will have to if it wants to survive.

"It needs a bath. You sure it's male?" she calls to Devon.

He answers, "How the hell should I know? You think the first thing I do when I'm pissed is gawk at a dog's bollocks?"

The puppy follows Ciere out of the bathroom. She leans up against the dresser while Devon plugs in the coffeemaker. When she tells him about the cops, he looks startled. "Christ. Talk about close calls. I know I'm supposed to be the manly-slash-brave type, but I've got a new plan. I say we find a rock to hide under."

"We're going to Philadelphia," Ciere says. "Kit texted me. He has a new job for us."

Sitting together on the mussed bed, sipping cups of coffee, they watch as the puppy tries to dig a hole in the floor. This is the first time Devon has partnered with her as a fellow crook. The alliance is only temporary—Devon's summer break ends in August. He'll be shipped back to some elite prep school where he'll show up drunk to every class, if he shows at all. As an eidos, he could ace everything. Which is exactly why he flunks out. It's safer to go unnoticed.

But for the moment, none of that matters.

They are young. They are criminals. They are glorious.

They are immune.

2

CIERE

When Ciere was eight, her mother told her the story of how the immunities came into existence.

Once upon a time, there was a pandemic.

It was a new strain of meningococcal disease. Named Meningococcas Krinotas—or simply the MK plague—it embodied the worst traits of both viral and bacterial meningitis. Because it was a virus, antibiotics had no effect, and the current viral vaccines were ineffective.

The result was a disease that, when diagnosed, was always followed by a funeral.

In 2017, the virus first cropped up in Chad and it went mostly unnoticed. Even when the disease spread to Niger, Mali, and Algeria, only a few virologists took notice. But when Egypt's morgues overflowed, the rest of the globe finally woke up.

Countries scrambled to make sense of the new disease, and governments advised their citizens to avoid Africa. The warnings came too late. A woman returned from a trip to the pyramids. She took one step into John F. Kennedy International Airport and there was no going back. The disease swiftly spread throughout America, to Europe, to the Middle East, and into Asia.

Schools shut down; children stayed indoors; public areas were avoided; hospitals had to turn people away. A black market in useless antibiotics raged, some of them genuine but most of them not. People who usually dealt in pot or coke found themselves selling penicillin. Not that it helped.

About six months after the MK plague landed on American soil, a spot of hope finally appeared. Fiacre Pharmaceuticals announced a new vaccine called Praevenir. It wasn't a cure, but the vaccine provided immunity against MK. Almost immediately the vaccine sold out, and Fiacre Pharmaceuticals was hard-pressed to keep up with the demand. The company, small by industry standards, was headed by owner and CEO Brenton Fiacre. His company enjoyed overnight success. The commercials for Praevenir flashed on televisions worldwide.

We exist in uncertain times. But there is one thing you can count on. Praevenir—the only vaccine that protects against the deadly MK virus. Protect yourself and your loved ones. Be certain. Praevenir. (Side effects may include itching at the site of injection, dizziness, weakness, fever, and rash. More serious side effects may include fainting, convulsions, and difficulty breathing. Praevenir is not recommended for women who are nursing or pregnant.)

Later, the blame was placed on undue pressure to distribute the vaccine. Fiacre Pharmaceuticals simply did not take the time it needed to thoroughly test the vaccine. It was pushed through and approved by the FDA in a matter of months.

If the truth had been known, the commercials would have sounded something like this:

Side effects may include itching at the site of injection, dizziness, weakness, fever, and rash. Approximately 0.003% of those vaccinated may experience one of the following adverse effects: telepathy, perfect recall, increased intuition, the ability to create illusions, levitation, body manipulation, and hypnosis. Praevenir is not recommended for a world that wants to avoid global conflict.

And so everything humanity had thought about itself came crumbling down. Scientists scrambled to make sense of the side effects. Everyone had questions. How many had been vaccinated? Millions? Billions? How many had these powers? What was the extent of the new abilities?

Chaos broke out. Six months after Praevenir's release, Brenton Fiacre locked himself and his family in a warehouse full of the vaccine. He blew it to pieces, killing everyone inside and destroying what was left of his creation.

Some claimed the vaccine's side effects were meant to change the world for the better. This would be the beginning of a new world order—an age of real superheroes, here to solve humanity's problems. Those with powers would fight crime and put things right. However, there was one flaw with that reasoning.

Human physiology was altered. Human nature wasn't.

Barely a year after Praevenir hit the market, the Pacific War broke out.

3

CIERE

"We ready to go yet?" Ciere asks, poking her head out of the bathroom. Her curls are damp from the shower, but there's no time to let them dry properly.

Devon sits on the bed, his tablet cradled on his knees. "Hold on," he says, and his brow creases in concentration.

"Well, hurry up."

Devon huffs out a breath. "Fetch your things. By the time you're finished, we'll be ready to go."

Each immunity has weaknesses, limitations. Illusions only fool human senses. If the human element is eliminated—say, by a security camera—then the illusion crumbles. Unfortunately, cameras are impervious to suggestion.

For that reason, Ciere usually wears a physical mask of some sort—a ski mask or a balaclava. That way, if a camera catches her, all that will be seen is a petite teenage girl wearing a mask. There will be no record of her facial features. But her usual mask is missing. She vaguely remembers it vanishing in the midst of a mosh pit.

"So are we taking or leaving the dog?" Ciere asks. She tries to ignore the way the puppy leans against her ankle and pants up at her. The stupid thing looks so happy to see her. "I'm not exactly the pet-owning type."

"Come on," Devon says. He has wedged a hotel pen between his teeth and chews on it absentmindedly. "Doesn't every great hero need a mascot?"

"I'm not a hero," Ciere grumbles. "And I thought you fulfilled the mascot requirement."

Devon makes a disgruntled noise. "Shut up. Mascots are just there to look cute. I'm useful."

She can't argue with that. Devon has been studying security systems for years. Specifically, he's studied how to hack security with his illegally modified tablet. "God, I love these wireless systems," he murmurs. "So much easier to break into. One more... just a minute... and there! Loop's in place—we've got about three minutes before it's blatant that something's off." He takes the pen from his mouth and uses it to gesture at Ciere. "Well, go on, then. Do your thing."

Ciere closes her eyes. She conjures up an image of an old woman—white hair pooled into a bun, wrinkles settling in around her features—and her clothes shift into sagging polyester. She darkens her skin, altering its shade to match Devon's. A young man and his grandmother will look perfectly innocent.

Devon shakes his head, grinning. "You have no idea how mad it is to see that."

Arm in arm, she and Devon emerge into downtown Manhattan. Despite the fact it isn't yet noon, the sun already beats down on the back of Ciere's neck. She sucks in lungfuls of hot, humid air, tasting sweat and exhaust. Steam flows up from sewer grates, and people swarm the sidewalks—everyone from the homeless with their blackened teeth and sunken eyes to businessmen with tailored suits and briefcases. Ciere has to dodge several tourists as they shuffle past. She tilts her head back and gazes at the city. The buildings are an odd mix of classical arches, sleek skyscrapers, and the grunge that has taken root in the urban areas like mold in an old bag of bread.

Devon releases her arm, hand raised to flag down a taxi. One screeches to a stop, and Ciere slides gratefully into the backseat, the leather upholstery sticking to her bare legs. In her illusion, she wears a pantsuit. In reality, she wears a sundress. It's too hot for anything heavier.

The cab driver gives Ciere's dog a doubtful look, and she smiles. "Don't worry," she lies, trying to sound old. Illusions won't change her voice. "The dog's trained."

The cabbie turns away with a grunt of acceptance, and

Devon rattles off the name of the train station. The car flies forward and Ciere digs her nails into the worn leather of the seats. The cab swings into traffic in a move both terrifying and utterly illegal. Ciere quickly fumbles for her seat belt. Once she's firmly belted in, she closes her eyes, hoping for enough time to rest.

Only minutes later, Devon touches her arm and his voice is in her ear, low and urgent. "Four turns," he says.

It takes her a moment to bring her mind around, and when she does, she jerks fully awake. There are ways to tell if you're being followed, either on foot or by car. One of the more reliable ways is to count how many turns a person behind you takes.

"We're being followed?" Ciere asks softly.

Devon nods. His eyes are intent on the rearview mirror. "Black Honda Pilot, looks like the 2016 make. Didn't know those things still ran. Tinted windows. I've got the plate numbers, too."

"Feds?"

"Not government-issue plates, but you never know," Devon murmurs. "Options?"

Ciere frowns. "Not a lot we can do in a cab. Not if we don't want to seem suspicious. Hopefully there'll be a lot of traffic around the station and we can duck into the crowd."

It's not a good plan, but they're not swamped with options.

When the cab pulls up in front of the station, Devon shoves a handful of twenties at the cabbie and scrambles out of the car, following Ciere. She's already slammed her door, and she strides into the train station, holding the dog in her arms. There isn't a huge crowd, but there are enough people around to make Ciere relax. Devon falls into step beside her. "I think the tail drove on," he says.

"So our plan worked?" she replies.

"Actually, I think there wasn't any place for them to park."

"Can we pretend our plan worked?"

"If anyone asks, we made a daring escape."

They find an empty bench just inside the station. They've got a good twenty minutes to waste, so to pass the time, Ciere says, "I spy..." They have their own version of this game. Instead of spying objects, they look for security. There are two types of deadly agents, and it's a point of pride that good crooks can tell the two apart.

"Man lurking near the women's toilet," Devon mutters.

Ciere squints through the crowd. She can just make out the man—he wears a baseball cap. His eyes continually roam over the crowd and there is a slight bulge around his left ankle. "Mobster," Ciere says firmly.

Devon nods and gestures to a woman lounging against another wall. She pretends to check her cell phone. She wears business casual, a matching skirt and blazer. Her blouse's neckline is low enough that Devon looks interested in more than the game. This time the bulge is under her right shoulder. "Fed," Ciere says.

"Damn," Devon says. "Can't hit on a fed."

"Can't hit on a mobster, either," Ciere points out.

The fed eyes the mobster. The mobster grins and touches two fingers to the rim of his baseball cap in a mocking acknowledgment. Eyes narrowing, the fed turns away from the taunt. The feds used to go after organized crime, but that was before the war.

As she and Devon wait, Ciere digs into her backpack for the Hello Kitty bobblehead she swiped from the Newark bank. She's not one for sentimental keepsakes, but when she saw it on the teller's desk, it triggered a rush of memories—the smell of trees, a warm hand in hers, and the scent of lavender. Taking the bobblehead seemed like a harmless way to hold on to those sensations.

Devon makes a concerned noise. "He's looking at us," he says under his breath. "Mob bloke with the hat is giving us the interested eye."

Ciere forces herself not to look. It would be an amateurish slip. "He can't see us—not the real us. My illusion's still up and he's not using a camera."

Devon's mouth creases into a thin line. "Still staring."

"Stop panicking. Maybe you're his type."

"I'm not panicking, I'm just calmly noting the armed mobster who keeps looking at us. What's there to be panicky about?"

Ciere grits her teeth, and says, "Pet the dog—you'll feel better."

Obediently, Devon's hand rises and falls over the dog's head. The puppy leans into his touch, tongue lolling as it pants. Ciere lets her eyes wander everywhere but the mobster; she glances at the crowds, at the fed, at the clock announcing that it's nearly noon on June 26, 2034.

Although she keeps her gaze forward, the rest of her senses strain toward the mobster. That's how she notices another man walking toward him. She glances over and takes in both men, quickly absorbing the details before pretending to study the dog on her lap.

The first man, the mobster with the baseball cap, has sandy brown hair and about a thousand teeth. He bares all of them in a grin. Combine that grin with his six-foot-something height and the way his sleeves strain over thickly muscled arms, and it's a shudder-worthy sight. The man looks like he wrestles great white sharks for fun and probably wins.

The second man is less terrifying. His face is lean and tanned, his blond hair bleached by sun. He isn't an imposing figure—about five and a half feet tall and thin-shouldered. But he has a steady expression.

Devon makes a disgruntled noise and focuses his gaze on the men, apparently giving up on subterfuge. "What are they saying?" Ciere asks. Devon learned to lip-read a long time ago.

("Mostly to spy on my older sister and her friends," he once admitted.)

"Not English. Think it's, uh, give me a second." Devon darts a look at the men. "I could be wrong, but I think it's German."

Ciere frowns. "You never learned German? Come on, it's not like it'd be hard for you."

"Hey, we've all got our priorities," Devon protests. "And from what I can tell, knowing security systems and hacking seems a lot more useful than learning the languages of unallied countries." He pauses mid-rant, and then adds, "Also, I flunked out of all my language classes."

"Don't tell me—you refused to learn anything that wasn't a curse or a pickup line."

"Nothing so elaborate. I just didn't show up."

Out of the corner of her eye, Ciere sees the first man point a hand at the crowd, dragging his index finger through the air. When he stops, the tip of that finger is aimed squarely at Ciere and Devon.

"They're walking toward us," Devon says, and his voice shoots up a few octaves.

"Look casual," Ciere says. "My illusion's still up. I'm old and you're a nice young boy who's escorting his granny around. Smile."

Devon forces his mouth into a twitching, teeth-baring parody of a smile. "This good?"

"Hold that expression," Ciere says, "and they'll think you're having a stroke."

A shadow falls over the bench and Ciere looks up, feigning surprise. "Oh," she says, in her best creaky voice, "can I help you, sirs?"

The blond man smiles down at Ciere. "Actually, you can." His English is unaccented, perfectly precise. "Take down your illusion."

Ciere's heart stutters and picks up at double speed. "W-what?"

"It's a good illusion," the man says. "Drop it." The last part isn't a request. His voice holds a confidence that indicates he is used to giving orders and having those orders be obeyed.

Ciere hesitates.

The man raises a finger, twirling it around in a circular gesture. "Chop, chop."

Ciere doesn't move.

He smiles and slips a hand into his jacket pocket, grasping a small, rectangular sheet of paper. "We'll see if this can change your mind."

"Polaroid," Devon mutters, as if he can't help regurgitating the information. "Antique form of instant camera without a digital platform."

The man's smile widens. "Ah, the lad knows his history. Now, if you'll take a look at this..." He holds out the picture and Ciere can't help but glance at it.

She sees a girl with hair that is curly, blonde, and chopped short. The face is round, the chin pointed. To Ciere's eyes, there is something rodentlike about the features. The picture girl is petite, grinning, and sitting at a bus stop beside a tall black boy in designer jeans and a T-shirt. The girl is holding a Hello Kitty bobblehead, gesturing at it like it is the most glorious of trophies. Ciere recognizes the scene immediately. She should—it happened last night.

"I can't," she says, and her voice comes out strangled. "Not here. The fed will see."

The dark-haired mobster slips out of his jacket and holds it out to Ciere. She flinches, but then understands. He drapes it over her head and shoulders, and it's large enough to cover everything but her legs, shielding her from sight. She closes her eyes and inhales. The jacket smells like cheap laundry detergent, with hints of aftershave. Ciere releases the breath—along with her illusion.

The girl who hands the jacket back is identical to the one in the photo.

"Who are you?" she says, and to her credit her voice remains steady. "What do you want?"

It's the blond man who replies. "My name," he says, "is Brandt Guntram."

Brandt Guntram is a mobster. He and the other man, whom Guntram introduces as Conrad, sit on either side of the bench, effectively trapping Ciere and Devon. They could cry for help—the fed nearby would have to react—but neither Ciere nor Devon wants to be on the government's radar. Besides, the fed has begun searching train passengers. She stops people at random and asks them for their ID tags. When one woman doesn't get them off her neck quickly enough, the fed yanks them over the woman's head, heedless of the hair tangled in the chain.

Ciere turns her attention back to the mobsters. These men aren't your garden-variety mobsters. No—when Ciere's luck dives, it dives hard.

"We represent the Gyr Syndicate," Guntram says.

Devon's lips form a silent curse.

The Gyr Syndicate are from Nevada, where they rose to power and eliminated the Mafia, the Triad, and every other gang or cartel that dared enter its territory. Ciere hasn't heard much, but what she does know is enough to frighten any sane criminal. The Syndicate doesn't function like a normal crime family—there are no blood feuds or old entanglements to settle. They operate more like a deadly corporation. Any lawbreakers must answer to the Syndicate when they want to work within their dominion.

"But the Gyr don't come here," Ciere says, feeling slow.

Brandt Guntram nods. "We've been expanding our reach. We thought the East Coast might benefit from a little . . . order."

Ciere bites back a reply, unsure what to say.

Devon has no such problem. "Order?" he says, with such obvious contempt that Ciere feels a thrill of fear.

Guntram seems to finally notice Devon. "This area has been thrown into chaos by the actions of the local criminal element. We're here to remedy that." In other words, Ciere thinks, they're here to stamp out all the competition so their own organization will thrive.

"Also, East Coast cities tend to be more profitable than the Midwest," Devon says.

Ciere yearns to tell him to shut up.

"That, too," Guntram agrees. "And you would know about profitability, wouldn't you? Nice job in Newark. If you hadn't used stolen cash to book that hotel room, no one would have found you." He holds the Polaroid between thumb and forefinger and uses it to gesture at the bobblehead.

At that moment, a voice rings out. It's the fed, raising her voice to a middle-aged man. "Give me your tags," the fed says.

The man scrabbles at his collar, and his hand comes up empty. "I told you," he says heatedly, "I don't know where they are. I think I forgot them—"

"Then you will come with me to the security office."

The man gapes at her. "I haven't done anything wrong. You can't detain me."

Wrong answer. Feds don't back down from such obvious challenges. Predictably, this fed pulls a long baton from her belt.

By now the entire train station is watching, captivated by the drama. No one is paying attention to the two teens on the bench or the two men sitting beside them. "What do you want?" Ciere repeats.

Guntram speaks quietly. "You're to the point. I like that in a person. Well, Ms. Kitty, it's not all that complicated. I want the money you stole."

"I don't have it." Ciere holds the puppy a little closer. "Not anymore."

"I assumed that might be the case," Guntram says. "But I recommend you dig the cash out of whatever hole you stashed it in. That is, unless you'd like this picture and a note slipped under the door of the nearest federal bureau's office."

Ciere's jaw drops. Mobsters don't give the feds tips. It's unthinkable. "You wouldn't. You're lying."

"I'll be entirely honest," Guntram says evenly. "I hate the feds. I just happen to hate poachers more."

A sharp snap breaks through their conversation, the sound of a baton hitting flesh. Ciere winces and briefly closes her eyes. She doesn't need to turn around to see what is happening. The fed must have gotten tired of arguing. When Ciere opens her eyes, she sees Guntram watching her. "You're what, fifteen?" he asks.

Her lips twitch, and she barely manages to voice the correct answer: "Seventeen."

"Too young." Guntram's eyes wander past Ciere to the

scene that's taking place behind her. She hears the thud of the baton, the cries of the man, and the silence of the crowd.

"You wouldn't remember when the Allegiant Act was signed. When everyone was rounded up," Guntram continues. "Like cattle, only with less dignity. People forced into lines, pricked with needles, tested for antibodies, and then told to wear dog tags or else they'd be considered a threat to national security." He reaches out and his fingertip traces the silver chain encircling Ciere's throat. Her own tags are tucked under her dress. "You're too young," he repeats. "Your generation can't remember a time when we all weren't collared. Speaking of which..."

His hand suddenly clamps around her forearm. His fingers are calloused and surprisingly warm. When she instinctively yanks back, his grip doesn't break. Devon makes a sound like he's choking back a shout, but Conrad's hand clamps down on his shoulder, holding him in place. Ciere wants to thrash, to start hitting this man until he lets go, but with that fed only a few feet away, she doesn't dare.

It's over after barely a second. Guntram releases her and she recoils, a strange prickling running through her arm. Her wrist is heavy and cold, weighted down by a silver bracelet.

It's smooth, the only decoration a slight indentation where someone might slip a key. It looks like any normal metal bangle. Ciere tries to pull it over her hand, but it catches. The metal rests snugly against her skin.

"This," Guntram says, and he sounds remarkably calm, "is a little device developed for Alzheimer's patients. Don't bother trying to take it off." He holds up a hand, and Ciere sees something gold glitter in his palm. "Unless you use this key, it'll automatically begin broadcasting a signal to emergency services. For your own good, of course." His smile is an unpleasant thing.

"That's a tracker," Devon says, like Ciere hasn't already figured it out.

"We like a little insurance on our investments," Conrad pipes up, and his deep voice sounds amused. Unlike Guntram's, his speech carries a thick German accent.

Ciere chances one more look at the fed. She is threading zip ties around the man's wrists. She drags him to his feet and hustles him roughly past the crowds, towing him in the direction of the security office. Only after the pair has disappeared does the chatter pick up again.

"You saw what a fed just did to a man who probably left his tags at his motel," Guntram says evenly. "He probably took them off to shower and forgot to put them on again. Now, what do you think those same feds will do to an illusionist who walked out of a Newark bank with forty thousand dollars?"

Ciere shivers, and her fingers twine around the bracelet.

Guntram leans in. "You will give us that money, or I'll give the feds this picture and your location."

"Why are you doing this?" she whispers. "You don't own that bank. Your Syndicate wasn't hurt when I robbed it."

Guntram rolls his shoulder. "That bank was in our territory—territory we're investing in. And we protect our investments."

A memory tugs at her, the voice of the old mantra Ciere has lived her life by: *Don't let anyone see what you are, understand?*

"All right," she says.

"No," says Devon.

"All right," Ciere repeats. "I'll get the money. But…I need some time."

Guntram nods. "That's fair." He pulls a small tablet from his pocket and unfolds it. He glances over the screen and nods again, as if to himself. "I'll be in this general area for a week. I assume that's more than enough time to collect your cash?"

No. "Yes."

Guntram fishes something out of his jacket—a business card. A picture of a falcon in flight stretches from corner to corner, and there's a name and number spelled out in black lettering. "You can use this to get in touch with me." She reaches out to take the card and the tracking bracelet slips a few inches down her arm, settling in around the muscles. Her pulse beats hard against the icy metal.

4

CIERE

Wynnewood is one of the many Philadelphia suburbs. Like most of its neighboring townships, Wynnewood is classified as an elsec—an elite sector. The houses are all brick and stone, tall and proud, their owners competing with one another to see who can grow the most perfect lawn.

A taxi approaches the Montgomery County elsec gate, the car grinding to a halt. The gate looks like a toll station, only with armed guards. A man with an automatic rifle slung over his shoulder strides forward.

Ciere fishes her tags out. They hang from a loose chain around her neck. Other people tuck them into wallets or attach them to bracelets; she has even seen one woman who wore each dog tag as an earring. The government doesn't care, so long as a person has their tags on them at all times.

Ciere doesn't bother to conjure any illusions—there are too many cameras at the gate and little point in fooling the gate guards. Her ID tags will confirm her face and false name. The tags themselves are counterfeit. Kit knows a woman in Minneapolis who can create the microchips and implant the correct government codes.

This guard leans through the open window and says in an uninterested tone, "Tags?"

Ciere hands him both hers and Devon's. His are likewise programmed to let him into any sector—the difference is that the tags are legit.

The guard flashes both sets of tags under a scanner and hands them back. "Go on through."

The gate creaks open and the cabbie edges forward. Past the gate, it's obvious the area is an elsec: perfectly shiny cars sit in driveways, people wearing designer clothes stroll along the sidewalk holding the leashes of designer dogs, and every house is at least three stories tall. There is no sign of homelessness or poverty—that kind of thing upsets the neighbors.

When the cabbie asks for directions, Ciere says, "Turn left onto Penn Road, then left again onto Bolsover Road."

Kit's house is a clone of its elsec neighbors. In other words, it's ostentatious and worth an absolute fortune. The garden wraps around the front of the house, and while Kit's beloved tulips are no longer in bloom, his calla lilies are. A wrought-iron fence, evergreen trees, and Asian bamboo wall separate the house apart from its neighbors. But while the whole effect is pretty, Ciere knows from experience that poison ivy weaves through the bamboo and the wrought-iron fence holds an electrical charge capable of knocking a full-grown man off his feet. To top it off, she once saw Kit researching miniature land mines.

The house is pretty, but it's also nearly impenetrable.

A red light blinks on the house's gate—another one of Kit's safeguards. Ciere waves her tags in front of the sensor and the light blinks green, the gate snapping open. "Come on," Ciere says when Devon hesitates.

"You know he hates me," Devon says.

"Kit doesn't hate you," Ciere hedges, fumbling for her house keys, when the door swings open.

Kit Copperfield is a lean man in his thirties. He has stark features with hollow cheeks, wide at the cheekbones and narrow at the chin. His red hair is long enough to brush his shoulders. Along with the house and neighborhood, his outfit gives the impression of wealth—he wears pressed slacks, a crisp white shirt, and a waistcoat. He looks like a successful businessman. From the eighteenth century.

"I told you," he says, "to keep a low profile."

Ciere winces. "Yeah, about that…"

Kit points his index finger at her. "You. Inside. Now."

Ciere ducks her head and scurries through the open door.

"You," Kit says, seeing Devon for the first time. "I didn't know you'd be bringing a dog with you," he adds to Ciere. He glances at the puppy in Devon's arms. "And a pet."

Devon edges past Kit into the foyer, keeping close to Ciere's back.

"Copperfield," Devon replies with a grim little smile. "Found a buyer for that Pollock yet?"

It's an old jab. Kit fences a lot of stolen property, but he specializes in art. He collects what he can, bits taken from museums and private collections. He once mistakenly bought a counterfeit Pollock ("Number 33"), and Devon pointed it out. Devon knew because the real "Number 33" was on a wall in his father's office. It's still a sore point for Kit, that he hadn't recognized the forgery immediately.

He shuts the door and locks it. "This is why I never had children," he mutters, scowling. "Tell them to clean their rooms, and they leave their socks everywhere. Tell them to eat their vegetables, and you find them sneaking candy. Tell them to keep a low profile, and they rob a bank in the middle of Newark!"

Ciere stomps into the living room and drops her backpack by the couch. It is a gorgeously decorated room, complete with a circular staircase winding upward to the second story. Two of the rear-facing walls hold wide stretches of windows with ironwork wrought into them. Paintings grace the rest of the walls, and the furniture is ornate and older than Devon and Ciere put together. What most people don't know is that the front windows are tinted against outside observers, the paintings mask several safes, and most of the furniture is stolen.

"Yeah, well, you didn't bother to tell me that Jersey is being invaded by the Gyr Syndicate," Ciere says. "I had to find out through other channels."

"I told you to keep your head down."

"But if you'd given me a reason, I might have actually listened to you." Ciere flops onto the couch and crosses her arms. "All you said was, 'I think you should keep a low profile for a while. Safer that way.' Instead I had to find out that the Gyr Syndicate is sniffing around on my own."

"And would you have laid low?" Kit asks.

Ciere thinks about it. "I might have robbed a safer mark."

Kit frowns. He carries all his emotion in his mouth—in the curve and dip of his lips. Ciere has spent years watching that mouth thin out in anger, twitch in amusement, or turn down in scorn. It's the only way she can tell what he's thinking. His eyes are always cold.

"At least nothing went wrong," says Kit.

Ciere's hand flutters to the band of metal encircling her wrist. Involuntarily, her eyes stray to the door and windows—her mind automatically cataloging how long it would take to sprint to them. It's a stupid response; she's safe here. But part of her still yearns to run, to flee, to escape. She opens her mouth to tell Kit that *no, something went wrong*, but what comes out is, "Yeah. We got lucky, I guess."

Devon starts to say something and abruptly changes his mind and clears his throat instead. "Dry throat," he says.

Kit stands. "Let me get you both something to drink. I have a feeling this conversation will require tea." He vanishes in the direction of the kitchen, leaving Devon and Ciere alone in the living room.

Devon rounds on Ciere. "You cheeky little liar."

"What was I supposed to say?" Ciere hisses, dropping her voice to a whisper. " 'Yeah, sorry, Kit, but I'm being blackmailed by a mob boss. Got any cookies to go with our tea?' "

"Of course not," Devon replies, straight-faced. "Ask for the biscuits and *then* tell him about the blackmail. I doubt he'll be inclined to feed us when hears your news."

Sometimes Ciere wonders what it would be like if her life were normal. If she hadn't been vaccinated, hadn't ended up with an immunity. If Kit really were her uncle, like he pretends to be, and Devon really just her best friend instead of her best friend/hacker/partner in crime. If this were a normal house, and its inhabitants weren't criminals. Maybe she'd go to school like Devon, or live away from the city, or—

Or maybe her mother would be alive.

She cuts off that line of thinking as quickly as possible. Because her mother isn't alive. Ciere isn't normal. And Kit isn't her uncle. He's a crew leader, which means putting the welfare of the crew over that of the individual. If Ciere brings the wrath of the Gyr Syndicate down upon them all, Kit will have no choice but to cut her off.

"He doesn't need to know!" She taps her foot against the hardwood floor. "We can handle this."

"We?"

"You were the one who demanded to come along," says Ciere. "Hey, you become a thief—you deal with the consequences."

"Consequences like finding yourself in a river with concrete shoes?"

"Exactly. Or in our case, having the feds on our ass." Ciere grimaces. "Actually, I think I'd prefer the concrete."

"So we're really not going to tell him?" Devon jerks his head in the direction of the kitchen.

Ciere thinks about how Kit's mouth would turn down, how his eyes would fix her with that cold stare. She's not a child—specifically, she's not *his* child. There's nothing like blood binding them together, and Ciere knows that no one is irreplaceable. Illusionists are rare, but it's not like Kit couldn't find another one eventually. The thought of being kicked out, of finding herself on the street, makes her feel sick and cold. She can't do that again.

"No," Ciere says firmly. "He doesn't need to know. We'll do his job, get paid, and then give the money to Guntram."

"That's our plan?"

"And it's not open for discussion."

Devon wisely chooses not to pursue the topic, instead scratching the puppy's ears. The puppy thus far has been content to sit in Devon's lap and eye the room curiously. "You notice he didn't kick the dog outside?" Devon says. "Maybe he's softening up. I thought we were going to have to take drastic measures to get the puppy past the front door."

Ciere groans. "I'm sure he'll have something to say later." The pup, oblivious to the fact it is probably unwelcome in this house, begins chewing on its own paw.

When Kit returns, he holds a tea tray. His fingers dart over the teapot with deft precision, pouring tea into porcelain cups as thin and delicate as flower petals.

Ciere eyes her cup doubtfully. "Nothing stronger?"

"No." Kit straightens and strides in the direction of the kitchen. He calls over his shoulder, "And don't think I haven't noticed the reek of smoke and booze on you. I will not have two drunkards in my house."

This lack of alcohol is to be expected. Kit isn't a drinker—he says it makes criminals sloppy. Ciere has always been curious about what secrets Kit might let slip while drunk, but the one and only time Kit drank too much whiskey, he ranted about how Dada was an offense to modern art.

"That man's sense of smell is mad," Devon mutters, staring at his cup of tea. "He wouldn't poison mine, right?"

"Kit wouldn't. He's got this thing about hospitality in his home. Honor among thieves, blah, blah, blah."

"That's reassuring." Devon gives his tea another narrow-eyed look. "But I'm not a thief."

Ciere opens her mouth to reply, but a tinny electronic jingle cuts her off. *Ding a ling ling, a ling ling ling.* It's the sound of a default ringtone, and Devon rolls his eyes as he goes for his pocket.

"Your dad calling you again?" she asks.

Devon glances at the caller ID before pocketing the phone again. "Of course."

"Why don't you change the ringtone?" Ciere wrinkles her nose. "Honestly, who keeps their cell phone's ringtone set to the default?"

"Boring people," Kit says, gliding back into the room. He fixes Devon with a glare. "And rude people who don't silence their phones in the presence of company." He perches in his favorite high-backed chair and looks every inch the aristocrat he isn't. When he speaks again, he directs the words at Ciere. "So what in the world did you want to rob a bank for?"

Ciere shrugs. "Just stocking up on some emergency cash."

"Nice bracelet," says Kit. "New acquistion?"

Ciere locks her expression down. She can't afford to let him see her sudden surge of panic. "Took it from the bank teller," she says, "along with the bobblehead. Figured I deserved a reward for a job well done."

"I would've thought the money would be enough," says Kit.

She shifts uncomfortably on the couch, feels the hard metal of the bracelet around her wrist and tries to ignore it. "The money is never enough."

She has lost count of how much she's squirreled away in offshore bank accounts. She allows herself a little paranoia; she knows exactly how easily a life can unravel.

After all, a sprig of lavender unraveled hers.

"So you said you had a job for us?" she says, changing the subject. "What is it? Deliveries? Message-running? Acquisitions?"

Devon snorts. "Translation, please?"

"Smuggling, acting as messengers, or more thefts," Ciere says.

"Why couldn't you just say that?" Devon says.

Kit's smile freezes in place. "You," he says coolly, "have yet to be invited to join this little undertaking."

Ciere sets her teacup back in its saucer with more force than she should. "He's invited," she snaps.

Kit's smile melts away entirely. "Ciere, what is that boy doing here?" He says "that boy" the way people say "rotting garbage."

"He's an eidos," Ciere says.

"He's a straight." Kit turns his glare on Devon. "In fact, he's heir to one of the most profitable investing empires in the US. He's the straightest of the straight."

Ciere glares right back at him. "He's not like that. He wants out."

"Out of wealth?" Kit scoffs. "Out of security? Of luxury? My God, what a horror that must be. Growing up in safety, even with an immunity."

Devon raises a hand to Ciere, silencing her argument. "You can trust me. I'm not about to turn you in."

"Well, obviously," Kit retorts. "If you were *that* type you'd already be buried out back underneath the tulip garden. It's not a question of your affiliations, it's your upbringing."

Devon looks bewildered. "My what?"

Kit laces his fingers together and sets them in his lap. "You're not like us. Sure, you have an immunity, but you've never had to use it for profit. I'm sure you've shown off to your friends—cheated at cards a few times, memorized and sold test answers at school, but in case you hadn't noticed, this isn't boarding school. We're not breaking into a teacher's desk, and there won't be detention if we're caught. We take risks. We break laws. Are you ready for that?"

Devon seems to be making a conscious effort to appear even taller. "In case you hadn't noticed, Ciere didn't break into that Newark bank on her own. I was an accomplice to a felony."

Kit huffs out a sigh. "Let me guess, you used your oh-so-special hacking skills to hijack the bank's security cameras to run a loop while Ciere made herself look like one of the bank's employees, using his keycard to enter the bank vault and walk out with the money. You were probably sitting in a coffee shop a block away, safe from the immediate fallout if anything had gone wrong."

Devon and Ciere goggle at each other. "How the hell," Devon says, "did he know that?"

"Oh, honestly, who do you think taught Ciere that trick?" Kit says contemptuously. "Now give me one good reason to include you on this job, Mr. *Lyre*." He puts a less than subtle emphasis on Devon's last name.

Devon hunches as he tries to come up with an answer. "I just—I just want to spend some time with people who aren't telling me that I should shut up and do what I'm supposed to." He fidgets with his teacup. "I may be a Lyre, but I'm loyal, I'm clever, and I'm willing to work for free."

"Where does your family think you are right now?" Kit asks.

"On a bender in Hemsedal—some skiing resort in Norway,"

Devon admits. "I downloaded a free translation program so I can sound like I'm speaking the language. I also send my family some photo manips every few days. Usually it's a picture of me sitting on a mountain, holding a bottle of vodka."

"And they believe you?"

Devon's smile is twisted. "Honestly, they don't care. Dad's got my older sister to inherit the company. I'm just the bad-boy younger-son stereotype. Boring." He picks up his cup of tea again, studies it, and then sets it down.

Kit traces the line of his teacup with his fingernail. "Ciere, why did you decide to make him your partner now?"

"He's technically an adult," she says. "And he wouldn't shut up until I agreed to let him tag along."

"Why do I feel like the fat kid being picked last at football?" Devon mutters.

Kit smiles. "It's not a bad analogy."

"Simile," Devon corrects.

Kit's smile pulls tight. "If I didn't have other things to worry about, I'd argue further. This isn't a good idea, Ciere, but since you're standing up for the boy, he can stay. And it's on your head if anything goes wrong."

"What else are you worrying about?" asks Ciere.

Kit purses his lips and says, "Daniel was the one to find this job. He put me in contact with our client."

"And?"

"I haven't heard from him since."

She draws in a sharp breath. Daniel Burkhart. A seventeen-year-old eludere she's known almost as long as she's known Kit. He passed on tricks to evade cops, taught her how to cheat at poker, and stole beer when Kit wasn't around. Daniel is crew, which means he's as close to family as she'll ever get. "H-how long?"

"Long enough," Kit says quietly. "He called me about this job and then vanished."

The word "vanished" is different when it comes from Kit's lips. It doesn't mean a person has gone missing. It means that a person has gone missing and *Kit can't find them*. Ciere can only think of one place where Kit's influence won't reach.

"You think he's been arrested," Ciere says. Her hands tremble, and she clasps them over her knees.

"Perhaps." Kit takes another sip of his tea. "He could be in hiding. Either way, we cannot reach him right now. Which means our crew is short a member." He aims a sharp glance at Devon. "For the job I have in mind, we'll need an eidos and a mentalist. An eludere would've been nice, but I guess we'll have to do without."

He's already talking like Daniel's a lost cause. It makes Ciere feel out of step, like the world has shifted and she's still trying to adjust. A job without Daniel. Without his keen instincts and deadpan humor. It feels wrong.

Devon, who has never met Daniel, isn't overly concerned. "Good luck finding a mentalist," Devon snorts. "I may be new to this, but even I know how rare those lot are."

"I know a man," Kit says. "He is unaffiliated."

Ciere can't help but ask. "You sure he can be trusted?"

"I'd stake my reputation on it. Which is exactly what I'm going to do when I hire him."

"Is he willing?" Ciere asks.

Kit shrugs. "I haven't approached him yet. I thought I'd leave that little assignment to you."

"Because I'm so charming?"

"Because we had a slight falling-out the last time we worked together," Kit replies. "I figure he'll be more amenable to you."

"All right," Ciere says, "so we'll talk to him. Got it. But I expect a bonus for that." She counts off on her fingers. "An eidos, an illusionist, a levitas, and a mentalist. This is a hell of a team."

"It's a hell of a gig."

"What's the target?" Devon asks, sounding impatient. "Where are we hitting?"

Kit rises to his feet; it isn't an angry gesture but a smooth one. He strides to the center of the room. And then he simply *lifts* into the air.

It looks like a trick—like there should be wires attached

to his body, or a platform under his feet. But there isn't. Gravity and Kit have an understanding of sorts—Kit can ignore it when he likes. He can't fly—not really. That's what it means to be a levitas.

Kit touches the ceiling fan, which is at least thirty feet high. He reaches up and pulls something free. A file. He must have taped the file to the upper portion of the fan, where it would be out of sight of anyone who wasn't a levitas or wasn't using a very tall ladder.

When his feet touch the ground again, Kit returns to the couch. He holds out the file, and as he does so, his sleeve rides up on his right arm. Ciere catches a glimpse of ink on pale skin. It's a strange tattoo, a series of roman numerals etched into the smooth skin of his inner wrist. Kit usually keeps it covered, and Ciere has never had the courage to ask about it.

She takes the file and opens it. The first page is that of a copied blueprint, complete with the builder's notes. It takes her a moment to find the title scribbled in the left-hand corner.

"We're breaking into a lawyer's office?" she asks.

Kit's only answer is a wicked smile.

5

DANIEL

Daniel Burkhart sits in a room with blank white walls, no windows, and furniture that is bolted to the floor. He can't see the cameras, but he knows he's being watched. The cameras' gaze registers as a buzzing itch along his skin. He can easily imagine what the cameras see—a seventeen-year-old with dirty brown hair and a crooked nose. He shifts, trying to find a more comfortable position, but his handcuff clinks and the chain prevents him from standing.

He runs a hand over the table—long, rectangular, and steel. Whoever designed this room didn't have its occupant's comfort (physical or mental) in mind.

He has visited this room seven times—one for each day of his captivity. It's how he keeps track of the time; there are no windows to track the sun, and so far the FBI agents haven't offered him a watch. *A week*, Daniel thinks. It's long enough for the FBI to let their guard down. They think he's been beaten.

Daniel rests his forehead on his arm. To an observer, he simply looks like a criminal who is trying to take a nap. But rest is the last thing on his mind.

They searched him, of course. But since no one bothered to wrench his jaw open and point a flashlight inside his mouth, he still has the bobby pin tucked into the space between his teeth and lip. An old trick, but it's proved useful again and again. Under the guise of rest, with his arm blocking the camera's sight, he reaches into his mouth with his other hand and takes hold of the pin. It's warm and sticky with saliva, and he has to dry it on his sleeve—a tricky matter without lifting his head—and then he slips one end into the handcuff's lock. The pin's tip is bent at a ninety-degree angle, and it's a simple matter to twist and... there.

At once the pressure on his right wrist lets up. They only used the single lock, Daniel thinks scornfully. It is almost a professional insult.

As an eludere, Daniel can escape anything.

Freed, he cocks an ear and listens for footfalls in the hallway. *One man*, his instincts whisper. Then the lock clicks and the door opens. Sure enough, a single man steps into the room, his hand lingering on the door handle.

It's one of the FBI agents who arrested Daniel—Special Agent Something-or-Other Carson. He's just shy of his forties, with black hair, a clean jaw, and faintly Latino coloring. He also has a sour expression, which is par for the course.

"You've got some visitors," Carson says when a loud *ding a ling ling, a ling ling ling* reverberates through the small room, interrupting him. Daniel recognizes the sound as a default ringtone. Honestly, who keeps a phone's ringtone set at default?

Carson lets go of the doorknob and raises his phone to his ear. That's when Daniel moves.

He lashes out, swinging the now unlocked cuffs at Carson's eyes. The blow connects and there is the sound of metal slapping flesh, followed by a cry of pain. Daniel doesn't wait to see how badly he hurt the agent; he grabs the door before it can click shut, before the automatic lock can slide into place. He darts through and pulls the heavy door shut behind him. That door cannot be unlocked from the inside; it's one of the clever security arrangements meant to keep crooks from escaping. Even so, it's not soundproof. Carson's furious yell is the sweetest sound Daniel has heard in days.

One fed down.

Daniel takes stock of his surroundings. The hallways are dimly lit—it's night after all—and he can easily see into numerous interrogation rooms. Some are empty. Most are not.

For a moment, he pauses. He considers finding a way to free the others—a desire that is half mercy and half calculation. If the feds are occupied with a group of escapees, it will be easier for one lone eludere to slip away. But the door controls are probably locked away in the heart of this building, which would undoubtedly be heavily guarded. There's not enough time.

Daniel closes his eyes and takes a deep breath. He balances on the balls of his feet, waiting for the old senses to kick in. He spins around, like a compass finding north, and then he sprints down the hallway to his left.

A fed is emerging from one of the interrogation rooms. The fed hears the clatter of footsteps and glances up, his expression almost bored. He must think it's another agent, so when he sees Daniel his jaw goes slack and there is the slightest moment of pause.

Daniel reaches out and *listens.*

The man's shoe squeaks on the linoleum floor. He is shifting to his left, preparing to throw his weight into a tackle. *Ex-football player,* Daniel thinks, seeing the man's heavy muscle and bristling haircut. It takes Daniel back to when he played backyard football with his friends after school. He pretends he doesn't notice the fed's impending move; he continues to barrel to the left. At the last second, he spins to the right, those handcuffs swinging up. There are places you can hit a man, no matter his size or weight, and the strike will always be effective. Daniel goes for the eyes.

The blow doesn't have to blind the fed—but there will be

enough pain to temporarily put him out of the game. The cuff hits the man across his brow and he lets out a bellow. Daniel darts past, barely catching a glimpse of the man mashing his hand against his right eye, trying to see through the pain and the tears.

Daniel isn't in the habit of injuring people. He's a con artist and a thief, not a thug. A distant part of him knows he should feel bad for nearly blinding two men, but here's another thing Daniel has learned from years of conning people: empathy will get a person killed.

As Daniel sprints down the hallway, an instinct howls at him to lift his feet. He hears the slight buzz and leaps into the air, catching the briefest glimpse of a near invisible laser trip wire. Then he's moving again, charging for an emergency exit. There will be alarms, but he'll be gone before anyone can investigate them.

Daniel listens as he charges down the hall. There is no sign of a general pursuit. Not yet. He hurtles forward, throwing himself through another set of doors. He's almost out. He can feel the outside beckoning, hear the wind and the sky. He can hear freedom.

There. The exit is in view now—a large door with a red handle and the words ALARM WILL SOUND painted on it. It's his ticket out of here. The only other doors are slightly ajar, with the words VENDING MACHINES flaking off. Daniel grins.

That's when the woman walks out of the last room.

She's dressed in a gray pencil skirt and blouse—not ideal for chasing criminals. Her sandy hair is curly and pulled back into a loose ponytail. Even without makeup, she has pretty features. She looks fresh, youthful, and untested. She is unwrapping a candy bar when she sees Daniel. Her thin brows draw together in confusion. When her eyes alight on the half-open cuffs still looped around one of his wrists, a smile breaks across her face.

It's not the reaction Daniel is expecting. He tilts his head and listens.

The world is silent for a long second, and then he hears the soft thud of a racing heart. His own.

All of Daniel's senses scream at him to turn around, to back up, to get out of there. His immunity tells him that she's not benign, and he needs to get out of there before she—

She springs forward, quicker than he could have imagined, and her fingers tangle in his shirt. She yanks him forward, and he staggers in an attempt to keep his balance. Her right leg sweeps sideways, her foot hooking around his ankle and pulling it out from under him.

His back slams into the linoleum floor, and the shock jostles his whole body. He blinks and realizes the woman is on top of him, her hands fisted in his shirt. Her knee is poised between his legs; any struggle, and he'll definitely come off on the worse end of things.

He's pinned.

The woman gives him a shake, the way a dog might shake a rabbit in its jaws. "And to think, all I wanted was a candy bar," she says.

Now he understands what his instincts knew first. She is immune. More specifically, she's a dauthus. Only a dauthus could lift Daniel so easily into the air, setting him easily on his feet.

"Eludere," she says. "Your type always tries to run. Ever thought of fighting back?" She yanks him down the hallway, retracing his wild rush to freedom. She moves confidently through the building; she's obviously been here before.

Back at the interrogation room, she gives him a push, and he stumbles through the door, bracing himself for a blow. But it never comes; the woman remains standing in the doorway—a human barrier between Daniel and freedom—with her arms crossed and eyebrows raised. Her gaze flicks up, and Daniel realizes that he's not alone.

There's a man standing in the middle of the room. He has a right-angle chin, and the rest of his features are equally sharp. His black hair is carefully clipped. He's not FBI. That's made evident by the VISITOR badge the man has clipped to his lapel. He isn't carrying—there's no telltale bulge at his ankle, hip, or shoulder. An analyst, then? But why would the feds bring in an analyst?

"Ah, Mr. Burkhart," the man says warmly. "I was hoping we could have a talk."

6

CIERE

A hand seizes her shoulder, and Ciere comes awake with a start.

Two brown eyes, set in a wrinkled face, glare down at her. Ciere recoils and kicks the blankets free, ready to run if necessary. It takes her a moment to calm down, even after she realizes that the so-called threat is an old woman holding a broom. "Crap," Ciere groans, flopping back onto her bed. "Liz, I was busted by NYPD at seven in the morning and *that* was less terrifying than your wake-up call."

Lizaveta's lips pinch together. "You," the old woman says in a reedy voice thick with a Russian accent. "Copperfield wants you." Her worn hands tighten on the broom handle.

Ciere scrambles out of the bed. She's had that broom aimed at her more than once.

Lizaveta Elstov is yet another occupant of the Bolsover house. She rents a room on the third story, and Kit's rationale is that she has no family to take care of her and she wants to live in the safety of an elsec. Ciere can't blame her; the elsecs are one of the few places where the feds won't meddle—if only not to anger their constituents.

Nearly sixteen years ago, after Praevenir's adverse effects were formally acknowledged by both the public and the medical community, the world was stunned. So many expectations subverted, so many theories dashed, and so many lives irrevocably altered. Humanity reeled, at a loss for what to do.

The US government couldn't decide how to classify this new minority group—it was calculated that hundreds of thousands of Americans were affected. The government scrambled to react, and the first course of action was a massive identification program. They needed a way to single out people who had been vaccinated.

Things improved once the seven immunities were categorized and named: dauthus, eidos, levitas, eludere, mentalist, illusionist, and dominus.

Although there was no way to test for adverse effects, testing for Praevenir was another matter. The antibody titer was a quick blood sample that could determine exactly who had been vaccinated. If the blood had MK antibodies, then that person had been vaccinated and there was a chance they could be immune. The titer test, as it soon became known, helped narrow things down, and was systematically and methodically administered at schools, hospitals, pharmacies, and clinics. After testing, individuals were required to wear identification tags at all times.

Testing became mandatory. Civilians who avoided it found their bank accounts frozen, their social security checks withheld. The government claimed testing was in society's best interests. Kit says they were recruiting. Within a matter of months, many who identified as immune were snapped up for government work. The military scrambled to collect as many dauthus as possible, while mentalists joined up with the TSA. Eludere and eidos went to any number of agencies. Illusionists were considered a rare commodity and could be siphoned into the more elite intelligence teams.

Only two groups of people escaped the rampant recruitment.

The first were the criminals.

Criminals didn't worry about things like tax returns or social security checks. An underground market for counterfeit tags sprang up, allowing the crooked to circulate in normal society. Even people who had previously obeyed the law suddenly found themselves on the other side of it, unwilling to become pawns of the government.

The second group were those rich enough to bribe their way into normalcy. They banded together, moved into prosperous neighborhoods, and blended into elite communities. Neighborhood organizations formed that were supposed to "improve" their communities, but in reality were meant to keep the neighborhoods privileged. Anyone with an annual income that wasn't at least three hundred grand need not apply. These elite sectors petitioned the government, requesting their own security forces. To protect themselves, they said. And so the elsecs were born.

Picking a house in an elsec was a risky move, but Kit had enough fake IDs and money to pull it off. And once he'd established himself here, the neighbors hadn't questioned him. Kit Copperfield, his niece Ciere, and their Russian housekeeper were just a few more rich eccentrics in the neighborhood.

Lizaveta's guise as a housekeeper is half-true. While Kit is perfectly fine doing his own cooking, cleaning, and gardening—actually, he's rather possessive of his house in general—Liz picks up some of the slack. Her English is limited, her disapproval of Ciere high, and if Liz knows anything about her landlord's criminal activities, Ciere hasn't heard about it. Not that she could, since Ciere never learned Russian.

Ciere thuds down the stairs and into the kitchen. This particular room is the house's one nod to modernity. Marble counters frame two stainless-steel sinks, and a large refrigerator hums contentedly in the background. Ciere settles onto one of the stools at the large breakfast bar and rests her chin on the counter.

Kit is already at work. A skillet warms on the stove and a carton of eggs rests beside it. Ciere plucks a strip of bacon from a plate covered by a layer of greasy napkins. Kit has propped a tablet up against a napkin holder; Ciere glances at it and sees a video of men in suits.

"Give me a moment," Kit says, "and everything will be ready. And don't touch that bacon—you'll only ruin your appetite." He nimbly picks up an egg in each hand and cracks them.

Ciere chews on her piece of bacon. "What're you watching?"

"The EU conference." Kit's arm is a blur as he whips the eggs with a fork. "Europe is annoyed with us."

"Same old, then."

Devon strides into the kitchen, sees the bacon in Ciere's hand, and follows her line of sight to the plate. "Leave the bacon alone," Kit says, taking a cutting board down from its hook. He pulls a bundle of freshly washed parsley from the sink. "There's supposed to be a broadcast of the Republic's newest speech later."

Devon slides into the seat next to Ciere. "Really?" He sounds interested—then again, he's always been able to muster more enthusiasm for politics than Ciere. She settles on stealing another slice of bacon. "What about?"

"The newest treaties," Kit says. He reaches into a drawer

and selects a long knife. He tests the edge with his thumb. "I can already guess what they'll say. China's going to say that it would never use immune individuals as weapons—"

"Ha!" Devon snorts.

"—and would do so only if America did first," Kit says.

"But America already has," Devon points out.

"Exactly." Kit goes to work on the parsley. "It's all empty reassurances. But we world powers have to at least pretend to not despise one another."

Devon beams. "Speaking of which." He reaches out and takes a slice of the forbidden bacon. He eyes Kit, as if in challenge. "I have to say—nice apron. Ever consider leaving the crime business and becoming someone's manservant?"

Kit also smiles—it's a rather scary expression. He rinses off the wooden cutting board and hangs it back on its hook. The knife also goes under the running water and he dries it off with a napkin. Then Kit turns on his heel, tosses the knife into the air, catches it by the hilt, and throws it. The knife spins and slams into the cutting board. The knife shivers, its blade sunk deep into the wood.

Devon puts his slice of bacon down.

Fellow criminals have seen Kit's domestic habits and deemed him harmless. All they see is a man who fusses over plate garnishes and prunes rosebushes. But Kit's domesticity is carefully arranged over previously existing, deadlier habits.

He sprinkles the parsley onto two omelets and slides the plates across the counter to Ciere and Devon.

"Lizaveta says her knees haven't been feeling well," Kit says brightly. "So I'll deliver breakfast to her room. You two enjoy the bacon."

Devon stares at him until he disappears. "Mental," he says. "That man is completely mental. And," he adds hastily, seeing Ciere open her mouth, "don't you dare try some horrible pun about him 'making a point.' "

Ciere closes her mouth.

The knife remains stuck in place.

A gig always requires certain steps. Whether it's a robbery, a con, forgery, or smuggling, there are always routines that must be followed. First, the gig must be found. Either a client will come to them, or else Kit will spot an opening in the market and exploit it. Second, Kit plans things. Kit always plans things—that's his role. Once he has found a gig, he decides which players are best for the job. If Ciere, Daniel, or another one of Kit's usual crew is not available (or qualified), he will go recruiting.

Recruiting is always risky.

Bringing in freelancers means trusting them with information best kept hidden. Most good crooks like Kit have built up a network, relying on the same individuals for certain skills. It minimizes the chances of information being leaked;

also, it lends to building bonds between those individuals, discouraging deliberate betrayal.

But for all of Kit's contacts, he doesn't have a mentalist on retainer. Mentalists are scarce, and most of them are snapped up by the government or by the various mobs.

Around eleven in the morning, Ciere and Devon climb into Kit's oldest car—a 2030 Dodge Journey. "Take the SUV. I don't want you relying on public transportation for this," Kit says, pressing the keys into Ciere's hand. "And don't go into downtown DC today. I heard that Aditi Sen woman is heading up another protest, and the last thing I want is to retrieve you from a riot."

Ciere lets Devon drive; she has many skills, but she's never been all that good with cars. Devon sits behind the wheel comfortably, resting one hand on the window and using the other to steer. He guides the car past the elsec fences and out into the normal world.

Devon makes a disgruntled noise. His eyes drift to the car's dashboard, where there is a small hole. It looks like a cavity in a healthy mouth. "Did someone steal Copperfield's stereo?"

Ciere forces herself not to snort. "It's where Kit dug out the GPS."

Devon casts a glance toward the bracelet. "If he managed to do that . . . you think . . . ?"

"No," she says after a moment's thought. "It took Kit hours to fix the car so it couldn't be tracked. I don't think he could take the bracelet off." She tucks her hands into her lap, trying to look anywhere but down.

Something in her face must give Devon pause, because he changes the subject. "So, no GPS. We're using written directions. It's like we're back in the Stone Age." He's used to being able to simply plug in an address and rely on a tinny voice to tell him when to turn.

"When you're crooked," Ciere reminds him, "you operate off the grid."

Devon doesn't look happy, but he follows her instructions and guides the car to an on-ramp.

"I tried yanking it out," Devon says after a minute or so of companionable silence.

"What?" she says, bewildered, wondering if he's still talking about the GPS.

"The knife," says Devon. "After breakfast, when Kit was still in the shower. And you were changing clothes. I tried yanking the knife out of that cutting board."

"And you couldn't?"

Devon glances over one shoulder and eases the car into the left lane. "What do you know about him?"

"Who?"

"Copperfield."

Ciere taps her fingers on her bare knee. She wears another loose sundress, since Kit assured her this meeting wouldn't require business clothes. Otherwise, she'd be dressed in black, with a mask shoved in her pocket. "He's sort of a crooked agent," she says. "You know, handling the careers of us criminals who don't care about things like contacts. He's in charge of our crew."

"Yeah, yeah, I got that." Devon fiddles with the steering wheel. "But what do we really *know* about him?"

Involuntarily, Ciere is drawn into her own memories. She met Kit when she was eleven years old and on the verge of starvation. She remembers the ache in her middle, the gnawing hunger. Dirt crusted her face and hands, her curly hair a mess. She stood in an alley, clutching the pink backpack her mother had forced into her hands. (*"Don't let anyone see what you are, understand?"*) Then he was there, a stranger asking if she needed help. She ran from him, just like she ran from everyone else. Running was what she did—it was the only way to stay alive. Then the stranger lifted into the air, and she saw he was floating. "It's all right. I'm like you," he said.

She never found out how he knew. She assumes he must have seen her use an illusion to pick someone's pocket.

Looking back, Ciere knows how lucky she was. Kit could have been anyone: a murderer, someone looking to sell her to the highest bidder, or worse. But Kit simply took her to his apartment and fixed her the first hot meal she'd had in weeks. After a long shower, she put on one of his shirts, which fit her like an oversized dress. She slept on the bed he made up on the couch, and when she asked him why he would take her in, like some sort of stray cat, he said, "Why wouldn't I?"

Six months later, when he moved to the East Coast to expand his business, Ciere went with him. She's been with him ever since.

Ciere frowns. "I know he's a good person," she says, fighting back a surge of annoyance. "He's helped people like us stay off the government radar."

"He's our very own Fagin," Devon mutters.

This close to the country's capital, the signs of the government crop up everywhere. Billboards proudly display federally funded messages along with their usual commercials. The animated scripts blink over and over, trying to draw attention to themselves.

"TRUE AMERICANS WEAR THEIR TAGS WITH PRIDE."

"HE HAS STOOD STRONG FOR FOUR YEARS—LET HIM STAND FOR YOU AGAIN. REELECT ROBERTS FOR PRESIDENT. (I am Edward Roberts, and I approve this message.)"

"USING SMUGGLED GOODS IS A CRIME."

"SUPPORT YOUR COUNTRY—BUY ALLEGIANT BONDS."

"OUR FAMILY VALUES ARE IN JEOPARDY; LET A FAMILY MAN REPRESENT OUR COUNTRY. ELECT JOHNSON FOR PRESIDENT. (I am William Johnson, and I approve this message.)"

"YOUR VIGILANCE PROTECTS YOUR FELLOW CITIZENS—REPORT ADVERSE EFFECTS."

"Adverse effects" is the technical term for immunities. According to Kit, the government's PR team had a tough time coming up with a name for the powers introduced to the population. The widely used term "immune" was considered, but ultimately thrown away in favor of "adverse effects." After all, that's what the immunities are—bad side effects. It makes those with powers sound like an unfortunate accident.

Once Devon and Ciere enter the DC borders, it's not long before they arrive at their destination, the Sun Horizons Hotel. It's in an older part of the city, an area that still sports things like cobblestone streets. The hotel's automatic glass doors glide open before Devon and Ciere when they approach. They stand in the air-conditioned lobby and get their bearings. To their left is the concierge and check-in; to their right is what looks like the restaurant and bar.

According to Kit's instructions, they're to meet the mentalist in the bar. "Magnus Fugaré," Ciere reads aloud, then tucks the note card into her pocket.

Devon turns disbelieving eyes on her. "You're joking."

"Nope."

"That poor kid," Devon says. "Imagine going to primary school with a name like Magnus."

"It's probably an alias," Ciere replies.

Ciere is an alias. Ciere Giba in full. It's just another false name, one created with a French dictionary and a laugh. Ciere wears this name like a comfortable old T-shirt; she can put on other identities with ease, but at the end of the day it's nice to slip into something old and familiar. Now that Ciere thinks about it, she can name only a few people who still use their birth names. Most crooks end up ditching their old identities as soon as they pull off a job or move to a new location; those with immunities do so more frequently. It's a matter of survival, of staying hidden and untraceable. Daniel Burkhart uses his real name, and Ciere has never figured out why. Birth names are a luxury none of them can afford.

Devon Lyre uses his real name. He hasn't needed a false one.

Ciere and Devon find an open table near the hotel bar. It's in the odd hours between lunch and dinner, and there is a lull in the customer flow. The empty room makes it easier for Kit's contact to find them.

The contact turns out to be a woman in her mid-thirties. When she catches sight of Ciere and Devon, she glides to their table. "You must be Ms. Giba," she says, offering a manicured hand for Ciere to shake. "I'm Mr. Fugaré's personal assistant, Bellevue."

"Hi," Devon says at the same moment Ciere says, "Heya."

Bellevue's eyes linger on Devon and her polite smile freezes in place. "I wasn't informed there would be two of you," she says.

Devon and Ciere exchange looks. Kit never explained what this Magnus does for a living. What they're supposed to be meeting him for. Kit simply handed Ciere an envelope, rattled off the directions, and then waved them off.

Hesitantly, Ciere offers Bellevue the envelope. It bulges with twenties—Ciere never counted the bills, but she's got a good instinct for money. She hazards a guess that she just paid about one grand for this meeting.

Bellevue glances inside the envelope and her smile becomes more genuine. "Thank you for your kind donation. This way, please."

She leads them past reception and to the elevators. It's a quick jaunt to the sixth floor, and Bellevue obviously knows her way around. She walks unerringly to room 615 and slides a card into the lock. Once inside, she retrieves two robes from the closet. "Why don't you both enjoy a nice shower," she says. "Magnus will be along soon." Then she is smiling, pulling the door shut behind her.

Devon and Ciere stand in the hotel room, robes in hand, staring at each other.

"All right, I give up. What game are we playing?" says Devon.

Ciere looks from the robe to the hotel room, and then something in her mind clicks. She grins, relieved to finally understand what Kit sent them into. "Think about it," she says. "What do people come to hotels for? And what job could a telepath do really well? What would pay the bills without linking this guy to a crime family or the feds?"

It takes Devon a moment. His fingers fumble, and he flings the robe away like it's on fire. "He's a tom," he says, comprehension dawning on his face.

"Actually, I was thinking prostitute." Ciere raises her eyebrows and gestures at the room. "And judging by the fact that we handed over a thousand dollars for a one-hour appointment, I'd say he's a damn good one."

Devon's head whips back and forth. "Sod this. We've got to get out of here."

"Why do you always sound more British when you're embarrassed?" Ciere plops down into one of the plush chairs. "Come on and sit." She can't help but laugh. Now that she knows what Magnus is, she feels at ease. "Calm down."

"Copperfield," Devon says, furious. "That bastard did this on purpose."

"Probably," Ciere agrees. She giggles. "Heh. Magnus."

"Oh, dear lord." Devon buries his face in his hands. "Stop talking. Stop thinking."

When the door opens, Devon looks like he wants to either run or scurry under the bed; he settles for perching on the edge of the other chair. Ciere straightens and eyes the newcomer with interest.

This must be Magnus Fugaré. He's muscular, but not in a bulky way. His lips are full and his brown eyes large, balancing out his prominent nose. His dark brown hair contrasts with his light skin, and his brows are long and closely set over his eyes. Underneath his beauty there is something gaunt about his face. He looks haunted, like some of the veterans Ciere has known.

"You must be Ciere," Magnus says, and a smile chases the grimness from his eyes.

Ciere jabs an elbow into Devon's side. "Yep. This is Devon. Say hi, honey," she adds, making her voice sound artificially sweet.

Devon jumps as if Ciere's elbow is live with electricity. "What?" he says.

"He's so shy," Ciere tells Magnus confidentially, wrapping an arm around Devon's waist.

"I'm Magnus Fugaré," Magnus says, holding out a hand. She takes Magnus's fingers in her own and squeezes lightly.

The moment Ciere touches him, Magnus goes rigid. His shoulders draw forward, and his eyelids flutter shut.

He retreats and sinks onto a corner of the bed. When he rests his elbows on his knees, Ciere sees how pale he's gone. He reaches into a pocket and withdraws a small box. A cigarette appears between two of his trembling fingers. In a moment, the cigarette is alight, and Magnus closes his eyes on the first pull, savoring it. Only after he's exhaled does he give Ciere a calculating look.

"Kit Copperfield sent you," he says.

Devon sits up straighter. "It's true. He's really a mentalist, then." He presses his palms to the sides of his face and begins humming, as if trying to block out an annoying noise. "Lalalalalalalalala—stay out of my sodding brain—lalalalalalala."

Magnus stares at Devon doubtfully. "What exactly is he? I know you're a thief, but what is he?"

"Eidos," Devon says, sounding annoyed. "And I'm right here."

"Ah." Magnus nods. "I wasn't referring to your immunity, Mr. Eidos. I wanted to know *what* you are. Your expensive clothing would make me think you're a thief, but you don't move like one."

Devon's jaw sets. "Rotting hell. I was just an accomplice to a *felony*. What do I have to do to get into your crooked club?"

"For one thing," Magnus says, looking amused, "we don't use terms like 'accomplice to a felony.'"

Ciere rests a hand on Devon's arm. "He's one of us," she

says, and Magnus leaves it at that. "Like you said, I'm here representing Kit Copperfield. He mentioned you'd worked together before."

All the humor vanishes from Magnus's eyes, leaving behind a man with a controlled expression. "You can tell Kit that I'm done," he says. "I'm done with all of it. I'm out of the game."

"But it's just a—"

"Jobs are never simple," Magnus interrupts her. "And they're never just jobs."

Ciere rocks back, startled by his vehemence. She's never dealt with a mentalist before, so she's not sure how to convince him.

"Tell Copperfield I'm not his mentalist," Magnus says curtly. "Now leave. Please."

Ciere wavers, uncertain. She'd suspected they might have to convince the mentalist—after all, Kit said he and Magnus hadn't parted on good terms—but she didn't expect this kind of open hostility. Magnus, who is strangling his cigarette between two fingers, clearly wants nothing to do with them.

Before Ciere can string together a new argument, there is a pounding on the door. It swings open and Bellevue stands there, her knuckles gone white as she grips the doorknob.

"A SWAT team just pulled up in front of the hotel," she says, breathless.

7

DANIEL

Daniel sits inside his interrogation chamber and tries to look nonchalant. Like there aren't four feds, all staring at him like he's a deer and they're wolves. Like they're already divvying up who gets the finest hunk of meat.

Of the three men, the first is FBI Agent Carson. With a sharp jaw and black hair, he might be good-looking. If not for that cut above his right eyebrow and the bruise. His youth and clean-cut good looks are a stark contrast to his partner. Special Agent Avery Gervais is a man with craggy, worn features. He's older than Carson, with peppery gray hair. They stand a few feet from the metal table, angled away from the two new feds.

The third man is the analyst. He stands with his hands in his pockets and his eyes trained on Daniel. The woman—the dauthus who dragged Daniel away from freedom—leans against the far wall. She has crossed her arms behind her head like she's in a lounge rather than an interrogation chamber.

Carson holds a strip of cloth to his forehead, but it's done little to stanch the bleeding. "Head wounds are a bitch, aren't they?" Daniel says, unable to hide his grin. Carson takes a step forward, looking like he wants to pummel Daniel.

The analyst darts into his path. "Agent," he says, his voice a quiet rebuke.

Gervais says, "He attacked two federal agents while trying to escape; whatever deal you were going to cut him is void."

The analyst raises his hand in entreaty. "I still haven't had my meeting."

"Screw your meeting," Carson snarls.

"No. If it wasn't for Morana, Burkhart would already be gone," the analyst says. "You owe us."

Color pools in Carson's cheeks. With obvious effort, he reins in his temper. "Five minutes," he grates out.

Something has changed within the room; something's missing. Daniel rolls his shoulders, as if trying to work out kinks, but he's reaching out with that sense of his. His eyelids fall partly closed, and he *listens*. His immunity doesn't have anything to do with hearing, but *listening* is the closest word Daniel has for what he does. He *listens* for sirens, for the hum of a silent alarm, for the footfall of a pursuing cop, for a soft inhalation that means someone is waiting out of sight, for a heartbeat, for the click of a lock's tumblers.

The eludere immunity is the hardest one for scientists to quantify. It's been called clairvoyance, increased intuition, even the sixth sense. Eludere sense things others can't—sometimes even before they happen—and they use that knowledge to their advantage. It's nearly impossible to catch someone who can sense the waiting trap or feel the pinprick of crosshairs.

His immunity is how Daniel knows something has changed. It's not what he hears, but what he *doesn't.* He doesn't hear the security cameras. They've been turned off. Before Daniel can process that fact, the analyst sits in the chair across the table and offers him a brief smile.

"You have an interesting file," the analyst says. "Quite the varied career for one so young. I look forward to hearing about it." He folds his fingers together, and Daniel catches a glimpse of ink along the analyst's wrist.

"Don't hold your breath," Daniel says. He leans back in his seat, trying to convey nonchalance. In reality, his every instinct is screaming to put distance between himself and the feds. He's still keyed up from his escape attempt.

"You will talk to us."

Daniel snorts out a bitter laugh. "I know the US military has free rein to hold anyone they think is a terrorist. Too bad you're not military and I'm not a terrorist."

The man tilts his head. "How did you know?"

"You're too skinny—no muscle, and your hair isn't buzzed. And you're not FBI, because you've got that visitor's badge."

A frown. "That's correct," the man says.

That's when Daniel suddenly understands. His mouth goes dry.

"UAI." The word springs to Daniel's lips of its own accord. "You're with the UAI."

The man inclines his head. "Call me Aristeus. My partner, Morana, was the one who prevented your escape." The dauthus woman holds up a hand and waggles her fingers in silent greeting. Aristeus points at the two FBI agents lurking in the corner. "You, of course, already know Special Agent Avery Gervais and his partner, Eduardo Carson. They were the ones who apprehended you."

The animosity between the UAI agents and the FBI agents is palpable. Daniel hears it when Gervais flexes a fist inside his pocket and pops his knuckles, in the whisper of silk over metal when the dauthus woman shifts her stance; he hears the barely-there curse that Eduardo Carson exhales, his eyes fastened on Aristeus's back. Daniel tucks this information away for later.

Aristeus picks up a piece of paper from the folder and glances over it. "Mr. Burkhart, you should know that I'm not interested in you personally."

“That’s a relief,” Daniel says dryly.

Aristeus continues, “You’ve worked for many employers, including the group known as TATE. I know one of their agents contacted you—a Frieda Fuller. She wanted you to steal something for her. I’d like you to tell me about it.”

“I’d like a more comfortable chair,” Daniel retorts. “And a warm meal. Oh, and a pony while you’re at it.”

“I’m willing to make you a deal,” Aristeus says.

A deal. Yeah, right. Deals are less than worthless; the moment a person finds himself or herself with an immunity, they lose all their rights. Daniel knows that better than anyone. It’s why he ran away from home, leaving his family with nothing more than a scribbled note. It’s why he has ten different fake tags, why he steals, why he cons, why he’s become the perfect escape artist.

Too bad it was all for nothing.

The bitterness gives Daniel bravery. Or maybe it’s just recklessness. He hasn’t got a lot to lose at this point. “Go fuck yourself. I know what kind of deals you feds make.”

Aristeus doesn’t so much as blink. “If you tell us everything about your job,” he says, “I’ll unlock that door and give you an hour.” He leans forward. “Exactly one hour before I report your escape.”

It’s a lie. It has to be. No fed would simply let Daniel walk out of here.

Carson makes a noise—it sounds like a curse has caught in his throat. "What—*no!* You don't have that kind of authority—"

"Actually," Aristeus says coldly, "I do."

Carson's heavy jaw bulges as he grinds his teeth. "The UAI can't—" He is cut off by his partner, who seizes his arm and squeezes. It's a silent warning.

The UAI woman, Morana, straightens. Her posture is deceptively loose and relaxed, but the facade is wasted on Daniel. A dauthus could take down these two in a matter of seconds.

Aristeus raises a palm to Morana, and she slouches back against the wall. "Do not tell me what the UAI can and cannot do," Aristeus says. "We hold as much authority as the federal bureau."

"Don't kid yourself, Agent," Carson says. The last word is tangled up with a bitter laugh. "You've got as much authority as the president gives you. He's enamored with what you freaks can do for him." Gervais moves to grab at Carson again, but Carson steps out of his reach. "The moment we get someone sane in office, you and your agency will be the first ones rounded up and—"

Aristeus turns on Carson and his words drop to a low hiss. "*Shut up.*" Something in his voice changes. Daniel hears it, *hears* it, the way normal people can't. That voice is poison, cold and creeping—a silent hand that reaches and chokes the voice out of Carson.

Carson's mouth clamps shut and he staggers backward. Daniel can't see Aristeus's expression but it must be something to behold, because the look on Carson's face is close to panic.

Together, Gervais and Carson take several more steps backward, until they are—literally—backed into a corner. Gervais moves in front of Carson, and there is nothing subtle about the way his hand rests on the gun at his belt.

Aristeus simply turns away, as if the two agents are no longer worthy of his attention. "Damn FBI," he mutters.

Morana speaks up. "I think they're cute," she says, as if Gervais and Carson have gone deaf as well as mute.

"You would." Aristeus hooks a finger through the knot of his tie and loosens it, trying to gather himself. He returns to the seat across from Daniel. "Now," he says, "where were we?"

"You were making him a deal," Morana says.

"Ah, right. The deal." Aristeus folds his hand on the table. "Mr. Burkhart, I am not like those agents," he nods to the corner, "who would lock you away until you rot. You've made them look incompetent. Of course, they're part of the Adverse Effects Division, so they should be used to that sort of thing."

Daniel smiles.

Aristeus continues, "To them, you're just a criminal

eludere. They know what that means intellectually, of course, but they've never experienced adverse effects themselves. That's why you were able to escape. As much as the FBI thinks they can deal with our kind, they can't."

"Our kind?" Daniel scoffs, but it's a bluff. If this Aristeus is with the UAI, it's certain. He's immune, too.

Aristeus looks as if he knows what Daniel is thinking. "We're all equals here. We're all on the same side. Please." He leans forward, his expression surprisingly earnest. His voice goes low, pleading, *reasonable*—that's the word Daniel settles on. It's disarming how *reasonable* this man is, with his dark eyes and youthful face. He's not much older than Daniel—probably in his mid-twenties.

"You think I'm that naive?" Daniel says. "That I'm going to give up any leverage I have for a deal I know you won't honor?"

Daniel catches the flicker of unhappiness in Aristeus's eyes, and he barks out a laugh. He's scored a hit. "Or maybe," he says, "it's you that's naive. You think the government's going to support you for long?" He nods in the direction of Gervais and Carson. "Those feds have it right. Us immune—we're criminals. The only difference between you and me is that you're willing to whore whatever talents you've got out to the people who're trying to hunt us."

Aristeus's face shuts down. "I'm working to help people like us."

Daniel gestures at the interrogation room and then at the places on his wrists where the handcuffs chafed. "Great job you're doing."

There are few lines that Daniel won't cross. He's conned innocents, stolen plenty of valuables, and even let blame be pinned on others. But he won't betray people he cares about. Kit Copperfield and Ciere Giba are the closest thing he still has to family. If his choices come down to rotting in a cell or selling them out—he'll choose the cell.

"You were right before." Aristeus folds his arms over his chest and leans back in his chair. "Legally, the UAI can't touch you. We cannot conduct interrogations under the Allegiant Act. We are not military." He inclines his head, as if conceding a point in a duel. "So, I won't touch you. But here's the rub—I don't need to." He shifts his attention to the dauthus in the corner. "Morana, would you mind watching the door? I would rather not have anyone walk in on this."

Morana nods and steps outside. The lock clicks into place, and something about it makes Daniel shiver.

Aristeus's voice rings out in a sharp command. "Look at me," he says, and reflexively Daniel meets Aristeus's eyes.

"You will not use your immunity," Aristeus says, and his voice is different. Softer and ice cold.

The world around Daniel goes silent.

It's like he's slipped underwater—he feels as if every sound is muffled, muddied. He doesn't realize what's happened until Aristeus's earlier words sink in: his immunity is gone.

It's gone.

Just...gone.

This has never happened before. His senses have never failed him. They've always been there, whispering to him, telling him where the lock is weakest, which wire will start the car, the direction the security camera is facing. He's been relying on his instincts for so long that having them taken away is crippling.

"It feels odd, doesn't it?" Aristeus says. "It's like your sense of smell. You never notice it until it's gone."

"W-what did you do to me?" Daniel says, and each word is carried on a shaky exhalation.

"Oh, that's a parlor trick." A smile lifts the corner of Aristeus's mouth. "Want to see something much more interesting?" His voice takes on that tone again—cold and soft. *"Stop breathing."*

Daniel's lungs freeze in mid-exhalation. His whole chest seizes up and he cannot draw breath. He tries—oh god, he tries. At first it's just uncomfortable, a tightness around his throat and nose. But then his chest begins to burn. He needs to breathe. He chokes on the effort, wants to gag, but he can't. He's scrabbling at his own collar, trying to open something. There is a pounding in his head, nausea in his stomach. Under normal circumstances, a person cannot hold his breath until unconsciousness. The body will not allow it. But these circumstances are anything but normal. Gray spots begin to dance at the edges of his vision. His fingers tingle like they've fallen asleep.

Then Aristeus says, *"Breathe."*

Daniel's breath hitches in his throat, and he has trouble restarting his lungs. He cannot suck in enough air; he presses his fists to the table to keep himself upright while he pants.

Aristeus's smile widens.

Daniel has heard of this. There have always been rumors, but Daniel thought of the most rare immunities the way people do about albinos—sure, they exist, but what are the odds of ever meeting one? Mentalists and illusionists are unusual enough, but even they are considered common next to... It takes Daniel a moment to remember the name. *Dominus.*

The implications make Daniel reel. The US government has a dominus. This information has to be top secret. If other governments find out—if the Republic or the Union find out—who knows what it could trigger. That's why the cameras are turned off. There can't be a record of this.

The fact that Daniel has been allowed to see Aristeus, to understand what this man is... It means they have no intention of letting Daniel out of here. Not alive. Not carrying this knowledge. Which means, he realizes, that this is no simple interrogation. If the UAI is desperate enough to unleash a dominus, it means they know exactly what Daniel was sent to steal. They know about his job.

The job that Daniel told Kit about.

"Do you think the FBI can shut down the UAI?" Aristeus asks. "You think they can control us?"

Daniel glances over and sees the two FBI agents; their expressions are torn between panic and shock.

Daniel slumps forward onto the table.

"I did offer to make you a deal," Aristeus says, chiding.

Daniel cannot bring himself to reply—he's too busy dragging breath after breath into his lungs. A small line of saliva escapes his lips and pools on the table's metal surface.

Aristeus rests his chin in the palm of one hand. It's a casual pose, one usually reserved for friends conversing with one another. He says, almost lazily, "You were recently contacted by a woman called Frieda Fuller, one of the leaders of the terrorist group called TATE. *I'd like you to tell me about it.*"

Daniel's lips crack open. They'll overflow with secrets, he realizes. In a moment, he'll be telling this Aristeus whatever he wants to know.

Daniel is an eludere. He is supposed to be able to escape anything.

Except his own mind.

8

CIERE

Magnus rises to his feet in one graceful movement, getting to the window in two strides. His fingers twitch the blinds open. "Well," he says, "there is no chance I'm meeting that accountant at five, is there?" He grinds his cigarette out on the windowsill.

Ciere is already moving. "I think this is our cue to run."

"They're after you?" Magnus says, but he sounds more surprised than accusatory.

Ciere blinks. "What, you thought they were after you?"

"Maybe," Bellevue says in a faint voice, "they're not after any of us."

"Maybe." Magnus moves away from the window. "But we should still leave. Call the agency. Warn them that if there are any coworkers in the area, they should evacuate now."

Bellevue looks desperately glad for something to do; she

fumbles in her pocket and withdraws a small tablet, unfolding it with trembling fingers.

Already, Ciere can hear the shuffling feet, the cries of alarm, and then a siren screeches to life. "And there it goes," Magnus says, satisfied. "Someone's already pulled the fire alarm. That's why I love this hotel." He moves out into the corridor and gestures for the others to follow. Ciere immediately swerves to their left, but Magnus grips her arm. "What are you doing?"

"Escaping," she says, incredulous. "What are you doing?"

Magnus's long fingers encircle Ciere's wrist. His fingers catch on the tracker bracelet. "You ever dealt with SWAT before?"

Once. Just once. A long time ago.

"No," Ciere lies.

Magnus draws her back against the wall, out of the path of two businessmen, who nearly flatten each other in their haste to get to the stairs. Magnus says, "The back exits are the first routes they'll cover. Men will already be in place before they allow the main team to be seen. They're smoking us out. Like rabbits from a hole. Whoever goes running out the back will be taken into custody."

It's a frightening prospect, even more so because Ciere would have done exactly that. Sure, she could have shielded herself from sight, but Devon would be visible. And if there were any cameras, she'd be spotted.

"But," Ciere says, "where are we going?"

Magnus's eyes are drawn tight. "Where any really good criminals would go—through the front doors."

Clamoring shouts and raised voices drown out anything else Magnus might have wanted to say. Words like "smoke," "fire," and "stairs" ring out above the din. Obviously, not everyone has realized exactly what's going on, but they do know something is wrong. The tide of bodies flows in the direction of the stairs, and Magnus glides in amid them. He still grips Ciere's wrist, and she grabs for Devon's arm. She will not lose him in the chaos. Out of the corner of her eye, she sees Devon clasp hands with Bellevue.

The stair doors swing open before them, and it's all Ciere can do to keep her feet. They are rushing, stumbling, flying down the stairs. If this swell of people resembles a river, then this is white water. If anyone falls, they'll be trampled. The air is thick with fear; all it will take is one spark to start something that might turn deadly. Ciere is suddenly grateful for Magnus's firm grasp, and she clings even harder to Devon. They're a human chain, linked by their crooked status, holding on for dear life.

Getting out of the lobby is easier said than done. The crowd bottlenecks at the front doors, but Magnus leads the others through the bar and out the restaurant entrance into the parking lot.

There are at least two hundred people in the lot, all of them fenced in by cops. The crowd's instinct is to huddle together. They clutch at one another—parents' fingers twined with those of children, couples with arms around each others' waists, friends who stand so closely that their shoulders touch; even people who have obviously never exchanged a word find themselves bunched together. Ciere finds herself watching a family with a girl about her age. The girl stands between a man and woman. She looks safe, sheltered by family. It sends a pang of yearning through Ciere. She can't remember the last time she felt that secure.

The SWAT officers begin separating the crowds. Batons in hand, the black-clad men and women direct everyone into orderly lines. It's a shuffling mess, and only fear of the officers brings order to the chaos. Ciere finds herself in the third line back, with Magnus on her left and Devon on her right.

Once the lines are established, a man with a tag scanner begins at the first row. He holds out a hand, fingers twitching in a silent question. A moment later, the first set of tags is produced and then run through the handheld machine. Ciere's eyes narrow. If the feds are scanning tags, it means one thing.

They're looking for someone.

Devon shifts nervously from foot to foot. "They're FBI," he mutters.

Ciere shoots him an incredulous look. This is a whole new level of ignorance, even for him. "Please tell me you didn't just figure that out. It's written on their vests."

"No," Devon retorts, then pauses. "Well, yes, but that's

not what I meant." He turns his attention back to the officers, his brows knitting together. "What I mean is, they're FBI and they're working with a SWAT team. SWAT do hostage situations, riots, terrorists. They take on only the most dangerous tasks." He clears his throat significantly and lowers his voice to a whisper. "What are they doing in the tourist district of DC?"

Her stomach sinks. His meaning is all too clear.

"They also," Ciere adds, "take down immune threats."

Abruptly her tags feel heavy around her throat. She cups her hand around the two slips of metal and weighs them in her palm. Could these feds be looking for her? Could Guntram have already gone through with his threat to inform the feds of her crime? He couldn't give them her name—he doesn't know it—but the feds' facial-recognition software is easily capable of tracking her movements through the CCTV network. Those cameras are how most criminals are caught. Could they have tracked her here?

Don't let anyone see what you are, understand?

The urge to break out of the line is nearly unbearable. Ciere wants to pump her legs, sprint away from this crowd and throw an illusion around herself. She wants to disappear. But the moment she takes a step out of line, she'll draw attention. And to run would be to invite chase.

Anxiety forms a lump in her throat that she desperately tries to swallow. A hand falls on her shoulder and she looks up. "Kit should've taught you how to hide in plain sight by now," Magnus says quietly.

She forces a shuddering breath into her lungs. "He has. Tried, anyway. I—I'm not good at that."

"You want to run, to change your face, and hide where no one can find you," he says.

She rolls her shoulder, dislodging his hand. "Are you reading my mind?"

Magnus laughs, but it's a rueful little sound. "Your face speaks quite well on its own."

It takes a few minutes for an officer to get to Ciere's row. She isn't dressed like the SWAT officers, and it takes Ciere a moment to see the letters embroidered on the woman's bulletproof vest: FBI—ADVERSE EFFECTS DIVISION.

Ciere clenches her fists, feels her bitten nails dig into her palms, and tries to ready an illusion. Just in case.

The fed gets to Devon first. Wordlessly she holds out her hand for his tags.

"Officer," Devon says, giving her one of those flirty smiles.

Can't hit on a fed, my ass, Ciere thinks.

Unfazed, the woman takes his tags and passes the scanner over them. Ciere can see the information flash on its screen—an official headshot of Devon, his name, birth date, current address, passport, and other information. Above all of it, three lines are bolded.

DEVON LYRE

TITER: POSITIVE

NO SYMPTOMS OF ADVERSE EFFECTS

Translation: while the government knows Devon was vaccinated, they have no proof that he has an immunity. They don't know if he's one of the 0.003 percent. Since he's been vaccinated, he's required to undergo an annual physical and fill out a questionnaire. It's a system put in place to supposedly weed out those who have immunities, but there's an inherent flaw: everybody lies.

Devon's used to pretending. It's one of the few times Ciere's seen him lie flawlessly. It's a skill drilled into him by his own father—or so Devon has said, with an edge of bitterness. Now that skill comes in handy; Devon grins unabashedly at the pretty officer. He looks just like any teenage perv, not a guilty eidos.

The officer takes a note, scribbling something down before shoving Devon's tags back into his hands. Ciere doesn't have time to breathe a sigh of relief—the fed is gesturing for her tags. She shakily holds them out. The chain is yanked from her hand and the officer brings the tags to the scanner's glittering surface.

A red light winks and the tags spell out one of Ciere's many aliases.

SARAH GRAVES

TITER: NEGATIVE

Translation: according to these tags, Sarah Graves was never vaccinated. No Praevenir, no immunity. What follows is a dummy address and other false information. In fact, the only truths on those tags are her height and weight.

Ciere holds her breath; if the officers are here for her, then this is the moment. They will arrest her now. While the officer's attention is focused on the scanner, Ciere's tags dangle between her fingers like an afterthought.

The officer looks up. Ciere feels her tags pressed back into her hands, but she doesn't react fast enough. The chain slips and her tags hit the pavement. Immediately she drops to her knees and scoops them up, pressing them protectively to her chest. She chances a look upward and sees that the officer has moved on to Magnus. He hands his tags over with the slightest hesitation, and Ciere sees his fingertips lightly brush the bare skin of the officer's wrist.

Once the officer is out of earshot, Magnus murmurs, "Bellevue was right—they aren't here for either of us."

"How do you know?" Ciere asks.

Magnus rubs his fingertips together. "Our faces weren't in her head. It's—"

A loud, wordless cry cuts him off. The quiet hum of the crowd dies in the wake of the shout. Ciere cranes her head and her eyes widen.

It's an older man. He's being dragged out of their line,

caught between two feds. He struggles, his face contorted with fear and anger, and as he fights back, Ciere catches a glimpse of something around his wrist.

A heavy silver bracelet.

The old man snarls curses at the two as they drag him to the SWAT van. As he nears the van, the man's curses become pleas and he's begging the crowd for help. He has a family, he says desperately. He has a wife. Grandkids. A life. A home. Please, can't somebody—?

The van's door slams shut, and the man's cries are silenced.

The crowd watches, paralyzed.

Bellevue closes her eyes; Magnus stares on. Devon makes a move as if to step forward, but Ciere seizes his arm. He says something, but she doesn't hear it. Her attention has narrowed, contracted to a pinpoint. All she can think about is that silver bracelet, heavy and seamless, just like the one encircling her own wrist. Her whole body feels heavy and cold, her muscles rigid with dread.

"Come on," Magnus says quietly, tugging on her arm. She stumbles and just catches herself. Her legs feel numb, but she manages to follow Magnus as he walks away.

The feds let them pass. Magnus and company have already been IDed and released; there is no need to hold them.

Magnus strides ahead and the others fall into step; after ten minutes or so, he leads them into a graveyard, of all places—one of the historic gravesites, complete with an informative plaque. Overhanging branches block out the sunlight and provide cover. The ground is lumpy and some of the headstones have begun to crumble.

"There are no cameras here," Magnus says. "Mourners and tourists have little to hide."

Bellevue slumps onto the grass, her eyes focused on her manicured hands. Magnus remains standing, with his arms loosely at his sides. "Another raid," Bellevue says. "That's the third this month." She slides a calculating look toward Magnus. "What was it this time?"

Magnus looks more self-assured than before; all his earlier fragility has vanished, and he looks cold and detatched. "I didn't get much out of that fed's head, but I do know that the old man works—ah, *worked* for the Alkanov family. Racketeering, mostly. The feds were there because there was some anonymous tip. Someone planted a tracking device on him and then called it in."

Devon and Ciere glance at each other, and Ciere sees her own dread echoed in his face. He looks like he might be sick. He begins pacing back and forth, his steps quick and jerky. "No one—no one did anything."

"What were they supposed to do?" Magnus pulls his tablet from a pocket and hits a button. "Looks like no one else from the agency was in the area. Good."

"They should've done something." Devon sounds like he's choking on his own words. "Someone should've—"

"Gotten shot?" Magnus says mildly. "An adverse effects FBI team won't hesitate to gun down anyone who tries to stop them. I've seen it happen before."

So has Ciere. But she keeps her mouth shut. The memory is too painful.

"They shouldn't be able to just do that, just pull people off the street," Devon says.

Ciere remains quiet. She isn't one to rage against the way society works; she's lived in this world long enough that its sharp edges have dulled for her.

"They shouldn't," Magnus agrees. "But there's nothing we can do about it." He checks his watch. "We should get going." He fumbles in his jacket pocket for a moment before coming up with something. It's the envelope Ciere gave Bellevue. Magnus pries Ciere's hand open and wraps her fingers around the thick envelope. "Full refund," he says curtly. He starts to pull away, but in a sudden flash of insight Ciere grabs him. She remembers his lingering handshake, the way he knew what the fed was thinking when she brushed his hand. If she's right, then his mentalism is linked to touch. It's the only time he's seemed to truly know what she was thinking.

So she brings to mind the last memory of Kit as he showed them out the door that morning. *"Tell him that I'm sorry,"*

Kit said, and there was something in his voice that Ciere had never heard before. *"Tell him I did it for his own good."*

Magnus jerks backward, out of her grasp. He turns away, but not before she sees the flash of hurt in his eyes. "Damn," Magnus says. "Damn him." He presses his thumb into the crease between his brows. He looks tired and limp, like all the emotion has been wrung out of him.

"Let's get out of here," he says, and Bellevue nods. Together, they stride out of the graveyard and disappear around a corner, vanishing from sight. Devon remains sitting on the headstone, leaning over his own knees like they're all he can depend on.

Ciere sits down, curling her legs beneath her. She can feel the grass on her bare skin, the prickle of a ladybug as it crawls over her ankle, and hear the whisper of wind through the overhanging branches. It's an idyllic scene—a summer day in an old graveyard. She shivers.

They wait another hour before returning to the hotel parking lot for their car. There is no sign of the earlier chaos, but Ciere can still see the marks where the old man's feet dragged.

"Well, that could've gone better," Ciere says, just to say something.

It's a quiet drive home.

9

CIERE

When Ciere was twelve, she robbed the Lyre residence.

The Lyres were the perfect mark. They were obscenely wealthy, and they'd just relocated from England "to pursue new business opportunities"—or so the press release had said. Kit's contacts indicated that tax evasion might have played a role. So Mr. Lyre migrated across the Atlantic and took up residence in an elsec in Boston.

A week after the Lyres relocated, Kit and Ciere made their move. They slipped into the elsec under the guise of a gardener and his young niece. Nobody gave them a second glance, not when they were sweeping the sidewalks and pruning the hedges.

"Mr. Lyre is leaving," Kit murmured, and Ciere glanced up from her broom. Sure enough, a tall, dark-skinned man was climbing into a Bentley. He was followed by a slim, doe-eyed girl wearing a designer jacket.

"Is that all of them?" she said quietly.

Kit nodded. "My sources report seeing only his daughter. And they haven't had time to settle in or hire maids yet." He gave her a small smile. "You can do this."

Ciere smiled back, grateful for the praise.

Her ability to conjure illusions had faded since her mother died. Ciere found that her illusions were like cobwebs—fragile, unable to hold any real weight. But Kit had her practicing regularly, trying to help her regain some of the talent she had lost. Standing beside their rented truck, Ciere used her immunity to draw the world in around her. She wasn't invisible; it was more of a chameleon effect. Colors washed over her skin until she blended in with the greenery. When she crossed the street and darted over the picketed fence, no one noticed.

There was an unlocked window on the first floor. Honestly, these people were asking to be robbed, she thought. Ciere squirmed through the small space and found herself standing in a hallway. The decor was nearly nonexistent: bare gray walls, wooden floors, and very little furniture. Boxes were piled everywhere; it was obvious the Lyres hadn't yet settled into their new home.

She began silently moving from room to room, trying to find anything that looked valuable. Most of the boxes had labels like GOOD DISHES or COMPUTER CORDS. She paused for a moment next to a box labeled SILVER, but moved on. If she didn't find anything better, she'd come back to it.

The master bedroom was tucked away in the northern corner of the house. Ciere knew it had to be the master bedroom, because the bed alone was bigger than Kit's whole living room. And there was a safe resting in the open closet.

Jackpot.

Illusion still up, she crossed the room and studied the safe. She knew how to crack it. But that would take time and... and the safe was already open.

Hesitantly, her fingers found the knob and pulled. The safe's door swung open, and she peered inside.

Empty. No stacks of money or expensive jewels. There was only a sheet of paper.

Curious, Ciere reached in and picked up the sheet. It had been clumsily folded over several times, and when she managed to pry the edges apart, she saw there were only a few words scrawled onto it.

I'm leaving. Don't look for me.

A soft thud made Ciere whirl around.

A boy stood in the doorway. He looked about Ciere's age, and he had the same clean good looks as Mr. Lyre—even teeth, brown eyes, dark skin, and curly hair. The noise had been when he'd dropped a canvas bag onto the floor.

"Y-you're..." he said.

She knew how this must look—a sheet of paper floating in the air. She wondered for the briefest second if she could pretend to be a ghost. Fear lanced through her, and she released the paper, turning to run. There was a window she might be able to squeeze out of—

"Wait," the boy said, surging into the room. But it wasn't the movement that stopped her. It was his voice, which was thick with tears and unexpectedly fragile. She froze.

"Please don't go," he said. "Please. I won't hurt you." He fumbled blindly ahead with one hand, and out of sheer luck he ended up grabbing Ciere's shoulder. The moment he touched her skin, the illusion broke apart.

Ciere watched several emotions play out on his face: shock, fear, dawning comprehension, and then... elation?

"Hi," he whispered.

This wasn't what Ciere had expected. He should've been afraid of her; he should've been calling the police; he should've been doing anything but stare at her like she was the greatest thing he'd ever seen.

Her own gaze darted around the room and landed on the canvas bag. The boy saw what she was staring at, and said, "This what you're looking for?" He picked up the bag and held it open. Inside were stacks and stacks of cash. More than Ciere had ever hoped for. No wonder the safe was empty; it had already been raided, by Lyre's own son.

"You're—" she said, her voice coming to a shuddering halt. "You're—not supposed to be here."

Kit had said the house was supposed to be empty.

"Yeah," the boy said, and there was no mistaking the bitterness in his voice. "My dad keeps me hidden. At least until he can find a boarding school for me.

"You're one of them, though, aren't you?" he said, almost desperately. "One of those immune criminals?"

Unsure of what to say, Ciere nodded.

The boy smiled, and for the first time Ciere saw something of herself in him—a quiet yearning, a desperation that she felt when looking at whole families. He looked hungry, even though he probably had never experienced the empty gnaw of physical starvation.

The boy inhaled. "Take me with you. I can't—I can't say here."

Shock made Ciere's voice sharper than she intended. "I just met you," she said incredulously.

He recoiled a few inches, realization settling over his face. "Yeah. Right. Sorry—I—It's just, I've never met another..."

His voice trailed off, and he seemed to be fighting some internal battle. Then he picked up the fallen sheet of paper and drew a pen from his pocket. He scribbled on the back and crammed it into the bag.

"Take this," he said, hurriedly shoving the canvas bag—cash and all—into her hands. "We don't need it. Honestly, I don't even know why my dad keeps so much cash around."

She stared at him. He couldn't be serious.

"My e-mail is inside," he said. "It's untraceable. Please—I won't turn you in. I just...please. I can't be the only person like this."

She opened the bag after she'd clambered through the window and hidden herself behind a large tree. With unsteady hands, she touched the bundles of cash before her fingers alighted on the paper.

Sure enough, there was an e-mail address. And beneath it:

Devon Lyre—Eidos
Wannabe Criminal

10

CIERE

That night Ciere dreams. Flashes of white-hot fire, the taste of ashes on her tongue, the rip-roar of automatic rifle fire, and a child's wobbly voice repeating the same word over and over again. She jolts awake, half expecting to find herself barefoot and standing on a cliff overlooking the Pacific Ocean. But she's in her bed, in the Bolsover house, and she's as safe as she'll ever be. She wonders if it's time to get up, if she can drown the nightmares—*memories, really*—in a cup of coffee.

Her digital clock says it's four in the morning.

Ciere flops back onto her bed, eyes wandering to the spackled ceiling. Her throbbing heart begins to slow, and her limbs feel cold.

Her room hasn't changed much, not since she and Kit first

moved here. It's still patterned in pink-and-white wallpaper, with frilly curtains and a closet full of sundresses.

Ciere reaches out, flicks on a lamp, and picks up the business card sitting on her bedside table. It's plain white with a single image embossed on it—a bird in flight, its wings stretching from one corner to the other. Centered are the words BRANDT GUNTRAM written in all caps and, underneath it, a phone number.

The Gyr Syndicate was responsible for the raid in DC. They tagged that man and then called the authorities. She's heard horror stories of what mobs do to people who don't pay debts. Mobs have been known to collect interest by taking fingers. And when they run out of digits, bodies start turning up.

But as gruesome as that sounds, what Guntram can do—what Ciere just witnessed—is scarier.

She'll be hunted down like the valuable commodity she is. Taken into custody just like that man. Given a choice: recruitment or imprisonment. She could run, smash the bracelet and try to make a break for it. But all her emergency cash is stored overseas, and she doesn't have time to arrange for safe—by which she means, illegal—travel to Europe. Her only course would be to take a commercial flight, but there are far too many mentalists working for the TSA. It would be the ultimate gamble.

Yesterday, when Ciere told Kit about the raid, he was less

than pleased. "I entrusted you with a simple task: recruit a freelancer. Apparently that was too difficult."

"But why do we need a mentalist?" Ciere asked, honestly curious.

Kit grimaced. "When dealing with lawyers, you need someone who can tell what's going through their twisty little minds."

Ciere spent the rest of the day in the backyard, trying to teach her new dog to play fetch. Devon tried to help, but when his phone blared that *ding a ling ling, a ling ling ling* ring-tone, he panicked. "Here," he said, shoving the phone at her. "Answer it with an accent."

"This is ridiculous," she said. "Your family knows you're not in Norway."

"They have no proof, and as long as they can pretend I'm pissing my way through some ski resort, they won't come looking for me," Devon said. "Now repeat after me: '*norsken min er dårlig.*' "

After a subdued dinner, they all went their separate ways. Ciere retreated to her own room, hoping an early bedtime would calm her nerves. Obviously, it didn't work, because she's staring at the ceiling at four in the morning, wondering how prison food would taste.

Ciere swings her legs over the side of her bed and scans her room. This house is large, with its three stories, six bedrooms, and four baths. It's a picture of what an elsec home should be—expensive, safe. It should make her feel secure.

It doesn't.

Ciere isn't the only one to have a bad night. When Devon comes downstairs for breakfast, Ciere nearly spits out her mouthful of coffee. Devon's hair, previously curly and dark, is buzzed short in one, long strip. It looks like a reverse Mohawk.

"Wha—?" she begins to say, but is cut off by an incensed Devon relating the story of how he was attacked in the dead of night by a madman with a razor.

"It was seven in the morning," Kit says. "Hardly the dead of night."

"Oh," Ciere says, relieved, "so Kit just tried to shave you. Why are you making such a big deal out of it?"

Devon gapes at her. "Please repeat that sentence and realize just how ridiculous you sound."

Lizaveta sputters when she sees Devon's half-buzzed hair and makes a concerned clucking noise. "Trust me," Devon tells her, "this wasn't a deliberate fashion statement."

"Oh, calm down," Ciere says.

Devon rounds on her. "Are you mad?"

"Kit's, uh—I don't know the word. Hazing?" Ciere explains. Her fingers wrap around her cup of coffee and she holds it close, savoring the warmth.

Devon's brow furrows. "Indoctrinating?"

"Yeah, that sounds better. The whole hair-cutting thing is standard. Less chance of a hair being left at a scene, less chance someone could grab a fistful—that sort of thing." She lifts a hand to her own hair—curly and blonde, it probably would be striking if she'd let it grow out. But it's cropped short around her ears. "Kit cut my hair when I went out on my first job."

Ciere remembers sitting in the wooden chair, facing the mirror, as Kit's nimble fingers parted her wet hair. The cool steel of the scissors sent chills down her neck as he snip-snipped away at her curls. His hand brushed the stray hairs from her shoulders and nose, the touches light and quick.

Kit spends the day attached to his phone, making all sorts of calls. From what Ciere can tell, he's trying to find a new mentalist. But like Devon said, mentalists are rare and valuable commodities. Known mentalists are either recruited by the government or various mobs. And inviting a mentalist with conflicting loyalties onto a job could be disastrous.

Ciere ghosts through the house, wandering in search of something to do. She ends up giving the dog a bath and brushing its matted fur.

"It's male," she says, sure this time.

Devon is eying his hair in the bathroom mirror. "You ever going to name the thing?"

Ciere yanks a knot of fur out of the brush and goes back

to work on the dog's back. Luckily, he doesn't seem bothered by all the fuss. He sits on Ciere's lap, tongue lolling and eyes bright. "Tulip," Ciere says.

"But you said he's a bloke." Devon's brow wrinkles. "Why not take the final step and call him Pretty Flower Daisy? Might as well strip him of all masculinity while you're at it."

Ciere pats the dog's head. "We need another tulip around here, because this little guy dug up all the tulip bulbs in Kit's garden. Kit doesn't know yet—I sort of shoved them all back in the ground."

Devon eyes the dog with new fondness. "All right, then. We're calling him the Great Tulip Destroyer. Tulip for short."

A bell rings out, echoing through the hallway. A moment later Kit's voice follows.

"Someone at the gate!" he calls.

Ciere shuts the bathroom door behind her—no sense in incurring Kit's wrath by letting a wet Tulip loose on the antique furniture—and thuds down the stairs with Devon at her heels. When she drags the door open, her jaw goes slack.

Magnus Fugaré stands on the porch.

"Um, hi," Ciere says. After their encounter, she was sure he would never join them. Yet here he is, duffel bag in hand. She tries to make sense of his arrival, but her brain seems to have short-circuited. "How'd you know where to find us?" is all she can come up with.

"Kit always did like ostentatious houses," Magnus says.

"Well," Devon says. "Thought we'd seen the last of you."

Magnus's lips thin out. "Circumstances change."

Kit comes into the foyer, his phone still cradled between ear and shoulder, a folder in his hands. "Yes, I understand," he is saying, until he catches sight of the three people standing in the doorway. The folder slips from his hand and the papers scatter. "I'll call you back," Kit says vaguely, and snaps the phone shut. Ciere has never seen him look so startled. It's as if his usual mask has cracked open, giving her a glimpse of someone young and hopeful.

Magnus goes still. A shadow passes behind his eyes, and he sets his duffel bag on the floor.

"Magnus," Kit says. His steps lengthen and he rushes to the door, a tentative smile breaking across his face.

And that is when Magnus's gloved fist connects with Kit's jaw. It happens so fast that Ciere's eyes don't register the movement—all she sees is Magnus's arm draw backward, and then Kit is on the foyer floor, gingerly touching a spot on his jaw. Magnus doesn't say a word. He picks up his bag and steps over Kit's fallen form, his long strides carrying him into the house and out of sight. It takes Kit a second to recover. When he rises to his feet, Ciere cannot decipher the look on his face.

"Well," Devon says, suddenly cheerful, "we have our mentalist. Let's rob some lawyers."

PART TWO

Many of the scientists who have been working on S-1 have expressed considerable concern about the future dangers of the development of atomic power. Some are fearful that no safe system of international control can be established. They, therefore, envisage the possibility of an armament race that may threaten civilization.

—George L. Harrison, Memorandum for the Secretary of War, June 26, 1945

11

CIERE

The Richard & Cole law firm is located on the fourth story of an office building in downtown Baltimore. The streets are crowded with cars, buses, and taxis, and a constant haze of smog drifts through the city, along with the sounds of car engines and the droning of air conditioners.

At one in the afternoon, a man strides into the office building. His tags identify him as Massimiliano Paterni. Security doesn't give him a second glance; he looks like any other businessman. He pauses at the front desk and tells the receptionist he has an appointment with Matilda Cole. The receptionist smiles vaguely and makes a phone call.

"Fourth floor," she tells him, pulling a visitor's pass from her desk drawer. Massimiliano Paterni takes it and clips it to his lapel. With a word of thanks, he makes for the elevator. He nods once to the security guard, who smiles back. All is well.

One block away, three criminals sit in a silver SUV and watch the office building's hacked security feed on Devon's largest tablet.

The planning session for The Lawyer Job (as Devon titled it) occurred the same day Magnus arrived. No time to delay, Kit said. Especially not with Daniel missing.

Kit brought in a platter of tea and scones, set it down, and headed to the far wall. A large portion of that wall—about five feet by four feet—appeared to be nothing more than a landscape painted on glass. Kit reached out and touched it; the colors shimmered and then faded to transparency. It was the patch of the high-def enamel Kit installed when they'd first moved in. Capable of syncing with any tablet or computer, it functioned as a large screen when it wasn't masquerading as a painting.

The large wall screen showed the blueprints of a multistory office building. Kit's fingers darted over his tablet and the picture zoomed in, focusing on a specific area. "This is the building where Richard and Cole practice law. It's in downtown Baltimore. Eight stories. The building also houses other law practices, three real estate agents, a politician's headquarters, and a pretty affluent artist." He paused. "What does this tell us?" The question was aimed at Ciere, who froze in the act of reaching for a scone.

She sat up straighter, trying to give the impression she hadn't zoned out halfway through his description. "Um, all the tenants are loaded."

"Which means tight security," Devon said. He already had his own tablet out and was typing with one hand. "The building is owned by a rental company that owns several other corporate offices in the area," he said. "They've outsourced security to a private agency. All guests are buzzed in from the lobby reception area, and tags are scanned for records. Cameras everywhere. Two security guards in the lobby at all times. Oh, and every office is equipped with a safe. At night, there's the usual lockdown—motion-detecting sensors around the doors and windows and a single guard bunking in the lobby."

Kit nodded with grudging approval. "Looks like you're not a complete disappointment."

"So how are we going to get someone inside? Walk in through the front door?"

Kit looked at Magnus. "Exactly."

It occurs to Ciere that confining Devon and Kit to a car together is a bad idea. The quarters are too close—they keep bumping elbows. The SUV's backseats are folded down, and the three of them sit in their makeshift crooked headquarters.

The immediate plan is for them to remain in the SUV while Magnus does his thing. Hacking into the building's security system is Devon's job.

Devon grumbles to himself as he works, his fingers a blur on his tablet. All Ciere can see are streams of code. "Wireless systems again," Devon mutters. "My God, when will people learn that wireless is about as secure as an unlocked car?"

"For our sakes," Kit drawls, "hopefully never."

Ciere leans over the tablet. "Well, at least Magnus is in the building," she says. It's not the most graceful segue into a new conversation, but it distracts Kit.

"Of course he got in." Kit shifts uncomfortably, trying to find a place to sit. "His alias is flawless."

"Who is Massimiliano Paterni?" Ciere asked. She wasn't sure if she'd pronounced the name correctly. Frowning, she brushed the scone crumbles from her lap. Kit still stood in front of the HDE screen, his tablet in hand. His fingers moved, and a new picture appeared on the screen. It was a government-issued ID, the kind programmed into tags.

MASSIMILIANO PATERNI

TITER: POSITIVE

The picture showed a young man with a long neck and dark hair. It looked like a younger Magnus. Devon whistled in admiration. "Nice bit of forgery."

Magnus's lip curled. "Oh god, not that name again."

"Massimiliano Paterni is an identity we worked under a long time ago," Kit said, ignoring Magnus. "Youngest son of the Paterni family. They own several large vineyards in Italy. Unfortunately for poor Massimiliano, he had a falling-out with his father and was disowned. That's why he needs an estate lawyer."

Devon frowned and leaned forward. "Wait, so one of us is going to impersonate some fake Italian wine bloke?"

"Oh, the family is quite real," Kit said. "And Massimiliano is also real—well, he *was* real. He died in the war. And you," he added to Devon, "will not be donning any aliases. The tags are programmed for Magnus."

Ciere understood. "You resurrected this Paterni's social security code, his titer test, and his birth certificate."

Kit inclined his head in an approving nod. "It's more reliable to resurrect an identity than to create one. Good to see you were listening for that lecture."

"That's sort of morbid," Devon said, pulling a disgusted expression. "Using a dead man's info like that."

"We're crooks. Morbidity is the least of our worries." Kit's smile sharpened. "And if you're disturbed by Magnus's alias, then you won't like what we're stealing."

"A will," Devon says, for what must be the fifth time. He shifts uncomfortably, trying to stretch his long legs inside the SUV.

"I can't believe we're going to all this fuss for some dead bird's will."

A muscle near Kit's eye spasms. "Richard and Cole specialize in estate law. What'd you *think* we were acquiring?"

"I don't know." Devon smirks down at his tablet as he scrolls through the many security feeds. "Maybe you finally decided to *acquire* that Pollock piece. I think my dad sold it to a lawyer a year ago."

Magnus pushes the door open and steps into the offices of Richard and Cole. The offices are plushly decorated, with a dark carpet and leather furniture. The receptionist is a man in his early thirties, with wire-rimmed glasses and an impeccable suit. He's typing away on his old-fashioned desktop computer. He sees Magnus and his lips form words.

Ciere cannot see Magnus's face—he is angled away from the security cam. But he must say something amusing, because the receptionist smiles.

As if on cue, the office door swings open and a woman appears. She's in her mid-forties, with graying hair swept back into a bun. She wears a dark skirt and blazer, both conservatively cut.

"Mr. Paterni," Devon says in a breathy parody of a woman's voice. "We spoke on the phone. I'm Matilda Cole."

There is an exchange of hands. Bare hands, Ciere notes, because Magnus isn't wearing his gloves.

Kit switched the wall screen to the building blueprints while Magnus poured a second cup of tea and Devon reached for another scone. "This is Cole's office," Kit said, pointing at the HDE screen. "Now"—he drew a box inside the office—"this is the safe. The will of Marie Louis should be inside."

"Who is Marie Louis?" Ciere asked.

Devon perked up. "Yeah. You never did tell us why the client wants the will, anyway."

"Or," Magnus murmured, stirring his tea delicately, "*who* the client is."

Kit's expression smoothed out. "Her name is Frieda Fuller. Daniel has freelanced for her before. She works for a conglomerate of hackers. As for why she wants the will, I wouldn't know."

Magnus looked as if he wanted to ask another question, but Kit cut him off. "It is our job to make a copy of Marie Louis's will and deliver it to Ms. Fuller by the day after tomorrow." He spread his hands wide, opening up the conversation. "Now, how are we going to get the will? According to Fuller, it's being kept in the safe in Cole's office."

Ciere narrowed her eyes at the HDE wall screen. The office was on the fourth floor, which would've posed a problem if their crew didn't have a levitas. She glanced at the blueprints again and saw that the office in question had a window just large enough for someone to squeeze through.

"Break in through the window," she said, "and pick the safe's lock."

Devon snorted. "Not unless you find a way to disable the entire building's security. Motion sensors on the windows. The moment you break in, you've got about two minutes before the police show up."

"Precisely," Kit said. Then his face twisted into an expression of disgust, as if he realized he and Devon agreed on something. "Cracking the safe's combination would take far too long."

"Then we'll take the safe with us," Ciere said. "Tear it out of the wall and chuck it out the window."

"I considered it." Kit tapped the HDE screen with a fingernail, pointing at the safe. "But our odds of getting that very heavy safe out of the office and to the car wouldn't be ideal. Also, we're not taking the will with us. Lyre should memorize it and put it back into the safe. Then he'll dictate it to me afterward." He directs a gaze at Ciere. "Magnus gets us the code. You buy us time. Lyre and I will do the actual breaking in."

"Why don't we just steal it?" Devon said.

"Smart thieves," said Ciere, "don't leave behind clues. Like obviously missing property." *Like that Hello Kitty bobblehead*, she thinks, but doesn't say aloud. "Anyone who investigates the break-in will have no idea why we did it, so they won't know who to suspect."

Kit nodded in approval. "Exactly. As for how we get the safe's combination, that's a task best suited for our mentalist."

Devon shot Magnus a derisive look, and said, "Sorry, but what's a rent boy going to do for a job like this? He going to shag the combination out of the lawyer?" Ciere winced; Devon's habit of blurting out his every thought was sometimes mortifying.

Magnus let the silence draw out into an uncomfortable length. He never said a word, but he let the full weight of his gaze rest on Devon. Devon shifted restlessly in his seat, his mouth pulled down in an expression that was half embarrassment, half defiance.

"I have other uses," Magnus said once a full thirty seconds had passed.

Devon, looking thoroughly spooked, said, "Right. So what are you going to do?"

Magnus set his cup on its saucer. With his free hand, pinched the tip of one leather glove and tugged. The glove slipped off, revealing a long-fingered, pale hand. His every movement was deliberate, careful, the way a man might handle a grenade.

"As a mentalist, I can experience what a person feels and thinks so long as I am touching them," he said, flexing his fingers. Suddenly the fact that Magnus wore a turtleneck sweater, pants, shoes, and gloves even on a hot summer day made sense. Ciere's eyes raked over him—besides his hands, the only bare skin she could find was on his face. Magnus rubbed his thumb and forefinger together. "When this lawyer opens the safe, the numbers will be in her head, even if it is subconscious."

"You can't just grab her while she's getting into her safe," Ciere said. "That would look suspicious."

Magnus began pulling his gloves back on. "Like I said—I can do things other than seduce people."

Kit, Devon, and Ciere watch the security feed as Cole and Magnus exchange the usual greetings. The lawyer slides a key into her office door and unlocks it.

As the door shuts behind Magnus, Ciere draws in a sharp breath. "We're blind now, aren't we?"

Devon nods. "No cameras in the offices." He taps his tablet again and Ciere can see several feeds at once—all miniature.

Kit rises from his crouch, his knees making painful creaking sounds. With a groan, he drags himself into the driver's seat. "Might as well be comfortable while we wait," he says, angling the seat into a reclining position.

Ciere wishes she could adopt such a leisurely attitude about this job, but the thought of Brandt Guntram and his tracker has her on edge. Its heavy weight is a constant reminder of the power he holds over her. She rocks back and forth, waiting impatiently for any sign of Magnus's return. Devon seems as jumpy as she is; he doesn't put his tablet down. Instead, he channel surfs through the security feeds, bouncing through them so quickly that Ciere can't keep up. But then again, she's not an eidos. Devon is probably taking in the scenes at a glance, storing the information, and then going on to the next feed. It's a good strategy, and Ciere tells him so.

Devon blinks. "Actually, I was trying to see how many people in this building are picking their noses. So far I'm at three."

Ciere is only half-sure he's joking.

The minutes crawl past. It's at least an hour before Devon makes a noise. "Sighting," he says abruptly, and Ciere sits up so quickly she slams her elbow into the car door. "It's Magnus—he's leaving the lawyer's office."

Kit's eyes don't open, but a smile tugs at his mouth. "About time."

A few minutes later, Magnus swings into the passenger seat. Without a word, he opens the glove compartment and digs out his leather gloves. "Combination digital lock and password," he says without preamble. "Eight, three, five, nine, six, one. The password is 'ad valorem.' " He twists in his seat so he can look at Devon. "And I didn't even have to remove any of her clothing."

Devon seems instantly fascinated with the floor. Ciere grins. All that's left is to wait for nightfall.

12

DANIEL

When Daniel was fourteen, he met Kit Copperfield for the first time.

Daniel had been hanging around a bus station—he was new to Philadelphia and looking for a few easy marks. Picking pockets was easy when you could sense things other people couldn't, and it wouldn't take Daniel long to collect enough cash to stay at a local hostel.

A girl walked into the station. She looked about Daniel's age. Five feet tall, with short blonde hair and small, sharp features. Kind of pretty, in a mousy way. She wore a white sundress with no pockets. Not a good mark. Daniel would've dismissed her completely if she hadn't been carrying an awkward, rectangular-shaped package. Her hands trembled slightly, and her steps were quick. Daniel's instincts whispered a silent warning, and for the briefest second, his gaze found that of the girl. Their eyes locked, and Daniel felt a surge of recognition. It wasn't anything physical, but something familiar in the way this girl carried herself. Then the girl looked away, staggered up to the counter, and said, "I'm sorry, but can I set this thing here for a second?"

The clerk blinked at her. He was a man firmly ensconced in middle age, with jowls and an unamused stare.

The girl took his silence as an affirmative and heaved the package onto the counter. "Thank you," she said, undaunted. She bought a ticket to some station in the city center, and then confided, "I bought this thing at a garage sale for Father's Day, but it's a pain to carry around."

The clerk grunted and handed back her change.

"Want to see?" the girl said brightly, and before the man could wave her off, she pulled something out of the package. It was a painting. The whole thing was a mass of scribbles and blotches. Not worth stealing.

"Pretty, right?" the girl said. "My dad loves art."

The clerk grunted again.

The girl's smile faded as she scanned the small building. Her knees squeezed together and her expression pinched. "I need to use the restroom," the girl said, turning back to the clerk. "Can I leave this here, just for a second?"

The clerk waved her off.

"Thank you!" The girl grinned and hurried in the direction of the ladies' room.

The whole exchange wouldn't have caught Daniel's interest if another man hadn't entered the bus stop. He was out of place in this grungy building; his red hair was pulled back into a ponytail, and he wore clean slacks and a pressed shirt. Daniel just caught a glimpse of a black tattoo on the man's wrist, but it wasn't jail ink. The letters were stylized, printed in deepest black, and obviously professionally done. Everything about the man screamed money. Now *that* was a mark. The man brushed past Daniel—close enough to pick his pocket, but a flicker of uneasiness made Daniel hesitate. Why would someone who was loaded be taking a bus?

The man glided up to the counter and pulled out an antique money clip. He spoke in a light, clear voice, asking for tickets to some downtown location. But he cut off in mid-sentence when his eyes settled on the painting that the girl left behind.

"What is this?" the man said, setting a pale hand on the frame.

The clerk grunted. "Painting."

The man's eyes brightened. "May I?"

"Knock yourself out."

The man picked up the painting and studied it with undisguised delight. "Oh my goodness," the man murmured. He carefully slid a finger over the paint. "This can't—but I'm sure it is." He looked up, and when he spoke, his voice shook with excitement. "This is an original Pollock. See the signature?"

"A what?" the clerk said, cocking an eyebrow.

"Pollock, Pollock," the man said, like this should mean something. It certainly didn't mean anything to Daniel. "One of the greatest modern artists of all time! Jackson Pollock! If I'm not mistaken, this is his 'Number Thirty-Three'! It's been missing—where did you find it?"

The clerk finally began to perk up. He uncoiled himself from his seat and leaned over the counter to really look at the painting. "S'not mine. Belongs to a girl."

"To have a real Pollock in my collection," the man said reverently. "Goodness. If I can find this girl... but, damn," he looked at his watch. "Damn, if the bus didn't leave now... I really have to go." He focused all his attention on the clerk. "This is my card. If you could ask the girl to get in touch with me, tell her that I will pay anything she wants."

Then he flounced out of the bus stop, striding so close to Daniel that he felt a whisper of cotton brush his left arm and smelled woodsy cologne. Then the man was gone.

The teenage girl emerged from the restroom and skipped back over to the counter. "Thank you for watching this, sir!" she beamed, reaching for the painting.

The clerk put a hand down on the frame. "Wait," he said slowly.

The girl stopped and blinked up at him.

"This is a really pretty painting," said the clerk. "What... what do you want for it?"

The girl scratched at the back of her neck. "I dunno. I was planning to give it to my dad." She started to turn away, but the clerk spoke more quickly, his voice sharp with urgency.

"I'll give you a hundred dollars for it!"

The girl froze. "What?"

"A hundred dollars," the clerk said. "You can buy your father another present. And you'll still have some money left over."

The girl bit her lip. "I don't know...." Something in her face made Daniel think that the nervousness wasn't false—her fingers twisted together and she bounced on the balls of her feet.

"Two hundred."

Her face broke into a smile. "Okay!"

There was an exchange—the clerk handed over several rumpled twenties, and the girl gave him the painting. "Thanks," the girl said brightly as she pocketed the money. She turned and skipped out of the bus station. The clerk stroked his thumb over the painting's frame and smiled to himself.

It was perfect. A perfectly executed little drama for anyone gullible enough to believe it. And for all his flaws, Daniel had never been gullible. He finally understood what his immunity had been telling him—that flash of understanding when he'd met the girl's eyes. It was the recognition of two predators among a herd of sheep.

He stole out of the station and after the girl. He caught a glimpse of a white sundress and followed it around the corner.

There stood the man, arms crossed and expression cool, all his flamboyance gone. The girl hastened to his side and pulled out the handful of worn bills. "Two hundred," she said.

"Not bad," the man sighed. "At least that damn forgery is good for something. There's a back door. Retrieve the painting when that idiot goes on break. There's an art collector in King of Prussia we'll hit next."

The girl grinned, and it caught Daniel off balance. This girl looked nothing like his sister, but the wicked glee in her face reminded him of the times Bethany would poke his shoulder and plan a prank on the neighbors. She carried herself with the same mixture of hesitancy and defiance—a young immune criminal in the making. It made Daniel want to pick up the phone, to call home, but he knew that wasn't an option. It wasn't safe. So Daniel did the next best thing.

When the two walked past him, Daniel took care to brush against the man. Daniel slipped two fingers into a silk-lined pocket and found the antique money clip. He left something in return—a note with his phone number and the message: *Call me if you're looking for a new employee.*

Daniel was a member of Kit's crew for three years, but he knew it wouldn't last. Jobs come and go. It was only a matter of time until he'd be forced to move on. But he hadn't thought it would happen so soon, and he hadn't anticipated trading in his thieving crew for a pack of feds.

And he *really* hadn't anticipated becoming some dominus's lapdog. Aristeus's words still ring in his ears. Each was a command that Daniel can't break—and if he does, he'll have the nice little side effect of not breathing.

You will answer my questions truthfully.

You will not try to escape.

You will not harm my allies or myself.

You will go no farther than a three-mile radius from me without express permission.

You will not warn any of your former criminal allies about us.

You will aid the UAI in our cause.

You are one of us now.

That was it. No place to sign, no papers to initial, no legalese to sort through. Aristeus looked Daniel in the eye and laid down the law. Each order wrapped around Daniel's insides, tight and unyielding. He can still feel the words inside his brain, like worms infesting an apple. "My team is lacking an eludere," Aristeus said, which made both FBI agents goggle at

Daniel. "And we'll need him to identify Frieda Fuller when we find her."

That was how Daniel became part of Aristeus's team as a confidential informant. To the feds, he's an invaluable source of information. To his fellow crooks, Daniel is a traitor.

He feels like a turncoat, sitting in the back of an FBI van headed for Baltimore in the middle of the night. "For the love of all things holy, can't you guys ever do anything at a decent hour?" he says.

Gervais and Carson don't spare him a glance. They are both on their cell phones, busy talking with the other FBI agents and the local Baltimore police department. Looks like organizing a raid isn't an easy feat.

It's the dauthus woman, Morana, who speaks up. She's traded in the office-wear for a bulletproof vest. "Daylight is overrated," she says, clapping the shoulder of a distracted FBI agent. He jumps visibly, and Morana laughs. When he turns to glare, she winks. "Besides, if you're going to get the drop on a terrorist group, it's best to do it at night."

Daniel swallows whatever he might have said. It's no longer relevant. "T-terrorist?" he says, and the slight stutter gives him away. He's worked for Frieda before, and he can't reconcile the word "terrorist" with the comfortably plump woman he knows who has silvery blonde hair and can hack a government server without so much as blinking.

Morana picks up a knife and tucks it into her sleeve. "Turns out that your employer happens to work for some unsavory people."

One of the FBI agents snorts. "I want to know why you'd steal a will for her. I mean, really—a will? Usually it's jewels or bonds or something valuable."

The FBI doesn't know. Which means the UAI hasn't told them.

Daniel tries to keep his face impassive. "I don't ask—I just get paid."

Morana twists her curly hair back into a ponytail. "I guess that's understandable." She flashes a grin. "You've got some shady friends, don't you?"

Daniel glances around the interior of the van, at the feds strapping on riot gear. "Yeah. I really do."

13

CIERE

Robberies happen late at night for a couple of reasons: fewer people and the cover of darkness. Even if they spot something, witnesses out at three in the morning are usually doing something unsavory themselves and are less likely to go to the police. Crooks revel in the night, while the straights stay inside and keep their doors locked.

Ciere greets the night like an old friend as she steps out of the SUV. The fresh air is welcome, even if it's still heavy with humidity and heat. Devon all but falls out of the car in his haste to get outside. He staggers, grabs a lamppost to catch himself, and then straightens, obviously trying to give the impression the fall was on purpose.

"Keep the car running," Kit says.

Magnus slides into the driver's seat, his fingers curling

around the steering wheel. "Go get your score. I'll be waiting right here."

Kit, Devon, and Ciere make their way down the sidewalk, keeping out of the lamplight. Ciere is wearing her usual work outfit—black shirt, black leggings, worn black tennis shoes, and a ski mask clutched in her left hand. Kit is dressed a little more conservatively in dark slacks and a black shirt, his long hair pulled back. He looks strange without the waistcoat. Devon tried his best, but his designer tee and stylishly ripped jeans stand out. He's dressed like a model of rebellious youth, not an experienced thief. All he needs is a can of spray paint and a pierced eyebrow to complete the image. He catches Ciere staring. "What?"

"Nothing," she says automatically, turning to look at their quarry. The office building is tall and silent, its windows opaque. The whole scene looks deceptively benign, like it wouldn't take a single broken window to summon every nearby cop.

Kit leads them into a neighboring alley. The good news is that the alley is situated with Cole's office above. The bad news is that the alley also houses the trash.

"This is disgusting," Devon mutters, pressing his sleeve to his nose.

"Thieving isn't always stolen diamonds and cocktail parties," Kit replies.

Devon glowers at the garbage cans. "Right. Sometimes it's garbage and dead people."

"As long as we get paid," Ciere says, "who cares?"

Kit turns to face Devon. "All right. You remember the plan?"

"Eidos, right?"

"Humor me."

"Fine. We go up to the fourth floor, and I bust in through the window. Ciere provides the distraction while I open the safe. I find the will of some bird called Marie Louis and memorize it. Then I pop it back in the safe, and we all run."

Kit aims a glare skyward. "Two hours of intricate planning condensed into four sentences. If only I had your razor intellect." He heaves a sigh and holds out both arms, as if inviting Devon to embrace him.

Devon flinches, taking a step backward.

Kit cocks his head. "How did you *think* you were going to get to a fourth-story window? Climb?"

Devon understands. "Oh, hell. I'm riding the human elevator, aren't I?"

"Believe me," Kit says vehemently, "I'm not looking forward to this any more than you."

Reluctantly, Devon steps into Kit's personal space. He starts to put his arms around Kit's neck, then recoils and tries again. It's like watching two children trying to hug but too afraid to actually make contact. Ciere places her palm between Devon's shoulder blades and pushes. Devon stumbles into Kit, instinctively grabbing at the older man's shirt to keep his balance. Before Devon can let go, Kit shoots into the air and hovers at about ten feet.

Devon swallows a shriek and wraps both arms around Kit's neck, his legs hooking around Kit's waist. "Why do I always end up as the pack mule?" says Kit, straining under his burden.

"Don't drop him," Ciere calls, keeping her tone quiet.

"Two minutes," Kit mouths. His face smoothes out and he relaxes, a faint smile on his lips. He turns his gaze to the dark sky, as if welcoming the open air, and he soars upward.

Devon's squeak of terror vanishes into the night.

Ciere reaches down and presses the timer on her watch. Numbers begin to slide by, seconds blinking past. She closes her eyes and concentrates, illusioning herself into a homeless man with dirty jeans and worn shoes. Smudged skin, haunted eyes, broken fingernails.

A buzzing sets up around her temples, but it's nothing like the sharp, blinding flash of pain when she tries to illusion anything beyond herself. She tugs the mask into place, pushing her curls back as the rough wool slides over her face. There—if a camera catches her now, all they'll see is a tiny figure dressed all in black. Nothing to ID her.

A quick glance at her watch tells her she still has a minute. The front of the office building is heavy with shadow, and Ciere takes up residence next to a row of potted plants. A cement bench provides a place to sit while she watches the seconds tick past. Forty seconds.

Her heartbeat picks up, her pulse fluttering through her neck and wrists. She loves this part, loves the moment before she pulls off a job—the heat, the cold, the rush. It's terrifying and delicious, like teetering out over the edge of a building, her fingers tight on the safety railing. She can see how everything could go horribly wrong, but that rational part of her is tamped down, silenced by the beauty of the fall.

Thirty seconds.

She glances around. The potted plants aren't bolted down, and they'll work well for what she has in mind. She squats and grabs the rim of a particularly heavy pot. It creaks as she lifts, dry dirt crumbling over the edge. She staggers under its weight.

Ten seconds.

Each step is a struggle, and soon her arms are screaming in protest, her joints straining under the load. She uses the weight to add to her momentum as she jogs toward the windows.

Five seconds.

Ciere spins around once, twice, like an Olympic shot-putter, and then, as dizziness begins to swirl the edges of her vision, she slams the potted plant through the window.

The alarm kicks to life. Beyond the sound, she hears a male voice snarling out a stream of curses.

Ciere has played her role—the alarm she's created will cover the sound of the second break-in, the one at the fourth-floor window. Devon should be inside by now, already at work on the safe. It's time for her to escape.

A silhouette appears in the lobby—large and roundish, probably an underpaid mall cop who was never supposed to deal with a break-in. Ciere grins, skipping backward, still in the illusioned body of the homeless man. She revels in the sound and the chaos. This is the part she loves best. She laughs and turns, readying herself for the sprint back to the car.

Something slams into her.

Her chest is set ablaze and her muscles seize. The pavement rushes up to meet her and she crashes into it, unable to catch herself. Her legs tangle beneath her, useless and unresponsive.

She's not sure how many seconds pass before the sensation abruptly vanishes. She goes limp, slumping against the ground. She only registers the rough texture of the pavement on her cheek and the taste of copper in her mouth. Her arm is twisted awkwardly beneath her, and the tracker bracelet digs into her ribs. She rolls over, trying to see what the hell just happened, and she finds a black form blocking out the lamplight. A man stands a few feet away.

A second security guard.

There can't be a second guard. Devon researched this. There is supposed to be a single guard who is middle-aged, with a paunch, and whose most dangerous weapon is a flashlight. This lean young man isn't supposed to be here.

He holds something in both hands; it looks like a gun, but the shape is off. Ciere finally feels the twin pinpricks of pain in her chest, and her fingers come up, touching cold barbs of metal embedded in her skin. Lines of wire trail from the gun's barrel to her chest and that's when she realizes that it's a Taser.

"You basta—" she starts to croak. The guard's thumb moves, and her muscles are set on fire. She wants to scream; her lips are pulled tight over her teeth, and fuck it all—she can't move.

The searing pain fades and she gasps, able to breathe again. She blinks several times, trying to see through the haze and the tears.

The guard looks like a college student—maybe someone taking a few classes while working part-time. He stares down at Ciere, disbelief reflected in his eyes. His mouth slackens and the Taser trembles in his grip.

For a moment, Ciere is confused. Her mind moves sluggishly, trying to work out why a security guard would be terrified of a downed homeless man. As the paralysis begins to wear off, she realizes something is missing—that pressure around her skull, that comforting hum through her temples.

Her illusion is gone.

The guard electrocuted an old homeless man and ended up with a masked criminal. He knows. He knows.

Don't let anyone see what you are, understand?

It's a little late for that. She's prone on the ground with a man twice her size standing over her. In a moment, the Taser will recharge and she'll be in for another shock. Ciere doesn't fool herself into thinking he will take mercy on her because of her youth or gender.

Her arms shake as she pushes herself to a half-sitting position. The guard's hands tighten on his weapon and his mouth opens in a shout. If Ciere is scared, this man is terrified.

"Charles," the second guard says, speaking for the first time. It takes Ciere a moment to realize that he isn't speaking to her but to the other guard. "Get over here!"

The first guard, the paunchy one, waddles out of the building. He aims a flashlight at Ciere and his eyes widen. "What the hell?"

"She's one of them," the second guard says. "She's got adverse effects."

The first guard, Charles or whatever the hell his name is, gapes at Ciere. "What do we do?"

"Radio the cops," the second guard snaps. "They should already be on the way, but they'll haul ass if they know we've got some adverse effects Mafia assassin."

The first guard turns away, his hand going to the radio at his belt. There is a hiss of static and the man begins rattling off a code.

"Dammit, how long until the cops get here?" the second guard snaps.

Ciere rolls over onto her side, trying to rise to her elbows. Her voice is little more than a ragged exhalation. "Wait," she says, and her mind scrambles for a lie, for an illusion—for anything that can get her out of this.

"Shut up," the younger man snarls. His grip on the Taser wavers and Ciere sees the wires glinting in the lamplight. The wires run from the barbs embedded in her skin to the gun itself, binding her to the weapon.

"BPD will take at least fifteen minutes," the first guard says. "They said something about a raid. Just... keep her there, right?"

They're both so afraid, it would be funny under other circumstances. Ciere is just an illusionist—it's not like she can fly into the air like a levitas, read their thoughts like a mentalist, fight them like a dauthus, or escape like an eludere. She might be able to disappear, but her head is throbbing and her concentration shot.

Her eyes flick over both security guards. They're not armed beyond the Tasers and flashlights, and that thought gives her an idea.

Ciere brings to mind a gun. She imagines a heavy black pistol and pushes the thought out of her mind and into reality.

The pain spikes through her brain, as sharp and bright as a lightning strike. The pistol forms in her right fist. It's clumsily done, lacking the form and detail she would need to fool more rational men. But the guards are already on edge, making them easy marks.

When she swings her arm up and aims the false weapon at the second guard, his eyes go wide and he falls to one side, trying to put something between himself and the bullet he thinks is coming. The first guard screams and scurries backward.

Ciere rolls. The wires on a Taser aren't easily broken, but the guard's retreat and her own momentum snap the cables. She darts to her feet and rushes away. The older one is screaming into his radio, the young man desperately fiddling with the Taser. When Ciere looks over her shoulder, she catches his eye, and for a moment they lock gazes. Despite the layers of wool on her face, she feels naked. He stares into her with abject terror, like he is the hunted and she is the hunter. She catches the silent word on his lips: "Immune."

The ground feels unsteady beneath her sneakers and she nearly falls going down the steps to the sidewalk. The world tips sideways and she catches herself on a bench.

Her panicked breaths drag through her lungs and throat, but it still feels like she isn't getting enough air. The mask is suffocating her, the heavy wool catching the sweat from her hairline and holding the moisture against her skin, an uncomfortable presence she wants to rip away. But she can't—not yet.

The shadows beckon, and Ciere follows them into an alley. It's not the way she came, but it's dark and gloriously empty. She pauses, a hand on the brick wall to steady herself, as she glances over her shoulder. She can still hear the guards' shouts and the building's alarm, but there is no sign of the cops.

Going back the way she came might draw attention to the others, so she takes a roundabout route to the car—through a parking lot and behind another office building. In the flash of illumination from a lamp, Ciere sees wires ghosting through the air near her chest, trailing behind her as she moves. She grabs at the wires. They are a cold, alien presence beneath her collarbone, their tiny spikes fixed in her skin. She tangles the wires around her fist—a good yank, a blaze of pain, and the barbs come free.

The SUV sits where it should be, engine running and exhaust drifting around the tires. Ciere fumbles with the back door and it swings open from the inside, nearly smacking her in the face. Devon is perched there, his grin lighting up the inside of the car. "What took you?" he says, and he is obviously riding the high from the job, still gleeful and triumphant.

She can't bear to ruin his moment of victory. With his shining eyes and grin, she can tell he's still infatuated with being a crook. And the thought of explaining herself to Kit—explaining how she was nearly caught—is almost too daunting to contemplate.

Ciere pulls herself into the car and slumps against her seat. Her fingers scrabble at the ski mask and she yanks it off, tossing it on the floor. Her freed skin is damp and cold, and she presses the back of her hand to one cheek, trying to rub some feeling into it. She'll explain about the guard tomorrow, when things have settled down. The wires remain a cold lump in her pocket.

Ciere spends most of the drive staring out her window, fingers touching the cool glass as she watches the lights of other cars. The others' chatter barely registers in her ears.

"You know, this actually wasn't that different from the time I broke into the headmistress's office at my third school," says Devon. "Only that time, I had a friend give me a boost through the window."

"And I'm sure you didn't kick that friend in the groin," says Kit.

"For the last time," says Devon, "that was an accident."

Magnus chuckles. "Count your blessings, Kit. I would've done it on purpose."

Once they're done bickering, Devon dictates the will's words to Kit, whose nimble fingers sketch the will anew on a fresh piece of paper. Magnus guides the SUV through back roads, avoiding the highway. Highways are too easily watched. Going through smaller neighborhoods and winding streets may take longer and use more gas, but there is less chance of being tailed. By now, the night is slowly creeping toward morning. Kit assures them that their contact, Frieda Fuller, will be awake at this hour.

It takes about half an hour to get to their destination. Magnus finds an empty parking lot beside a warehouse. Many of the lampposts are unlit, casting the entire area into darkness. Magnus parks the car underneath a couple of scraggly trees on the edge of the lot.

"We're meeting Frieda Fuller in a park about half a mile away," Kit says, unbuckling his seat belt.

"Too bad I left my hiking gear at home," Devon says dryly.

"Don't strain yourself. Magnus and I will go—you can stay and watch the car." Kit pushes open the passenger-side door. The smell is the first thing that Ciere notices. It smells like the Fourth of July—fireworks and smoke. There's the distant sound of something popping.

"It's a bit early for Fourth celebrations," Magnus observes.

"Holidays," Kit says sourly. "They keep getting pushed forward. We'll be seeing Christmas decorations any day now." He gives Ciere a stern look. "Stay."

"Yeah, yeah," she says wearily.

Kit and Magnus stride away from the car. They fall into a synchronous step and vanish around the street corner.

Devon squirms in his seat. "I know Copperfield said to stay put, but can we please at least sit outside of the car? I've been stuck in this bloody thing all day."

Ciere gives him a tired grin. "If you want to live the crooked life, you've got to get used to it." But she pushes the door open and leads the way out of the car. She knows exactly how he feels—stifled and constricted.

They lean against the side of the SUV. Ciere tilts her head back and watches the wispy clouds pass overhead, ghostly white in the moonlight. "Bit burnt out here," Devon says, and Ciere has to agree. Smoke drifts through the air, smudging the sharp lines of the city. Another series of pops echoes off a nearby building, and human voices follow the noise.

"Who sets off fireworks a week before your Independence Day?" Devon asks.

Another crackle and a shout. Lights flicker in the distance, oranges and yellows blinking on the horizon. Ciere takes a step forward, her eyes squinting to find the source of the light. *Crack. Crack, crack.* The noises get louder. One of the booms seems to resonate in her chest, like an overly loud bass from a speaker. More smoke rolls along the street. From somewhere behind her, Devon says, "Wait... what's that?"

There are other noises now. Screams. Another series of snaps that echo off the warehouse walls.

Ciere understands before Devon does. Those are not fireworks; the smoke is not from a bonfire or cookout or any kind of celebration. And those are not the kind of sounds people make when they are having fun.

The city is burning.

And before she can say a word, an explosion of gunfire shatters the SUV's windows.

14

CIERE

Most crooks tangle with the cops eventually. It's inevitable—breaking the law repeatedly means attracting the attention of those who uphold the law. The first encounter is often seen by fellow crooks as a rite of passage—a person isn't truly a crook until they've looked the enemy in the eye and walked away (preferably with their wallet). First encounters are often talked about in the crooked community. They're trotted out in bars or at parties. Ciere's heard many "firsts." According to Daniel, he was nearly caught by a cop in Detroit when he was fourteen. Even Kit, who never talks about his own past, will admit that his "first" involved a fed, a cliff, and a bulletproof vest disguised as a waistcoat.

Ciere never talks about her past, because she's sure most

people wouldn't believe it. Her first encounter with the law was when an entire SWAT team came for her.

She was eleven years old.

When Ciere was eleven, her mother taught her The Game.

As far as Ciere could tell, it was a modified combination of tag and hide-and-go-seek. The rules were simple:

1. Using her immunity, Ciere had to either make herself invisible or camouflage into the background.

2. Mom would attempt to find her.

3. If found, Ciere would run and find a better hiding place.

Back in those days, Ciere and her mother lived in Washington State, on the northwest coast. The woods were thick, tall strands of red cedar and hemlock, towering giants that threw the world into shade. Not much sunlight escaped the near constant cloud cover. They lived far beyond the reach of the nearest city, their house tucked away in the woods with the ocean in view. The years drifted by with variations on the moderate temperatures and overcast skies, punctuated by the occasional rainstorm. The forests were the perfect place to play The Game. Ciere wasn't allowed near the sea cliffs, so she would turn inland and find a tree or some thick undergrowth. There, she'd try to make herself disappear.

She didn't try hard. What was the point? She liked it when

her mom found her, liked being hugged and told to go hide again.

The forest had other uses. The huge trees were clotted with moss and ideal for making forts. Ciere found a particularly large one and slowly, methodically piled rocks around the trunk and called it her castle. One by one, she stacked them one on top of another until they formed a stone wall that reached her waist. She fashioned a table out of fallen branches and used old, broken mugs taken from the kitchen for tea parties. Her illusions came easier to her in those days; she could conjure new friends easily.

She hadn't gone to school since... well, Ciere couldn't ever remember going to school. She had dim memories of living in a crowded city—her mother said they originally were from Seattle—but these forests were all she'd ever known.

She was playing in those woods the day the feds came for her.

On that day, Ciere heard the the sound of cars on the gravel road. It was a far-off noise, but there were so few visitors that she immediately scrambled out of her castle, leaving behind the remnants of a peanut butter sandwich and apple juice.

The house stood at the bottom of a hill, and the driveway wound around for half a mile from the main road. As Ciere peeked through the trees, she saw two black cars kicking up dust on the road. They weren't to the house yet—not even close.

Ciere's mother was outside. She wasn't running to meet the cars, Ciere realized, but was sprinting away from the house and toward Ciere. It was only then she noticed the rifle clamped under her mother's arm. She stared at it in confusion; the rifle was meant to scare off coyotes and raccoons and she couldn't imagine why her mother would need it now.

Ciere tentatively started down the hill. A strange scent caught her attention. It smelled like barbecue, like a bonfire, like the times Mom accidentally burned their toast.

Something was wrong with the house. The windows were shattered, and there were lights flickering inside. It wasn't until she saw the flames that she realized the house was burning. Great rolls of smoke billowed through the broken windows.

She stood in slack-jawed astonishment for a second, paralyzed by the sight of her home in flames.

By that time, Ciere's mother was at her side. "Mom?" she said, her eyes fixed on the house. It came out as a question, a quivering entreaty. Her heartbeat picked up; something was wrong. Fear took hold in her stomach, her chest, drew tight around her throat.

Her mother called her name. It wasn't "Ciere," because that wasn't what she was called then. "Come on," her mother said, her voice sharp. Her hand clamped down on Ciere's wrist, and then she was running. Ciere stumbled and then was forced to pump her short legs to keep up.

"The house—" she started to say, but she was cut off by the sound of cars screeching to halt and the grinding of gravel under tires. She looked back. Their house was nearly consumed by the fire, collapsing in on itself, pieces of the roof caving in. Ciere nearly stopped running then—she had toys and books in that house.

"Not now," Mom said, yanking hard on Ciere's arm. She ran faster, her feet barely touching the ground in an attempt to keep up.

The trees rose up all around them and the house vanished from sight. The pair tore through the forest, heedless of the scratches and cuts accumulated from the underbrush. Mom's hand remained clamped around Ciere's wrist, and without it, she was sure she couldn't have kept up. Her feet tangled with the ferns and fallen branches, and Mom kept that tight grip on her. Soon Ciere's lungs ached, her tiny chest heaving.

She wasn't sure how far or how long they ran. The forest flew by in flashes of green and brown. Terror kept her moving as much as her mother's hand. Something horrible was chasing them, that much Ciere knew. Something was coming for them.

They ran until Ciere stumbled and nearly fell. Her mother was sweating, her breath coming in ragged gasps, and then she skidded to a halt. Her eyes swept over Ciere, and something in her face hardened. She dropped the rifle and pulled a pink backpack off her shoulder. It was the one with the kitty on it.

She knelt and forced the backpack's straps over Ciere's arms and shoulders. "Take it," Mom said. Her fingers dug into Ciere's arms so hard that she later found tiny bruises.

"Now listen," her mother said, adjusting the backpack's straps. "We're going to play The Game, all right? But this time, you can't wait for me to find you." She threw a glance over her shoulder, and her fingers tightened on Ciere's shoulders.

Then Ciere was being crushed against her mother's chest, and it was only then she realized that her mother was trembling. She was held there for a moment, breathing in the familiar scent of clean clothes and fresh air, and then Mom pulled back.

"Don't let anyone see what you are, understand?" she whispered, rising to her feet with the rifle in hand.

Ciere couldn't run; her legs wouldn't respond. She simply stared at her mother, uncomprehending. Only when her mother gave her a hard shove did she respond, staggering backward. "Now!" Mom said urgently, her voice sharp.

Ciere took one more step backward. She heard it now: the sounds of other voices. Male voices. People crashing through the undergrowth, coming after them.

She took one last look at her mother, who had raised the rifle to her shoulder.

Ciere ran. The Game meant she had to hide. She had to disappear.

She found a nearby tree; its roots were huge, coiled and raised above the ground. Ciere threw herself beneath them, her fingers sinking into the damp moss and dirt as she burrowed into the dirt and roots.

Then she reached into her mind and *yanked*. She took the colors of the leaves, the texture of the bark, the softness of the moss, and she enfolded those images around her own skin. She huddled as close to the tree trunk as she could, hoping her illusion would be enough to make her invisible.

By now, there were other sounds. Unfamiliar raised voices.

"Put the weapon on the ground and your hands behind your head—"

CRACKCRACK.

A hoarse shout.

"PUT YOUR WEAPON DOWN!" Someone else now, a man's voice pitched in a scream.

Ciere closed her eyes, turned her face to press into the bark. Her cold fingers tightened around the branch.

"PUT YOUR WEAP—"

Another gun went off. A different gun. The sound was lower and more controlled, and the silence that followed it seemed to flood Ciere's ears. The echo of the shot bounced through the forest, replaying over and over again. It was so loud that Ciere didn't even hear her own lips form the word.

Mom?

15

CIERE

Glass bounces off the pavement. The tiny, glimmering shards remind Ciere of hail. Part of her strains to hear the tinkling sound, but her ears are torn apart by the sound of gunfire.

It takes her a moment to realize that while she has dropped to the ground, Devon remains upright. He appears frozen, mouth still open in a soundless question, pupils blown wide. She slams her fist into the back of Devon's knee and he crumples, catching himself on his palms. His mouth snaps shut and he turns huge eyes on her, annoyance kindling to life. She jams a finger to her lips and gestures at the car. Without a sound, she presses herself to the pavement and worms her way under the vehicle. Devon follows.

They're lucky Kit drives an SUV—they wouldn't fit under

any other car. Even so, Ciere can feel the car's underbelly scratching at her hair, tiny metal bits catching on her shirt, the heavy scent of gasoline all around them.

Another two shots. One hits the SUV, and the car rocks. All she can see is the few inches of space between the car and where the ground rushes up in the horizon. It's enough, though, to catch a glimpse of moving shadows. Two people rush out of the shadows.

One figure carries what can only be a gun. Two more shots ring out, and there is answering fire from somewhere in the distance.

"What the hell?" Devon whispers.

"Shut up," Ciere hisses. She presses herself closer to the ground and cranes her head. The angle allows her to see what is going on.

The two runners rush past the SUV—a woman and a man. The man fires several shots over his shoulder with a handgun, aiming carelessly at their pursuers.

Two new figures sprint along the sidewalk. They are dressed all in black, complete with masks and night-vision goggles.

The letters *FBI* stand out on their jackets.

One of the feds fires, and Ciere hears the skid of gravel and the sickening impact of a human body slamming into the pavement. The man cries out, but he pauses for only a fraction of a second. Then he's sprinting away.

Ciere can see the outline of the body—it is utterly still, its limbs splayed along the pavement. It reminds her of a fallen bird, of something that belonged in the air brought crashing down to earth.

One fed runs past the car without giving it a second glance. The other pauses beside the fallen body, probably searching for a pulse. The fed's hand falls away from the figure's neck and he moves on, apparently satisfied.

A raid. That's what this is. And judging from the smoke and the sound of guns off in the distance, it's a massive one. The voice of the security guard back at the lawyer's office comes back to her: *"BPD will take at least fifteen minutes. They said something about a raid. Just... keep her there, right?"*

"They must be taking down a crime family," Ciere breathes. *Let it be the Gyr Syndicate, let it be the Gyr Syndicate.* The thought makes her whole body clench, the desire so strong it's almost a physical ache. She yearns for it to be true, for these feds to be taking down Guntram. It would make things so much easier.

She turns to look at Devon. "Can you call the others?"

Devon stares at her.

"Devon!" she snaps. No reaction. "Devon?" Still no reaction.

Gritting her teeth, Ciere adjusts her weight so that she can strike out with a leg.

That snaps Devon to life. "What the hell?"

"Call the others now!" Ciere says sharply.

The anger vanishes from Devon's face, replaced by fear. His fingers fumble on his cell phone, but he manages to dial a number. A second later, he is swearing and snapping the phone shut, only to reopen it. "What's wrong?" Ciere asks.

"There's no signal," he says.

"But we're surrounded by cities!"

Devon nods, his face drawn tight. "Which means it's deliberate."

Ciere lets out a growl. "Stay here," she says, making a snap decision. Squirming out from under the car isn't easy, but she manages it. Devon's hand clamps down on her ankle.

"What are you doing?!"

"I'm going to find Kit and Magnus." Ciere shakes him off. "We can't leave them out there, especially if they don't know what's going on."

"You can't go out there!"

Ciere pulls her lips back into what she hopes is a confident smile. "Yes, I can." She rises to her feet.

"But you saw—they're *killing* people—"

Ciere closes her eyes, focusing in on herself. "They can't kill," she says, "what they can't see." Enfolding the night in around herself, Ciere skips back a few steps and turns on her heel, jogging in the direction she saw Kit and Magnus go.

Despite her brave words, her pulse races and she can feel

clammy sweat break out on her forehead. If those officers have infrared goggles, they'll see her. Illusions can't hide things like body heat.

The wind carries the chokingly thick smell of burning rubber and plastic. She covers her nose with her sleeve in a futile attempt to block it out. Her shoes slap the pavement as she runs past the warehouse doors and deserted crates. The alley remains unlit, and Ciere welcomes the darkness, using it to mask her movements.

At the end of the alley, the street breaks in two directions. Ciere slows and glances both ways: one leads to what looks like the town's edge. There are trees and fences, and fewer buildings. The other way appears to lead back into town. The sounds of gunfire and human terror drift in from that direction, carried on a humid summer breeze.

She is so focused on finding Kit that she doesn't immediately notice the young man standing only forty feet away.

He stands on a street corner. His arms are crossed, and his face is turned toward her. He steps into the lamplight. He's young—seventeen, to be exact—with brown hair, a crooked nose, and very green eyes. A shock of recognition goes through Ciere, and when she drops her illusion, her disbelief is mirrored on his face.

"Ciere?" he says, aghast.

"Daniel," Ciere says. Relief courses through her, and she's

suddenly warm, a little giddy, and she finds herself laughing. She hasn't let herself think about him. She's pushed him out of her mind, tried to forget that he ever existed, so that she wouldn't have to acknowledge his absence. But he's here. Before he can say anything, Ciere runs to him on unsteady legs and throws her arms around his neck. He feels steady and familiar.

Daniel is stiff at first, but then relaxes into the embrace. "You ass," she says into his ear. "You scared us. We thought something happened to you." She satisfies herself with studying his uninjured face.

"What happened?" says Ciere. "Where've you been?"

Daniel licks his lips. "What—why are you here?"

"We're delivering a package to Frieda Fuller—you know, the job you told Kit about. Where have you been? Kit's been calling you for days." She vaguely waves her hand around, trying to encompass the smoke and the chaos in the gesture. "What the hell is going on?"

Daniel's mouth works silently, like he's trying to bring up words and failing. "Oh god," he says softly. "Kit went through with the job. I thought—I thought he wouldn't take it after I vanished." His throat convulses and he gags, coughing wildly, like he's inhaled something rotten.

Ciere takes a step forward. "What? What are you talking about?"

Pain flares in Daniel's eyes, and when he speaks, each word sounds like it's tearing up his throat. "I—I—It is not safe," he croaks.

"Well, obviously," Ciere retorts. "That's why I'm looking for Kit—we need to get out of here. We've got a car, in case you don't have one. We should—"

"Run." The word is spoken so quietly that Ciere doesn't hear it at first. When it sinks in, she looks up again. "Run." His voice cracks. "Not safe. I—not safe. Run." His throat seems to close up on the last word.

Ciere stares at him, uncomprehending. She turns in a circle, expecting to see a squadron of soldiers or something equally horrible. But there's nothing. Just Daniel. Just her and Daniel and—

"Burkhart! What are you doing?" A voice rends the air, sharp and female. Before Ciere can react, a woman strides around the street corner. In the dim light, all Ciere can make out is that the woman is tall and has wildly curly hair. The woman freezes, mid-step, when she sees Daniel and Ciere.

"You caught one," the woman says, a small smile flitting across her mouth. She turns that smile on Ciere.

One second, the woman is standing on the street corner; the next, she is sprinting toward Ciere.

Ciere's vision seems to narrow, and, for a second, all she

can see is the government-issue vest, the holstered gun, the baton, and the handcuffs on the woman's belt. Ciere knows what she is. A fed. She's a fed—and she's coming for her.

Ciere turns to Daniel and she finally recognizes the look on his face. Grief. Regret. Guilt.

That's when she gets it.

Daniel isn't here because of a job or simple coincidence. He isn't running from the feds. He's working with them.

16

CIERE

Ciere runs. She doesn't have time to think about Daniel or even Kit. She has a fed on her heels. It's time to vanish. She ducks around a parked truck and a bike rack, hoping the roundabout route will trip up the fed. As she runs, she reaches out and yanks a trash can off balance. It teeters and crashes to the ground.

Ciere chances a look back.

The fed vaults over the bike rack and uses one hand to propel herself effortlessly over the fallen trash can. The fed's eyes are wide, lips pulled back into a grin, and her movements are sinuous, graceful. She moves through the shadowy street like it is full day.

A fresh burst of adrenaline helps Ciere to scramble around another corner, and she skids into an alley. She's lost track of her direction and she probably won't be able to find the car again, but that doesn't matter. Not now. Now she just needs a few seconds of lead time.

She throws down another trash can and rushes around a corner. The fed is out of sight and Ciere slows her mad dash, skidding to a halt. She throws herself against a wall, trying to take in its rough texture.

She dredges up what little concentration she has left. Invisible. She needs to be invisible. Or at least she needs to blend into this wall as closely as she can. If her plan works, the fed will rush past her, chasing someone that isn't running anymore. It's an old trick, but with Ciere's immunity it has a good chance of success. She turns her skin, her clothes, her hair—all of herself—into the dull gray color of the wall.

When the fed turns the corner, Ciere sucks in a breath and holds it. It's hard; her breathing verges on panting and her chest aches.

The fed slows to a jog as she takes in the empty street. She isn't even breathing hard, like that mad run was nothing. The woman's eyes slide over the street, taking in the shadows, the nooks, and the crannies. She takes a step forward. "Come out," she says softly. Her voice might be pleasant if it wasn't edged with mockery. "Come out, come out, wherever you are." Another step, and she is glancing from side to side, cocking her head in a distinctly doglike manner.

Ciere tries to inhale without making a sound.

"I'm not going to hurt you," the fed says. "Really, I promise I won't. We only want to talk to you. You and all your other TATE friends... you have something we want."

Tate? Ciere has never heard the name before.

The fed takes another step. Ciere grits her teeth, feels her jaw ache, and tries to stay as still as possible. Her illusion holds.

The fed moves slowly, her head still tilted at that angle. She appears to be trying to draw in the entire street with her senses, to rake through the air until she finds her prey.

Ten feet.

Ciere stays utterly still, her breaths short and silent, her knees locked and fingers splayed on the wall. It feels solid and steady behind her, but she's well aware that she can't run.

And then the fed is even with Ciere's hiding spot. She pauses, her gaze still scouring the street. Ciere tries not to move, not to think, not to do anything that could give her location away. *Move on,* she silently urges. *Just move on. Please.*

To Ciere's relief, the fed does. She takes another step, and another. She's moving farther on, apparently unaware of the fact that her prey is behind her.

Ciere lets out the tiniest, shuddering breath.

The fed's head whips around, her eyes scouring the cement

wall. Her teeth flash in a sharp grin, and then she's moving in the direction of Ciere.

But surely the fed can't see Ciere—she's still hidden, still out of sight.

No one can see her.

Which apparently doesn't matter.

The fed's hand closes on Ciere's shirt, yanking her free of the wall. The illusion breaks apart, and Ciere finds herself staring up into the fed's face.

"There you are," the woman murmurs.

Ciere can't stop herself from gasping. Her breath comes in ragged jerks, and she is surprised to hear a slight vocalization when she inhales—it sounds a little like a tiny, suppressed sob. She wants to ask *how*. She can't understand *how* this happened, how this woman was able to find Ciere when no normal person could—

When no normal person could.

Ciere finally notices the insignia attached to the fed's vest. It doesn't spell out FBI or any of the usual markers. Rather, it's a simple symbol: two circles overlapping each other. Ciere would recognize it anywhere.

UAI. United American Immunities. And beneath the UAI's symbol is a word embroidered into the fed's vest: MORANA.

This fed is one of them—an immune person working for the UAI. A dauthus. Only a dauthus, with that freaky ability to mess with her own body, to shut down all her senses but the one she needs, could have found Ciere this easily.

Ciere's heart thumps at her rib cage, a prisoner screaming to get out. The UAI doesn't go after mobs. Their job is to deal with "threats to national and foreign security."

"An illusionist," Morana, says. She barks out an incredulous laugh. "I didn't know you guys recruited so well."

Ciere wants to tell this fed that she isn't supposed to be here. Whatever's happening, she isn't part of it.

"Let's go," Morana says. "Aristeus will want to talk with you."

The dauthus takes hold of Ciere's arm, but she pauses. Her brow creases and she angles herself onto the balls of her feet, like she has heard something no normal human can. Then Ciere hears it, too.

It's a whistling sound, like the hum of a Frisbee, and then a *freaking hubcap* flies out of nowhere and nearly brains Morana. But her dauthus reactions kick in and she springs out of the hubcap's path. Ciere goes flying and hits the pavement, rolling several times. The hubcap slams into the side of a wall with a loud *clang* and rattles to a halt on the ground.

For a second, all Ciere can do to stare. She's never believed in any kind of divinity, but this might be enough to convert her. But... what kind of god drops hubcaps from the sky?

The sound of feet hitting the pavement brings Ciere back

to herself. A figure charges down the street, his long legs eating up the distance. Without hesitation, he draws his arm back and throws a punch at Morana's face.

Ciere doesn't recognize him immediately. He moves differently—his comfortable, poised posture is replaced with a predatory tension. In the dim light, she sees the dark hair, pale skin, and long neck.

Magnus.

Magnus is attacking a dauthus.

The sheer idiocy staggers Ciere. A dauthus's immunity allows her to consciously alter her body—muscles can be strengthened, senses heightened, extra adrenaline pumped into the body; organs can even be moved slightly out of alignment, making lethal blows nearly impossible to deliver. A single dauthus can take down multiple attackers in a fight.

Morana reacts to the attack with inhuman speed, sizing up her opponent with narrowed eyes and a flash of teeth. Her hands flex and she springs forward, loose and easy, as she takes a return swing.

Ciere rises to her feet. She stands, frozen in half step, unsure if she wants to help. She teeters on the edge of action, paralyzed by her own uselessness.

Magnus dodges the blow with ease; Ciere expects to see anger on his face, but his tranquil expression is untouched by the violence.

He fights like the moves are more familiar to him than his own name—like the punches and the kicks are instinctive. He knows what he's doing; every move is both calculated and graceful. Morana is faster, so he does not let her use that speed. His arms wrap around her, in a parody of an embrace, while his knee flies up and plows into her gut, her groin, her thighs. Over and over, until she's gasping and writhing, wriggling out of his embrace and flitting backward. Magnus pushes forward, keeping himself between Morana and Ciere. Morana's hand moves, twitches to her belt, and Magnus lunges at her.

Morana is quicker. Her hand flashes out, a glint of silver between her fingers, and Magnus staggers. Red blossoms along his hairline. Blood streams into his left eye and he struggles to wipe it away.

Morana isn't smiling anymore. She dances from side to side, her eyes fixed on Magnus as she readjusts her grip on the knife. She swings around, lunging at Magnus, the tip of the blade aimed for his gut. A cry lodges in Ciere's throat—he can't see, not with blood leaking into his eye. With a hiss of expelled air, Magnus's arm lashes out and deflects the knife; at the same moment, his other fist hits Morana squarely in the collarbone.

The knife skitters along the pavement, far out of Morana's reach. She doesn't so much as blink. With Magnus so close, she presses her advantage.

Her arm coils around his throat, but he falls to his knees,

his hand clamping down on her arm. He angles his weight forward and throws her over his shoulder. She flips over, and any normal person would've hit the ground on her back. But Morana isn't normal; she manages to catch herself on her heels, her whole torso bucking free of Magnus's grip. She's on her feet in less than a second.

Magnus has yet to stand.

Her leg flashes around, singing through the air with the kind of force only a dauthus can manage. It's a blow meant to shatter bones.

Magnus slides one foot backward, easing into a sprinter's stance. The kick slams into his forearms and before Morana can react he wraps one arm around that leg, holding it in place. He twists it hard and she's off balance, trying to hop backward to escape his grip. But it's too late.

Her back slams into the pavement. Magnus drives a fist into her gut the moment she falls, his arm drawing back and repeating the blow a good five times. There is a sharp cry of pain, but it is cut off, swallowed up by the sound of fist hitting flesh. Morana's flailing arms and legs go still.

Ciere stands there, paralyzed. When Magnus rises to his full height, she finds herself shrinking back. He's changed—that demure, well-mannered man has vanished and in his place is a soldier with eyes like granite and blood staining his knuckles.

"Are you okay?" he asks.

Ciere forces herself to nod.

Magnus squats down to pick up the fallen knife and tests its edge with his thumb. "Military grade," he says. "She's wearing a vest. And that insignia..." He trails off as he stares down at the symbol on the woman's vest.

"Damn," Magnus says quietly. "She's UAI." Fresh blood spills over from the cut above his eye, dripping down his face and settling into the faint lines around his mouth. He wipes at it irritably as he strides back to Ciere.

"We need to get out of here," he says.

Ciere falls into step behind him. The night's events are changing too quickly for her to process. Honestly, she's a little grateful for the orders—it means less chance of her getting something else wrong.

"W-what are you doing here?" Her voice trembles and she clears her throat, trying to sound steady. "Where's Kit?"

"Back at the car. We realized something was wrong and returned, only to find you gone." Magnus stops at the corner, pausing to glance both ways before gesturing at Ciere to keep close.

Ciere glances over her shoulder. "Is she...?"

Magnus strides ahead, his eyes scanning the street. "She's a dauthus; she'll live."

"You can fight." It's a ridiculous understatement.

Magnus wipes at his cut again, and fresh blood stains his hand. "Kit wasn't always an art fence. I wasn't always an escort. Some skills stay with you."

Ciere gapes at him. "You threw a hubcap at her."

"Found a parked car. Sometimes you have to scrounge for weapons," Magnus says, then suddenly he blinks and his hand clamps down over her mouth.

He spins around, dragging Ciere backward. He ducks behind a pair of trash cans and drops to a crouch.

A car trundles down the street. The windows are rolled down and the man in the passenger's seat is clearly visible. All Ciere catches is a glimpse of black hair and male features before the car turns a corner.

Ciere pulls away from Magnus, and this time he lets her. "Aristeus," he says, his face gone pale.

Ciere recognizes it as the same name Morana mentioned earlier. "Who?"

A muscle works in Magnus's throat. "Not now." He slowly rises from his crouch, taking hold of Ciere's wrist. "Come on." He begins to run, forsaking silence for speed. With his grip on her wrist, Ciere has little choice but to keep up. For a second, it's all too familiar—she's eleven again and her mother is pulling her through the forest.

The parking lot swings into view as they veer around a corner and Ciere realizes they're coming at it from the opposite end. She ran farther than she thought when trying to get away from Morana.

The SUV is a mess. Half its windows are shambles of broken glass and one of the headlights is gone.

Devon stands beside the car. When he sees Ciere, his face breaks into an anxious smile. "You're okay. Christ, what happened to Magnus's face?"

"Not now," Magnus says tightly, getting into the passenger's seat. Ciere barely has time to climb in herself before Kit turns the key in the ignition and hits the gas.

The car flies forward, rolls over the sidewalk and onto the street. They careen through a red light, and Kit wrenches the car into a wild turn, going for one of the side roads.

Magnus's knuckles stretch tight around his seat belt. "Aristeus."

"Aristeus?" Kit says the name with a simmering undercurrent of heat.

"I saw him," Magnus says. "He's here."

Kit presses hard on the gas, and the car spins around another corner. Ciere fumbles for her seat belt; the bouncing car ride seems like it's only going to get worse. Devon yelps and makes a grab for the armrest as Kit throws the car into another turn, skidding onto a path that is certainly not a road.

"Pretty sure this is a park," Devon says grimly, grabbing his own seat belt.

"Pretty sure they'll be setting up barricades on every major road right about now," Kit shoots back. "Ciere?"

Ciere feels disconnected from this scene, like she's watching everything happen from a distance. Her mouth takes a moment to respond. "What?"

"You have to hide us."

His words aren't registering. "What?"

"If you want us to escape," Kit says harshly, "you'll illusion this car to get us past whatever barricades the feds have set up."

This cannot be happening. She can't illusion something like a car. That hotel room in Manhattan was hard enough, but a room is static. This car is a moving, shifting, changing object. It's far beyond anything she's ever tried. Digging her fingernails into the fabric of the seat, she sucks in a breath and feels the illusion ripple through her brain. She instinctively wants to wrap it around her own skin, to make herself disappear, but that's not what is needed right now. She pushes harder, trying to force her immunity outside of herself.

Darkness creeps in at the edges of her vision, shadows framing a world she no longer recognizes; she blinks several times.

"Ciere," Kit says sharply.

The worst part is that she's *trying*. She is reaching inside and pulling hard, but it's as impractical and agonizing as trying to rip out her own intestines. She can't do it.

"She's turning blue," Devon says, sounding alarmed. "Ciere, breathe!"

"Ciere!" Kit says again.

"Sod off," Devon snarls at him. "It's hurting her. She can't do it and you can't make her!"

Ciere opens her eyes, finds that she's been pulled against Devon's shoulder, his arms around her, his fingers touching the line of her jaw. "You all right?" His voice is soft in her ear.

She reaches up and tangles her fingers in his shirt, trying to push herself upright. "I'm okay." The engine revs again and she feels it vibrate through her bones.

"All right, boys," Kit mutters. "Chicken, it is."

Ciere sees them—two feds with rifles, standing beyond a line of yellow cones. "They don't want to fire yet," Kit says. "Magnus!"

"Kit," Magnus says, in exactly the same tone. "Where?"

"Underneath your seat."

Magnus bends over. When he straightens, he's holding a pistol, a silencer screwed into the barrel. Without even looking at it, he flicks off the safety, raises it to eye level, and fires two shots directly through the windshield. Cracks spider out along the glass and wind howls through the freshly made holes.

"I thought your lot didn't carry guns," Devon says.

Kit pays him no attention. "Magnus, if they hit the tires,

we are—" he begins to say, and then swerves hard, a loud chatter ringing out above the sound of the car's engine.

"I see it!" Magnus leans out of his open window and aims at something Ciere can't see.

Shots ricochet off the SUV, and one shatters the last remaining window. "Angle, angle," Kit says over the racket. "Compensate for the windshield's angle!"

"I know how to fire a gun, Kit!"

The car bounces into the air and Ciere's head nearly hits the ceiling. Devon, taller than she is, cries out and begins frantically rubbing the top of his head. Ciere glances back and sees the line of yellow cones scattered along the road, bent and tossed about by the SUV's tires.

The two feds stand on both sides of the road, apparently just having jumped out of the SUV's path. One fed raises her rifle in a flash of light and sound.

Something explodes in a shower of sparks. Ciere feels a stir of air and the impact of a bullet slamming through the car. She throws herself to the side and sees the smoking hole carved through the SUV's seat. It's inches from where she was sitting.

She looks up, frantic to see if any more damage has been done.

"I don't want to alarm anyone," Kit says, in a tight voice, "but I think something hit me."

Magnus shoves his pistol onto the dashboard and leans over. "Where?"

"Right side, beneath the ribs." Each word is forced out from between Kit's clenched teeth. Ciere edges forward, her hand coming to rest on the back of Magnus's seat. It isn't easy to see blood on Kit's black shirt, but even she can tell that something wet is soaking through the fabric.

Magnus slowly peels the sodden cloth away from Kit's side. "It's not too bad." He doesn't look at Ciere, but adds, "You and Devon keep an eye on the back—see if there's anyone coming after us."

Ciere cranes her head around. Seeing through the rear-facing window is easy, since that window no longer exists. When she speaks, she has to raise her voice above the wind. "No one's following us. Not yet."

"Good." Kit sucks in a deep breath and holds it for a second. "I'm going to keep driving. Any delay now could be fatal." Ciere hears a soft noise; she doesn't realize that it came from her throat until Kit adds, "Sorry. Bad choice of words."

"Shouldn't he pull over if he's been shot?" Devon asks. "I mean, if he passes out...?"

"Ah," Kit says, grinning. "Friends don't let friends drive while hemorrhaging?"

"You're not hemorrhaging." Magnus presses the wadded-up

cloth to Kit's side. "It's a graze." He reaches beneath his seat again, and this time he comes up with a plastic first-aid kit.

Kit lets out a breathless little laugh. "God, that stings. I'd forgotten how much being shot hurts."

"I'd forgotten how much getting shot makes you whine," Magnus replies, cracking open the first-aid kit.

"You certainly know how to make someone feel better." Kit's fingers tighten on the steering wheel as Magnus goes to work.

Soon the only noises are Kit's occasional complaints and the wind roaring through the broken windows. Ciere continues to watch the car's rear, keeping an eye out for a tail. As they flee the city, she can see the smoke from the raid. It billows up, illuminated by searchlights. The whine of sirens recedes into the distance.

17

DANIEL

No matter how long Daniel spends in the shower, he can still smell the smoke on his skin.

The bathroom is all black marble and polished silver. The hotel's signature line of soap adorns the sink, and the towels are folded in the shape of swans or some other ridiculous bird. The UAI definitely like their ritzy hotel rooms.

His bedroom is part of a larger suite that joins with Aristeus's and Morana's rooms. Well, Daniel corrects himself, now it's only Aristeus. Morana was taken away on a stretcher and rushed to a Baltimore hospital. Daniel can't say he's heartbroken. In fact, he's bordering on smug.

He tries to hold on to that feeling. It's better than the sharp stab of pain when he remembers Ciere's betrayed face. When she looked at him, not like a friend, but as an enemy.

The ache in his chest feels physical—like he's being ripped apart from the inside. He and Ciere are friends. They're crew. She's the closest thing to family Daniel has left.

She'll never forgive him. None of them will. Daniel digs his hand into his eyes, desperate to erase the memories.

Leaving the bathroom is a calculated risk. Daniel considers just staying in here, taking a towel and bunking down in the bathtub for the night, but then Aristeus will realize that he's hiding.

Feel the fear, but do not let anyone see it.

It was an old saying that Kit was fond of repeating. When he would say it, Daniel and Ciere would share an exasperated look, and say, *"Jeez, why can't you just say 'never let them see you sweat'?"*

"Because," Kit would say, *"my way sounds more intelligent."*

Daniel lets out a small laugh. It keeps hitting him. He'll never listen to Kit's pompous advice again. That part of his life is over, and that thought rubs at already raw wounds. Desperate for something new to think about, he strides out of the bathroom.

The suite is large and opulent, with a wall of windows overlooking the western horizon. A large leather couch faces another wall where the entire surface is covered with HDE; it's probably programmed with all the television channels a person could want, but Aristeus hasn't gone near it. Instead, he stands by the windows with his arms crossed over his chest. But that's not what draws Daniel's attention.

The hotel door is open just a crack.

Daniel takes a step toward it. That door is an offer of freedom, a lure. To escape, all Daniel would have to do is walk through it. But he can't. Aristeus knows that, so he didn't bother shutting it. It's a deliberate gesture—a way to show Daniel exactly who is in charge here. Aristeus probably gets off on these power plays.

Two can play this game.

"Any word on your partner?" Daniel asks.

Aristeus doesn't turn, but Daniel can see his dour expression reflected in the window.

"Concussion and broken ribs," Aristeus says, without looking at Daniel. "Internal bleeding. They're taking her into surgery."

Daniel makes no attempt to hide the smile in his voice. "That's too bad."

Aristeus continues to stare out the window. "Morana will be fine. She's one of us after all."

One of us. Like being immune is some great privilege. Like it makes a person special. In Daniel's experience, having an immunity doesn't improve one's life at all—it makes one a target.

"Are you sure you didn't see anything?" Aristeus asks. He

doesn't have to layer his immunity over his words to ensure that Daniel tells the truth. His earlier injunctions took care of that.

Daniel swallows. Aristeus's present question is open-ended—it allows for Daniel to smudge the truth. Just a little. That's how he manages to swallow down Ciere's name and immunity. He will not betray her unless explicitly forced.

"I told you," Daniel says, "I saw Morana run after a girl. I would've followed, but that would have put me out of your three-mile radius."

"No normal girl could have taken down Morana," Aristeus murmurs.

It's not a question, so Daniel doesn't have to answer. His gaze slides to the door again. He can see the hallway lights peeking through the sliver of open space and he can just make out the sound of footfalls. Daniel's immunity sends a jolt through him—someone's coming. Before he can say anything, Aristeus speaks. He leans against the window, hands in his pockets. "You're uncomfortable here."

Daniel considers denying it, and then weighs the pros and cons of outright admitting he'd rather be spending time with a cobra than with Aristeus. Finally, he settles on saying, "The hotel's a little out of my price range."

"Right." Aristeus nods. "You've been on the run since you were thirteen. You ran away from home." He moves away from the window. "I had some of my people run a background check on you. There're no reports of domestic violence and your grades were fine. You played sports, had friends. From what I can tell, you were a surprisingly well-adjusted young man. Did you run away because you were immune?"

Now that is a question, and Daniel can't ignore it. Aristeus's order to *tell the truth* yanks the words through his lips.

"No," he says. "That wasn't it."

"Then why?" Aristeus asks. He seems genuinely curious. He's playing good cop, trying to forge some kind of bond between them.

Again, Daniel cannot remain silent. "I did it for my sister."

A flicker of surprise crosses Aristeus's features. "Your sister? Tell me."

No. Daniel can't say it aloud; it will tear him apart. He sinks his own nails into his arm and blood wells up. But the pain cannot halt his words. "I ran away so that if anyone in my family were to catch the government's attention, it would be me. That's why I never used an alias. My twin sister is immune, too. I didn't want her to be recruited."

There it is. Daniel has never told anyone about his sister. He waits for the inevitable question—*What's your sister's immunity?* He'll have to answer, and then his sister will be part of the system, forcibly recruited just like Daniel.

But Aristeus doesn't ask. Instead, he's looking at Daniel

like he just became more interesting. "How did you figure out you were an eludere?"

"Accidentally revealed my power by scoring a goal in a football game blindfolded," Daniel says, relief making the words easier. His own secrets are of little value to him. "Did it on a dare. I'd never realized that everyone didn't have a sixth sense, so I didn't know any better. How'd you figure out you were a dominus?"

The briefest flicker of hesitation crosses Aristeus's face. "I commanded my father to stop hitting my mother."

Before he can say anything else, a whisper of instinct snaps Daniel's head up. Aristeus follows his gaze to the door, and a moment later there is a knock.

Agents Eduardo Carson and Avery Gervais fill the doorway. Carson openly gapes at the room in a way that makes Daniel think the FBI agents must be staying in a very cheap motel.

"Glad to see you two came through the raid unharmed," Aristeus says.

The two agents stand awkwardly in the doorway for a second before Gervais huffs out an impatient breath and steps inside, pulling Carson with him.

"You, too," Gervais says. "Although I heard your partner had a . . . setback."

Aristeus's mouth draws tight. "She'll make a full recovery."

"Glad to hear it," says Gervais. Without asking permission, he walks to the HDE wall and digs out his cell phone. He presses the phone to the enamel's smooth surface. A shimmer runs along the wall, a ripple of light, before the screen powers up. The hotel logo appears in the center while the HDE syncs up to Gervais's phone.

"We've got good news and bad news," Gervais says. "First, the good news is that the raid on the TATE cell went well. There were no fatalities on our end, and only four or five injuries, including your partner. We managed to round up most of the perps suspected of working for TATE, although a few did manage to slip past the barricades." He clears his throat. "We could have avoided that if we'd had more time to prepare."

Aristeus seats himself at the couch and waves his hand in a gesture of dismissal. Keeping the FBI agents in the loop is obviously the least of his worries. "Has everyone been IDed?"

Carson, who has so far remained near the door, moves farther into the room. "We're still working it," he says. "Not everyone we found at the compound had legitimate tags, and many of them lack obvious criminal records. We're trying to corroborate fingerprints with medical records at the moment."

"And was this Frieda Fuller among them?"

Gervais and Carson exchange a look. Gervais punches in a command on his phone. The HDE wall glitters and a picture appears on its smooth surface. It's of a woman sprawled facedown in a parking lot, her head tilted at an unnatural angle and her limbs tossed about.

Daniel bows his head—he doesn't want the agents to see him grieve. Fuller is dead. A rush of relief follows his initial shock. He's sorry she's murdered, but at least dead people can't become traitors. Fuller's secrets will die with her.

"This is the bad news," Gervais says after a moment's pause.

"Fuller is dead?" Aristeus looks at Gervais for confirmation.

"No, she's just resting," Carson deadpans, and Daniel balls his hand into a fist. Choking suffocation might be worth breaking Carson's nose.

Gervais gives his partner a quelling glare. "Two of our agents pursued TATE members who managed to escape the main compound. They fired, and we fought back. This woman here was later IDed as Frieda Fuller."

"I wanted her alive," Aristeus comments.

Carson throws his hands up. "They were armed—they fired at federal agents. If you thought we were going to lie down and play dead—"

"She was the head of that TATE cell."

"Then I don't see why you're upset," Carson says. "The woman probably would've faced a death sentence anyway. Just happened without the court or jury fees."

"I wanted to question her," Aristeus replies. "She was trying to obtain information that could be a matter of national security. I need to know if she found it."

Gervais and Carson look at each other again. An entire conversation takes place in that moment. It ends when Gervais twitches his shoulders in a shrug. "You know," he says to Aristeus, "this... uh, joint mission between the UAI and FBI would probably go a lot smoother if we actually knew what we were looking for."

"I second that motion," Carson says, holding his hand up as if in a mock vote.

Aristeus's gaze is fixed on Fuller's picture. He doesn't answer right away; his eyes unfocus and he lets out a small sigh. "Tell me what you know about TATE."

Gervais speaks. "It's one of the lesser-known terrorist groups currently active in the US. Known primarily for cyberterrorism—distributing sensitive information, breaking into government sites, and taking down the federally instituted firewalls. The name stands for Total Anarchy, Total Efficiency."

Aristeus shifts restlessly. "Do you know who Richelle Fiacre is?"

Gervais snorts. "Is your next question going to be if I know the current president, too? Of course I know who Richelle Fiacre is. She's the one surviving member of the Fiacre family.

The last remnant of that godforsaken pharmaceutical empire. Whereabouts currently unknown, although we'd love to find her. I think she was in Italy the last time US intelligence knew her location."

A cold smile touches Aristeus's lips. "Not living. Not anymore."

"What?" Carson says, startled. "Seriously? She's dead?"

"Yes, I'm pretty sure that's the definition of 'not living,'" Aristeus says smoothly. "Or maybe she's just resting."

"How?" Gervais demands.

"Liver cancer." Aristeus rolls his shoulder in a shrug. "It took her rather quickly, as she never sought treatment. Checking into a hospital would've given her position away, and her anonymity was important to her. We only found out when she was identified at a morgue in New York. She had already had her will delivered to an estate lawyer in Baltimore under the alias of 'Marie Louis.'"

"So the last Fiacre finally bit it. It's something for the history books. Doesn't explain why we raided a Baltimore suburb," Carson says impatiently. "What does this have to do with TATE?"

The words take a moment to register, but Daniel feels it when everyone comes to the same conclusion. The silence is so complete that he hears Carson swallow. "Shit. You mean those terrorists were after the last Fiacre's will? Why?"

There is only one thing that the Fiacres are known for—only one legacy they gave the world. One thing that people would kill or die for. "But the formula doesn't exist anymore," Gervais says quietly. "Fiacre destroyed it when he killed his family. It's a fool's dream."

"I disagree," Aristeus says. "Do you know what Fiacre's last message was? He posted it on his website just before he set off those explosives. One word: Pandora. A box that could never be closed."

"You think it's still out there," Daniel says, and he tries to sound as incredulous as possible. He's a good liar. Maybe if he sounds startled enough, the feds won't figure out that Daniel has already pieced this together. "You think the magic vaccine formula is just floating around, waiting for someone to find it."

Aristeus turns a cold smile on him. "I know it is."

18

CIERE

Ciere opens her eyes. She is curled up in the SUV's backseat. Warm air drifts in through the car's shattered windows, carrying the scent of trees and earth. Somewhere to her right, she can hear Devon's soft snores. Kit sprawls in the passenger's seat, and Magnus is nowhere to be seen.

When she peers through the car's broken window, she sees the forest. Shockingly green trees surround the car, their canopy blocking out most of the afternoon light.

Ciere has no idea where they are. All she remembers is Kit driving farther and farther west, his eyes determinedly on the road while the car ran from the rising dawn. Eventually, he found a gravel road leading into a forested area. They spent a good half an hour jostling up and down in their seats while

Kit took the car on long-deserted dirt roads, finding the most remote location he could.

As soon as the engine clicked off, Ciere flopped onto her side and fell asleep. Devon must have clambered into the open trunk and decided to rest there. When she peers over the seat, she sees him splayed on his back, limbs pointing in all different directions, his jaw hanging open.

Kit sleeps in a more dignified manner, with his arms crossed over his chest and head nodded forward. Someone must have bandaged his wound after Ciere fell asleep. As quietly as she can, Ciere opens the back door and slides out of the car. Her bare feet touch gravel, and she carefully makes her way off the road and deeper into the forest. There is an uncomfortable weight in her bladder, and without any access to a nearby toilet, the cover of a tree will have to do. The sensation of dirt, grass, and twigs on her bare feet remind her of when she was young.

When she picks her way back to the SUV, she sees Magnus. He sits with his back to one of the larger trees. Morana's knife and Kit's pistol sit beside him, within easy reach. His eyes are half-lidded, but something about his posture makes Ciere think he is alert. This theory is confirmed when she steps on a twig and Magnus doesn't so much as twitch.

"Get some sleep?" he asks.

She finds a fallen log and settles on it. "Yeah. You?"

"I'm fine."

She gestures at the forest. "So where are we?"

"West Virginia," Magnus says. "If you want more specifics, I have no idea." He reaches down and picks something up: a water bottle. Silently, he holds it out to Ciere. She takes it with a grateful nod.

She feels strangely displaced, sitting on a log, drinking warm water, and trying to drown the bitter taste at the back of her throat. There is something surreal in being outdoors, with the sunlight dappling through the trees, birds chirping, and fresh, smokeless air. Last night she saw the SUV riddled with bullets; she saw buildings burning in the distance; she saw someone she thought was a friend stand by and watch as a fed chased her down. She squeezes her eyes shut, her fingers going tight around the bottle. Has it been less than a week since she and Devon were staking out a Newark bank? Everything seems to be unraveling. She takes a shuddering breath and tries to steady herself. When she reopens her eyes, Ciere finds Magnus studying her.

He's going to say something about the raid, she just knows it. So she opens her mouth first. "What's it like? Being a mentalist."

That throws him. A line appears on his forehead. "What?"

"You," she gestures at him, "reading minds. I've never met a mentalist before. What's it like?"

"What's it like being an illusionist?" he says.

Phantom pain makes her rub the heel of one hand into her temple. "Mostly, it's a literal headache."

That earns her a smile. "You know," Magnus says slowly, "how when you're watching TV and a commercial comes on, and it's twice as loud as the show itself? You'll jump, maybe flinch, and then hit the mute button as fast as you can." He touches the collar of his shirt. "Now imagine that happening every time you touch someone. And there's no mute button."

She lets that sink in.

"What now?" she says finally.

"We wake Kit," Magnus replies grimly, and rises to his feet. "And then we get some answers."

Waking Kit is usually a simple matter of putting the wrong china in the dishwasher or going near his tulip bed—he has a sixth sense about these things. It doesn't matter if he's dead asleep or in an entirely different part of the house; he'll come awake with a start, mumbling about disemboweling whoever is defiling his home. Rousing Kit today is a different story. The skin around his eyes is drawn tight and his usually pale skin is downright chalky. His hand shakes when he takes the proffered water bottle. "Eat this," Magnus says, unearthing a protein bar from the backseat. Kit looks at it with distaste, but manages to take a few bites.

Ciere and Devon settle on the ground. She crosses her legs

and puts her back to a young tree with broad-shaped leaves. Devon begins fidgeting with a stick.

Only after Kit has finished eating the protein bar does Magnus speak up. "So," he says, in an all-too-casual tone. "A hacking conglomerate?"

Kit glances up. "What?"

Magnus's face is frozen in a neutral expression. "Our employers. You said they were a hacking conglomerate."

Kit runs his thumb over his mouth, brushing away crumbs. "Maybe I altered the truth a bit."

"A hacking conglomerate?" Magnus repeats. His voice hardens, and for once there is real emotion in it. "That was TATE. Your so-called client, Frieda Fuller, is an operative of TATE."

"Tate?" Ciere asks. It's the same name Morana said last night, and Ciere still has no idea what it means.

Magnus throws a narrow-eyed look her way, like he suspects she might have been part of this. "You led me to believe we were working for an individual," he says to Kit, "not a terrorist cell."

Devon chokes.

"They're not a terrorist cell," Kit retorts. "They're... a resistance group."

"A fanatical organization," says Magnus.

"Freedom fighters," says Kit.

"Cyberterrorists," says Magnus.

"Aggressive computer experts," says Kit.

"Semantics," Magnus snarls. "You lied to me, Kit. Again."

"I didn't so much lie," Kit says evasively, "as not tell you everything."

"You lied."

"I misled."

"You misinformed."

This time it is Kit who says, "Semantics. Whatever I did—it's not important now. We've got much bigger things to worry about."

"Bigger than the fact we contracted out to terrorists?" Devon croaks.

Ciere catches on first. "The feds took down TATE," she says. "Why?"

"Other than the fact they're terrorists?" Devon says.

Ciere shakes her head. "No—I mean, why now? Why did the feds move now? Why was it so important that they used local cops, as well as both the feds and the UAI?" She swallows. "What were they looking for?"

"Yes, Kit," Magnus says evenly, "what were they looking for?"

"What makes you think I know?" Kit says.

"Because you've been holding out on us this whole time."

Kit replies, "I haven't been holding out so much as—"

"Concealing?" Magnus says darkly.

"Fucking hell," says Devon. "If either one of you says 'semantics' one more time..."

This is getting nowhere. Ciere shoves her index finger and thumb between her lips. A loud whistle cracks the air and everyone winces, turning to look at her.

"Everybody needs to shut up for a second," she says. "Calm down." She doesn't mention the fact she's trembling, and she clasps her sweaty hands behind her back.

"She's right," Magnus says. "We need to be calm. Logical." For a moment, everyone just stares at one another. Then Magnus adds, "Kit, you are going to tell us everything or so help me I will pin you to the ground and listen to your thoughts until I know everything you do."

Oh, well. The calmness lasted a second longer than Ciere expected it to.

Magnus looks like he might be making good on his threat—he starts pulling at his gloves.

Devon cracks his knuckles. "I'll get his left arm. Magnus, you get his legs."

"Now, now," Kit protests. He turns a beseeching expression on Ciere. She still remembers the cold touch of the dauthus's fingers on her, the sting of the Taser's barbs when they bit into her flesh, the running, the smell of smoke, and the taste of her own terror.

"I'll get his right arm," she volunteers.

"The will," Kit says abruptly. "All right? They must have found out about the will. They probably thought that we'd already delivered the will to TATE."

A pause. Ciere and Devon share a confused glance before she understands. The will. The whole point of this job.

"The will we just stole?" Ciere says slowly.

Devon gets it. "The will I have permanently stuck in my brain?"

"No, some other will," Kit snaps. "Of course *that* will!"

"Kit," Magnus says, and there is that deadly calm in his voice. "Exactly whose will did we steal?"

Another pause. Kit seems to be steeling himself, bracing for their reactions.

"Marie Louis was an alias," he says.

Devon leans forward. He is staining the knees of his designer jeans with dirt and moss, but he doesn't seem to care. "For...?"

Ciere swallows. The air has a new quality to it. It feels like the moment before a lightning strike, when everything goes quiet and dark, only to be set alight.

"Richelle Fiacre," Kit says.

The words hit Ciere like a blow. Richelle Fiacre. A Fiacre. Why in the world would Kit send them after the last Fiacre's will?

"Now," Kit says, "answer me this. What information

would the feds kill for? What information would a cyberterrorist group hire thieves to go after? And what's the only thing the Fiacre family is famous for?"

"You cannot be serious," Devon says, but he sounds more terrified than unconvinced.

"The formula," Ciere whispers.

Kit's crew has completed a few big jobs. They've fenced a genuine Manet, forged a Jacques-Louis David, and stolen one of Thomas Cole's collections from a museum. They've lifted diamonds from a crooked cop's vault. They once ran a con on the head of a crime family. Ciere is used to high-stakes games, to playing her part, and hoping no one gets caught.

But nothing compares to this.

"But," Devon says, and he sounds younger. "Why?"

"You know what immune individuals are to the government," Kit says quietly. "We kill. We evade. We levitate. We make people see things that don't exist. We listen to their thoughts. It's no wonder the feds want to control us—we're worse than any weapon they could have knowingly devised. And you know what the Praevenir formula could do? Create more of us. Create armies. Right now they can't make more of us—Brenton Fiacre made sure of that. The vaccine is impossible to duplicate—the MK virus wiped itself out with its mortality rate. Today, there are only about six samples of virus for the entire world to experiment on. That's why the armament race stalled. But Richelle Fiacre's will, if it does hold the key to the formula, could change all that."

"And you were going to sell it to a terrorist group," Magnus replies.

Kit shakes his head. "For the last time, TATE is no more a terrorist group than we are. They're hackers, and I thought they were going to publish the will for everyone to see."

That makes Ciere blink. "What?"

"According to the TATE manifesto, they're dedicated to freedom of the press," Kit says. "It made sense that they'd want to publish something like this."

"They wanted to end the armament race," Magnus breathes. "But that..."

"Would let anyone in the world have access to the formula," Kit says. "The European Union. The Chinese Republic. Our former allies and our current enemies. It's no wonder the feds came down so hard. They can't have information like this leak out."

"And you wanted that information," Ciere says. "Because it would be worth a fortune."

"I figured we could make a few disposable copies of the will," Kit says. "In case TATE didn't leak the information too quickly, we could sell it."

Devon blinks. "Disposable? One of those copies is in my head."

Kit looks unruffled.

"You son of a—"

"Fiacre," Magnus breaks in. "Are you sure that this belonged to Richelle Fiacre and not some impostor?"

Kit nods. "Yes. Daniel worked for TATE and Frieda Fuller on a number of occasions, and she trusted him. She sent him to verify Marie Louis's identity, and when he did, she gave him the job of retrieving the will. Daniel called and left me a message the night before he vanished. He thought the will would be a trinket, a rarity. Something he could profit off of. I don't think he truly knew what he was getting into. After talking to Frieda Fuller, I understood a bit better what the risks were. And what could be gained."

"Daniel?" Magnus asks.

"One of my protégés."

"Daniel's not missing," Ciere says, and three pairs of eyes turn to her. She quickly lays out exactly what happened when she was separated from the others, beginning with her search for Kit and ending with Magnus's rescue. As she speaks, the last remnants of color drain from Kit's face.

"Daniel is in the hands of the UAI," Kit says.

"Not just the UAI," Magnus murmurs. He repeats the name he said last night: "Aristeus."

"Okay, I'll bite." Devon taps the ground with his foot. "Who's Aristeus?"

Magnus hesitates before saying, "Aristeus is one of the highest-ranked operative agents of the UAI."

Ciere's stomach tightens with anxiety. "What is his immunity?"

Magnus and Kit exchange a long look. "Dominus," Kit finally says.

Devon makes a disbelieving noise. "No. That's impossible. The feds can't have a dominus—people would know."

"Why?" Kit asks. "Because the government is so free with information these days?"

Devon opens his mouth and then closes it again. He looks at a loss for words, and Ciere is reminded that Devon grew up as a straight. He was raised believing in the government—first in the UK and then in America. While Devon could be skeptical, he wasn't raised with instinctive distrust.

Ciere holds up a hand, trying to ward off any argument. "Wait...dominus. So they're real? That whole mind-controlling thing exists?"

Kit scowls at her, like he suspects this is one of the lectures Ciere dozed through.

"It's not mind control. It's hypnosis," Kit explains. "Except on a massively powerful scale. The first command requires eye contact, but after that he could be standing behind you and tell you to jump into a river. You would do it without hesitating."

Devon adds, "Rarest of the immunities—hell, dominuses

make us look common and useless." He looks up, confusion chasing the fear from his face. "Wait, dominuses? Or would the plural be dominii?"

"I don't think anyone truly knows or cares," Kit replies, "since the plural has never been an issue."

"And if one has Daniel," Ciere says, suppressing a shiver, "then he has to do what this guy says. But—but, can't we get him out?" Determination bubbles up in her chest. Maybe there's some way to save the situation, to rescue a little piece of her old life. "We can get him out, right? We can rescue him."

The look Magnus gives her is full of pity. "He's not safe anymore," he says, not without compassion. "This Daniel will already have been forced to listen to Aristeus's commands. Even if you manage to get him back, there's no telling what kind of orders Daniel will be carrying with him. He could spy on you—even try to kill you."

Ciere tries to swallow the lump in her throat. "No."

"He's right," Kit says coolly. "I don't like it any more than you do, Ciere, but Magnus is right. Daniel's gone, and even if we could retrieve him, I'm not sure we should try." He takes a breath, wincing as his arm goes around his injured side. "Daniel should've known better. He didn't think, and it got him caught by the feds. We can't afford to associate with such carelessness."

Ciere shifts, and the heavy silver bracelet settles more

closely around her wrist. A chill prickles its way up her arms. "So you'll just leave him there?"

Kit regards her with his flattest stare. "There's nothing I can do."

"Wait," Devon interrupts. "Back up. How do you know this dominus bloke? You tangle with him before?"

Magnus and Kit exchange a look, and in that moment Ciere knows that neither is going to tell the truth. Something silent passes between them, an acknowledgement, before Kit turns on Devon, and says coolly, "That's not important right now. The government knows about the will. They're going to come after anyone they think might have had knowledge of it. I'll have to burn a few aliases, but my information won't be traceable. There's no way the feds know we have the will, and that's how things are going to stay."

Ciere pushes a hand into her pocket, her fingers wrapping around Guntram's card. "So the job's over...?" She trails off, unsure.

Kit nods and shakily rises to his feet. He ignores Magnus's proffered hand and says, "This information is too hot. We're going to leave it, for now anyway. The feds will be trying to root out anyone who might have had contact with Fiacre or her will.

"This job is over. We're done."

Which means, Ciere thinks, they won't be getting paid. And her only hope of freeing herself from Guntram is gone.

19

CIERE

The drive back to Philadelphia eats up the rest of the afternoon. Kit takes care to avoid the highways and sticks to less populated areas. The sound of the wind blowing through the car makes conversation nearly impossible. Ciere doesn't mind the silence. She spends most of the drive with her hand in her pocket, her fingers wrapped around Brandt Guntram's business card.

They stop at a gas station on the fringes of Harrisburg. Kit chooses a location that looks a little too run-down for many people to frequent, and vanishes into the station to pay with cash. "I need to stretch my legs," Ciere says. Magnus nods. He's taken over driving from Kit and remains in the SUV, his hand resting on the steering wheel.

Ciere leads Devon around the corner and out of sight. The restroom door is rusty, and the faded picture of a woman hangs from a single nail. "Charming," Devon says. His face shifts—he seems to gather himself. "You all right?"

"Fine." But she doesn't put any effort into the lie.

"Of course," Devon says blandly. "We just tried to deliver the world's most dangerous weapon to a terrorist group and nearly got nabbed by the feds. Kit got shot and Magnus looks like an extra in a slasher flick. I thought I signed on with a crew of competent criminals."

She considers reaching up and smacking him, but she's too tired. She also considers making a cutting remark, but she can't think of one. Sleep deprivation must be getting to her.

Before she can say anything, Devon leans down and wraps an arm around her shoulders and draws her into a hug. It's awkward for one or two heartbeats, but then Ciere leans into his warm chest and lets herself relax for the first time since Baltimore. He feels familiar and steady—it's easy to close her eyes and pretend for just a second that nothing's wrong. That it's just the two of them hanging out in Manhattan again, sitting in a park and discussing how to pick someone's pocket.

Devon breaks the hug first. "Thank you for not getting shot and saving me from a lifetime of therapy," he says sincerely. He straightens his shoulders and takes a step toward the restroom.

"We're not here to pee," Ciere says.

"Speak for yourself," Devon replies, poking at the door. It

swings open, and he makes a face. A horrible stench wafts out, and he takes a step back. "On second thought, you're right."

Ciere holds out her hand. "Cell phone, please."

Still looking bewildered, Devon hands it over. She fumbles with the phone in one hand and Brandt Guntram's card in the other. "Wait," says Devon. "You're calling him?"

Ciere ignores him and punches in the number. Swallowing hard, she tries to clear her throat. Confident. She needs to sound confident.

The phone rings once. Then a deep, accented voice says, "This is Conrad."

It takes her a moment to remember him—Conrad. Guntram's bodyguard. When she speaks, she tries to infuse her voice with a breezy boredom. "I need to talk to Guntram."

"Who is this?"

She hesitates. She hasn't told Guntram her name, and she wants to keep it that way. If he does turn her in to the feds, that's one more bit of information he'd have on her. Then she remembers Kit's words about the bank robbery. "The Kitty Burglar," she says.

A deep-throated laugh crackles over the line. "Ah," Conrad says. "Yes. Hold on a second." There is some shuffling, a moment of static, and then a new voice speaks.

"Good timing," Guntram says. "I just finished eating a late lunch. So where would you like to meet?"

He thinks she has the forty grand. He thinks their business is about to be concluded.

If only.

"Um, yeah," she says, and her confident facade crumbles. "I don't have your money yet."

Silence.

"Then why are you calling me?"

Because according to their deal, she has only two days to get forty thousand dollars. She's a good thief, but she's not that good.

She considers several possibilities: she could tell Kit about Guntram and let him handle it. But the thought of telling him sends a cold chill through her whole body. She's not sure how he'd react to her predicament, and to the fact she's been keeping this situation a secret. She's already lost Daniel. She can't risk losing Kit, too.

She resists the urge to pull at the tracker bracelet. Her skin crawls, and even if it's just her imagination, her whole right arm feels contaminated by its very presence. As long as she's wearing it, she's a danger to everyone around her. Any moment, the cops could come swooping down on her. All it would take would be for Guntram to make one phone call.

Leaving the country is a last resort; there are mentalists at every international airport just waiting to catch immune criminals. She might not make it out. If she did, she could never come back. And what if Guntram has international contacts?

"I—I need more time," she says. "I'll get you the money, I swear, but I need more time."

Guntram makes a thoughtful sound. "Ah. You see, that's where we have a problem, Ms. Kitty. The Gyr Syndicate has a reputation to uphold. We don't give extensions."

"But—"

"I suggest you check the papers," Guntram interrupts. "Look over some of today's headlines. Go home. Think it over. It'll give you some perspective."

Before she can argue further, the call ends. Ciere stares at the cell phone's screen as it fades to black. The bracelet slides along her wrist and she has the sudden—and unwise—urge to smash it against the restroom door.

Devon touches her shoulder. "Not good?"

"Not good," she says grimly. "We need today's newspapers."

In addition to gasoline, the station also sells out-of-date snack food, boxes of beer, some emergency car equipment, and other odds and ends. Kit is handing several bills to the clerk when Ciere steps inside. There's a rack of newspapers to the right of the counter and Ciere picks up one of each. "These, too," she says.

Kit takes them without a word and pays. When they step out of the station, Kit says, "Good idea. We need to know what the press is saying about the raid."

"Exactly what we were thinking," replies Devon, without missing a beat.

Back in the car, Magnus forces Kit to drink half a bottle of water. Kit quietly argues with him about eating a donut, while Devon and Ciere try to remain unnoticed in the backseat. Ciere opens the newspaper and begins scanning headlines.

Devon finds the right one. Silently, he points a finger to it.

ALLEGED MOB BOSS BEHIND BARS. The article that follows details how the head of a New York crime family was recently caught red-handed in a drug bust, thanks to an anonymous tip.

The headline below reads *ACCUSED MURDERER'S BODY FOUND NEAR FORT WADSWORTH.*

And below that: *POLICE LOCATE CACHE OF GANG WEAPONS.*

"They're taking out their enemies," Ciere whispers. "One by one. Anonymous tips. Assassinations. Cutting off resources."

Devon folds the paper shut, obviously trying to cover up their conversation with the crackle of the newsprint. "You really think they're behind all of this? But—but they're using the feds. I mean, literally using them." Devon jabs a finger at the paper. "It's like in DC—they're letting the feds do their dirty work. I thought criminals didn't do that."

Guntram's words come back to her. *I'll be entirely honest. I hate the feds. I just happen to hate poachers more.*

"The Syndicate isn't playing by the rules," she says. "That's why they're winning this war. By calling in anonymous tips and using these trackers. Without ever getting their hands bloody."

"The enemy of my enemy," Devon says. "It means, either way, we're royally screwed."

They ditch the SUV at a junkyard on the outskirts of Philadelphia. What's left of the car would draw too much attention in an elsec, so they leave it, and Kit calls for a taxi. Someone will come by later to tow the SUV and quietly repair the damage, no questions asked.

The taxi driver doesn't comment on Kit's bloody shirt, Magnus's appearance, or the smell of smoke. Ciere isn't sure, but she thinks she sees Kit slip him a few extra bills.

Magnus steps up to the gate and flashes his tags before the alarm sensor. Ciere hurries forward to tell him that Kit's security will probably shoot lasers or grenades at him if he tries to get through. Then the tiny light blinks from red to green and the lock comes undone. Magnus pushes the gate open like it's nothing, and Ciere is left standing there, hand still outstretched, wondering how Magnus has access to Kit's stringent security.

"Kit's careful to ensure that certain people always have access to him," Magnus says, and Ciere jumps. She didn't notice him watching her. "And then there are those who would flash their tags and trigger a few anti-personnel mines."

Ciere honestly doesn't know if that statement is comforting or terrifying. Maybe both. "And if that dominus, Aristeus, walked up to the gates...?" she says tentatively.

Magnus turns away so quickly Ciere only catches the briefest gimpse of his expression—a twisted, jagged smile. "Kit's always been fond of his protégés," he says, so quietly that Ciere almost doesn't make out the words. "Aristeus is no exception." Before Ciere can reply, Magnus leaves her side to go help Kit.

Ciere pushes the gate open and steps into the front yard. A day ago, she would've scoffed at the sight of the pristine lawn and carefully tended gardens.

As she steps onto the cobblestone path, a crinkling noise catches her attention. She glances down; her foot has landed on a crumpled paper airplane. She picks it up, smoothing the paper between her fingers. This elsec is full of families, so it's not uncommon for things like baseballs or Frisbees to find their way into Kit's yard. Sometimes he even tosses them back.

The paper is crisp, and she almost throws it away, but the letterhead catches her eye. It's not an address or even a name—it's a picture of a falcon in flight.

Her fingers begin to tremble. She unwraps the rest of the airplane and finds two handwritten words.

TWO DAYS

She crumples the paper before anyone can see it, shoving it deep into a pocket. She doesn't look back; she can't let the others see her face. She can't imagine what expression she's wearing. When she steps into the house, she barely notices that Lizaveta is sitting in the living room, her knobby hands clutching knitting needles. What looks like the beginnings of a scarf is draped over the couch. Tulip sits next to her, his head resting on her knee and his eyes fixed on the yarn ball. "You are back now?" Liz asks.

Ciere doesn't even try to answer. She sweeps past the living room and up the stairs, taking them two at a time. Only after she's safe in her room does she dig out the flyer. She uncrumples the page and sets it on her bed before digging out Guntram's business card.

The falcons on the card and the flyer are identical.

They were here. The Gyr Syndicate was here. At her home—at the Bolsover house.

Guntram's words come back to her, making her feel physically sick. *Go home. Think it over. It'll give you some perspective.*

This shouldn't come as such a shock. They've got a tracker on her, and Guntram must have at least one operative in every major city on the East Coast.

That's when it hits her.

There's no place she can hide. Someone got close, close enough to slip a note under the gate. What if someone else had found the note—what if Kit or Magnus had found it? They'd abandon her just like they did Daniel.

When Devon enters the room, Ciere is sitting on the floor, her legs folded up beneath her. Concern flashes over his face and he kneels next to her. "What is it?"

Her eyes wander to the flyer and he snatches it up.

"Shit," he says.

For a long minute, they both sit like that—on the floor, with the flyer between them. Devon traces the outline of the falcon with a finger, his expression gone hard with thought. "I could ask my dad for access to my trust fund," he finally says.

"Would he actually give it to you?"

A shake of his head. "No. And even if he would, he still thinks I'm in Norway." He chews on his lip, as if trying to hold something back, and then blurts out, "Why don't we just ask Copperfield for help? You know he would."

Ciere's throat draws tight. "'We can't afford to associate with such carelessness,'" she says softly. "That's what he said. If one of us gets caught, it's our own fault. He's letting Daniel rot with the feds—what makes you think I'm any different?"

"Well," Devon retorts, "for one thing, you haven't stupidly tried to acquire the will of perhaps the most infamous person alive. From what I can tell, that Daniel bloke had it coming. You'd never..." His voice trails off in the wake of her expression.

Because it's dawning on her. Sudden hope, hot and desperate, flares to life in her chest. They do have one valuable thing. If they could find it, it'd definitely be worth forty thousand dollars.

"Oh, no," Devon says. "The last time I saw that face, we went and robbed a bank. Please tell me you're not thinking what I think you're thinking."

Ciere forces a confident smile onto her lips. "You've got the will. We're going to use it and find that formula. And then we sell it to Guntram, get the Gyr Syndicate off our backs, and no one will ever know."

Devon stares at Ciere like he's never truly seen her before. "Are you serious? You want to find the formula? The one that the FBI and the UAI are hunting?"

Ciere forces herself to nod.

"You want to find the formula that the entire world has been trying to re-create for nearly sixteen bleeding years?" says Devon. "You want to find the formula that could potentially turn normal people into preternaturally powered soldiers. And then you want to sell it to a bloodthirsty mobster?"

Well, when he puts it like that... "Yeah. That's pretty much the plan," Ciere mumbles.

Devon presses a hand against his eyes. "The next time my dad says I have no ambition, I might have to tell him about this."

20

CIERE

Ciere and Devon spend most of the night studying the will. Devon rewrote it from memory on several sheets of pink stationery. But no matter how many times they look over the scrawled words, they find nothing. Devon tries every cipher he knows, including a few he made up himself. They cross out every other word, reverse the letters, scramble and unscramble whole sentences. But if there is a hidden message in Richelle Fiacre's will, it's hidden too well.

When morning light begins to peek through her frilly white curtains, Ciere lets out a groan. Her eyes feel grainy and her hair unwashed. She flops onto her bed and rolls over, facing Devon. He's perched sideways on her desk chair, his long legs sprawled over the arm. The will sits in his lap.

"What do you know about the Fiacres?" she asks. "I mean,

besides the obvious." Maybe there is something here: a clue that would only be visible to someone who knew Richelle Fiacre better.

"Family of bloody lunatics," Devon mutters. "Effing Brenton Fiacre and his Praevenir vaccine."

"He did cure the MK plague," Ciere feels obligated to point out.

Devon shoots the will a poisonous look. "Only for those who had the money to pay." He pushes himself to his feet and begins to pace, his long strides eating up the small space between the desk and wall. "He also got the vaccine through with minimal testing."

Ciere touches the place on her collarbone where the Taser barbs hit her. "Which explains the unexpected side effects."

Devon snorts derisively. "That's a mild way of putting it. Poor bastard realized what he'd done, though. Locked himself and his family in a warehouse full of the vaccine, along with all the research, and bid the world adieu with C4 and a reference to a Greek myth."

"What was that again?"

"Pandora?" Devon asks, confirming. He waves his hand vaguely around, as if to indicate a box. "It's a story about a woman who opened a box full of horrors like grief and misery and—ironically enough—disease. Once it was open, she couldn't close it. Guess that Brenton Fiacre sympathized with her when he realized what he'd created. A box that could never be closed and all that."

"Well, he closed it." Ciere rolls over, burying her face in

a pillow. The soft cotton feels comforting, and she draws the duvet over her head. "Good-bye, Pandora's box. Good-bye, formula. Good-bye, freedom. Hello, government cell."

"So long as it has a toilet," Devon says from somewhere behind her. "I need to take a piss."

She listens to the sound of his footfalls as he strides through the door. Then she sits up and surveys her room. The last few days haven't been kind to her bedroom. The place is a mess—scattered papers everywhere, empty teacups, dirtied plates, and an empty chip bag. This is not the abode of a master crook. This is not even the abode of a competent crook.

She begins picking up the papers, trying to fix some of the clutter. As she gathers the sheets, she glances over the will again. So many words, all of them seemingly meaningless. If there is a formula or a clue or even a damn crossword puzzle, then she's too dumb to see it. Her eyes slide over the now-familiar legalese and then down to the signatures. Richelle Fiacre's loopy scrawl is perfectly duplicated by Devon's eidetic memory. Ciere lets her finger trace the name and wander down the page. Beneath Fiacre's signature are three others—the witnesses.

She reads the words: "*We believe Marie Louis is sound of mind and not acting under duress, menace, fraud, misrepresentation, or undue influence. We declare under penalty of perjury under the laws of the State of New York that the foregoing is true and correct.*" Ciere blinks and stops reading. Turns out that legal language is even better than counting sheep. She's about to put the will down and admit defeat when something catches her eye—

The name of the first witness. Ciere sits bolt upright, her grip on the paper so tight that it rips around her fingers.

Pandora Marton
689 Rybak Rd.
Endicott, NY

Ciere feels her breath catch.

Still clutching the paper, she runs from her room and down to the first floor. Without so much as a warning, she pushes the bathroom door open. Devon, washing his hands and humming contentedly to himself, jumps. "Ever heard of privacy?" he says. "What if I wasn't finished?"

She thrusts the paper into his still-damp hand. "Look at the witnesses."

Devon is still staring at Ciere like she's utterly lost her mind. He rolls his eyes and glances down at the paper. She knows the moment that the knowledge sinks into Devon: he stops fidgeting and goes still.

"Rotting hell," he says, the words coming out jerky and ragged.

"You memorize the directions to Endicott, New York," Ciere says. "I'll get the car keys."

21

DANIEL

Daniel is self-aware enough to admit that there is some irony in his current position. Specifically, the fact that he wants to ride in the car with the two FBI agents. As far as Aristeus knows, Daniel rides with the agents to ensure they aren't about to pull a double cross. With Aristeus's permission, Daniel was released from his three-mile radius to spy on the agents. But that's not the real reason that Daniel volunteered for the job.

The two agents are a lot less creepy than Aristeus.

The morning after the raid, Aristeus wanted to get the will from the lawyers who unknowingly possessed the most dangerous piece of information currently in existence. Aristeus would have barged into the office and simply taken it, but Gervais stood firm. "Due process," Gervais said firmly. "We'll get a warrant."

Aristeus looked as if he wanted to get a warrant by hypnotizing the nearest judge, and he probably would have if not for Morana's surgery. While he spent the day at the hospital, Carson and Gervais got the warrant and obtained the will.

It took only a moment for Aristeus to scan the will and plan their next move. "Endicott, New York," he said.

So here Daniel sits, in the backseat of a government-issue car, with the two agents who captured and put him in this situation to begin with. He should hate them, try to plot his escape, or think about how much he despises the establishment. Instead, all he can think about is how relieved he is to be out of Aristeus's presence. Carson and Gervais do normal things like bitch to each other about work, handcuff Daniel to his armrest, and buy food. There is comfort in the normalcy of it all.

At their only pit stop, Gervais goes inside to restock on snacks while Carson fills up the gas tank. Daniel peers out the window. The drive from Baltimore to Endicott takes about five hours—although the trip was delayed again by Gervais's insistence on following the law and obtaining a second warrant to search Pandora Marton's house.

"We're not simply going into someone's house based on the wild conspiracy theory of a terrorist," Gervais said when Aristeus protested.

As soon as the warrant was in their hands, the journey

northward began. The agents and Daniel took Gervais's car, while Aristeus went to commandeer a van.

Carson drives quickly; they maintain a speed that's well over the limit. Unlike his partner, Carson seems perfectly willing to disobey laws. When Daniel helpfully points out the fact that Carson is doing something illegal, the agent snorts. "Want to get there first" is all he'll say.

Daniel perks up. The rivalry between the UAI and FBI is turning out to be amusing as well as informative. "Before Aristeus?"

Carson and Gervais glance at each other, but neither says a word. Daniel interprets this as: *You work for him; you're not to be trusted.*

"Hey, I'm just another guy who was pulled into this investigation against his will." Daniel drums his fingers on the armrest. "Out of curiosity, how'd you two end up getting this gig, anyway? The FBI can't be happy to have two of its finest at the UAI's beck and call." He is pretty sure that neither agent will answer him, but it's fun needling them. And he has a feeling that fun will be a limited commodity for the rest of his life, so he might as well find it where he can.

"By the way," Daniel says, "did you notice that your car is missing a hubcap?"

Carson's crazy driving pays off—they arrive at Endicott before Aristeus. Carson pulls off the freeway and they drive north. The landscape is a brilliant green; even in summer the humidity keeps the trees and grass lush. When they're on the boundary between suburbs and country, Carson guides the car to the curb and parks it. "That's it," he says.

The house looks normal. It's an old farmhouse, with two stories, yellow paint, and a porch that wraps around the entire first floor. Both Carson and Gervais swing out of the car and approach. "You going to leave me here?" Daniel calls. Carson looks over his shoulder.

"We cracked your window," he says, like Daniel is an unruly dog. "You're fine."

Unless this is a trap. If anyone fires on the agents, the car will be the first target. And judging from Carson's cheery wave, he knows it.

Gervais gestures for Carson to cover the rear. Carson nods and leaps over the porch railing, disappearing around a tangled rosebush. It's obvious they've done this before. Gervais waits thirty seconds before he shifts, never standing directly in the path of the front door as he rings the bell.

Daniel realizes he's holding his breath and forces himself to breathe normally. Gervais waits, poised like a cat above a mouse hole, all tense shoulders and crouched posture, ready to pounce or run.

Gervais shouts to Carson, confirming that no one has left the premises. Then Gervais lunges forward, his heel slamming into the door. The door is a cheap fixture, and it buckles beneath the blow. "Going in," Gervais says loudly. He has his gun out and ready now, aimed at the ground as he darts into the hallway and out of Daniel's sight.

Daniel watches and waits, feeling exposed, as he glances up at the second story and imagines how easy it would be to put a sniper in any of those windows. In fact, any of these houses could easily be hiding vengeful members of TATE. They can't be happy at having one of their bases raided. If Richelle Fiacre was involved, and if this place is hiding the Praevenir formula, it must be protected.

Daniel feels as if his every muscle has been drawn tight. The silence presses down on him and he scuffs his shoe against the floor for some noise. The house sits there, silent and disarmingly benign.

A screech of tires makes Daniel jump. His head swings around so fast that his forehead makes contact with the half-open window, and pain flares through his skull. His eyes flood and he rubs angrily at the aching spot on his forehead. When his vision clears, he sees a van.

Aristeus pushes the car door open. As he strides toward the house, his eyes go to the front door and fix there, like he's seeing something extraordinary. He must realize he's not alone, because he abruptly turns to face the FBI agents' car. "What are you doing out here?" he says, jerking the car door open.

This is a bad thing, because Daniel is still handcuffed to said door's armrest. He staggers out onto the pavement, barely managing to keep his feet as he's dragged out into the open. Aristeus sees the handcuff and his brows draw together. "Oh, sorry," he says, like he means it.

"No problem. Never liked that arm much, anyway." Daniel grips the door tightly with his other hand.

"They cuffed you?"

"Well, if they didn't, then this bracelet is more trouble than it's worth."

Aristeus makes a disgruntled noise. "And you couldn't break out because I told you not to escape. Really, you'd think those two agents would have more faith in me." He rummages in his suit pocket and comes up with a set of keys. "You're no danger to anyone. Not anymore." He locates the right key and slides it into the cuff. The metal falls away.

"Come on." Aristeus moves away from the cars and to the house, obviously expecting Daniel to follow.

Heel, Daniel thinks. *Good dog.*

The hallway has a hardwood floor covered with a pink-and-yellow rug. There are generic pictures on the wall—panes of glass over photos of flowers, landscapes, and a few classical prints. But no family portraits, Daniel notes. No identifying information.

Aristeus walks into the kitchen and Daniel follows. It

looks pretty normal—a timer shaped like a pig rests next to the oven, and cutlery dangles from a hanger next to the fridge. Aristeus pulls a pen out of his pocket and uses it to lift a single mug out of the sink.

"Look at this," he says.

It's not the sound of the dominus's voice that lures Daniel to the sink—it's his own curiosity. The mug is plain white and holds a layer of brown sludge. Daniel sniffs. "Moldy coffee," he says. Aristeus gives him an expectant look, and then he understands. "No one's been here for at least a few days."

"Exactly," Aristeus agrees. His fingers brush over a toaster, plucking a slice of burnt bread from its interior. "They left toast in the toaster."

"They left in a hurry." Daniel feels himself relax. "There's nothing here."

"Let's hope," Aristeus says, "that you're wrong."

The ensuing search is less interesting than Aristeus made it sound. After all, saying, "*We're going to look for the famed Praevenir formula,*" sounds good in theory, but in reality it involves a lot of grunt work. Aristeus declares they're taking anything that could potentially hide a formula—tablets, the family computer, notebooks, even the books left beside the upstairs toilet.

There's also a safe. It's small—about the size of a microwave oven and settled in a corner on the floor. Aristeus reacts like it's the Holy Grail. Jittery with excitement, he paces back and forth, eager to see its contents. However, getting the safe open provides a challenge. Besides being a heavy SOB, it's also bolted to the wall.

"Shoot it," Daniel says to Gervais.

"It's bulletproof," Gervais replies, eyeing the cables.

"We are on a time schedule," Aristeus calls from the hallway.

"Shoot him," Daniel says quietly.

Gervais says, "The paperwork would be horrendous." He runs a hand over the cables and looks to Daniel. "Why haven't you offered to help?"

"Shoot Aristeus? Sorry, but I was expressly ordered not to."

"No, I mean with this." Gervais raps a knuckle against the safe and rises from his crouch. "Could you break this open?"

"I wasn't expressly ordered to."

"Could you?"

Daniel cracks his knuckles and surveys the safe with professional interest. It's not cheap, but it's not top of the line, either. Strictly middle-range home security, usually for important documents or valuables. It's a stupid place to hide them. Safes are the first thing any crook will go after. If a person is smart, they'll hide their valuables in their dirty laundry hamper, an old closet, or a fake toaster.

"Tell you what," Gervais says. "You get this safe open and

you guarantee yourself another spot in the FBI car on the way home."

Daniel considers, and says, "And donuts."

"Really?"

"You want out of here?"

"Deal."

When Aristeus comes to investigate, Daniel is on hands and knees, edging a slip of wire and a nail file into the locking mechanism while Gervais and Carson watch with rapt attention.

"I think that's all of it," Aristeus says briskly. "How's this coming along?"

"It'd be a lot easier if all my tools weren't confiscated when I was arrested," Daniel mutters. "Ah, ah. Come on, you stubborn little hunk of—HA!" The lock springs open and Daniel yanks the door free, revealing the safe's contents.

Money.

Twenty-dollar bills, mostly. They are all bound together, like money in a bank vault, and he would estimate the value at about five thousand.

Aristeus tries to hide his disappointment; he must have thought there would be a giant folder with the words SECRET PRAEVENIR FORMULA printed across it.

"Well, bag it," Aristeus says. "I'm going to take what's in the van back to DC."

"If you don't mind," Gervais says quickly, "we'd like to take Burkhart with us for one last sweep of the house."

Aristeus nods. "Not a bad idea. We should also leave someone here, to make sure that no one returns without our knowledge."

"Who's going to take that job?" Carson scoffs.

Aristeus smiles. "I think you nominated yourself."

"You can't leave a single agent here alone," Gervais says. "It's not safe."

"It's a stakeout," Aristeus replies. "I'll make some calls and get someone I trust out here to relieve him." Gervais opens his mouth to argue, but Aristeus continues on. "Do you think we can trust something this sensitive to the local police force?"

The silence speaks for itself.

Aristeus says, "It's about a six-hour drive from DC to here, so it should take that long for one of my operatives to arrive." He turns to face Carson. "Do you think you can handle watching an empty house for that long?"

If it were phrased any other way, Carson might have been able to back down. But this is a challenge, and Carson's hackles are up. A vein appears on his forehead. "I got this."

"Good." Aristeus rubs his hands together and surveys the office—the torn-up furniture and scoured bookshelves.

Daniel and the FBI agents return to their car, and Daniel finds himself once again in the backseat with his right wrist encased in metal. They will drop Carson off at a local police station, where he'll requisition an unmarked vehicle for his stakeout. (Daniel is well-versed in fed-speak enough to know that "requisition" means Carson will throw his badge around until he gets what he wants.)

"Productive morning," Gervais says as they drive back toward town. There are more cars here, more people, and Daniel contents himself with gazing through the window, watching car after car pass them by. As they slow at an intersection, he catches a glimpse of a blue sedan turning down the road they just came from.

Through the sedan's half-open window, Daniel sees a flash of short blonde curls.

22

CIERE

"Welcome to Endicott, New York," Devon announces as they pull off the freeway.

The town of Endicott doesn't look like much—mostly some fast-food restaurants and the usual small-town businesses. Beyond the concrete and steel, green hills rise up to form a verdant horizon. "The address is a little out of town," Devon says. "Which makes sense. If you're going to hide a super-secret formula, do it where no one would look: the middle of nowhere."

He's right—the address takes them to an off-yellow house with a large porch and a lot of dead flowers. "Homey," Devon says, slowing the car. "You reckon it's safe?"

Ciere glances around. There is no obvious sign of surveillance—no cop cars, no eyes peering through nearby windows—but she's not taking any chances. "Keep driving," she says. "Pull around the corner and park somewhere out of sight. We're going in the back."

The backyard turns out to be surrounded by a six-foot wooden fence, brambles, and a tangle of rusted wire.

Ciere runs her hand over the fence and squats, trying to see if there's a place to slip underneath. No luck. The fence is solid, leaving no room for thieves.

They'll go over instead.

"It's a good thing I'm tall," Devon says, coming to the same conclusion. He flashes a grin at her. "Otherwise you and your five foot nothing would be screwed."

"Five foot two," Ciere replies, too used to short jokes to be offended.

Getting over the fence is a matter of being boosted up by Devon. Her hand falls on his shoulder and he cups one of her feet in both of his hands. When he hoists her upward, she teeters in the air, supported only by her grip on Devon's shirt and his own strength. She can smell him—there's that faint odor of smoke, but there's a hint of something clean beneath it, like soap or clothing detergent. Before it has time to register, she nears the top of the fence and steadies herself by latching on to the rough wood. She hauls herself up and over, scraping her shins, and drops over the other side. Her feet hit the ground and she surveys the backyard for possible threats. It looks like any normal yard—overgrown grass, a birdbath, and a few discarded garden tools. The porch wraps around the side of the house and there is a small back door with a screen.

She hears the sound of running feet, then the fence shudders as Devon vaults into sight. His strategy of running and scaling the fence is anything but graceful, but it is effective. He hits the ground with a small yelp and falls to his knees.

"You're lucky this place looks empty," Ciere says, "and there are trees all around. Could you be any louder?"

He rubs his palms together. "Not everyone spent their childhood scaling fences and breaking into bank vaults."

"I've never broken into a bank vault," she replies. Stealing a bank teller's keycard doesn't count.

Getting inside is laughably easy. The door is locked, but the window isn't. Ciere pops the screen out and squeezes through.

A quick search proves that Ciere's assumption was correct: the house is empty. The interior is like any other middle-class dwelling. There are scuffed floors, worn carpets, knickknacks on the shelves, and mismatched furniture. A print magazine sits on a coffee table, and Devon looks at the date. "Four weeks old," he says.

"People sometimes keep old magazines," she answers.

Devon isn't dissuaded. "Did you see the kitchen? There's still toast in the toaster—burnt, too." He surveys the room again. "Whoever lived here must've legged it."

Ciere shivers. This whole situation feels eerily familiar.

Leaving behind a house, trying to hide information about its occupants. She remembers fleeing through the woods, leaving behind her childhood home in flames. At first, Ciere didn't understand why her mom would set their house on fire. Later, she realized it was for her own protection. There were papers in their house: birth certificates, social security cards, medical records, and titer tests. Setting that fire was her mother's final attempt to hide her daughter.

When she ventures upstairs, Ciere finds more evidence to support her theory. There is a room that must have been an office. It is completely gutted—the shelves empty, the computer desk tipped on its side, and a broken safe on the floor.

"You think someone pinched all of this?" Devon asks, leaning over the computer desk. "Or was this a quick-moving job?"

Ciere isn't listening. She strides across the room and kneels beside the safe. It's made of layers of metal, boxes encased in more boxes, with a heavy lock punched through the door. It's small and bolted to the wall, its door pulled wide open. The sight makes her draw inward, an instinctive need to make herself a small target.

"This place was searched," she says. "Whoever lived here didn't do this."

"How'd you figure?"

Ciere studies the safe's broken lock. "If the person who lived here took all of this stuff, they wouldn't have needed to break their own safe open."

“Oh.” Devon sounds as if he’s trying to stay calm. “So who got here before us?”

She opens her mouth to answer, but in the silence between her words and Devon’s, there is the sound of a door being forced open. It isn’t quiet or subtle—the crash of someone hitting into the back door, followed by the distinctive crack of shattering glass.

Someone else is in the house.

It could be a fellow crook, here to steal what they can. Or maybe a member of TATE. Or a fed. Or Pandora Marton herself. No, Ciere corrects herself. Pandora Marton wouldn’t break into her own house.

Ciere freezes in place, her senses straining downstairs. Listening through the walls and floor isn’t easy, and she spends a furious moment wishing to be a dauthus rather than an illusionist.

It is almost a relief when Ciere hears the creak of floorboards. Someone is definitely downstairs.

She considers opening the window and crawling onto the roof. The sound would draw the attention of whoever is downstairs, but she would escape. Devon couldn’t follow, though. The window is too small for his lanky arms and legs.

Don’t let anyone see what you are, understand?

For one horrible moment, Ciere still weighs the option. Open the window, run, leave Devon behind, get as far away as she can—

No. She squeezes her eyes shut and forces herself to slow down, to think. Isn't that what Kit has been trying to instill in her for years? *Listen*, she tells herself.

The intruder is moving through the house slowly, deliberately. The fact that this person isn't simply rushing through from room to room implies they've broken into houses before. And by breaking open the door, they've indicated they do not fear repercussions.

Feds. Or one of Guntram's agents. She isn't sure which is worse.

Silently, Ciere raises a finger to her lips, then points at the closet. Devon, his face tight with fear, gently pulls at the closet door. Inside are coats and shoes.

A squeak comes from the direction of the stairs.

Devon eases in among the coats, folding his long limbs into the confined space. The closet looks too small, but Ciere grits her teeth and squeezes inside.

This closet was obviously used to house winter clothes that won't be used for months to come. The scent of old wool and dust make Ciere's nose itch, and she begins pawing at the hanging coats, trying to arrange them so they'll block the two teenagers.

The footsteps pause at the top of the stairs, and she waits, her heart thumping, trying to listen for the direction that the intruder will go.

Something touches Ciere and she flinches before realizing it's Devon's hand. She grips it hard and he does the same, his sweaty fingers a comfort in the dark, stuffy space. She can feel his heartbeat, quick against her own skin. Footsteps grow nearer. The air is too close, the walls too near, the space too small; bitter fear floods her mouth, and she can't slow her breathing.

There is no warning.

The closet door is wrenched open, the coats thrown aside, and a hand appears. It seizes Ciere by the shoulder, fingers digging into her skin and shirt, the grip painfully tight. Devon lets out a shout.

She sinks her teeth into the hand, and there is a shouted curse, a snarl of pain, and the hand moves, trying to shake her off. Ciere doesn't let go. The intruder steps backward, dragging Ciere into the light. She blinks her eyes into focus, staring up for the first time into the face of her attacker.

Kit.

It's Kit.

They simply stare at each other, Kit's hand between Ciere's teeth. Slowly, never taking her eyes off of him, she loosens her jaw and releases him. When she runs her tongue over her teeth, her mouth floods with the taste of copper.

Kit glares down at her, cradling his bleeding hand. "I thought we got that biting tendency of yours under control when you were eleven," he says in a scarily calm voice. Ciere expects him to start shouting, but he keeps looking at her.

Something like a sob grips her throat, and she chokes it back. The sight of Kit, with his long hair and waistcoat and shiny shoes, has never been so welcome. "How'd you know where to find us?"

"You left the will in your room," says Kit. "You drove away in a car that you had to get out of the garage, which makes a particularly loud clanking noise when opened." His jaw works, and when he speaks, it is through gritted teeth. "How—do—you—think—I—found—you?"

In hindsight, it's not the most brilliant plan Ciere has ever pulled off.

"Sorry?" she offers, but her words are the spark that sets his temper ablaze.

"Do you know how dangerous this could have been?" Kit snarls. "You had no idea what was waiting here—there could have been more TATE members, there could have been feds, there could have been mobsters—"

"No one here, though," Devon pipes up. He remains half in, half out of the closet. "We're pretty sure the place has already been stripped. Whoever did it must have moved on."

Kit rounds on him. "I can't believe you went along with this! Aren't you supposed to be the smart one?"

"Hey," Ciere says, offended.

"You—hush." Kit jabs a finger at her. "You," he aims that finger at Devon, who is still half in the closet. "Where did you park my car?"

"Out back."

Kit's nostrils flare and he seems to be making an effort to control his breathing. "All right. Magnus is in a station wagon down a side road."

Ciere blinks. "How…?"

"We borrowed a car," Kit says tightly.

So he hot-wired one.

"One of our neighbors is under the impression I had a fight with my niece," Kit continues, "and that she ran away in my car. They kindly offered to lend me their spare vehicle so I could retrieve her."

"Oh, you mean you actually *borrowed* one?" Ciere asks, startled.

Kit bares his teeth. "Sometimes being a criminal means *being smart.*"

Ciere winces.

With a muttered curse, Kit walks to the door. Ciere can tell he's already focusing on the next task. She can imagine the gears turning in his brain: *Idiot kids found. Must get home now and bake a soufflé to calm my nerves.*

"We can't go yet," Ciere calls.

Kit pauses in the hallway and gives her such a venomous look that she bites down on her lip. "And, pray tell, why not?"

Ciere raises an arm, holding it out to encompass the room. "There could be something valuable here. Isn't that why Frieda Fuller and TATE wanted the will? So they could get this address? Something...something to do with Pandora? And the formula?"

Kit's face changes—his hot temper seems to harden, to coalesce into something sharper and more focused. "That's what you two came here for?" he asks. "The Praevenir formula? You think Richelle Fiacre hid it here, like this is some sort of scavenger hunt with a magical prize at the end?" His steps lengthen and abruptly he's in front of Ciere, looming over her. "Do you think this is a game?"

Ciere forces herself to meet his gaze without blinking. "Of course this isn't a game," she says, her own temper rising to the surface. "Why do you think I did this? I knew exactly what kind of danger could be here, but I thought it was worth the risk!"

"You thought it would be—"

"I'll go to jail!" The words burst from her, and she claps a hand over her mouth.

Kit rocks back. It's rare to see him so startled. "What?" he says, and draws the word out to twice its normal length. "What are you talking about?"

She tells him. She tells him everything—Guntram finding Ciere and Devon at the train station, the picture, about how Guntram threatened to take proof of her theft to the feds if she failed to pay him, and how her deadline of one week is nearly up. She tells him about the bracelet, about the note, and for a second, she sees something like concern flicker across Kit's face. He can't like that the Syndiate knows where he lives. When she finishes, the look he is gives her is undecipherable. His hand goes to the bracelet and he runs his thumb over the smooth metal.

"You kept this from me?" he says.

Ciere manages to shrug. "I—I—" She doesn't know what to say; she feels limp and exhausted, ready to sit down on the floor and not get up again. "I didn't—" She doesn't know how to say, *I didn't want you to hate me. I didn't want to lose you.*

Kit's hand rests on her shoulder. "You should have told me."

"I know," she replies, miserable. "I just couldn't."

"No," says Kit, "I mean you should have told me, because I could've paid your debt and this would all be over. I have a Francis Bacon in our basement—trust me, it's not like we can't afford to pay off a crime syndicate. And even if I didn't have the money, you still should've told me."

"You said it yourself," she says, suddenly feeling tired. "Those who are stupid enough to get caught should be left behind."

Kit's eyes narrow. "You're talking about Daniel? Ciere, that's different."

"I don't see how."

"Because Daniel has been compromised by a very dangerous man," says Kit, and his voice lowers. "Daniel is out of our reach now. Aristeus will go to any lengths to achieve his ends."

"How do you know that?" The question slips out before she can stop it.

Kit's face hardens. "Because that's how Magnus and I taught him to function. It's a story that I'm not going into now. And I'm sorry about Daniel, I truly am. But there's an enormous difference between the head of the UAI and some new Syndicate enforcer. Guntram we can deal with." Kit's hand falls on her shoulder, and he squeezes tight. "I will stop him if I have to."

Ciere closes her eyes, lets out a small breath, and tries to steady herself. "Thank you."

That is when Devon pipes up. "Um, guys? I understand this is a touching mentor/student moment and I hate to interrupt, but I think I'm stuck."

Ciere turns back to the closet. Sure enough, Devon's legs are tangled in a coat. She bends over Devon and surveys the damage—he's sprawled on top of several shoes, and the coat looks as if it is trying to strangle the life out of his legs.

"Can we leave him like this?" Kit asks.

Getting Devon out of the closet is a matter of angling him sideways and yanking hard. He yelps as a stiletto heel digs into his thigh. When he rises to his full height, he tries to brush the dust from his jeans, and scowls at the coat still tangled around one leg.

Trying to hide her grin, Ciere ducks her head and yanks the coat free. She turns back to the closet and throws the coat inside when something catches her eye. In her haste to hide, she didn't see that something is out of place. The wall leading into the closet is ordinary: wood-paneled and obviously cheap. But the far wall of the closet is different. The color matches the dark wood, but there is no paneling and the surface is oddly reflective. She reaches past the coats and runs her fingertips over the wall. It's cold. Metallic.

"Out of curiosity," Ciere says, "why does the closet have a metal wall?"

The others quickly examine her findings. "Interesting," Kit says. He takes an armful of coats and dumps them onto the floor. Ciere ducks down and scoops out the piles of shoes—and really, why is there a coat closet in an office, anyway? The careless way things were tossed about in the closet seems like a calculated effort to appear chaotic.

When all the clothes are piled on the floor, the metal wall is plainly visible. In the farthest, darkest corner, Ciere sees a panel with a keypad and screen.

"If this is a safe, then it's huge," Kit remarks.

"Whoever stripped the house didn't find this," Ciere says eagerly.

Even Kit doesn't try to discourage her excitement; she can see it mirrored in his eyes. He taps Devon on the shoulder and says, "Get Magnus—there should be a flashlight in the car. I'll look for a crowbar or something we can use to get this open." In a moment, the two of them are gone, thudding down the stairs, stealth utterly forgotten.

Ciere slides into the closet, for once glad she's so small. Devon or Kit could never have managed this. She eyes the panel. Gently, she reaches down and brushes a finger over the keypad. Part of her expects to hear a siren go off. Something this heavily guarded should have a security system. Or maybe she'll get an electric shock if she tries to open it.

The panel flares to life, and in the dim light of the closet, the flickering illumination is blinding. Words form on the screen:

ENTER PASSWORD

She bites her lip, her hand frozen over the panel. There is security. A password. But what would...?

The answer comes to her before she fully realizes the question.

The whole situation has an air of inevitability about it, like everything has been leading up to this moment. Ciere only hesitates a fraction of a second before typing in a single word:

P-A-N-D-O-R-A

She hits the Enter key and braces herself for an alarm or shock. If she's wrong, who knows what the security will do to her. The screen flickers again, and there is the sound of mechanized bolts sliding into place. Before she has time to flinch, the door comes free with a hiss of expelled air.

Her heart in her throat, Ciere reaches for the door and pushes. It opens on silent hinges, and she sucks in a breath, a surprised cry hovering on her lips.

This is what Richelle Fiacre was hiding.

It's not the formula.

It looks like a miniature bedroom—but only if the decorator was into panic-room chic. The walls are all obviously bulletproof, windowless, and the only source of light is a small camping lantern. There is a cot on the floor and a portable toilet in the corner.

And a young man stands in the middle of the room.

23

CIERE

Ciere reaches out a hand to steady herself. She's used to upheaval during a job. You can never tell which way a gig will go, and uncertainty has taught her to be flexible—to respond quickly to change, recalculate plans, and justify losses.

But nothing could have prepared her for this.

It's not the formula.

It's a guy about her age with slick black hair, coppery skin, dark eyes, and full lips. He's lean, angular. He looks to be maybe seventeen or eighteen. Panic flashes across his face.

She slowly raises both hands, her empty palms out in an attempt to reassure him. "It's all right," she says. Her voice cracks and she swallows, trying to wet her dry tongue. "I—I'm not armed."

His eyes flick over her, looking for places she could stash

a weapon. Then his gaze falls to the floor, and he angles his face to one side, his hair falling into his eyes. But even with his hair in the way, Ciere can see the expression on his face. It shifts from fear to something softer. When he speaks, his voice sounds hopeful. Yearning, almost.

"Are you Frieda Fuller?" he asks. His voice is startlingly resonant.

It takes her a moment to understand the question. This guy thinks she's Frieda Fuller. Which means... which means that Fuller was in on this somehow. Getting the will must have been what she wanted all along. Maybe Richelle Fiacre meant for Fuller to have it, but something went wrong. Maybe she died before she could get a copy to Fuller. Maybe Fuller, seeing no other options, hired a crew of thieves to steal the information she needed that would lead her to this.

"No," Ciere says, uncertain of how to respond. She takes several steps back, until she's free of the closet.

A voice rings out from behind her and she jumps.

"Fuller's not coming," Kit says. He is frozen in the office doorway, his freckled fingers splayed on the frame as if he needs something to hold on to. "She's probably in government custody."

Ciere turns to look at Kit, grateful for his presence. He steps into the room, Magnus and Devon at his back. Magnus holds a crowbar, while Devon clings to a flashlight.

The guy's gaze roams over all of them in turn, coming to rest on Ciere. "You're not cops," he says. "Are you part of TATE?"

"No," Kit replies, and he appears to be regaining his usual calm. The momentary shock of seeing a boy in this abandoned house has passed. "We're not affiliated with TATE—we're freelancers."

The guy rakes his fingers through his black hair in a gesture that's more resigned than annoyed. "Criminals."

A beat of silence before Kit says simply, "Yes."

He glances back at his panic room, and says, "How did you find this place?"

Magnus speaks. "Richelle Fiacre's will. We thought—"

Kit lets out a small laugh, more bitter than amused. "That's not important. Who are you?"

The guy's eyes narrow, as if he is surprised that Kit doesn't already know. A cold, creeping certainty takes hold in Ciere. She knows who he is. At least, she knows his last name.

"Fiacre," she says, and waits for a denial. Because there must be a denial. This guy can't be—he just can't—

The stranger's eyes fall to the floor, and he doesn't say a word.

The silence that fills the room is heavy, and it seeps into her lungs, choking off anything she might say.

Devon has no such problem: "Holy shit."

PART THREE

[T]here had been brought into being something big and something new that would prove to be immeasurably more important than the discovery of electricity or any of the other great discoveries which have so affected our existence. The effects could well be called unprecedented, magnificent, beautiful, stupendous and terrifying.

—Brigadier General Thomas F. Farrell,
Eyewitness Account of the First Nuclear
Weapon Test, July 16, 1945

24

CIERE

The Fiacres are dead.

Or they're supposed to be. This is how the story goes: Brenton Fiacre killed himself along with his wife and son; extremists shot his younger sister and brother; his grandparents were arrested, and vanished from public knowledge. The only Fiacre who escaped the backlash of the Praevenir vaccine was Richelle Fiacre, the oldest sister. And now she's dead, too.

"Hell," Devon says desperately. "Rotting hell." He's taken to pacing back and forth, uttering a long stream of never-ending curses. Part of Ciere itches to hit him upside the head, but she can clearly see the panic in his face. They're all dealing in their own way. Devon's way just happens to be louder than most.

"Pandora," Magnus says softly. "The message that Brenton Fiacre posted on his website. It didn't refer to the formula at all. He must have been trying to get a message to his sister that his son was alive." He squints, as if delving into old memories. "Correct me if I'm wrong, but your name is Alan Fiacre."

Alan Fiacre—if that is his name—glances up quickly before looking down again. This close up, Ciere can see that he must have spent days inside that room: he needs a shower, and his clothes are stained with wear. He's taller than she first thought—outside of the room, Fiacre stands with his shoulders hunched and head ducked.

Kit turns and opens the office's window, presumably to let some fresh air in. The panic room was obviously a last resort, a secret place to stash Fiacre until someone could retrieve him. *Retrieve*, Ciere repeats the word to herself. Like he was another object in Richelle Fiacre's will, to be passed along to a new owner.

The more Ciere stares at him, the more she wants to look away. Fiacre is dangerous, a magnet for attention. The feds will stop at nothing to find him—hell, every government on the planet would pay a hefty sum for him.

They need to get out of here. They need to leave Alan Fiacre behind, get back to Philadelphia, and forget about the whole gig. While Ciere wouldn't be proud of leaving Fiacre on his own, if it comes down to her skin or his—well, it's an easy decision.

"I need to talk to you," Ciere says to Kit, hoping that Fiacre will not hear.

"Stay here a moment," Kit calls to Fiacre.

He shrugs as if to ask: *Where would I go?*

"Stay with him," Kit adds to Devon.

"What?" Devon asks, breaking the rhythm of his profanity-laden chant. "Why me?"

"Because you're the most expendable," Kit replies. He nods at Magnus to join them. Silently, Magnus hands Devon his crowbar—which only makes Devon look more freaked. Kit leads the way out of the office and down the hall. The bathroom is a less-than-dignified spot for a chat, but it has a door and a lock, and that's all they need for a private meeting. It's a tiny room, with barely enough space to fit a narrow bath and toilet. Everything is decorated in shades of faded yellow and blue, and the scent of lemon wafts from an air freshener.

Kit shuts the door before turning to Magnus and Ciere. "Well, this changes things."

"Understatement," Magnus replies, unsmiling.

"We should leave," Ciere says. "Now."

Magnus leans against the sink and crosses his arms, his gaze focused on something faraway. "You think he's truly a Fiacre?"

"Definitely," Kit replies. "He looks like Brenton Fiacre. If he's not the son, then he's related somehow. And what would he have to gain by lying? No. The real question is what we do with him."

"Leave him here," Ciere puts in.

"You'd do that?" Magnus asks. "Leave him here?"

Ciere moves toward the toilet, sitting down on its closed lid. She runs her hands up and down over her bare arms, trying to rub some heat back into her chilled skin. Everything is too close, too tight—the bathroom walls seem to creep in on her. The smell of old lemon air freshener turns her stomach and she clasps her cold fingers together, leaning over her knees in an attempt to block out her sudden nausea.

"We were supposed to find the formula," she says. "We weren't supposed to find a person!"

She came to this house to fix a problem, and instead found a whole new one. In Ciere's experience, there's a single solution to problems you can't solve: leave them behind. Run. Get far away, and then cover your tracks. It's a strategy that's kept her alive, and she sees no reason to alter it now. She rises to her feet and angles herself toward the door.

Magnus's hand falls upon the doorknob, blocking Ciere's escape. "We're not leaving him," he says.

Kit nods once. "I agree. He could be valuable."

Color floods Magnus's cheeks in a hot flush. "That's not what I meant," he snarls. "For fuck's sake, Kit, show a little humanity. If a clean-up crew arrives, they'll find the boy. I won't leave him to that." He leans closer to Kit and his voice softens into a hiss. "I—don't—abandon—people."

Kit looks as if he would like to have taken a step back, but there's no room. His hand goes to one of the yellow walls and he leans up against it. His jaw flexes, as if he is readying himself for an argument, but then his head drops and he remains silent. Ciere looks to him, waits for him to make things right, to get them out of here, but Kit doesn't make a move. Another surge of terrified anger burns through her. Why doesn't anyone understand how dangerous this is? Why is she the only one clamoring to get out of here? She turns her attention to Magnus, frantic for a way to get him to agree.

She tries to muster up an argument, but all she can come up with is: "He's a Fiacre."

There has to be a way to convince Magnus that this is too dangerous. He probably doesn't realize the risks. He isn't a crook like Ciere or Kit. He's just a whore, how would he know—

"He's a human being," Magnus says.

For Ciere, shame manifests as an uncomfortable prickling sensation on the back of her arms and legs.

"If you won't offer him any protection, I will," Magnus says. "I'll be damned before I let an innocent child get hurt for things his family did."

Kit exhales slowly. "Magnus..."

"Kit," Magnus says sharply, but Kit is already shaking his head.

"I know." He steps away from the wall and his hand goes to the doorknob, covering Magnus's fingers with his own. "I know."

When they return to the office, Devon is chanting in something that is definitely not English. "If he's started speaking in tongues, we're leaving him behind," Kit says.

"I think he's run out of English swearwords," says Magnus.

"It's Greek. I can translate, if you like," Alan Fiacre says. All eyes go to him, and he looks uncomfortable with the attention.

"Looks like we're taking you with us," Kit says.

Fiacre takes a step back. "And tell me," he says quietly, "why I'd go along with that?" He looks up for a fraction of a second, his gaze sliding over each of them in turn before returning to the floor. It's odd, the way he won't make eye contact. "You're thieves. You're probably going to sell me to whatever government can pay the most."

Magnus clears his throat. "Some people would," he says, "but we won't."

Ciere can almost see the escape plans working themselves out in Fiacre's brain—everything from jumping out the window to relocking himself in the panic room. She knows, because it's exactly what she'd be considering if she were in his place.

"I can't trust you," says Fiacre.

"You don't have a lot of choice." Impatience creeps into Kit's voice. "You stay here and it's only a matter of time until the feds show up. TATE was compromised."

"Maybe I want to go with the federal agents," says Fiacre.

"If you wanted the feds to find you, you'd be in one of *their* safe houses," replies Kit. "You're running from them. Now, we can do this two ways: either you come with us or you don't. We have a place in Philadelphia that's relatively safe until you figure out a plan. Or you can try your luck on your own."

Thick silence settles between them.

Devon inches toward the door. "Oh, just come with us. And can we please leave now, because I really don't want to explain to my dad why I'm in jail for harboring a supposedly dead guy."

Kit throws Devon an exasperated look, but somehow Devon's outburst seems to reassure Fiacre.

"You give me your word?" Fiacre says, and directs the question to Kit. "You won't let anyone else take me?"

Kit raises one palm level with his heart. "If you're taken into government custody, it's because someone is signing my death certificate. Happy now?"

Slowly, Fiacre nods. He picks his way back into the panic room and emerges a moment later with a backpack slung over his shoulder. He follows Devon out of the room. Ciere waits until the sound of their footsteps has faded into silence.

"That's a big promise you just made," she says.

Kit reaches out and tucks one of Ciere's stray curls behind her ear. "No, it wasn't," Magnus says, scowling. "I have a copy of his last death certificate taped to my fridge."

25

CIERE

The Bolsover house has seen its fair share of criminals. Kit has used it as a halfway house before. When he finds immune youths on the street, he takes them in—like he did Ciere—and gives them a place to stay. He offers them a bed in the basement, a plate of warm food, and clean clothes. He talks to his associates and finds the kids work. It's how Kit has built up his network—there are young criminals indebted to him nearly everywhere along the Eastern Seaboard.

Fiacre is led to the basement. It's a better deal than it sounds—the basement is one of Kit's most secure bolt-holes. It's not accessible by any visible doors. A person has to go through a walk-in closet in Kit's room and hit a hidden button underneath one of the loose floorboards to find the basement stairs. Once down the stairs, the basement itself isn't too bad. The cement floor is covered by many throw rugs. There are five tiny bedrooms, each with two bunk beds and a desk, and one small shared bathroom at the end of the hall. A final, locked room houses canned food, bottled water, and some of Kit's more sensitive acquisitions. Devon once commented that the whole place looked like a boarding school dormitory, that is, if one was getting an education from mole people.

Ciere can't argue with that. Despite Kit's attempts to make the basement habitable, the air is still cold, the walls are still gray, and there is a sense of heaviness about the place, as if the weight of the whole house presses down upon it. It's a place for the hunted to run and hide.

Fiacre takes a bedroom on the left. He tosses his backpack onto one of the top bunks. "May I use the shower?" he asks quietly.

Kit gestures down the hall. "All the way back. Towels are under the sink."

Kit then taps Ciere on the shoulder, and she follows him out of the room. The stairs are tall—it's two floors to Kit's room, and by the time they reach that point, Ciere's legs burn. She wants to sit, to fall backward onto her own bed and maybe stare at the familiar ceiling for a few hours. Kit steps into her path, and suddenly she's staring into the shiny buttons on his waistcoat.

"I want you to move some of your things to one of the basement rooms," he says.

Ciere gawks at him, uncomprehending.

"I want you to stay down there for a couple of nights—or however long we have our houseguest." Kit gestures vaguely in the direction of the closet. "Pick the room closest to the door, just in case."

"Just in case... what?" His meaning finally sinks in. She says, "You want me to stay in the basement? With him?"

"Take Lyre with you if you think you need a bodyguard," Kit says. "But Fiacre looks like a lightweight. I think even you could take him, if you had to."

Ciere feels her face twist into a scowl. "Oh, that's comforting. Why do you want me down there?"

"Two reasons." Kit turns on his heel and Ciere is forced to scurry after him to keep up. "First, I don't trust him. And I'd rather he didn't have access to the sensitive materials in the basement."

By "sensitive" Kit means valuable or dangerous. There are things in the basement that have to be kept out of the public eye—like that creepy painting by a guy called Bacon and those two antique Kalashnikovs. But Ciere still cringes at the plan—she hates sleeping in the basement. There is only one way out, and that door is heavy, bulletproof, and difficult to open. "Why can't he stay in a guest bedroom?"

"Because I don't want anyone to see him, even by accident.

I know he's supposed to be dead, but taking unnecessary risks is idiotic."

This argument would be simpler if Kit weren't making so much sense. Ciere tries to formulate another line of reasoning, but he has already moved back on to the original topic.

"Second," he says as he strides into the kitchen, "it was your brilliant plan to go to Endicott. So you get to babysit our score."

Magnus stands next to the fridge, pouring himself a glass of orange juice. There is something in the way he holds the glass that makes Ciere think that he could easily shatter it and use its edge as a weapon. But then the moment slips by and Magnus's expression is mild again. He says, "The boy is not a score, Kit."

Kit reaches out and takes the full glass from Magnus, leaning against the counter like this is nothing out of the ordinary. Magnus silently reaches into the cupboard for another glass. Kit says, "Yes, yes. You don't have to keep watching me, you know. The way you're acting, you'd think I was going to start an online bidding auction for Fiacre."

"I wouldn't put it past you," Magnus says, frowning. "But there's another thing we need to discuss. You do realize that I was only supposed to join this crew for a couple of days. The agency thinks I'm out on a family emergency, but I'm missing work."

"Oh, yes," Kit says. "Work."

Magnus straightens, his mouth drawn tight, and he takes a step toward Kit. They're about the same height, but Magnus is more heavily muscled. If this comes down to a physical confrontation, Ciere will put money on the mentalist.

"Oh, don't give me that," Magnus says. "How do you earn your living again? Conning and thieving? Selling stolen property? Between my job and yours, which is really more despicable?"

Ciere begins to edge out of the kitchen.

"That's not what I meant," Kit says, and without another word he reaches out and grabs Magnus's bare wrist. A shudder runs through Magnus. When Kit releases him a second later, Magnus turns away and rests both hands on the counter.

Ciere slips out of the room and goes back up the stairs. All she wants is to curl up on her bed for a while. But when she steps into her room, she finds that her bed is already occupied.

"Your bed smells like dog," Devon comments. Sure enough, Tulip is sitting next to him. Liz must have brushed out his fur; he looks fluffier. He's trying to nip at Devon's waggling fingers. "Everything settled?"

Ciere nods and slumps into her desk chair. "Fiacre's in the basement and Kit and Magnus are in the kitchen."

"They having a row?" Devon asks, jerking his hand back as Tulip leaps at him.

"Yup."

"Christ, it's like living with both of my parents again."

Devon tickles Tulip's ear. "So, what's to be done with Anastasia?"

"Anastasia?"

"You know—the Romanovs. Big powerful family that came to a bad end... and this metaphor is completely lost on you." Devon rolls his eyes. "Your history knowledge blows."

"Tell you what: I'll learn history when you learn German."

"Point taken."

They sit in silence for a few minutes, Devon playing with Tulip while Ciere stares out the window, not really seeing anything. "We screwed up, didn't we?" she finally says.

Devon squeaks as Tulip manages to clamp his jaws around his index finger. "What's this 'we' business? Going after Pandora was entirely your idea. I just went along with it."

"Well, I didn't think Pandora was going to lead us to a *dead guy.*"

"Not so dead," Devon corrects.

Isn't that the problem? Ciere almost says it, but manages to bite down before the words escape her. She would never truly want someone dead, but she has to admit that her life would be a lot less complicated if Alan Fiacre had perished along with the rest of his family.

"Well, what now?" Devon asks.

"Kit says he's going to see if he can get into contact with anyone from TATE."

"So we're pretty much done with Fiacre, then."

Ciere forces herself to stand. She needs to collect fresh blankets and pillows to bring to the basement. "Not exactly. We're rooming with him while he's here."

Devon looks alarmed. "What? You mean we're sleeping with the mole people?"

Ciere nods. Well, technically Devon wasn't ordered to sleep in the basement, but he doesn't need to know that. "Kit doesn't want to leave Fiacre alone downstairs with the valuables and the automatic rifles."

Devon looks torn between grim acceptance and apprehension. Before he can say anything, his phone clamors to life.

Ding a ling ling, a ling ling ling…

"Brilliant," Devon says grimly. "Time to see if that translation program is any good." He flips open his phone and slurs, "*Kan jeg få en flaske vodka*? Oh, heeeey, Dad. Din't see the caller ID. Howaroo?"

Ciere rises to her feet. Kit keeps extra blankets in a linen closet nearby, and this is the perfect excuse to get away before Devon wrangles her into pretending she is a Norwegian bartender.

She gathers several sets of fresh sheets, pillows, and an armful of blankets. By the time she carries them back to her room, Devon is trying to describe snow-capped mountains and milkmaids.

"Sorry, Dad, I've got to go," Devon says distractedly when he sees Ciere. She promptly dumps the armful of blankets into his lap and he lets out a small *"oompf."*

"Let's go," she says. "Anastasia awaits."

The voice on the other end of the line blares, *"Devon? Who was that? What was that? You're rooming with a girl called—"*

Devon snaps his phone shut and pinches the bridge of his nose. "Great. Now my dad not only thinks I'm drinking my way through a ski resort, but also that I'm probably shagging a local girl. Two girls, if he heard your voice. Thanks ever so much."

"You know you love me," Ciere calls over her shoulder.

She barely hears his muttered response of "God, life would be easier if—" before she shuts the door, cutting him off.

26

CIERE

Nighttime in the basement feels like sleeping in a prison cell.

Of course, Ciere has never been in a prison. There's only one for immune criminals: Blanchard Penitentiary, an offshore detention camp meant specifically for people like her. She imagines this must be what Blanchard is like, though—exposed concrete, dim lighting, utterly still air, and a sense of gloom and heaviness.

Devon took the room next to hers. He claimed he wanted to see if he could tap out messages through the walls, but since she hasn't heard any tapping, he must be asleep by now. It's well after eleven. Ciere's own body aches with weariness, but her mind won't shut off.

She sprawls on her bunk bed, the bulky wool blankets

pressing down on her. Despite the warm summer heat, it's cool enough down here to merit a heavy comforter. She draws the wool up to her chin and forces her eyelids shut. She draws in a breath and tries to settle down.

But it's too quiet.

She's used to the sounds of the neighborhood. They aren't loud—elsecs never are—but she misses the sounds of distant cars, of the occasional bark of a dog, of neighbors getting up in the morning. Down here, it's all heavy silence.

Like a grave.

Like being buried alive.

She needs to stop thinking like that. Maybe a glass of water will help.

The rooms have a system of lamps run by a generator—but Kit turns off the generator at night. The darkness is complete. No windows, no moonlight, not even the dim glow of nearby streetlights. All that's left to illuminate the basement are portable battery-powered lamps. One sits on the desk, and Ciere fumbles for it. Her fingers find the knob, and she twists. Light springs to life within the bulb, and she blinks at it gratefully. The light doesn't do much to relieve the general feeling of entrapment, but it's better than the utter blackness.

The bathroom is at the end of the hall, opposite the basement entrance. Ciere pads down the hall on her bare feet, grateful for the scratchy rugs Kit thought to arrange. The light flickers in her hand, and she gives it a nervous shake. It would be her luck for the batteries to die.

She is so intent on her light that she doesn't notice the figure standing in the bathroom doorway. They collide, and she lets out a small gasp. Her trembling hand lifts the lamp, the illumination spilling over Fiacre. "Crap," Ciere gasps out.

"I'm sorry," he says. "Are you all right?"

"Fine." She presses a hand to her chest and sucks in a deep breath. "What the hell are you doing up?"

Fiacre nods his head in the direction of the sink. "Water."

"Ah. Same here."

She follows him into the bathroom and rests her lamp on the counter. There are several cupboards, and one holds glasses. Ciere fishes out two and hands one to Fiacre. He accepts it with a murmur of thanks before filling it from the sink. He takes a step back, leaning against a concrete wall while he sips his water.

Ciere looks away and tries to pretend she wasn't watching. She reaches out and twists the faucet back to life, filling her own cup. The water isn't cold and tastes vaguely metallic, but she forces herself to drink it all.

"Good night," she says, reaching for her light. She is so focused on not looking at Fiacre that her elbow hits the lamp, knocking it from the counter. She makes a grab, but it's too late, and the lamp crashes into the floor. She leaps back, conscious of her bare feet and the glass skittering across the cement.

Hands fall on her bare arms and she realizes that she has moved far closer to Fiacre than she meant to. She can feel the heat of him through his shirt and her own cami, and his hands steady her, keeping her upright. He's surprisingly strong—he supports her with little effort.

"Sorry," she says.

Fiacre's hands drop, but he doesn't recoil from their proximity. "Is there a broom down here?" he asks.

She nods, grateful for the excuse to leave the bathroom. The closeness bothers her, although it's different from before. Little jolts of adrenaline keep sparking through her, and she can still feel the places where he touched her.

She finds the storage cupboard by touch, her fingers fumbling through the cleaning supplies until she retrieves the broom and dustpan. When she steps into the bathroom, she finds Fiacre kneeling on a towel. His own lamp rests on the floor, casting enough light for her to see his fingers dart among the shadows, coming up with tiny shards of glass. His quick, graceful movements remind Ciere of the way a bird picks for food amid blades of grass.

She hands him the broom and he goes to work, slanting

the dustpan so that he can sweep up the remaining pieces. When Fiacre speaks, it's so abrupt that it makes her flinch.

"Are you afraid of me?" He doesn't sound offended. If Ciere had to guess, he sounds curious.

"W-what do you mean?" she says.

He dumps the dustpan into the garbage can before kneeling again and angling the broom around the base of the toilet, searching for any missed shards. "You were shaking when I touched you. You're also sweating, and if I had to guess, your pulse is racing."

Ciere's hand flutters to her neck. Sure enough, she can feel her heart jumping beneath her skin. "I'm not scared of you."

Even with his back to her, Ciere can imagine she sees Fiacre's skepticism. His voice is saturated with it. "Right."

She shouldn't have to explain herself to him. But the idea that he thinks she's scared of him makes her both embarrassed and strangely defiant. "It's not you," she says. "It's—uh, this place."

Fiacre finishes sweeping and shakes the dustpan over the garbage. "This shelter?"

"Yeah."

He rises from his crouch, and holds out the broom and dustpan. She takes them with a tense smile, and replaces the broom in the cupboard. He pauses in the hallway, hand on the wall, and studies Ciere. It's an odd stare, with his head angled to one side, peering at her through the corner of one eye. It reminds Ciere of a raven cocking its head.

"You're claustrophobic," he says.

"No." Ciere finds herself rubbing her arms. "I just don't like it down here. It feels…I don't know. Like I'm trapped. Like if something went wrong, I couldn't get out of here on my own." She half expects him to smile or laugh, but a frown line appears between his brows.

"You're claustrophobic," he repeats. "Yet you're down here."

"Orders," Ciere says shortly.

Fiacre looks puzzled. "That Copperfield isn't your father, is he?"

"He's my…" Ciere searches for the right word. Not an adoptive father—more like an older brother, but not quite. There is no shared blood, no piece of paper binding them together. "Handler" is the word she settles on. "And he's head of our crew."

"You're all thieves." Fiacre's eyes wander to something beyond Ciere, and she realizes that one of the stolen paintings is stored behind her, propped up against the wall. In the dim light of Alan's lamp, the stark contrasts between the whites and darks, and the streaky paint, make the whole thing look even more eerie than usual. "Thomas Cole," Fiacre says. "From *The Course of Empire* series. I heard that it went missing a few years ago... I guess this is where it ended up." He takes a step toward the painting—this particular one depicts an ancient city in chaos. Ships burn, people throw themselves off docks, a bridge falls, people kill one another, and a statue leans precariously over the whole scene. Fiacre's hand comes up and his fingers hover reverentially over the tiny figures.

"I still don't know your name," Fiacre says, eyes on the painting. "I overheard the others talking in the car, though—you're Ciara?"

"Ciere," she corrects. "Take off the *a* at the end. Ciere Giba."

A smile flits across Fiacre's mouth. "Oh, I get it. Gibeciere."

Ciere jerks in surprise. No one has ever guessed the source of her name. "You know what that is?" she asks.

Fiacre's smile fades. "Magicians used them—back when there were stage magicians. A gibeciere was a bag they'd use to hide things in. I'm guessing that's not your real name."

Ciere tenses, feeling uncomfortably defensive. "It's my real name. It's just... not the one I was born with."

Fiacre's amusement fades. "I'm sorry. I—I'm not judging you. Names can be dangerous." Still ducking his head, he holds out his free hand, and Ciere hesitates, unsure of what he's doing. "I'm Alan," he says formally. "It's a pleasure to meet you, Ciere Giba."

Slowly, hesitantly, she extends her own hand. Fiacre takes her fingers in his own. The gesture is awkward, like he's not sure how firm his grip should be or how to move his hand. His skin is warm, a spot of heat in the chilled underground. Ciere expects him to let go, but Alan's hand lingers in hers and then he slowly shifts his grip so that he cradles the back of her hand in his palm.

Ciere might have been shocked or pulled away, but she waits, poised on the balls of her feet. He cradles her hand in his palm, his eyes raking over it, lifting the lantern with his other hand as if to get a better look. She glances down, trying to see what he sees. Her skin is much lighter than his, with a light dusting of blonde hair and a few bluish veins beneath her skin.

Alan releases her, and Ciere's arm drops. Feeling suddenly self-conscious, she scratches at her wrist.

"You have a thing for hands?"

She can't be sure in this darkness, but it looks like Alan is flushed. He tucks his chin and cants his head to one side. "Sorry. It's just—hands can tell you a lot about a person. I'm in the habit of noticing them."

"Huh?"

Alan gives her a sidelong glance. "You know I've been on the run for my whole life. My aunt told me... well, I was never supposed to look anyone in the eye. There was always a chance someone could recognize me. Aunt Richelle used to say I look like my dad." He speaks more quickly, as if in a rush to get the words out. "When I was a kid, I'd always just look at people's hands. It was something to focus on instead of looking at their faces. Eventually, it just became habit. Now I…" He trails off, and she doesn't need him to finish. Now he can't look anyone in the eye. It's too ingrained in him. And suddenly Ciere understands why he hasn't really looked at her—why she's only seen his eyes in darting little glances. Why he's always angled to one side, bangs hanging over his brow, head tilted downward. It's not that he's shy—it's a survival technique.

"You probably think I'm insane or something," Alan says quietly, turning away. But Ciere reaches out and grabs his wrist, holding him in place.

"No, it's fine," she says. And it is fine. She gets it.

Don't let anyone see what you are, understand?

"My mother used to teach me a game," she says. "A messed-up hide-and-go-seek where I'd have to hide again and again. Years later I realized it wasn't really a game." She forces a smile, and says, "So how does my hand measure up?"

Alan's mouth twitches. "You have broken nails."

"Comes from lock picking," she says. She glances at the painting again, wishing for something to look at. "Damn, it's dark down here."

"I've got another lantern in my room if you want it."

Ciere feels a rush of gratitude as Alan leads the way back to his room—it's not that she's afraid of the darkness, but she can feel it pressing in around her. His bedroom is identical to hers—raw concrete walls and minimal decor. Alan bends down under his bed and gropes for something. When he comes back up, he has another lantern in his hand. She reaches out for it, her fingers closing over its wire handle, but Alan doesn't let go. The lantern quivers, the wire drawn taut between both their hands, and Ciere realizes that she is still shaking. She grits her teeth and forces her arm to still.

Alan releases the lantern and sits on the lower bunk. "You sure you're not claustrophobic?"

"I'm fine," she snaps.

He lifts his chin and says, "You know, it would be all right. If you weren't fine, I mean. Everyone has something they deal with."

Ciere squirms. Part of her yearns for this conversation to end—as interesting as Alan is, all she really wants to do is vanish. Maybe if she became invisible, she could sneak upstairs and leave the basement behind. Kit would never know. Probably. Maybe.

"You—" Alan says abruptly, and Ciere's attention snaps back to him. "What are you...?" His voice trails off, and a thrill of horror goes through her.

She hadn't realized she was beginning to illusion herself. It wasn't even conscious; the desire to leave was so strong that she instinctively grasped for her immunity. She feels the blood draining from her face. She's never had to hide what she is—not here. This is home.

Alan is staring at her with a mixture of apprehension and wonder. "You're an..."

Ciere fumbles for something to say. Anything. "I'm an illusionist."

Okay, maybe she shouldn't have said that. The less people know, the better. But this boy is already carrying so many secrets—hell, the kid *is* a secret—what's one more? Who could he possibly tell?

He doesn't look at her, not really, but she sees a flash of teeth as he grins. "Really?"

She shrugs. "I'm not a very good one, so don't get excited."

Alan shifts on the mattress, edging closer to the wall. At first it looks like he is drawing away from Ciere, but she realizes he is making room for her to sit. She hesitates, her fingers still wrapped around the lantern handle. *He's not going to bite you*, she reassures herself.

"I've never met someone with an immunity," he says. "It's kind of amazing."

She feels her lips compress and her hands curl into fists, which she places beneath her legs. "You're...not...?"

His shrug somehow looks rueful. "Completely normal. Well, as normal as someone like me could be."

"So why do you want to go to TATE?" she asks. "Why would the last Fiacre hand himself over to a terrorist group?"

"You don't know anything about TATE." Alan's fingers twist together. "They're not a terrorist group."

"Freedom fighters?" Ciere suggests. "Rebels?" When he looks at her, she shrugs and says, "I know, I know. Semantics." She studies him and says, "Why're you talking to me?"

His smile is sad. "I've spent my whole life on the run. Is it weird I'd want to talk to someone else?"

She remembers the panic room in Endicott and shivers. The thought of being so enclosed, so trapped, makes her skin itch.

"How do you know I won't sell you out?" she asks. "You don't know anything about me."

When Ciere glances at Alan, something in his face has changed. It's a subtle difference, and Ciere couldn't pinpoint it if she tried. He says, "I know enough."

"What do you know?"

Alan's gaze slides down to her lap. "Your eyes never stop moving. You're always looking to the doors, to the windows. Your fingers twitch and your legs bounce."

Ciere stops bouncing her leg.

He continues, "You make yourself small. You hunch, you keep to walls and corners. You're always looking for escape routes. You're used to being hunted. You've trained yourself to run." He takes a breath. "Your family is gone. The government is responsible."

She wants to ask him how he knows that—how he managed to voice her secrets without knowing a single thing about her. She feels as if his words have peeled away her skin and he's staring into her insides, reading her life story in her bones.

"How . . . ?" she says, unable to continue.

"Because," he says, "my aunt always acted the exact same way." He leans forward a little, staring at his knees. "She spent her whole life in fear after my family was killed. She must've had fifty different aliases—I think you've come across some of them. Pandora Marton. Marie Louis. She never went by her real name if she could help it." His gaze slides back to her. "Ciere." He says the name carefully, testing it out.

Ciere's brain feels like it's jammed. Her mouth opens, and she thinks she's going to say something about how she is nothing like Richelle Fiacre, but what comes out of her mouth is "The government didn't kill your family." She can't say the last part aloud; it's too horrible: *Your father did.*

"Are you sure?"

She's not—not really. Not when she thinks about it.

She opens her mouth to ask another question, when a loud knocking makes her jump. Her heart leaps into her throat, and it's then she realizes how calm she's been for the last ten minutes. She hasn't thought about the heavy walls or cement floor since she sat down next to Alan. But now all the fear comes flooding back and her mouth is bitter and sticky.

The door cracks open and Devon pokes his head inside.

"Hey, Anastasia, you seen Ciere? She's not in her room and I've been tapping out messages for the last..." Devon's voice trails into silence, and he steps fully into the room. He stands there, hand still on the doorknob.

Ciere is suddenly hyperaware of the fact she's sitting on Alan's bed. During their conversation, she ended up right next to him, his leg inches from hers, and she realizes that from where Devon is standing, he can't see even those few inches.

Devon's confusion dries up. "Oh," he says stiffly. "Didn't realize you had company."

"Anastasia?" Alan repeats, bewildered.

"I needed a lantern," Ciere says. "He was keeping a lantern. Here. In his room."

"Riiiight." Devon stretches the word out. "You know, I've got a whole pile of the things under my bed. All you had to do was knock."

"Good to know," Alan says. If he's at all affected by the sudden tension in the room, he's doing a good job of hiding it. Ciere wishes she could do the same, but Devon's gaze is a weight she can't shake off.

"All right," Devon says, and his accent seems to thicken. "I'll leave you to it, then." He vanishes through the door, pulling it shut behind him with a loud clang. The silence he leaves behind is riddled with unspoken questions.

Ciere rises to her feet, lantern in hand. "So, yeah. Um, thanks for the lantern, Alan. I'll get out of your way." Before he can say anything, she hastens to the door. She's halfway through it before a hand falls on hers and she twists around in surprise.

Alan is looking at her. Truly looking at her. It's the first time she's seen him straight on. His face is even, symmetrical, and his eyes a startling shade of black. With his coppery skin and sharp jaw, he's . . . striking.

When his eyes meet hers, a hot flush spreads through her chest and neck. She feels pinned by those eyes, more visible than she has ever been. The instinct to draw upon her immunity—to disappear—is nearly impossible to resist. It's only when she realizes that Alan must be fighting the same urge to turn away that she lifts her chin and refuses to break eye contact. There's new strength in the set of his jaw and shoulders and it's the first time she's truly thought of him as something other than the last Fiacre.

"Thank you," he says.

"For what?"

The corners of his mouth lift. "Good night," he says before shutting his door.

Feeling unaccountably shaken by the encounter, Ciere

turns away from the door. But then she catches a flicker of movement as Devon slips silently into his room and firmly shuts the door behind him. He must have seen everything. Ciere stands in the hallway, lit lantern in her hands, frozen in mid-step. She wavers, torn between the two closed doors. Swallowing, she turns on her heel and trudges into her own room.

Breakfast doesn't go well. Magnus offers up a friendly smile, but he's the only one. Kit is too busy flipping pancakes, and Devon won't look at her. He sits at the bar, mutilating a pancake with a fork, twirling it around and around a pool of syrup until the whole thing is a sticky brown mess. She tries to catch his eye and fails.

"Morning," Magnus says cheerfully, and hands Ciere a glass of orange juice. She takes it and slides onto the stool next to Devon. He's mashing his pancake with the side of his knife.

"Where's Anastasia?" he says, without looking up from his plate.

This is ridiculous. Devon's acting like he walked in on her and Alan playing strip poker. And even then, it wouldn't be any of his business. "Still in the basement." Her temper flares and she can't hold back the words. "So you can stop acting like an ass."

The look Devon gives her is full of false innocence. It

crumbles under her glare. “I just think you shouldn’t get attached to Anastasia, all right?” He takes a sip of his orange juice. “Remember who his family was.”

She resists the urge to slap the glass out of his hand. “I’m not getting attached,” she hisses.

Devon slides her a skeptical look. “The last time you had that look on your face, you were dragging a puppy out of an alley.”

“He’s a person,” says Ciere, “and he can’t help who his dad was. I mean, look at your family.” The words slip out far too easily.

Devon sets his glass down a little too hard.

Ciere opens her mouth to apologize, but before she can come up with a suitably indignant response, a chime rings through the house.

No one moves.

“Someone’s at the gate,” Kit says as he pours another swirl of batter onto the hot skillet. “Ciere, if it’s your mob friends, please invite them in for coffee. Just because they’re blackmailing you doesn’t mean you shouldn’t be polite.”

“Then what?” says Ciere, her limbs suddenly gone cold with fear.

Kit reaches for a spatula. “Then I pay them and we forget this ever happened.”

Ciere slides off her stool and walks toward the door on legs she can't really feel. Of course she's the one to get the door. She's the person who ticked Guntram off—she should be the one to face him.

But she's forgotten there is one other full-time occupant of the house. Lizaveta has already buzzed their guest through the gate and is pulling open the front door when Ciere trudges into the foyer.

An unfamiliar man stands on the doorstep.

"I'm so sorry to bother you," the man says with an apologetic smile. "My car—it won't start." He points his thumb at a black car parked on the curb. "I left the lights on and I need a jump." He's dressed in a rumpled suit and he's attractive in a clean-cut sort of way.

Lizaveta appears to be thinking, and she lingers in the doorway for a second, her bony hand gripping the door. "Come in," she says. "I will get Copperfield." She turns her heavy-lidded glare on Ciere and adds, "Take him to the living room," as if Ciere wouldn't understand basic courtesy if it bit her in the ass.

Ciere scowls at Liz. "This way," she says to the man, and stomps through the hall into the living room. When she turns to tell him it'll only be a second, something makes her pause.

This man walks with the grace of someone who is completely comfortable with his own body; his eyes move ceaselessly; his suit fits him too well to hide the bulge under his left shoulder; but most of all, she notices that he walks into the house with no fear. Where a normal person would hesitate in the foyer, this man treats the house like conquered territory.

Crooks know fear. Most will argue the fact, but crooked life is choked with it. Crooks go places they shouldn't, do things they aren't allowed to, take property they have no right to, and sell things they don't own. No matter how good the crook, there is always that undercurrent of fear.

This man has no fear.

He's not a criminal. Which means he isn't working for Guntram.

"Sorry," Ciere says with false brightness. "I didn't catch your name."

"I'm Eduardo Carson," the man says as he settles on the couch. His mouth twitches like it can barely contain his smile.

27

CIERE

When Ciere was eleven, she caused her mother's death.

It was an accident, but she cannot forgive herself.

It was a rare sunny day in early summer. Ciere and her mother needed to buy the common necessities: gas, fertilizer, toilet paper, and so on. Ciere spent the entire morning pestering her mother, saying she was old enough to come along; she wanted to see the town; she'd help push the cart; she'd do anything—

"All right," her mother said fondly, exasperated. "You can come. But best behavior, all right?"

It was a big deal; the two of them lived so far from large cities that even the small local town seemed impossibly big to Ciere. They grew most of their own food, and Ciere's mother only ventured into town for the most necessary supplies. Ciere was usually left home with strict instructions not to play with anything sharp or flammable. But this time, Ciere was allowed to tag along. She was old enough to handle the responsibility, her mother told her.

The grocery store was their first stop—even Ciere's mom couldn't grow things like sugar or flour. Ciere was given the grocery list and told to read off the items while her mom pushed the cart. The second stop was at a gas station to fill up their car and extra containers for their generator. The third and final stop was a hardware store. It smelled like leather and metal, and everything seemed polished.

When they arrived at the gardening section, her mother paused to let Ciere pick out seeds for their summer garden. Ciere sorted through paper packets, eyeing the pictures of the colorful blooms and organizing them by color. Her mother found a large bushy plant and heaved it into the cart.

"It's lavender," her mother said, seeing Ciere's confusion. "Come here, I'll show you." She found a gardening book on a shelf and began flipping through its glossy pages. When she located the right picture, she held it out. The picture she pointed to was of a bushy plant with long purple blooms.

"We can use it to make our clothes smell good," her mother said, replacing the book on its shelf. She pinched a sprig from the lavender plant and offered it to Ciere. "Smell this."

Ciere took the sprig—it didn't have any flowers yet, so it wasn't as pretty as the photo. She sniffed. The plant smelled somehow smoky, clean, and sweet all at the same time. "Weird," she said.

Her mother laughed. "Trust me. You'll sleep better when your sheets are lavender scented." She took Ciere's hand and led her from the plants.

The store was mostly empty, and there wasn't a line at the register. The cashier was a young woman with pale skin and reddish brown hair pulled into a ponytail. When she saw Ciere, she smiled vaguely. "Going to plant that?" she said, and Ciere realized she still held the sprig of lavender.

Ciere smiled and held up the plant. "Yup."

"It'll look nice when it's all full grown and blooming," the cashier said. She was using a syrupy voice, the way adults sometimes speak to children, and it annoyed Ciere. She wasn't a kid. She knew the flowers would be pretty. Just to prove it, she held up the sprig and focused on it.

Her illusion coiled around the stem, making the tip appear in full bloom. Tiny purple flowers materialized as if from nowhere, until it looked like the photo from the gardening book.

It was effortless and gorgeous, and Ciere grinned in triumph.

The cashier gasped. Ciere looked up at her, expecting to see amusement in her mother's eyes.

But the cashier appeared frozen, her mouth agape. A sound rose in her throat. She looked... scared.

Ciere was so startled by the woman's reaction that her illusion shattered.

The next thing Ciere knew, she was grabbed by her mother and hustled out of the store so quickly that she didn't have a chance to complain or squirm. Air blew past as the automatic doors breezed open and her mother hurried through them. She didn't quite run, but her steps were quick and jerky. Ciere found herself swung up over her mother's shoulder, and she stared backward. The automatic doors were making a valiant effort to close, but kept jerking to a halt as they sensed the oblivious cashier standing between them, gaping after Ciere.

They never went back for their supplies. Ciere's mother drove straight home, her mouth a grim line and fingers gripping the steering wheel hard.

"You can't do that," her mom said, her voice tight. "Not everyone can do what you can, and showing off will only get you noticed. It's dangerous. Don't let anyone see what you are, understand?"

That was the first time Ciere understood that her immunity wasn't to be shared with others.

It was a lesson learned too late. That cashier must have managed to catch a glimpse of their license plate, and the reward for turning in an illusionist was too lucrative to pass up.

One week later, a SWAT team showed up.

28

CIERE

Kit greets Eduardo Carson as if they are old friends. He hasn't changed out of his cooking gear: his sleeves are still rolled up and his apron tied around his neck. "I'm sorry," Eduardo Carson says, standing. "I didn't mean to interrupt your breakfast."

Kit grins and offers Carson his hand. "Not at all. I'm Kit Copperfield, and I see you've already met my niece. I heard you have car trouble?"

"I'm staying with some friends across the street." Carson waved a hand toward the front door. "They left for work and it wasn't until a moment ago I realized my headlights were on, so now my battery is shot. Could you give me a jump?"

Kit's smile never falters. "To be honest, I'm not sure where I left my cables. I know they're in the garage somewhere, but it could be a few minutes." He touches the back of Ciere's elbow. "I think the cables are somewhere near my power tools. Go look for them?"

Ciere slants a look at Carson before nodding. As she turns and makes her way to the hall, she hears Kit say, "Can I get you a cup of coffee?"

To an outsider, the exchange would seem casual. Normal.

But Kit has never owned power tools.

She doesn't go to the garage. If that man is what she thinks he is, then there is one person who needs to know immediately. She breaks into a run and dashes up the stairs to Kit's room. Her fingers, slick with sweat, fumble on the doorknob of his closet. It takes two tries to punch in the correct code to the basement.

She finds Alan on his bed; he is scribbling away in what looks like a journal.

"Ciere?" he says absentmindedly. When he sees her face, his manner changes. "What's wrong?"

"Some guy showed up on our doorstep claiming his car needs a jump—but I don't think so. I saw something under his left arm. I think he's carrying. Maybe a fed."

Alan slips off his bed, landing lightly on his feet. In one fluid motion, he shoves the journal into his backpack and slides it over one shoulder. "You think they're here for me."

Ciere nods.

"What will Copperfield do?" Alan says.

"I—I'm not sure. He knows that something is up." Ciere wraps her arms around her roiling stomach. "You should be ready to move in case we need to run."

Alan inclines his head. "So, Copperfield won't sell me to them?"

Her jaw doesn't drop, but it is only because she's clenching her teeth. "What?"

"It's a logical solution," Alan says. "If the feds have finally come for me, your handler might cut a deal. Turn me over in exchange for his and your freedom. If he plays his cards right, he might even get a good amount of money out of it."

"I don't think he'd do that," she says.

Alan's lips press together, but he doesn't argue.

"I'm going back upstairs," she tells him. "You wait here for now. Okay?" She whirls, walking out of his room and bounding up the long flight of stairs, taking them two at a time. Suddenly, she's afraid to leave Kit alone with that Eduardo Carson. She's afraid of what Kit might do without anyone watching.

Apparently, he is serving coffee and chatting. When Ciere rushes back into the living room, she finds Carson perched on the couch while Kit reclines in his favorite chair. They're talking about the neighborhood.

Kit looks up and blinks at Ciere. "You didn't find those cables, did you?"

Oh. She's forgotten her alibi. "Um. Not really." She can feel Carson's watchful gaze resting on her, and she forces herself to go still. "It's been forever since you cleaned out that garage," she says, and pitches her voice into a whine. "I mean, you can't find anything in there."

Kit is an expert liar. His expression is half fondness, half annoyance. "That's because you were supposed to clean it out last summer, if I remember correctly." The smile he gives Carson is conspiratorial. "Teenagers..." he says, standing. "I'll look myself."

Carson sets his coffee cup down. "I'll help." He rises and takes a step. He looks confused, like something is out of place and he cannot figure out what.

"Something wrong?" Kit asks.

Carson blinks and his eyes unfocus, his pupils staring in different directions. He takes another step and falters. A look of alarm flashes across his face, and his hand darts toward his jacket—where the telltale bulge of a sidearm is visible.

Kit's hand gets there first. He snatches Carson's wrist from the air and jerks it back, gripping it tight. "Now, now," he says, in a soothing voice. "None of that."

Carson makes a valiant effort to hit him, but Kit takes hold of both his wrists, rendering his arms useless. Carson makes a noise of protest, but his body seems to be folding in on itself.

Kit guides him backward onto the couch, where Carson tries to sit up and fails. His rolling eyes drift shut and his lips go still.

Utter silence.

"What did you do?" Ciere says, aghast.

"I drugged that pot of coffee," Kit says, like it should be obvious. He's already at work, peeling Carson's coat off. The first thing he finds is a gun tucked into a shoulder rig. Kit weighs the pistol in his hand. "A Glock," he murmurs. "That means—damn." He hisses the curse through gritted teeth, and his fingers dart into Carson's pocket. He comes up with a leather badge. When he flips it open, a glimmer of gold catches Ciere's eye.

The letters are clearly visible: FEDERAL BUREAU OF INVESTIGATION—ADVERSE EFFECTS DIVISION.

A nervous giggle rises up Ciere's throat, and she cannot choke it back. She presses a hand to her mouth, but the laugh spills over. She tries to stifle it, her breaths coming quick and hard, each carrying another of those hysterical giggles. Her lungs are drawn tight with mirth. This is it. They've drugged a federal agent. This is the moment, the line, the threshold that they've all stepped over.

Kit regards her with narrowed eyes. "Nothing about this situation is funny."

A loud crash makes them jump. Ciere has only enough

time to think, *What now?* before her feet carry her down the hall and into the kitchen. Her mind is already coming up with an explanation for the noise: other agents are breaking in from the back and it's too late to run. She half expects to see the dancing red dots of laser sights and the black-garbed forms of a SWAT team when she skids into the kitchen.

Instead, she sees that Devon is sprawled on the floor, his barstool tipped over and lying on its side.

A cup of coffee rests on the counter.

"On the other hand," Kit says after a pause. "Maybe I spoke too soon."

It takes Devon a good hour to come around. He does so by degrees, his eyes flickering beneath their lids, muscles twitching in his face, and he finally manages to prop himself up on the couch. Ciere convinced Kit not to leave Devon lying where he fell, if only because his drooling might damage the floor. She sits beside him, watching Devon slowly come back to himself. All in all, the experience isn't much different from the mornings they've spent hungover together.

The FBI agent, Carson, is dragged down to the basement. It seems the shelter will also double as a holding cell. When she sees Carson dangling between Kit and Magnus, she is torn between gratification and squirming guilt. She wants him out of sight, if only so she can pretend this isn't happening. As long as she doesn't have to see the agent, it means he doesn't exist.

This coping mechanism manages to distract her until Kit reemerges from the basement with Alan trailing behind. Alan casts a quick look at Ciere before sitting gingerly on the recliner.

Kit doesn't speak at first. He pinches the bridge of his nose and inhales, as if he needs the moment to himself. "The basement is officially a no-minor zone," he finally says.

"Whereweposedtego?" Devon mumbles. He hasn't quite regained control of his tongue yet.

"You three stay up here for now. The adults will handle the agent."

Devon blearily points a finger in Kit's general direction. "Techcallyimadult."

"True," Kit agrees. "But as you can't even focus your eyes on me, I think you'll find navigating stairs a little difficult. As for the rest of you—stay."

"Do you think we're in danger here?" Alan asks, still keeping his head down.

"I don't know," Kit says grimly. "If an FBI agent is in here, odds are that his partner or a team is somewhere out there. That's what Magnus and I are going to find out."

Ciere swallows. Her throat feels tight with panic. This is her worst nightmare. Being trapped, most likely surrounded by feds. Unable to escape for fear of what might be waiting for them. And the only place they might be able to hide is underground.

There's a grim comfort in knowing that this situation really can't get much worse.

As he strides out of the room, Kit pauses by the door and makes a vague gesture at them. "Oh—one more thing. Keep away from the windows."

Three blank stares.

"In case of snipers," Kit says, like it should be obvious.

In hindsight, Ciere thinks, she should have been expecting that.

29

CIERE

In the end, the decision to disobey Kit isn't a decision at all. Ciere always knew she was going to do it.

"Let me get this straight," Alan says. "You're going to sneak down to the basement? I thought you trusted Copperfield."

Ciere shucks off her light robe—she's still wearing her cami and boxer shorts, but she can't be bothered to get dressed now. "I do trust him. But he's got this bad habit of keeping information from the rest of us. It's simpler to just illusion myself."

Devon appears vaguely horrified. "Wha...?" He looks at Alan and then back at Ciere, unable to come up with the right words. She understands.

"I told him about me," she says dismissively. "Alan knows about the illusions."

"Dan—danjur," Devon slurs, looks annoyed, and then amends his response to "Bad."

"He's not dangerous." Ciere shakes out her arms and legs, trying to focus her attention. She needs to get this right; Kit will see through anything other than a perfect illusion.

"If you're going to do this," Alan says, "I want to come with you."

Ciere shakes her head. "I can only vanish myself. Remember what I said about me being a crappy illusionist?"

"Then I'll hide while you do your thing," Alan replies. "That way I'll still be able to eavesdrop." He hesitates, and then lifts his head and briefly meets her eyes.

It's Ciere who looks away first. "Fine. But if you get us caught, I'll say this was your idea."

Alan grins, and the smile transforms his face. "One scapegoat, coming up."

"Me, too." Devon wobbles upright and tries to steady himself by placing his fists on his knees.

This time it's Alan who shoots him down. "You can't help her if you're too drugged to stand."

Devon struggles to sit up straight. "Yeah, Ana? And what would you know about helping criminals?"

Alan's eyes quickly glide over Devon's slouched form. "Probably more than you," he says, but without malice.

Devon looks to Ciere, expectation in his face. Probably

waiting for her to come to his defense. But the sight of him, splayed out on a couch, defenseless and useless, gives her pause. She can't honestly come up with a reason for him to accompany her.

Devon glares at them both.

She has imagined this scenario a thousand times: waking up in a daze, sitting in a stark room, handcuffed to a chair, surrounded by armed men, and facing an interrogation. She has imagined the bite of metal around her wrists, the mirrored walls, and the locks on the doors between her and freedom. She's imagined it so many times that she's not surprised to see that it plays out the way she thought it would.

Only she never expected to be on the side of the interrogators.

She creeps down the basement steps with Alan at her back. There are sounds coming from one of the rooms on the left—harsh light spills through the darkness and the grating noise of metal on cement fills Ciere's ears. A silhouette appears in the doorway and she begins backing up, desperate to get into the shadows. In her haste, she feels her back collide with Alan's chest, and the two of them reverse into a wall.

She throws up her hands and sucks in a sharp breath. *Darkness*, she thinks. She draws the shadows in around herself and Alan.

Not a moment too soon. Kit strides into the hallway. "It's fine," he is saying. "He's not going anywhere." He turns, continuing down the hall away from Ciere and Alan, ducking into one of the far-off rooms. Ciere remains still, holding the illusion in place. Fresh pain surges through her temples.

"Fascinating," Alan whispers. His hand falls on her shoulder. "You're still there, but I can't see you all that well. And I suspect I'm just as difficult to see at the moment." His thumb moves, stroking the nape of her neck as if to check whether she's solid. The touch sends a hot flush through her skin and into her spine.

"Trying to concentrate here," she says through gritted teeth.

"Sorry."

She chokes back the wild urge to laugh. "Okay, so you're not willing to look most people in the eye, but you'll grope them from behind—good to know."

"I—I was not," Alan says, sounding horrified, but the reemergence of Kit cuts him off. Kit strolls toward them this time, and Ciere is careful to hold the illusion of darkness up. *Don't see us,* she thinks. *Don't see us. We're not here.*

Then she sees what Kit is carrying. A pair of handcuffs.

A chill goes through her. She hasn't let herself think about what this interrogation will consist of. Part of her still doesn't want to know—she wants to flee upstairs and crack jokes with Devon.

But she can't.

She leaves Alan in one of the bedrooms—it's close enough that he will be able to hear what's going on, but he keeps the lights out and presses himself against the wall and out of sight. It's a relief to drop the illusion from around him. She coils it around herself, letting her skin drink in her surroundings. She is shadow and cement when she tiptoes into the room and presses herself to the wall nearest the door.

Carson has been handcuffed to a metal folding chair. He lists to one side, his bound arms keeping him upright.

Kit stands in front of the FBI agent. "About time," he says. "Can't keep the party waiting."

Carson's breathing is ragged, and a sheet of sweat covers his tanned skin. When he speaks, his voice is in tatters. "Y-you drugged me." A growl escapes his teeth. "You are all dead. You've kidnapped a federal agent—"

Kit cuts him off. "I'd love to hear all your incredibly clichéd attempts to intimidate me, but we don't have the time."

"You going to torture me?" Carson asks. His eyes have begun to wander around the room. Ciere recognizes the look; it's the same way a hunted animal's eyes roll, looking for escape routes.

"Torture?" Kit grins, and it's something she has never seen

before. When Kit smiles, it's usually a thin-lipped smirk. This new grin is wide, baring all his teeth and crinkling the corners of his eyes. It's the grin of a wolf, not a fox.

"Torture?" Kit repeats. "What kind of barbarians do you take us for? There are much cleaner ways to retrieve information."

Magnus takes a step forward.

Kit moves so suddenly that Carson doesn't have time to react; Kit grabs a handful of Carson's short hair and wrenches his head back, exposing the vulnerable skin of his throat. It's been a while since he shaved—Ciere can see the dark stubble peppering his jaw. His Adam's apple flinches in a convulsive swallow.

Magnus kneels and rests his bare hand on the agent's throat.

"Now," Kit says, "who sent you?"

There is silence, only broken by Carson's hoarse breathing.

"Dammit," Magnus says, and Ciere jumps. *"What's that—why are they doing this?"*

"Who sent you?" Kit says again.

"W-what are you doing? What—why?" says Magnus. His voice has changed—it's no longer mild and soft, but clipped and altogether different.

That's when Ciere realizes that it isn't Magnus speaking.

Not really. He's translating Carson's thoughts into audible words.

Kit's grip on Carson tightens. "Who sent you?"

Something flickers over Magnus's face, and it reminds Ciere of the way dogs sometimes twitch in their sleep, like they're seeing and hearing things no one else can. *"Jesus Christ, no. A mentalist. I will not—you cannot—I'll think of something else. They've got a mentalist, they've got a mentalist—"*

"Who sent you?" Kit never raises his voice; he simply repeats the same question over and over.

Magnus's mouth moves so quickly, it's a wonder that he doesn't trip over the words. *"No one. Not supposed to be here—Aristeus and Gervais—didn't wait for backup, dammit, I've got to stop thinking! Get off of me!"*

"Why did you come here?" Kit asks.

Magnus's lips form more soundless curses before he says, *"Saw you leave with him in Endicott. Was watching the house. That boy. Shit, he looks like Brenton Fiacre. Is he a Fiacre? No wonder the UAI was so eager."*

"Then why were you watching that house?"

Magnus shudders. *"F-formula,"* he says, face twitching. *"We were looking for the formula. Thought it was supposed to be hidden somewhere in that house—searched it. Aristeus took all the data. Left behind—bastard left me to stake out the house. This means—there is no formula, is there? Just a kid. This was all for nothing."*

Kit pauses before asking, "Who will look for you?"

Magnus's eyes roam beneath their closed lids. His lips fall open, and it's then Ciere realizes that he's panting, his breath coming in gasps. The fear that twists Carson's expression is mirrored on Magnus's face. It's not only Carson's thoughts that Magnus hears—it's his emotions, too.

Ciere stares incredulously at Magnus. She knows how it feels to be pinned down by an enemy. The terror is sickening, all-consuming. She cannot imagine willingly going through that for the sake of information.

"No one," Magnus says, and it comes out as a whisper.

She feels some of the tension leak out of her body—she hadn't even realized she was holding herself so tightly, her own fear wrapped around her like a vise. There's no one coming for Carson. There is no trap, no snipers, and no SWAT team waiting outside.

They're safe.

"All right," Kit says. "That's all we need to know for now." He doesn't release his grip on Carson's hair, but he moves so that the man's head is no longer held at that painful angle. "You can let go now, Magnus."

But Magnus isn't letting go. His lips are still shaping silent words, his eyes squeezed shut.

"Let go," Kit says sharply.

A shudder runs through Magnus's whole body.

Kit releases Carson, and in one swift movement, grabs Magnus by the collar and drags him back. Magnus skitters to the floor and remains there for a moment, panting. Still trembling, he manages to rise to his feet on his own. When he staggers from the room, Ciere quickly ducks to one side to make sure they won't accidentally touch.

Kit follows Magnus out of the room. Ciere scurries after him and manages to get through the door before it closes on her. The thought of being left alone in there with Carson makes her feel ill.

Magnus backs into a wall. He sinks to the floor, and Kit follows.

"It's okay," Kit says in a voice Ciere hasn't heard in years. It's the way Kit would speak to her when she was a kid and her dreams were riddled with nightmares. "You're not that man. You're not him. Remember your name."

Magnus lets out a shaky exhale. "Well," he finally manages to say. "Haven't done that in a few years. Hoped I'd never have to again."

Kit frowns. "You okay?"

"Fine."

The silence stretches out again.

"You think he was telling the truth?" Kit asks.

Magnus wraps an arm around himself. "Yes. No one knows where he is. When he thought about it, all I got was, 'Going to show that son of a bitch, Aristeus.' "

Kit lets out a startled laugh. "Good to see that Aristeus hasn't lost his charm."

For a moment, neither speaks. They simply sit there until Magnus looks up. "What now?"

Kit retreats a few inches, and Ciere catches a glimpse of his face. His mouth is a thin line. "We deal with that man."

Ciere doesn't understand what he means—not at first. Then understanding slams into her, and it's all she can do to keep her illusion in place. Kill him. Kit means to kill the FBI agent.

Magnus shifts, straightening, but his arm remained firmly wrapped around himself. "Carson's daughter's birthday is in four weeks," he says. His voice is barely above a whisper, and Ciere has to strain to hear it. "He's been fighting for the right to come to the party—his ex-wife is rather vindictive about it. His partner's name is Gervais, and he's bound to be worried about Carson. He's always tried to restrain Carson, to keep him from doing something stupid. Something like this. Carson's father was from Scotland and his mother from Chile. Both of them died in the first wave of the MK plague. Carson misses them both."

"What are you doing?" Kit asks, his voice equally quiet.

Magnus's steady expression never changes. "I'm telling

you all the little bits and pieces I heard while I was listening to Carson's thoughts."

"Why?"

"Because," Magnus says, "when you look at him, you see a fed. There's more to him than that."

Kit turns so that he faces Magnus head-on, and Ciere sees the subtle change in his posture—his rigid shoulders go slack and his head bows. "They kill our kind all the time. You remember what we are to them: Tools. Weapons. We're not people to them, Magnus."

Magnus doesn't look away. "And that's exactly why we're not going to kill him. We're not like them. I won't let us be like them. Not again."

"Damn," Kit murmurs, and runs a hand over his face. "You always have to do things the hard way, don't you?"

Magnus smiles faintly. "We'll figure something out. We always do. In the meantime," he rises to his feet, "I should check on the kids." Ciere silently fumes at the term. *Kids?*

Only after Magnus is gone does Kit return to Carson's room. He opens the door. "You still alive?" It doesn't sound as if Kit would be all too bothered by Carson's death.

"How's your friend?" Carson says hoarsely. Ciere flinches; she almost forgot he could speak for himself. He huffs out a dry laugh. "Mentalists. They all crack in the end."

Kit doesn't answer aloud. Instead, he regards Carson with

a flat stare. Then he kicks Carson's chair out from under him. The movement is swift, violent, and Ciere gasps. The sound is swallowed up as the chair screeches in protest, slamming into the cement floor. Handcuffed as he is, Carson can't get up; he can't even shift to a less awkward sprawl. All he can do is lie there and glare up at Kit with murder in his eyes.

Ciere claps a hand to her mouth to stifle another involuntary sound. Kit steps over Carson like he isn't there, slams the bedroom door, and stalks out of the basement.

The lamps power down, and Ciere is suddenly plunged into darkness. Great—she forgot that he'd shut off all the lights. She mutters a curse.

"Whoa," a voice says, and she whips around. It's Alan's voice, but she can't see him, not in this total darkness.

"Marco," she says, unsure if he'll know the right response.

"Polo." He sounds a little off to her left, maybe five feet away. "I'm getting a feeling of déjà vu. Didn't we just deal with this last night?"

"Oh, the wonders of the basement," Ciere says grimly. "You have a lantern this time?"

"No, sorry." There's a whisper of cloth and movement, and Ciere abruptly thuds into Alan. "Well, I think I found you. Come on—we can feel our way to my room." Alan's hand falls on her shoulder and trails down her arm until his fingers twine around hers. "Come on."

"Why do I feel like you know this basement better than I do?" Ciere complains in a whisper.

"Because I get the feeling you never come down here." Alan must have better night vision than she does, because he unerringly guides her down the hall and manages to find his room. She hears the creak of a door, and then abruptly her eyes flood with light. Alan stands before her, lantern in hand. Even its dim light is enough to illuminate the small room. "Eureka."

She can't help but laugh. Her mirth boils up and overflows, but there's a hysterical edge to it, and again she's not really sure *why* she's laughing—she only knows that she heard Kit talk about killing a fed, and she's standing in the basement with a guy who's supposed to be dead and—

Her laughter dissolves into a hiccup and she realizes there are tears in her eyes. "Sorry," she chokes out, and turns her back on Alan. Pressing her hand into her eyes helps to hold back the gathering tears. She has to hold it together.

"I'm sorry," says Alan.

Ciere turns to face him again. "Sorry?"

"About this—about all of this." Alan pushes a hand through his inky black hair. "I know you weren't looking for a person... when you found me. You didn't have to take me in."

"It's not your fault," she says.

Alan seems to go far away for a moment. He shivers, as if trying to shake something off. "It's not yours, either."

"Yeah, it is." It's the first time she's admitted this to him, and she feels ashamed. "I was, well, I was looking for the Praevenir formula. Just like the feds, just like everyone else, apparently. I'm kind of in trouble with a mobster. I thought I could sell the formula to him and save my own ass." The skin beneath her bracelet itches. She wants a shower; she feels sweaty and dirty and wants to scrub herself clean of this whole situation. "It's my fault. I went off on my own because I was afraid."

She keeps looking at the floor, unsure if she wants to see Alan's reaction. He's been so nice to her, so trusting, and she hates to admit that she never came looking for him out of any pure motive. She wasn't in this to save anyone. She was in it for the money. She swallows, and opens her mouth to speak, but her voice dies away. Something pricks at her, something out of place.

There's a sound. Not her. Not Alan. Not a voice at all. It sounds like metal—grinding metal. Squeaking and rubbing and protesting.

Alan carefully sets the lantern on the concrete floor. Cold dread trickles down her spine, and she brings a finger to her lips.

She moves to the door and pauses, hand on the frame, peering into the shadows. The silence swallows up her quick breaths and she finds herself hesitant to step into the hallway.

The lantern's light only goes so far, and if she moves forward, she'll be in the dark again.

She takes a slow step forward, edging into the dark hallway. Alan follows, and she can feel his warmth at her back, giving her some comfort.

A metal chair swings out of nowhere, slamming into Alan. He staggers and falls backward through the doorway to his room. He hits the cement floor with a sickening thud.

A figure stands in the hallway, and he grasps the door, yanking it shut and jamming that folding chair underneath the doorknob, effectively trapping Alan inside. When the figure twists, Ciere manages to make out the clean-cut features and wrinkled suit.

She opens her mouth to scream, but Carson's arm wraps around her throat and effectively silences her.

30

DANIEL

The gardens outside of Homeland Security have probably seen a lot of covert meetings. But none like this. *A UAI agent, an FBI agent, and a criminal walk into a garden*, Daniel thinks. It sounds like the beginning of a bad joke. They stand next to a large fountain, surrounded by classical statues, and the rhythmic thrum of the water drowns out the chance of being overheard.

"Do it again," says Aristeus. He crosses his arms and leans against a statue of a headless naked woman.

The sun beats down on Daniel. He's wearing one of Aristeus's shirts; it's too long in the sleeves and a little tight around the chest. The cotton clings to his hot, damp skin and he scratches at it irritably. If only covert meetings could take place in nice air-conditioned rooms.

"I told you," Gervais says, "I've called him. Repeatedly. He's not picking up."

"And I told you," Aristeus says, deadly calm, "that my team found absolutely no sign of him. There is no evidence to support he's been kidnapped or killed."

Daniel watches the confrontation with a vague sense of detachment. It's nice not to be at the center of things for once.

Gervais flushes. "He must be following a lead."

"Then why isn't he picking up his phone?"

Really, Daniel thinks. *It's like a verbal Ping-Pong match.* All he needs is a bag of popcorn.

Gervais edges closer to Aristeus. He's broader and more muscular, even if he is a fair bit older. He could probably take down the younger man in a fair fight. If Aristeus ever fought fair.

"The car he took from the Endicott PD is missing, too," says Aristeus. "We should just call the police and get them to activate the car's GPS system. It would take a minute—thirty seconds to call and thirty for them to track Carson."

"We can't do that." Gervais flushes. "If we call, then there will be a record saying we don't know where Carson is."

"Isn't that the whole point? We don't know where he is!"

"There'd be an investigation," says Gervais. He's obviously making an effort to keep his voice level. "Internal Affairs would love to pounce on Carson. We're already on the brink with the Bureau because they think we let one immune criminal escape. Which is completely unfounded. If you go get a warrant to track his car or even report this, it'll be the end of Carson's career."

"Of course," says Aristeus evenly. "But why does this affect me?"

"Because Carson is part of your team! If he's pursuing a lead, it's in your best interest to let it play out! What if he finds something?"

Daniel heaves a sigh. He has a feeling that, if he doesn't intervene, someone's going to lose an eye. "Maybe he lost his phone."

Gervais shakes his head. "Carson sometimes leaves his phone in his car, but never for over twelve hours and never when he's on duty. Either he's working or..."

"Or something's happened to him," Aristeus says flatly. "Either way, we need to know."

Gervais turns his back on Aristeus and stares into the fountain. His fists clench and relax. "I never should've let you put him in charge of that stakeout. It was too dangerous. I should've—" He cuts off. "Three hours. Just give me three more hours before we report his disappearance."

"Fine," Aristeus says. He is already picking up his briefcase. "I'll give you that. But this investigation is too important to protect the career of one agent. If he doesn't get in touch by then, it's on his head. Come along, Daniel," he adds.

So much for being part of the scenery. Daniel reluctantly follows Aristeus through the garden, glancing over his shoulder one last time. Gervais has his phone pressed to his ear again, his foot tapping the ground and his eyes closed.

Daniel almost feels sorry for him.

Almost.

Okay, not really.

Aristeus sets a hard pace out of the gardens, and Daniel has to scramble to keep up. "I'm guessing no one's found any clues about the formula in all that stuff we took from Endicott," says Daniel. It's not difficult to deduce, since Aristeus looks ready to strangle someone.

"No," Aristeus says curtly.

"If we find the formula," Daniel muses, "the feds could create more immune. Forget elite little subdepartments like the UAI—there'll be whole armies of freaks like us." It's a slightly terrifying thought; Daniel can't imagine thousands more like himself.

"If we find the formula," Aristeus says darkly, "then the United States will be the first country to manufacture human beings as weapons."

31

CIERE

The first thing Ciere registers is the heat. The presence of a warm body pressed up against her hips and legs. She is so close to Carson that she can feel the coiling tension in his muscles, the bite of a belt buckle, and the rise and fall of his chest. His heart *thudthudthud*s somewhere behind her own.

His arm is the second sensation she notices. The thick muscles of his bicep and forearm catch her throat like a vise. When he flexes those muscles, the world swims and goes gray at the edges. Her heart migrates to her temples. Each beat becomes painful, and she's going to black out. The arm abruptly slackens. It's not enough to free her, but it does allow the blood to rush to her head again. She's limp and useless, held up only by the grip this man has on her throat and waist.

She doesn't realize that he's moving until her feet hit the

bottom step. He drags her upward, taking the stairs to Kit's room. He must have already scoped out the basement and realized that this is the only way out.

The flight is difficult; her legs feel oddly numb and unresponsive, but Carson is strong enough to haul her up.

It's a mistake. The moment her legs are free of the floor, she kicks out at him.

It's a dangerous move—they're halfway up a tall staircase, and if he falls, she will fall, too. But she cannot simply allow herself to be taken prisoner. It's not so much an act of will as an instinctive response. Her urge to dislodge this man's grip is as primal a need as breathing.

Carson lets out a low grunt as her heel connects with his shin. He is unsteady, unable to continue up the stairs while trying to wrestle with her. She flings out an elbow and she feels the impact on his ribs. Another pained sound slips out from between his teeth.

Belatedly, Ciere realizes that the same adrenaline that is allowing her to thrash and struggle must be running through Carson, as well. He is probably pumped full of the stuff; his own pain is an afterthought.

"Stop it," Carson growls, and he takes hold of her hair, yanking her head back in exactly the same way Kit did to him. It hurts; her neck isn't meant to be bent at this angle, and she realizes how easy it would be for a bone to crack, for her windpipe to be crushed. With her throat so exposed, she is an easy target.

His arm tightens, his elbow squeezing relentlessly until she cannot fight back. He releases her throat before consciousness slips away.

Then they are in the walk-in closet, and the light is blinding. Ciere blinks hard, the sunlight stinging her eyes, while Carson drags her through the door. They pass through Kit's room, and there are more stairs—down this time. Belatedly, Ciere realizes they're moving toward the kitchen, where Carson can slip out through the backyard.

Abruptly, Carson stops walking. Ciere's eyes roll up, trying to see what has brought their mad flight to a halt. A figure stands in the hallway. Tall and leanly muscled, with dark hair.

"Get out of my way." Carson's voice rumbles.

Magnus says, "Let her go."

"Screw that." Carson shifts his grip on Ciere, twists her head even farther to one side. "Let me out of this house and I don't break her neck."

"Let her go now, and I won't stop you from leaving," Magnus replies. His voice is still mild, still calm.

"I swear to God," Carson snarls, "if you don't let me past—"

Magnus pulls something out of his belt. It's Carson's gun,

the one Kit took from him. Magnus holds it with ease, like it's an old friend rather than a deadly weapon.

"Don't move," Magnus says quietly.

Ciere makes a noise in her throat, but Carson's grip keeps it from reaching her lips. She wants to tell Magnus to put the gun down, to let Carson past, because there is no way that Magnus can make that shot without hitting her. He must realize it, too. She is twined around Carson, a human shield between him and any forward threats.

Any forward threats.

Ciere sucks in a ragged breath. Magnus isn't here to save Ciere. As they stand in this narrow hallway, staring at one another, Carson has left his back wide open.

Magnus is the distraction.

Carson must realize this, as well. He spins around, and Ciere goes with him, her legs hitting the wall. She sees him then—Kit, creeping up behind Carson. Carson lets out a wordless snarl and strikes with his left hand. At first, it looks like a ridiculous move—even Ciere can see that his fist will not connect with Kit's face. But she sees the glitter of silver and the handcuff still encircling Carson's wrist. The edges are sharp and rough, as if Carson worked them until the metal twisted and broke.

Kit barely manages to dodge the blow; the metal whispers past his left cheek, inches from his eye.

Ciere recognizes the strategy—it's an old trick that Daniel taught her, one used if criminals escape with their handcuffs intact. Using cuffs to go after someone's eyes is a desperate, but sometimes effective, move. It's a patently crooked strategy, one that no one would expect from a fed.

Kit raises an arm to protect his eyes and Carson throws a punch at Kit's exposed torso. It's probably bad luck or maybe an instinct on Carson's part, but when the agent hits him, Kit takes the blow on his right side—just above his bullet wound.

Kit's eyes roll up, and his whole body curls in on itself. In that moment, Carson whirls, and Ciere is being propelled forward. She's flying, hurtling toward Magnus, and she barely catches the panicked, wide look in his eyes before she crashes into him.

She hits Magnus hard and staggers, her wobbly legs crumpling beneath her. Her knees hitting the hardwood floor produces an electric shock of pain, and she barely hears the sound of Magnus crashing into the wall.

The gun goes off.

The world is nothing but noise. Noise and pain. Noise and pain and the scent of smoke. She expects to feel a bullet ripping through her, but the impact never comes. When she manages to crack her eyes open, she sees the pistol on the floor, its tip pointed at the wall. There is a smoking hole opposite its barrel a mere three feet from where Ciere sprawls.

She doesn't have time to register the shock, because her

hearing is returning, and with it comes the sound of another struggle. Fists hitting flesh—a grunt—someone being slammed into the floor.

Ciere sits up, instinctively scooting back until she sees Carson wrap his arm around Magnus's throat. A scream hovers on her lips. She wants to conjure an illusion, but she's paralyzed. Carson begins dragging Magnus down the hall. Toward the kitchen and the back door. Toward freedom and out of sight.

Kit swears loudly and snatches up the gun. She sees a flash of red on his shirt—his wound must have reopened—before he sprints around a corner.

Ciere's fingers clench, and she forces herself to stand. Her throat still burns, a steady fire on the back of her tongue. When she wobbles out of the hallway, she sees that Kit has confronted Carson.

Carson stands in the kitchen, directly behind the bar. His arm is around Magnus's throat, and he has one of Magnus's arms drawn tight, the joint held at a painful angle.

Kit stands on the opposite side of the bar, the gun trained on Carson. Ciere waits for him to pull the trigger, to end this standoff, but Kit doesn't move. His mouth is so tight that he doesn't look capable of speech, but his eyes say everything.

When he manages to speak, the words are clipped and his voice raw. "Release him or I drop you."

Any sane person would be trembling at Kit's tone, but Carson smiles. It's a jittery little smile, edged with adrenaline and triumph. "No, you won't."

Kit's finger twitches toward the trigger.

Carson doesn't so much as blink. "All right, go ahead. Do it." Ciere can't understand why he sounds so confident. He is one trigger-pull away from a quick death, and he must know it.

"You can kill me," Carson continues. "Go ahead. But you know you won't." He gives Magnus a shake. "He's a mentalist. I know what they can do—I know how touch affects them. He'll feel it. He'll feel the bullet rip into my skull." He laughs. "People don't experience that kind of trauma and come out whole. But, hey, you'll all be safe, right? What's one man's sanity in exchange for your lives?" When he looks at Kit, all the humor vanishes from his face. "Put the gun on the counter."

Kit doesn't move.

Carson's arm tightens around Magnus's throat, and Magnus makes a soft choking noise; he strains backward, as if to try to relieve some of the pressure.

Kit's lips finally move: "Ciere, get out." The words are barely an exhalation of breath, so quiet that there's no way Carson will hear.

She stares at Kit, uncomprehending. His mouth twitches, and she can make out the words: "Get out." She takes one step backward, prepared to run if necessary. He must be planning something.

Kit lowers the gun. Keeping every movement slow and deliberate, he sets the pistol on the counter.

"Now slide it over to me," Carson says.

Now, Ciere thinks. This is when Kit's brilliant plan will happen—

Kit gives the pistol a push and it skitters over the counter, coming to a halt directly in front of Carson.

—Or maybe his brilliant plan is to surrender.

Ciere's confidence ebbs away as she gapes at Kit, who is now empty-handed and holding both palms out.

"I walk out of here with him," Carson tells Kit. "I'll let him go once I'm at my car."

They can't let Carson go. They can't. He knows about Alan.

Ciere flexes her fingers and tries to take a steadying breath. They can't let Carson walk out of here. She can't let it happen. If she can illusion herself, maybe she can get the jump on Carson. There's got to be something in the kitchen she can hurt him with. Her whole body seizes at the thought of using a weapon on Carson, but she can't just stand here. She sets her jaw and begins drawing on her immunity, coloring her skin to match the white of the walls.

But before she can move, Carson releases his grip on Magnus's elbow and goes for the gun.

Magnus's whole body arches upward, bucking like a startled horse, and without his two-handed hold on him, Carson can't prevent Magnus from lunging forward.

Without so much as blinking, Magnus flings an arm out, his fingers spread wide and grasping for the only other weapon in the kitchen: the knife still embedded in the cutting board. The one Kit threw there, just to prove a point.

Magnus's fingers close around the hilt. The knife comes free, and the cutting board clatters to the floor. Carson lets out a wordless snarl of rage and swings the gun around.

But Magnus twists, and, before any of them can react, he drives the knife through the FBI agent's throat.

32

CIERE

Ciere's seen death before—on HDE screens, in television and movies. Movie deaths are silent, clean, and instantaneous. She's heard someone die—and it was nearly the same as the movies promised. But she's never intimately witnessed a death. Not until this moment.

Carson's death isn't silent, isn't clean, and isn't instantaneous.

He stands there for an eternity, his eyes so wide that she can see the whites rimming his irises. The knife has slid deeply into his throat, and she imagines the tip protruding, jutting out amid the short, bristly hairs that trail down the back of his head.

She hears the softest of breaths leave Carson's mouth, a quiet exhalation of air that is meant to be spent on a vocalized cry.

Magnus pulls the knife free, and Carson falls. All Ciere

registers is a flash of brilliant red, a splatter hitting the counter, and then the sound of Carson collapsing to the floor. Then he is gone from her sight, blocked by the bar.

It would be a relief not being able to see him, but she can still *hear* him. He's struggling to draw breath—struggling and failing. It reminds her of the time Kit had bronchitis and spent a week racked with coughing fits that tore up his throat and made him double over with pain. She wants to clamp her hands over her ears. She wants to block out those horrible noises.

There is one mercy—Carson's death isn't silent, isn't clean, and isn't instantaneous. But it is quick.

The sounds fade, and after about half a minute, they vanish completely.

The silence is somehow even worse. Ciere can hear her own labored breathing, and each inhalation feels like the worst crime she's ever committed. She is stealing oxygen that belongs in someone else's lungs.

Magnus doesn't move. He stares down at the floor, presumably at Carson, the knife held loosely in his hand. The look on Magnus's face is utterly still and emotionless, as if he is gazing at a floor tile that is out of place.

All at once, Ciere needs to check, to see Carson for herself. She needs to know if he is actually dead, if—

"No." Kit appears in front of her, and Ciere realizes that her feet moved without her conscious permission. She tries to dodge around him, but he moves with her. He seems to be trying to block her view with his body.

"I..." Ciere says, and her voice is so broken she barely recognizes it. "I need to—"

"No," Kit says sharply, and his hands are on her shoulders and he's fighting with her, struggling against her flailing fists. "No, Ciere!" He grips both her wrists and keeps at it, herding her backward until she is through the door, into Kit's study, and there are walls between her and the kitchen. She finds herself tumbling backward into the leather love seat.

"You stay here," Kit says, and then he adds over his shoulder to Devon, standing behind him and looking unsteady but fully awake, "Both of you, just stay put."

Ciere wants to move. She can't sit on this love seat. There is something she needs to remember, something she needs to do—

"Alan," she says, and Devon's head snaps up. "He's locked in the basement. Car—Carson..." She stumbles over the name and doesn't know how to continue.

Devon's lips part, as if he is going to speak, but no sound emerges. He must have seen the body, and even he can't think of anything to say. He gives her a quick nod and leaves the room.

A few minutes later, he returns with Alan in tow. Devon hesitates at the door as if unsure of what to do, but Alan strides inside. He sinks onto the love seat, and she sees blood leaking from a cut over his eyebrow. He must have been trying to free himself. Before she can say anything, he brings a hand to her chin and his fingertips ghost over her jaw.

"He didn't hurt you?" Alan says.

"No. But he got you good." Before she can stop herself, Ciere's fingertips brush his brow. Part of her wishes she was the type of person to pass out, to simply leave this consciousness behind and wake up several hours later—when the blood has been cleaned up and the body removed—but she feels horribly awake. She hears footsteps in the hall and looks up, her fingers gone still on Alan's forehead.

Lizaveta shuffles into view; she pauses by the open door. She sees Alan, Ciere, and Devon, and she doesn't look surprised. "Good," she says, in that heavily accented way of hers. "Children do not need to see."

It's then Ciere realizes that Liz doesn't have her usual broom. In her knobby, liver-spotted hands she holds a mop.

Well, looks like the question of whether or not Liz knows about Kit's line of work has been answered, she thinks.

For a second, she's sure there is another laugh bubbling up her throat. But then the bitter taste of acid floods her mouth, and she scurries into the bathroom, falls to her knees, and vomits into the bathtub.

Kit comes for them about an hour later. He is wearing fresh clothes—strangely casual clothes. Jeans and a T-shirt look odd on him. Ciere straightens; she has been sitting on the bathroom floor, her forehead pressed to the cool porcelain of the toilet. She takes one look at Kit's outfit, and says, "We're leaving?" It's the only thing that Kit would dress down for. They are going underground.

"Get your things," Kit says shortly. He turns his attention to the boys. "You, too. Both of you. It's too risky to stay around here." He reaches down, grasps Ciere by the arm, and helps her to her feet.

Packing is easy. Ciere retrieves her old Hello Kitty backpack and checks the contents—new cell phones, clothes, bottled water, flashlight, a tiny first-aid kit, balaclava, Swiss Army knife, backup lock-picking kit, duct tape, some protein bars, counterfeit ID, and about three hundred in cash.

That sprig of lavender—the one she cast an illusion on when she was eleven—is sealed in a sandwich bag and tucked into the bottom of her backpack. It is brown, faded, crumbling, but there is still the faintest sweet fragrance. Ciere found the sprig in her backpack when she was living on the street. Her mother must have packed it without Ciere's knowledge, and she has never had the heart to remove it. It's a reminder of who she is. Of what she can do. It's a reminder she has to hide all of that.

Sitting on the bed is a crumpled sheet of paper. She turns it over, thinking at first that it is Devon's copy of the will, but then she sees the falcon letterhead.

Her whole body is wound tight, and she feels like she might snap under the pressure. This is just one more thing she can't deal with right now.

As she trudges downstairs, she catches a glimpse of a bucket resting on the hardwood floor. The water is dirty, rust colored, and Ciere's stomach rolls over. She's flaunted her exploits, bragged about her crimes, but she's never done anything like this. She's not used to the sight and smell of death, or the knowledge that if she looks into the trash can, she'll see paper towels stained red.

He deserved it. He was a fed. He was going to turn us all in.

But another part of her whispers: *He had a daughter.*

She finds herself rubbing her throat, touching the places where Carson's skin met hers, and her fingertips find the beat of her own pulse and linger on the throb of her carotid artery.

"It was quick," says a quiet voice, and Ciere whirls around. Alan stands behind her, his backpack slung over one shoulder. His expression is something between understanding and pity.

"What?" says Ciere.

Alan's gaze drops to the bucket. "That man's death. I heard Copperfield say that his throat was cut—he would've only been conscious for a few seconds."

"So you're saying that makes it all right?" She's not sure

why, but Alan's words set her on even more on edge. "If it was quick? You think that makes it better?"

Alan reaches out, and it's only then that Ciere realizes her hand is still clasped around her neck. He gently pries her fingers free, briefly squeezing before letting go.

"It's okay," he says. "Everything you're feeling, everything you're thinking—I get it."

"How do you know?"

His gaze remains fixed on the bucket. "This isn't the first time someone's killed for me."

"You all ready?" Kit asks briskly, striding into the room. He has his own go-bags: two military-grade duffel bags, the contents much the same as Ciere's backpack—only his contain more food and specialized equipment.

Ciere realizes they all have bags that are easy to grab and swing over a shoulder—all except Devon. His luggage is the roller type with the plastic handle.

"Where are we going?" he asks.

Kit checks his watch. "There's a place about forty miles from here—by the Schuylkill River. It's out of sight. It'll take a bit of work, but we'll manage."

Devon's brow furrows. "Okay, we're running from the feds and you want to go camping?"

Ciere understands. "We're going to dump h—*the* body." The word "his" sticks in her throat. "In the river."

"Well, we can't leave it here, for obvious reasons," Kit says. "We've already wrapped and loaded it into our car. We're going to break into two groups—Devon, you are going to drive the fed's car. Ciere and Alan will ride with you. Magnus and I will take my car. You'll follow us to the dump site, where we'll torch the car. From there, we go to a bolt-hole and stick it out for a few weeks. If nothing happens, we'll assume that the fed was right and no one will know where to look for him." He rattles off the instructions like they're planning a trip to the grocery store.

Alan clears his throat. "How exactly did the agent escape?"

It's a good question, and for a moment Ciere is thrown by the fact she herself didn't think of it. In the chaos of Carson's getaway and subsequent death, she hadn't realized that he must have escaped his handcuffs somehow.

Kit's face freezes. It's eerie how still he goes, and it reminds Ciere of when he held the gun on Carson. It's the same deathly calm. "He fell on his side. The metal chair must have cracked in the fall and he worked himself free."

But Carson's chair didn't fall by itself; Kit kicked it out from under him in a fit of rage.

Your fault, Ciere wants to whisper, but she doesn't. Instead she says, "What about Liz?"

Kit casts a look toward the kitchen. "She will be staying here to keep an eye on things."

"But," Devon protests, "she's a helpless old lady, and you want to leave her where some feds might come looking?"

"She will be fine," says Kit. "She's not as helpless as she looks." He takes a second to glance at every person in the room, his gaze resting on each of them in turn. "Let's move."

Devon lets out a wordless grumble and heads for the garage. Alan follows. Ciere takes a step after them. Then she pauses and glances over her shoulder. Magnus still hasn't moved from his place on the couch. Ciere hasn't seen him speak since killing Carson. It's then that the fed's words return to her: *People don't experience that kind of trauma and come out whole.* But in the end it was Magnus himself who wielded the knife.

"He had a daughter," Magnus says finally.

"And we have a Fiacre." Kit leans over him. "We couldn't let the agent go, not with that kind of information. You know how the UAI would react. What you did was necessary."

Magnus blinks slowly, like it's an effort. "He's dead. I don't care how necessary it was—it's not right."

Kit hesitates, turning away and striding to the door. "I know," he says. "But I can live with it. And so can you."

Only after Kit has vanished does Magnus cover his face with a hand. He must think he's alone; he lets out a shuddering breath and his shoulders begin to shake.

33

CIERE

The fed's car is disturbingly normal. There's a fancy radio with a CB, but other than that, the car could have belonged to anyone. Interestingly enough, Ciere finds a tag inside the car that marks it as belonging to a police department in Endicott. It must be borrowed.

The ashtray is full, and when Devon takes a sharp turn, some of the ashes spill over and drift onto the floor. The scent of stale smoke and something spicy—old cologne, maybe—clings to the leather seats. The door handle is worn down by years of use, and Ciere's fingers stroke the smooth surface.

Alan sits in the backseat, his legs crossed under him and eyes closed. Either asleep or meditating. Devon seems too intent on following Kit's car to bother with conversation, and Ciere cannot imagine touching the radio. Probably the last person to use the radio was Carson, and somehow the thought of fiddling with the same buttons that he handled makes her nauseous.

Devon's phone goes off again: it's the second time that morning, and the familiar *ding a ling ling, a ling ling ling* is beginning to grate on her nerves. She feels jumpy enough as it is.

At least the body isn't in this car. She's not sure she could handle that.

Before they drove off, Kit gave Ciere and Devon a few last-minute instructions. If Kit and Magnus were to be stopped, if anything were to happen, Devon was to keep driving. "If we get pulled over," Kit said, "don't stop. Don't even look at us. There's no time to disconnect that car's GPS, so don't draw attention to yourselves. Don't speed, don't go too slow. Just stay on the highway. Wait for us at the coordinates. If we do not show up within two hours, assume the worst." His eyes moved to Ciere, and she felt the weight of the responsibility he was unloading on her. "If that occurs, Ciere is in charge. She knows whom to contact and where to go.

"You hear me?" Kit said firmly. "No matter what happens, you keep driving."

Ciere tries to turn her mind away from the memory and focuses on the landscape. The greenery whips past them: trees bursting with fresh leaves, wildflowers blooming along the road, and—

Out of the corner of her eye, she sees something flash red and blue.

Her head whips around, and she feels her breath catching, her fingers gone rigid around the armrest. A cop car is creeping up on their right, driving on the shoulder of the road, its lights bright and spinning.

"Eyes ahead," Devon mutters. "Eyes ahead, eyes ahead." It sounds like a mantra, like a chant meant to protect. It rings hollow in Ciere's ears.

The cop car is now even with them, and Ciere cannot help but glance at them, waiting to see the inevitable stare, the gesture for them to pull over, to hear the demands of the cops wanting to know why three kids are driving an undercover cop car.

But the cop's eyes are fastened on something in the distance, and he doesn't so much as look at them. The cop speeds past. For another second, Ciere is sure the car is going to swerve in front of Kit's sedan and force it to the side of the road, but it continues on. Its lights blur from red to blue and back again, and the car screams toward the horizon like an angry hornet.

"Not us," Devon says tightly. "Not after us."

Ciere knows he's right. That cop must be off on some other mission. Catching some other crooks. Taking down some other criminal empire.

But her heart won't stop pounding.

The drive takes over an hour. They pull off the main highway onto a rural road and pass fields that must have once been used for farming. Now the fields are dusty and dry, left untended. Kit takes a right onto a road that Ciere doesn't see until his car vanishes into the trees. Devon follows, and the *bumpbump* of driving on gravel jostles Ciere in her seat. Kit takes a left, and then there is a thick wall of foliage between them and the road. Kit's car comes to a halt, and Devon pulls the car up behind it.

Ciere pushes her door open and scurries outside with a feeling of relief. The air is fresher here than in the city. The sounds of the nearby river soothe her nerves. Even the canopy of trees is reassuring—it's another layer of protection.

"The hard part is done," Kit says matter-of-factly, pulling Ciere out of her thoughts. "We're here. Now all that's left are details." He snaps his fingers at something beyond Ciere. "You boys, gather all of Carson's personal belongings. Search the car for anything that could be used to ID him. We'll toss that into the river before we burn the car." He unlocks his trunk. It eases open slowly, and Ciere averts her gaze. She doesn't want to see who—*what*—lies within the trunk. "After that, we'll run."

"What about Guntram?" Ciere says, stepping forward. "I'm supposed to pay him today. We can't run as long as he's tracking me."

Kit's frown deepens. "I'll deal with him," he says, and his voice is as flat as when he interrogated Carson.

Devon and Alan are already at work inside the fed's car.

The doors are all open and they're crawling around inside, saying things like "Found a lighter," and "Bloody hell, how long has this donut hole been here?" and "Mind removing your elbow from my side, Ana?"

Ciere tries to keep her eyes down. She doesn't want to see Kit and Magnus heave the body toward the river. She doesn't want to see them weigh the garbage bag with rocks. She doesn't want to hear the sound of their grunts and straining as they carry the heavy load to the water. She doesn't want to witness Carson before he sinks beneath the gray surface of the river.

As soon as they shuffle awkwardly out of sight, Devon stops working. He doesn't speak at first, apparently judging how long it will take for the adults to be out of earshot.

"I guess this is something else I can add to that 'What I Did over My Summer' paper we're always required to write," he quips. "I mean, what professor doesn't want to hear about their students dumping bodies?"

Ciere lets out a snort. Good to see that no matter how dire the situation might be, Devon's sarcasm will always prevail.

"You wouldn't," Alan says, looking perplexed.

"He's kidding," she says, patting Alan's arm.

Devon's smirk never falters. "Yeah, that would require me to *write* an essay. Seriously, Ana, you never heard of sarcasm?"

"His name is Alan," Ciere says. "And lay off him."

Devon looks on the verge of another insult when a familiar

ringtone goes off again. *Ding a ling ling, a ling ling ling.* Devon redirects his glare at the phone—it's sitting on the gravel road amid Carson's possessions. It must have fallen from Devon's pocket.

"You know," Ciere says, "I think your dad's figured out you're not in Hemsedal."

Devon goes back to shuffling through Carson's things, tossing them into several piles. It looks like he's sorting them according to Kit's directions; they'll either be burned or tossed into the river. A small canister of gasoline rests against the tire of Kit's car, presumably to speed along the burning process. Ciere fetches it, along with two of the lighters that Kit keeps in the glove compartment. Might as well get this over with as soon as possible.

Ding a ling ling, a ling ling ling.

Alan looks politely puzzled. "Why is your phone ringing a bad thing?"

"Hiding from my family," Devon says shortly. He glares at the phone; it is lying only a few feet from where he kneels. It rings again and then goes silent. "He hasn't left a voice mail yet, which means he's saving all his rage for me."

"Why not just answer?" Alan suggests.

Devon heaves a sigh. "None of your business, Ana."

"Would you stop calling him that?" Ciere snaps. The constant ringing of the phone is grating.

Devon's patience unravels. "I will call him whatever I damn well please."

And then the phone goes off again. *Ding a ling ling, a ling ling ling...*

Devon *snaps.*

He lunges for the phone and snatches it up, his face twisted into an expression of reckless fury. He flicks the phone open and brings it to his ear. Apparently, he's decided to go on the offensive, because he doesn't give his father the time he needs to launch into a lecture.

"Yeah, hello. Hiya, Dad," Devon says with manic cheer. "All right. Fine. I'll admit it. Dad, we're not in Norway. I'm with my mates in Philadelphia. Got that? *Phil-a-del-phi-a.*"

Still grinning in that slightly deranged way, he holds the phone out, and his thumb strokes over the button marked SPEAKERPHONE. He probably wants to prove to the entire world that he's finally standing up to his father.

When the phone's speaker crackles, Ciere expects to hear the furious voice of Mr. Lyre. But the voice that speaks is gravelly. Unfamiliar.

"Who is this?" the voice says slowly. "And where the hell is Carson?"

Everything freezes, goes still and quiet. Ciere's heart just *stops* for a moment—and in that moment she understands what just happened. She whirls on the spot and throws a desperate, searching look at Devon's luggage. And there it is.

Devon's cell phone, identical to the one that Carson used, is sitting on top of his luggage. Untouched. It wasn't Devon's phone that rang.

Which means that—

"Whoever this is," that unfamiliar voice says, "you should know that we're currently tracking the location of his police car. There will be a squad to your location shortly. If you have injured Agent Carson in any way—"

—that isn't Devon's phone. It's Carson's.

"Turn it off!" Ciere says, her voice ragged with terror. "Turn it off!"

Devon snaps back to life. The phone tumbles from his grasp, hitting the gravel. Before anyone can move, his heel slams onto the phone again and again. It looks like he is trying to kill an insect that startled him.

When he steps backward, the phone is little more than a mess of plastic and metal. Devon's breathing comes in harsh pants, and he turns toward Ciere, a beseeching look in his eyes. He wants her to tell him that it's all right. It's just a stupid mistake. One that any of them might have made.

She can't give him that reassurance. Sounds seem far off, and she feels that odd disconnect again. She stares at the remnants of Carson's phone. The feds won't be able to track that, not anymore. It is too broken. But they could easily track the car.

"They're coming," Alan says. His voice is oddly inflectionless, as if he expected this.

He doesn't add what Ciere knows. The police will come, and they will all be arrested. She considers the canister of gasoline and imagines setting fire to the car, watching the blaze consume it. But even if they destroy the car, chances are they've already been tracked to this location.

Devon seems to be at a loss, his long arms dangling at his sides. "What—what do we do?"

Ciere's instincts kick in. The old words leap to the forefront of her mind: *Don't let anyone see what you are, understand?* She wants to comply. She wants to wrap herself in her surroundings, to take the images of the trees dappled with sunlight and shadow, and blend in so seamlessly that no one will find her. She wants to run, to leave this all behind. She wants someone else to take the fall. She cannot go to jail. She cannot face a firing squad. She will not work for the same organization that killed her mother. And if the feds catch her, those will be her only options.

"Get Kit," she says, turning to face Devon. He hesitates. "Get Kit!" she repeats shrilly. This time, he obeys and rushes into the forest.

When she turns to face him, Ciere sees Alan staring at the car. "They'll come for me," he says. "But not here." It's like he's already accepted that fact, like it's a foregone conclusion. Then his eyes flick to her, meeting her gaze. A spark goes through her, a blaze of adrenaline that has little to do with their situation. Then his gaze snaps to the car, and he moves toward it, fresh determination in his face.

It takes her a second to understand. He's running. But not away from danger—toward.

"You've got to be kidding." Her voice trembles slightly, heavy with the words she isn't saying.

"I take this car and they'll follow," says Alan, and there's something she's never seen in him before: iron. "You can run. All of you—this isn't your fight. You can be free."

There's so much wrong with that statement. Her mouth feels slow, and the seconds are slipping by too quickly. She's spent six years running, and she's never found freedom. There's no such thing as freedom. There are only places to hide, things to steal, and a life she's not sure she even wants anymore. A day ago, she probably would've taken Alan up on his offer. Let him take the fall while she grabbed her friends and ran. But now—now she's not so sure.

She tries to think of a way to say all of this, but what comes out of her mouth is, "Can you even drive?"

A grimace passes over Alan's face. "Theoretically, yes."

"So in reality, no?"

She's moving before she's truly conscious of the fact. She tosses the gasoline canister and her backpack into the backseat, throwing herself behind the steering wheel. "What are you doing?" Alan says, aghast.

"What does it look like?" She snaps her seat belt into place.

"You don't have to do this." The look on his face a mixture of incredulity and wonder.

"Shut up and get in the car," she snaps.

He's already sliding into the passenger seat. "Just so you know," he says, "that's probably the nicest thing anyone's ever said to me."

She laughs, but her throat is so tight that she nearly chokes on it.

Out of her rearview mirror, she sees Devon emerge from the forest. He pauses, frozen for a half second, his mouth dropping open. He makes for the car, his long legs eating up the distance. Ciere reacts automatically, hitting the door-lock button. She hears the resounding click as Devon tries to yank the back door open. When that fails, he lunges at her door, fingers clawing at the half-open window. "What are you doing?"

She twists the key in the ignition. The engine kicks to life, but Devon doesn't back off, and she can't drive away with him clinging to the car.

"Let go," she says.

"No," Devon repeats. "If you're going to do this, you're not leaving me behind."

No. She can't be responsible for him anymore—not when the stakes are this high. She can't be the reason Devon is arrested. He could have a normal life; it's within his grasp, if only he weren't so infatuated with the idea of being crooked. What he doesn't get is, crookedness isn't a lifestyle choice; it isn't a choice at all; it's the only way people like Ciere can survive. Devon has protection she never did: Money. Power. Connections. He can go on with his life. He doesn't have to be here. He doesn't have to risk his life and freedom.

"Devon, get off!" she says desperately.

"Ciere—"

He isn't going to let go. Ciere draws in a breath, and says harshly, "You can't come with us, okay? I don't want you to!" Devon's grip tightens on the open window. Ciere can read the refusal in his eyes—he's determined to risk his life for her. Because they're friends.

"You don't belong with us," she says.

The moment the words leave her lips, Ciere knows they were the worst things she could have said. Devon takes several shaky steps backward, as appalled as if she had just hit him. His face crumbles, and she sees the hurt in his eyes. The betrayal.

Kit sprints out of the trees. He shouts something, but

Ciere can't hear it over the engine. She hits the gas, and the car springs forward. They have to get away. That's all that matters now. She needs to get the car far away from her friends.

The car peels off the gravel road, and Ciere yanks the car onto the pavement, twisting the steering wheel until they make a sharp left. Out from under the trees, the fading sun is overly bright. Ciere squints and takes her hands off the wheel to pull down her visor. Alan grabs at his seat belt, the worried expression on his face clearly asking if he should be the one behind the wheel.

"So where are we going?" Alan asks.

Ciere responds by digging into the contents of her pocket—her disposable phone, lighter, and a business card. She tosses the latter at Alan. "Call that number."

"And what do I say?"

"Tell him to meet us in Philadelphia at the docks off Columbus Boulevard." She presses the gas pedal as far down as it will go, and she is slammed back into her seat. The tires squeal in protest, and then they are flying down the road, trees rushing past and the world vanishing underneath them.

When Alan hangs up the phone, he says, "Now what?"

"I have a plan," she says. And she tells him everything.

PART FOUR

Humanity has always defined itself by its weapons. The Stone Age, the Bronze Age, the Iron Age, the Atomic Age—we track our progress by how easily we can take another person's life. I wonder what future generations will call this age. We do not need stone or bronze or iron to kill.

The moment Praevenir was introduced to the population, humanity itself became the weapon.

—President Henry Caldwell, Address to the American People, September 21, 2019

34

DANIEL

Aristeus's office is exactly how Daniel imagined: industrial carpet, a large desk, two walls of windows looking out over the city, and a heavy door with a dead bolt that is definitely not standard issue. There are no pictures of family, no calendar featuring cute animals, and no ritzy paperweights. The place feels sterile and soulless.

Just like its occupant, Daniel thinks. He stole a crossword from Aristeus's secretary the last time he was sent out for coffee. It's easier not to think when he's contemplating a six-letter word for "catlike."

Gervais has taken to calling Carson from Aristeus's office phone. He sits with the receiver pressed to his forehead, his finger hovering over the redial button. *Ring. Ring. Ring.* Voice mail. *Ring. Ring. Ring.* Voice mail. The process repeats itself over and over. Worry is etched into the lines around Gervais's mouth. His time is slipping away, and his composure goes with it. He has less than an hour before Aristeus's deadline.

Aristeus, having been displaced from his desk chair, kneels on the floor. He has some of the files he took from Pandora Marton's home spread out on the carpet. "You find anything yet?" Daniel asks. He's finished with this crossword, and his brain feels too sluggish to start another.

Aristeus's long finger passes over a sheet of paper. "Bills. Financial records. Letters."

"But not the formula," says Daniel.

A muscle goes in Aristeus's cheek. "Not the formula."

"Maybe there's something else you'll find that will be useful," Daniel says in a tone that clearly states he doubts it. The formula is all that matters, and if Aristeus promised it to his superiors, then it's his ass on the line. The thought makes Daniel smile.

"Not a thing," Aristeus murmurs, so low that Daniel almost doesn't catch the words. "Him."

Before Daniel can ask, something in the room's atmosphere shifts. His instincts whisper a warning.

Ring. Ring. Ring.

"Yeah, hello." The voice is tinny, quiet, and it comes through the earpiece of Aristeus's phone.

Gervais lunges for the phone, and he slams his fist down

on the button labeled SPEAKER. For a second, Daniel is sure he's going to hear Carson's gruff voice snarl something about them interfering while he's doing all the work. But then—

"Hiya, Dad," says an unfamiliar voice. It sounds young, male, and vaguely British. Daniel's senses flare in a silent warning. "All right. Fine. I'll admit it. Dad, we're not in Norway. I'm with my mates in Philadelphia. Got that? *Phil-a-del-phi-a.*" The speaker isn't someone Daniel recognizes, and it's definitely not Agent Eduardo Carson.

There's a moment of dumbfounded silence.

"Who is this?" Gervais says. "And where the hell is Carson?"

Daniel's other sense kicks in, and he hears a soft intake of breath coming from the speaker. He just *knows* that whoever has Carson's phone is terrified.

Gervais's tone shifts. It's the voice he probably uses when telling someone that he's going to bust open their door if they don't open it. "Whoever this is, you should know that we're currently tracking the location of his police car. There will be a squad to your location shortly. If you have injured Agent Carson in any way—"

Another voice cuts him off. This one is high pitched, female, and chillingly familiar.

"Turn it off!" the voice cries. "Turn it off!"

The line goes dead, and Daniel feels himself slowly sinking to the floor. He is the one still point in a suddenly chaotic world. Aristeus is moving, Gervais is shouting, someone is opening the office door, and then Gervais is on the phone again. There's a whooshing sound, and it takes Daniel a second to realize it's his own heartbeat in his ears.

He barely hears Gervais rattling off his instructions to the Endicott Police Department. They're going to track Carson's borrowed vehicle. Then the phone is being slammed into its cradle, and Gervais says, "The car is north of Philadelphia."

Daniel jerks back to life. "Maybe I should stay here...."

Aristeus doesn't even look at Daniel—he just grabs Daniel's collar and uses it like a dog's leash. Daniel finds himself on his feet and yanked forward before he can voice a protest. His crossword falls to the floor. The three of them rush out of the office and into the hall.

"Helicopter?" Aristeus says.

"Helicopter," Gervais confirms.

It must be the first time they've ever agreed on anything.

Daniel's stomach rolls over, and he presses the back of his hand to his mouth. Throwing up feels like a distinct possibility.

He recognized that voice. He's heard that voice laugh, whisper his name, tell jokes, grumble in anger. He knows that voice as well as his own. Ciere.

What is Ciere doing with Carson's cell phone? If she was robbing him, she might have stolen his ride, too. But she should have ditched the car. Any good crook would ditch the car. Why hasn't she ditched the car? His mind fixates on this one detail, because the rest of him is frantic to avoid the obvious conclusion: they're going after whoever has Carson's phone. He heard Ciere's voice. He's part of a federal team going after Ciere.

He can only hope she knows what she's doing.

35

CIERE

Running isn't new to Ciere. Running away from danger has always been her standby. But running *toward* danger? Now, that's a new one.

She drives quickly, but not fast enough to draw attention. They can't get pulled over now. Alan helps with their navigation—he has a good memory and points out exits that she would have otherwise missed. An hour later, Ciere finds herself fighting traffic back into Philadelphia. She swerves around taxis and commuters alike, trying to find the best route to the docks.

The docks near Columbus Boulevard used to house many active shipping barges. The Delaware River was used to ferry materials from the ocean upriver, the barges providing a convenient form of transportation. In recent years, the river's use has waned, and now the docks are all but deserted. Some old barges remain; they are weighed down with empty cargo crates and abandoned freight, and they stand as the only remnants of the river's former life.

Ciere pulls a left turn until the car jostles, and she swerves into an area not meant for driving. There are crates stacked all over; spare boat parts litter the ground; the scent of dirty water drifts into the car.

Ciere's parking spot is determined by the nails that puncture her tires. The car shudders to a halt.

There is no escaping now. The decision has been made. And she can only hope it was the right one.

"Now what?" Alan asks.

"We wait," Ciere says shortly. She drums her fingers on the steering wheel and tries to pretend that each passing second doesn't set her on edge. Evening slowly leeches the light from the sky. She looks up and squints at the horizon. She gives it half an hour until full dark.

Alan sits with his hands folded in his lap, looking alert and composed. He's put his whole future in Ciere's hands, and he appears to have utter confidence in her. Which freaks Ciere out. She's never even managed to keep a goldfish alive, much less a Fiacre. Even her dog is with Lizaveta now.

Two headlights pierce the dusk. She sits up, her fingers tightening around the steering wheel. She can't see who is in the other car.

The car parks about fifty feet from Ciere. A man pushes the passenger door open and emerges into the illumination of the headlights.

It's Brandt Guntram.

Ciere lets out a breath that is half relief, half apprehension. Part one of the plan—get an extremely dangerous mobster to meet with her at the deserted docks—has succeeded. But, on the other hand, she's on the deserted docks with an extremely dangerous mobster. She sways, suddenly a little dizzy. Her body has taken control of her, adrenaline and fear putting her physical reactions on autopilot.

"On second thought," Ciere says, and her voice shakes, "this was a shitty plan."

She grabs her backpack and shoves the gasoline canister, lighter, and balaclava inside. They're not the best weapons, but they're all she has. She swings the backpack onto her shoulder, and she and Alan make their way toward the waiting mobster.

Brandt Guntram leans against the side of his old Honda Pilot. He looks just the way she remembers him from the train station. Blond, medium height, with a remote expression. He's not imposing, but he has a confidence that usually accompanies the well armed. Conrad emerges from the driver's side and grins at Ciere like they're old friends.

Guntram raises an eyebrow. "Who is this?" he asks, directing his attention to Alan.

"Bodyguard," Ciere says stoutly. She makes a conscious effort not to look at Conrad, who is about two feet taller and a hundred pounds heavier than Alan.

Alan crosses his arms and does his best to look threatening.

Ciere tries to keep her face emotionless. "We need to talk payment," she says, forcing confidence into her voice and posture.

Guntram's gaze flicks to the tracker bracelet. "Yes, we do. So where is our money?"

Ciere lifts her arms and bows slightly, indicating herself.

Guntram and Conrad exchange a look. "I'm sorry," Conrad says, "but did she just gesture at herself?"

"I think she did." Guntram looks torn between horror and amusement. "Conrad, have we expanded our business to involve human trafficking?"

"Not the last time I checked," Conrad replies, "but maybe Henry decided to branch out and didn't tell us."

Ciere finds it hard to maintain her confident stance with these two men talking to each other. She feels herself deflate, and her arms fall back to her sides. "I'm not selling myself."

"Then I'm confused," Guntram says. "What exactly are you proposing?"

"Six months," she says. "Immune criminals have been known to work for mobs. I'll work for the Gyr Syndicate to pay off my debt."

"Like a customer who can't pay at a restaurant," Conrad says, seemingly charmed by the idea. "Washing dishes."

Guntram snorts. "We're a professional organization, not a fast-food joint. What makes you think we'll take you up on your offer?"

"Because I can't get the money right now. And I'm not in a position to get it any time soon," Ciere replies. "So your choices are to either kill me and protect the Syndicate's reputation as a badass mob or else use me and let me work off my debt. And I'm worth a lot more alive."

"What's going to stop us from just kidnapping you and using you indefinitely?" Guntram asks.

Ciere points a finger at Alan. "Hello? Bodyguard. And he has instructions to tell my handler if you mistreat me in any way."

"Who's your handler?"

"Kit Copperfield."

Conrad lets out a laugh. "Wait, I heard about a Copperfield in the area—something about a stolen Thomas Cole and a forged Jacques-Louis David. He's an art fence, right?"

Guntram frowns. "An illusionist's handler is an art fence?" He must have thought she answered to some powerful mob family; he obviously never considered that she would work for a freelancer. "Let me get this straight—instead of meeting with us to deliver the money, you are handing us your résumé?"

"Pretty much," Ciere agrees.

Conrad and Guntram look at each other again, and she can almost see the silent dialogue pass between them. This is the moment that will decide everything. Her pulse quickens, and her feet and hands go icy cold. She wants to rub her hands together, to work some heat into them, but she doesn't dare move.

"She's a lunatic," says Conrad.

"Absolutely insane," says Guntram.

"Either completely fearless or utterly stupid," says Conrad.

"She's going to fit right in," says Guntram.

"Henry's going to love her," says Conrad.

"Should we send her with Henry?" Guntram says with a frown. "I was thinking keep her in Newark with our team."

Ciere closes her eyes for a moment. The relief is all-consuming, a sweetness like none other. She is not going to die. At least not right away. "So it's a deal?" she says.

Guntram considers her. Then he holds out his hand. "Might help if I knew your going name," he says.

Hesitantly, she shakes his hand. "Ciere," she says. Guntram's hand is surprisingly steady.

"All right, Ciere," he says. "Welcome to the Gyr Syndicate."

And that, of course, is the second they all hear the sound of an approaching police siren.

Guntram's grip is suddenly crushing, his fingers tight on Ciere's wrist.

"Oh, you have got to be kidding me," he says, his head darting around and searching for the source of the noise. He turns back to Ciere, his brow wrinkled in distaste. "Really?" He sounds disappointed, like this betrayal is less of a threat and more of a letdown.

Ciere grimaces. "Okay, so the deal is that I'm kind of being chased by the feds. But I'm serious about my offer. I'm willing to work off my debt, but it's going to be pretty hard doing that if I'm dead or in jail. So if you protect me, you're really protecting an investment."

Ciere got the idea from Guntram himself. He's taken down so many criminals by using the feds that turning his own trick against him seems a little... poetic. If she can use him to escape her fed problem, all the better. "You hate the feds," she reminds him. "And you've told me how you love protecting investments. This should be the highlight of your day."

Guntram regards her with new admiration. "A thief," he says. "An illusionist thief trying to manipulate me into fighting cops on her behalf. I'll say this for you: you're either incredibly brave or you've got a death wish."

"Semantics," says Ciere.

Conrad is already on a phone, rattling off instructions. "Backup is on the way," he tells Guntram. "Fifteen minutes." He ducks down, squatting behind the Honda, and pulls Alan and Ciere with him. "Get down, kiddies. Things are about to get loud."

Whatever Conrad was going to say is drowned in a flood of vehicles. Cop cars, black SUVs with government plates, and a silver sedan. There are more than Ciere can count, and her stomach falls. Too many. Guntram and Conrad may be good, but they're vastly outnumbered. This raid will go exactly the way it did for TATE—everyone will either be taken into custody or gunned down.

Ciere glances at Guntram, expecting to see fear.

But he's smiling. Guntram is *smiling.* And so is Conrad.

"If the government wants her this badly," Conrad says gleefully, "she must be a handful. Face it, Brandt, if she was ten years older she'd be your soul mate."

"My wife will be so glad to hear that." Guntram turns his attention back to the cops. "Looks like they pulled out all the stops," he says, reaching into his jacket and withdrawing a semiautomatic pistol. He weighs it in his hand, considering the gun and the oncoming cops. Without so much as blinking, he rises to his full height, squints, and then pulls the trigger, pausing a fraction of a second between each shot. The sound is deafening; Ciere feels each shot resonate in her bones.

Each round hits a tire on a separate vehicle. The cars swing out of control as metal sparks and screams, plowing into the pavement. Ciere watches in fascination as one spins around twice before slamming into a pile of crates.

Ciere gapes up at Guntram. He's not normal. The way he acts—he's someone who is used to power. And not just the kind of power a gun or a heavily muscled bodyguard might provide. He regards the feds with self-assured contempt.

Ciere has only seen this confidence in a few people, and they all shared one trait. "You're immune," she says.

A smile pulls at Guntram's thin mouth. "Nice of you to notice."

Possibilities flicker through Ciere's mind: *Eludere? Dauthus?*

"Admit it, you were getting bored in Newark," Conrad says, grinning. "You missed this."

"Sure, of course I missed nearly getting my head blown off." Guntram fires off two shots without even looking at his target. Ciere keeps waiting for one of the cops to shoot back, but none of them do. Guntram's just standing there, in plain view, like it doesn't matter that he's an obvious target. He adds to Conrad, "You're just lucky we've got backup coming, or else I'd dock your pay."

"Just hope our backup arrives soon," Conrad says, taking Guntram's pistol. He ejects his magazine and slams a fresh one home, still grinning all the while. "Otherwise my pay is the last thing we'll be worrying about."

Guntram glances at Ciere and Alan before edging over the car and firing off several more rounds. "The kids should probably get out of here."

"Why?" Ciere says. The last thing she wants is to be in the middle of a police raid without protection. And, to be honest, the best protection she is likely to find is these two mobsters.

Alan's lips press together. "This car will not provide adequate cover from small handguns," he says. "Never mind if those federal agents have rifles or armor-piercing rounds." As if to emphasize his point, one of the car's windows explodes and shards of safety glass skitter along the ground. Ciere ducks, covering her bare neck.

"Kid's got a point," Guntram says. "Conrad, cover me, please. I'll get these two out of the way before I take care of those agents. Come on, you two," he adds pleasantly, before yanking at Ciere's arm and dragging her away from the car. "I'd suggest heading for a barge and using your illusions to hide yourself and your"—his eyes flick toward Alan—"*bodyguard*."

"This the way you treat employees?" Ciere manages to say. Even in the twilight, she and Alan don't dare to rise to their full height. The result is an awkward scurry, with both of them staying as close to the pavement as possible. Only Guntram doesn't seem to fear the bullets that slam into nearby crates, kicking up dust and splintering wood.

"No," he says, without missing a beat. "If you were a real employee, I'd ask for references before shoving you out into a firefight."

They run in the only direction possible—toward the docks. Ciere weaves to avoid tripping over a mooring line, and Alan ducks around another abandoned shipping container. Guntram moves through the chaos with more confidence, leading the way to a barge with rusted sides, its blue paint flaking off.

He comes to a halt. "Go," he says. "Hide on that. We'll take care of those agents and then come back for you. But if something happens to us, I suggest you hide."

Ciere nods. "You think you can take them? There're so many."

Guntram grins openly, and Ciere is reminded of Devon's crazy smirk, of the face he wears right before he does something really stupid. "Trust me," he says, revolving on the spot. He begins jogging back down the docks. Alan and Ciere look at the boat, hesitating.

"You think we should do as he says?" Alan asks.

Guntram stops when he is about thirty feet away, spinning so that he runs backward for a few paces. He gestures at Ciere and then points at the boat. Ciere is about to follow his instructions when she sees something flicker out of the corner of her eye.

Her mouth opens, and a yell builds in her throat.

Guntram, facing Ciere and Alan, does not see the man slip out amid the shadows. He moves with the graceful stealth of a serpent. Before Guntram can react, the man slams a fist into Guntram's wrist. Guntram's gun clatters to the ground. Guntram whirls, his hand raised to strike back.

"Go to sleep," the man says.

Silently, Guntram falls. He hits the ground in a boneless heap and sprawls there, unmoving. He's either been knocked unconscious or is dead. From this distance, Ciere can't tell.

She feels frozen, her breath coming so hard that she can feel it scraping her lungs raw. The man steps over Guntram's body and begins a slow, almost lazy approach.

In the fading sunlight, Ciere can just make out that the man has sharp features, short black hair, and large eyes. She is struck by a horrible familiarity. She has seen this man on a night just like this one. During a raid in a town just outside of Baltimore. She remembers Magnus breathing the name.

Aristeus.

36

CIERE

The world slows down to a few infinite seconds.

Ciere stands on the dock, staring at the man who just destroyed her one chance at survival. She can still hear the distant sounds of the fight, of metal impacting metal, of shattering glass and screaming sirens.

Aristeus continues his advance. The distant flashes of red and blue lights make it look like he is walking in slow motion, giving his movements an eerie grace. Behind Aristeus is another man, a younger man with brown hair and a crooked nose. It's Daniel.

A wave of exhaustion sweeps over Ciere, loosening her muscles until she feels unsteady on her feet. The last few hours—the last few *days*—seem to weigh down on her shoulders, impossibly heavy, and she can no longer hold herself up.

It's too much. Too many flights, too many scares, too many moments of utter terror chased by the relief of survival.

She watches Aristeus approach with a feeling of detachment. It hasn't sunk in yet. Part of her is still waiting for Guntram to get up and win this battle for her. She was counting on him; he was her pocket ace. But Guntram isn't moving. He hasn't even twitched. He's either dead or incapacitated, and at this point, it doesn't matter which. He is out of the game. And judging from the wild sound of gunfire coming from Guntram's car, it is only a matter of time until Conrad is taken, too.

Ciere played her hand and it simply wasn't good enough. She lost.

Alan drags her backward. She stumbles, barely manages to keep her feet, and then finds herself running. Her body is quicker on the uptake than her mind. She sprints ahead, dashing toward the boat. She remembers Guntram's advice to hide there. Plenty of nooks and crannies for them to burrow into. And with her talent, they might have a chance at surviving this. Maybe.

Getting onto the boat is a matter of scurrying up a wooden plank. It looks old, nearly rotted through, and it wobbles beneath her as she clambers up on hands and knees. Splinters dig into her skin, and the scent of the river wafts up and over her—damp, somehow salty—but Ciere doesn't take any time to notice it. She is uncomfortably aware of how easy a target she is, out in the open like this. When her fingers touch the rough metal of the boat's railing, she pulls herself up and over with a huff of relief. Alan follows a second later. He reaches down to nudge the plank out of the way, maybe thinking to prevent anyone else from boarding, but the plank has all but molded itself to the surface of the boat. There's no budging it.

Ciere tries to get her bearings. The barge isn't too big—it's mostly a long, flat surface meant to hold cargo. Several hatches look like they lead to a lower level, but each one is bolted shut, and she dismisses them. At the end of the boat, what looks like a tiny shack juts up from the flat deck. It's got a door and four walls, and it's the most defensible place she can find. "Come on," she says.

They run the length of the barge to the door. The hinges are rusted and the paint is all but gone, worn down by age. She reaches out and grabs the handle. The door starts to pull open—

And then slams to a halt as soon as the chain looped through the handle reaches its limit. Ciere stares down at the padlock. It's just a normal lock. She can open it.

She tosses her backpack to the floor and begins frantically digging through it. Her lock-picking kit is in there somewhere. She scrabbles through clothes, a water bottle, her mask, the canister of gasoline. In her haste, she leaves most of her possessions scattered along the floor. The clothes fall lightly, while the gasoline canister hits the metal floor and cracks wide open, sending fluid gushing over the deck. Ciere slips in it as she kneels hastily next to the pile, her hands darting through the mess. The kit, the kit—where the hell is the kit? Her heart hammers in her chest.

She can't find it.

"Ciere," Alan says urgently. She glances up at him. "There's no way off this boat, is there?"

She shakes her head. She reaches up into her hair—she always has a bobby pin stuck behind her ear to keep her blonde curls in place. As soon as she has the metal between her fingers, she falls to her knees in front of the door and jams the two hooks into the padlock.

Lock picking usually takes a certain amount of finesse and control, but her trembling hands and gasping breaths make it a matter of trial and error. She fumbles with the chain, trying to untangle it from the lock and the door handle. Rusty edges bite into her skin, but she doesn't feel it. Ablaze with adrenaline and panic, she doesn't register the pain.

Alan's hand falls on her shoulder. "Illusion me," he says.

"What?"

"You're not getting through that." Alan glances from the lock to her bloodied fingers. "This is our chance—we can't run. So we'll fight. Illusion me. Make me invisible."

His words don't make sense at first. She isn't a fighter—Kit hasn't even taught her to fire a gun. Crooks carrying deadly weapons get harsher sentences than those who don't. There's also the fact that anyone can carry a weapon; anyone can be a thug; anyone can demand a purse at gunpoint. Physical confrontations mean you're not good enough to think yourself out of a situation. Kit once said the moment you raise your hand to a mark, you've already lost the game.

She scrambles to her feet and takes a breath. She doesn't need the physical action, but it centers her.

She reaches for the illusion and feels that resistance. Her immunity is inside her and shouldn't be shared, shouldn't be seen—her mother told her that. She feels like she's being told to paint a person in her own blood—there's only so much of it, and it belongs inside her.

"Damn," she breathes. "It's not happening."

"Ciere, look at me," Alan says quickly, holding out a hand. She skitters to one side, feeling nausea roll through her stomach. All at once, it's too much. Being on this boat, the fumes of gasoline, the adrenaline and panic. She's sure she's going to either throw up or throw herself over the edge, when Alan's fingers lock around her upper arms, holding her in place.

"Look at me," he says again. "Ciere, just breathe. Your immunity—it's part of you. You can't access it if you're fighting it."

Slowly, Ciere feels some of her panic recede. A bit of her

control comes back and she grasps at it, desperately clings to it. When she opens her eyes, she realizes she's already illusioned herself into nothing. She reaches down, finds her backpack, and instinctively picks up her mask. Technically, she doesn't need it right now. There are no cameras. But she feels better wearing it—she can pretend this is just another job. Just another illusion. She slips on the mask, and Alan doesn't say a word.

She extends her hand and presses it to Alan's chest, feels the skin and ribs and muscle, and tries to envelop all of that with her illusion. Darkness. There's so much darkness here that a little more won't draw attention. She takes hold of the night and pulls it around Alan. Pressure swells in her temples, and she tries to ignore it.

With the illusion in place, Ciere casts about, trying to find anything she could use as a weapon. There's some rotting wood, a few nails, half of a collapsed crate and—there. A rusty chain loops along the deck. She scrambles to pick it up. She has no idea what Alan is doing—he's invisible, just like she is.

A hand appears—pale and long-fingered—grasping at the railing. A moment later, Aristeus heaves himself up and swings one leg over the railing.

Ciere swings the chain at his face.

It's a good blow, and it might have sent Aristeus falling back over the railing if his reactions weren't so quick. While

Ciere is invisible, she doesn't have time to vanish the chain, too. Aristeus rolls over the railing and drops onto the deck in a crouch, his gaze locked on the chain. It must look like it's floating in midair.

A grin darts across his face, and he straightens. "Illus—" he starts to say, but that's when a long piece of rotten wood slams into the back of his knees. The wood shatters, sending Aristeus crashing to the deck.

Daniel appears, pulling himself up and over the railing. He freezes, taking in the odd situation. "The hell?" he says, seeing the airborne chain.

Ciere whirls, ready to strike at the newcomer, but she hesitates. This is Daniel. He's one of her crew, part of her adopted family. They're not supposed to be on opposing sides.

"Daniel," Aristeus says. *"Defend me."*

Daniel goes rigid, his eyelids falling half-closed as he inhales. Ciere knows what he's doing; he's drawing on his immunity. While an eludere's powers are usually used for evasion, their increased intuition can serve other purposes—like knowing where a threat lurks.

Daniel twists and rushes Ciere, reaching out and grabbing the chain. He wrestles the improvised weapon from her grasp and she stumbles, her knees hitting the wooden deck.

She feels the illusion shatter.

Daniel stands over her, and in the pale light she sees his

face. She stares up into his green eyes and swallows hard. "Daniel," she whispers.

He looks wrecked, like he's been ripped apart from the inside out. He opens his mouth, as if to say something, but then he squeezes his lips shut. Something moves behind him, and Ciere's attention is drawn to Aristeus. She abruptly sees Alan standing there—he's no longer invisible, either. He's holding another piece of rotten wood, drawing it back as if to hit the man over the head. Aristeus whips around, and he rips Alan's weapon from him.

Ciere tenses, expecting Aristeus to go for the gun he took from Guntram. But Aristeus just stands there. His head is slightly tilted to one side, as if in bewilderment. He looks so out of place in the midst of this rust and decay. His suit is too pristine, the whites too bright and the colors too rich. He turns around and his gaze slides over Alan. "Finally. I was getting tired of chasing after you." He sounds like a babysitter whose charges have run away from him. He is mildly disapproving, but there is no hint of the violence he showed Guntram. Daniel falls behind Aristeus, his eyes fixed on Ciere.

Alan leans up against the barge's railing, his hands locked around the rusted metal like he needs the support. Aristeus says, "You must be Alan Fiacre."

Alan doesn't reply; Daniel makes a surprised noise.

"And... I have no idea who you are," Aristeus says, turning to Ciere. "Nice mask."

Ciere is frozen in place, her knees digging into the hard deck. Aristeus is distracted, too caught up in his triumph to care about her. She forces herself to draw on her immunity. If she can use her illusions, she might be able to get the drop on him.

She begins to gather the darkness around her and prepares to fade into nothing. "Aristeus," Daniel warns.

Aristeus's sharp gaze snaps to Ciere and she finds herself fixed by his dark eyes. *"Stop that,"* he says, and his voice takes on a new tone.

Her burgeoning illusion vanishes.

That's when the ramifications of his immunity truly sink in. He's a dominus.

She is well and truly screwed.

"An illusionist," Aristeus says. "Interesting."

Ciere tries not to look at Daniel and fails. She expects that he's already told Aristeus everything; he must have. But Daniel's lips are tightly mashed together, like he's holding something in his mouth. He shakes his head slightly, and Ciere understands that to mean that Daniel is still protecting her secrets, somehow.

Aristeus watches her. The distant sounds of fighting fade into nothing, and even the touch of the warm breeze seems to still. Her world has shrunk to the size of this barge, and at the center of it all is Aristeus's astute gaze.

"Too bad I can't see you, not with that mask on. *Show me*

who you are," he says, and that voice is coiling around Ciere's body, restricting her movements, and she cannot help it when her hands rise to her face. The words reverberate within her. She feels like she's being pulled under, like she's already fallen into the river and is fighting the current.

The words of her mother ring through her, as fresh as the day she first heard them: *Don't let anyone see what you are, understand?*

Show me who you are.

Her body struggles against itself. Her lungs hitch and her shoulders shake. Her body desperately wants to comply with his command, but doesn't know what to do. He didn't say, "Tell me who you are," so her lips remain clamped shut. How is she supposed to show him?

The balaclava hits the deck, and Ciere finds herself staring at it.

Trembling, she looks up at Aristeus. He considers her, eyes sweeping over her face as if in surprise. "God, you're young," he says.

This cannot be happening. Nobody is supposed to know who she is or what she can do. But here he is—looking at her and seeing her for what she truly is.

Don't let anyone see what you are, understand?

The world feels like it is coming apart. Every reality she has built her life upon is crumbling beneath her. Aristeus's level gaze strips it all away—every mask, every lie, every half truth.

Show me who you are, was his command.

That would be a lot easier if she knew who she was.

She is a thief. A seventeen-year-old girl. An orphan. A survivor. She is someone who has scribbled out her own identity, given herself a new name, and all but forgotten her real one.

Don't let anyone see what you are, understand? The words come to her again, spoken in her mother's voice, but they're fighting against Aristeus's command.

Show me who you are.

While Ciere struggles, Aristeus turns to face Alan. Alan stands several feet away, the railing pressed to his back. "Well," Aristeus says, "we've been looking for you for a long time."

"I was under the impression," Alan says, still looking down, "that the world thought I was dead."

"The world, yes. The upper levels of the US government, no." Aristeus takes a step back, as if he needs some distance. He rubs a hand over his mouth, and Ciere hears the scritch of day-old stubble. He hasn't shaved, and she is forcibly reminded of Carson, with his shadow of bristles.

"We knew you had to exist," Aristeus said. "Brenton Fiacre would never let it die, not with him. Too arrogant, from what I've heard."

Alan doesn't move from his spot, but Ciere sees his fingers flex convulsively, like he's grasping at something only he can see. "What are you talking about?" he says.

Aristeus steps forward. "Our sources in TATE told me about you."

A shadow passes over Alan's face. "You don't know anything about TATE."

He straightens, as if to move away from the railing, but Aristeus snaps, *"Don't move,"* in that voice of his.

Alan freezes, his gaze fixed on the deck.

"I know that some of them can be bought." Aristeus shrugs. "Members of TATE are human, just like anyone else. Some of them have their price, and for a big enough sum, they were willing to tell all sorts of stories—stories about Richelle Fiacre living in the US. And her young nephew." Aristeus lifts his chin, and something in his voice hardens. "I knew it, then. I knew what you are."

"The last Fiacre?" Alan says. He's still frozen, unable to move even from his awkward lean against the barge's railing.

Aristeus's eyes rake over Alan, as if he's searching for something. He jerks his head at Ciere. "Does she even know?" he asks. "Did you tell her what she's protecting?"

"No," Alan says, and she isn't sure if it's a denial or if he's answering Aristeus's question.

Aristeus inhales sharply. "Should I tell her or should you?"

"No," Alan says again, and there's panic in his voice.

"What?" Ciere says, unable to keep silent. "Tell me what?" She looks to Alan, but he won't meet her eyes.

It's Aristeus who speaks up. "That he memorized everything about Praevenir. That he's an *eidos*. He is the literal living formula."

Ciere blinks. The world has gone fuzzy, and her pulse is pounding in her ears, the continual *whooshwhoosh* drowning out all other sounds. Then Aristeus's words truly sink in, and the world breaks apart, re-forming into a scene she doesn't recognize.

Her first instinct is denial. She wants to protest that there is no way Alan is an eidos. He's just... Alan. Awkward and lanky with shiny black hair and a shy, quick smile. He can't be immune. He *said* he wasn't immune.

She would deny it. She wants to deny it. But... he knew his way around Kit's basement without needing a light. He remembered how to get from their body-dumping site back to Philadelphia without using a map. He identified a random painting in Kit's basement. He offered to translate Devon's Greek profanity.

He knew the meaning of Ciere's name.

"Alan?" she says. Her voice is frayed, breaking apart.

Alan finally meets her eyes.

He's trembling. It's the first time she's ever seen him truly frightened. Even when facing the prospect of the FBI or the mobsters, he didn't flinch. But now he looks like the world is threatening to burn and there's nothing he can do about it.

"Your father made you memorize the formula before he died, didn't he?" Aristeus says. "There is no way that Brenton Fiacre would have allowed his work to die with him. He had to bury it somewhere." He raises a hand to Alan, gesturing at him. "Where better than the mind of his own son?"

Alan's gaze never leaves Ciere. She sees all his fears, reads them in the whites of his eyes and the tears brimming over his eyelashes.

Ciere moves her fingers, twitching them. She tries to gesture in a way that Aristeus won't see, flicking her eyes down to her feet and then back to Alan. *Come here*, she mouths. She needs him to move, to stand behind her. She can't explain her sudden surge of terror—she only knows that Aristeus is looking at Alan the way that Kit looks at a weed in his tulip garden. Like an object to be removed.

Alan's gaze locks with hers. "Come here," she whispers. Something in Alan's face flickers, and the very air seems to shift around him.

Without word or warning, Aristeus pulls the pistol out of his belt, flicks the safety off, and shoots Alan through the chest.

37

CIERE

When Ciere was eleven, she listened to a lot of poetry.

It was in those first few months after Kit took her in. Nightmares plagued her, and she'd wake up trembling, paralyzed by fresh grief and terror. She would rise from the couch and tiptoe into Kit's room. Being a light sleeper, he'd wake the moment she touched the door. "Again?" he would say. He sat her back on the couch and went to make her a mug of warm milk. When she was ensconced in blankets and clutching her drink, Kit would pick a tome from his shelf, sit down on a rickety kitchen chair, and read aloud until Ciere drifted to sleep. He preferred reading from his books of poetry. He said the rhythm would be calming.

On one such night, Ciere tried to force her eyes to close again while Kit murmured softly to her. "Some say the world will end in fire, some say in ice."

She had no idea what he was reading—the words bled together until all that mattered was the soothing cadence of his voice. But the next few lines of the poem broke through her fog of exhaustion.

"From what I've tasted of desire," Kit murmured, "I hold with those who favor fire."

Alan doesn't cry out. Only his eyes seem to register the shock. His brows draw together in an accusatory expression, like he cannot believe that Aristeus shot him.

His back hits the railing and he tips over it, his hands scrabbling at the metal desperately. Blood is already soaking through his shirt in an ugly crimson stain. Even as he tries to hold on, a shiver goes through his whole frame. He blinks over and over, and each time it looks like it is a struggle to open his eyes. His grip slackens.

And he falls.

The sound of the river lapping at the boat swallows up any noise Alan's body might make as it slams the water. Aristeus takes several swift steps forward and peers over the side of the barge, his gun still held at the ready. He scans the river below.

Ciere doesn't move. She can't move. The boat feels unsteady beneath her, rocking in the gentle current of the Delaware. Her hands have balled into fists without her realizing. She feels like she's been gripped tight, her muscles hard and stiff. She isn't sure she could move if she tried. A buzzing has set up around her temples.

Aristeus continues to examine the river. "Not even a splash," he murmurs. "It's like he never even existed. Which is the way it has to be." He moves back from the edge and turns to look at Ciere. She flinches, expecting him to aim the gun at her. Instead, Aristeus reactivates the safety and tucks the pistol into his jacket.

"It's a more dignified end than he would've received anywhere else." He sounds regretful. "Daniel, would you go back to the cars? Gervais and the others should have subdued those criminals by now. They'll want you to help search for Carson."

Daniel doesn't move at first. He hovers in place; his gaze is fixed where Alan fell over the railing. He's shaking.

He has to pass by Ciere on his way off the barge, and Ciere scurries backward, scrambling away from him on hands and knees.

Daniel sees her shy away, and something in his eyes shatters. "Ciere," he says, and what she hears is, *I'm sorry.*

Ciere tenses; she knows that he's not working with the feds voluntarily. She felt what that Aristeus could do. If Daniel is under orders to work for Aristeus, then it's not his fault.

But that doesn't change anything.

"Me, too," she replies.

Once Daniel is gone, Aristeus walks over to her. She's still on her knees, her unsteady legs unable to support her weight.

All the fierceness is gone from Aristeus's expression; he simply looks tired. He says, "You should know that if the US government had got their hands on Fiacre, they'd have tortured the formula out of him and erased his memory with a bullet through his temple. They couldn't be allowed to have him."

This makes no sense. Ciere shakes her head in mute denial. This man is working for the feds, not against them. "You're—you're UAI," she says.

Aristeus's smile is cold. "Only because it will further help our kind. People like you and me—we're different. We don't deserve to be hunted, to be forcibly recruited into armies and organized crime. We deserve the lives we want—whatever that might be." He kneels before her. Ciere cringes back, but Aristeus is only reaching for her mask. He picks it up; it has fallen in the spilled gasoline.

He holds it out, and Ciere snatches the mask back. It's unusable now, but somehow she wants something in her hands. Something solid.

"What would you have done with Fiacre?" Aristeus says, and his voice is startlingly gentle. "Taught him how to be like you? Would you damn someone else to this life? Running, scheming, killing?

"Look at you," he says. "Wearing a mask, unable to walk around with your real face because you know they'll find you." He moves slowly, as if not to startle her, and touches one long finger to the mask in her hand. "Do you want to spend your whole life wearing one of these? As long as Fiacre was alive, our kind faced that kind of prejudice. With him gone... I don't suppose you had a lot of time to learn economics while on the run. Let me lay it out for you: It's all about supply and demand. At the moment, the supply of immune American individuals is utterly insufficient to the demands of the government. That's why they have been so... *enthusiastic* about recruitment. We stand on the brink of war with several other countries—the Pacific War was only the beginning. And America's only advantage over our many enemies is our greater number of immune agents."

"The rest of the world has immune people, too," she says.

"Yes, but not as many. Fiacre Pharmaceuticals was based in America, so we received more shipments of the vaccine than other countries." Aristeus's face remains calm, like he is a teacher imparting lessons to an unruly student. *He sounds like Kit*, Ciere thinks, struck by the familiarity of it all. He continues, "We have the numbers, and that is the only advantage the US government holds. That is why we are so valuable. And as long as we are valuable, we hold power over the government. And as long as we hold that power, I can help people like us."

"You're trying to *help* immune people?" Ciere snarls, her anger simmering to the surface. She flings an arm out at where Alan stood, where his body vanished over the side of the boat. "Well, you're doing a fantastic job."

Aristeus flinches. "Why are you even telling me this?" Ciere says raggedly. "Just kill me already."

Aristeus rises to his full height. "I'm not going to kill you." He sounds like the suggestion is repulsive. Like he hasn't just shot someone. "However, if you want a meal, a change of clothes, and a job, I'd be happy to oblige."

Ciere gapes at him. "What?"

"Well, you're caught, aren't you?" Aristeus flaps one hand in a vague gesture. "The FBI will be here in a moment, and they'll want to arrest you. I could offer an alternative."

Ciere finally understands what Aristeus is getting at and she is so startled that she laughs. "You want to recruit me? For the UAI?"

"You're an illusionist, aren't you?" he says. "We could always use someone like you."

She laughs again. "Oh, sure. Of course I'll come with you—that makes total sense."

"Of course it does," Aristeus says sharply. "Because what other choice do you have? Go on living like this?" He throws a look of contempt at her mask.

"Is that what you offered Daniel?" Ciere says.

"You know Daniel." Comprehension flickers in his eyes and he nods. "Ah. You must be part of his crew. Good—that might help you transition easier. Daniel is no longer going to be accused of aiding and abetting terrorists. I saved him from being shipped off to one of the US's offshore prisons. He won't be beaten, tortured, or starved. He's going to help me create a safe haven for our kind." He inches closer. "Don't you get it? If we're rare enough, powerful enough, the government will have to bow to our demands. If all immune people are united, the government won't be able to stand against us—no one could. Not a single nation, and not the species that abandoned us as soon as we became dangerous.

"Come with me," he says. "I promise no one will hurt you. I won't let them hurt you."

And perhaps the most terrifying part is that Aristeus sounds sincere. His face is open, beseeching. The way he said those last sentences—*no one will hurt you; I won't let them hurt you*—sounds like a plea.

When Ciere stares up at him, all she can think is that she could've turned out like Aristeus. He's young enough that he must have lived most of his life with his immunity. He must know what it's like to run, to be hungry, to burrow into a dark corner. Maybe his parents are dead; maybe he ran away when he was young; maybe a government official found him the same way Kit found her: starving and dirty. Maybe they offered him a warm place, a safe place, and maybe he grew up there. Maybe that is why he is with the UAI—because it's the only place he could fit in. Maybe he truly thinks that if the UAI is powerful enough, they can change things for the better. Maybe he truly believes that killing Alan was the only way to keep the formula out of the government's hands. Maybe he truly regrets it.

Maybe.

She could go with him now. She could leave all this behind her. She lets herself imagine the future as Aristeus does—wearing clean clothes, standing in a stark office, surrounded by feds she wouldn't fear. They'd be her coworkers.

What Aristeus is offering her is a life without fear. A life without constantly looking over her shoulder.

It's all she's ever wanted.

All the money, all the gigs, all the plotting and the crimes—it has all been about consolidating power. But this man is offering her something she could never steal: a legitimate life.

"Come with me," he says again. "Please."

But it's his earlier words that echo through her still: *Show me who you are.* It's a command she cannot ignore, and she hasn't shown him everything yet. She crouches on the deck of a long-forgotten boat, surrounded by abandoned crates and cargo, inhaling the scent of gasoline and river water. She looks down and is almost surprised to see the mask still in her hand. The wool is soggy with gas, its surface shining in the dim light. She stares down at it and thinks of everything it has been to her: a shield, a wall to hide behind, and a security blanket. Slowly, she reaches a hand into her jeans pocket. There are several things still there—Guntram's business card, a pen, and... *there.*

"You're right," she says.

When her hand reemerges, she holds a slender plastic cylinder in her hand. It's the lighter.

Ciere looks down at it. "Time to stop hiding."

Aristeus doesn't understand at first. His gaze flicks from her face to the lighter, and then to the gasoline-soaked mask in her hand. He makes a sudden noise, a sharp cry of protest.

Ciere's thumb hits the lighter and a flame springs to life, tiny and quivering.

She touches the open flame to the mask. It catches instantly, flaring with sudden brilliance, and she drops it. The mask falls directly in the path of the spilled fuel.

Everything lights up.

Brilliant reds and yellows illuminate the previously dark barge. It is amazing how fast the fire spreads, greedily following the tendrils of gas. In moments, the fire is far beyond what anyone could hope to control. Aristeus skitters back, rushing toward the dock, but the fire has already caught hold on that side of the boat; there is no escape that way.

The look he throws her is confused and betrayed. He can't understand why she would reject his way of life.

Ciere smiles at him. She doesn't move, only watches as the fire takes hold on the boat, swirling around her. Aristeus runs for the side of the boat. Without hesitation, he launches himself over the railing and vanishes into the water with a loud splash. She barely catches a glimpse of him before he is swept away, pulled downstream.

By that time, the entire ship is alight. Ciere crouches in the midst of the flames.

The world is nothing but fire and smoke and ash, and she welcomes it.

Somewhere just beyond the dock, Brandt Guntram rises shakily to his feet. He stumbles once and presses his hand to the back of his head. He is bleeding from where his skull cracked against the dock. When he looks up, his jaw drops.

The boat is on fire.

He takes several unsteady steps forward until he stands at the edge of the dock. He looks as if he is on the verge of running, as if he wants to do something, but doesn't know what. The flames have consumed the boat, swallowing it whole. The sounds of the fight have vanished completely—the agents and Conrad have probably seen the fire and gone still. As for Guntram, he stands on the docks with an expression that appears almost regretful.

Then his eyes widen.

Two figures emerge from the flames.

They leap from the boat onto the docks. They should be on fire. They should burn. Their hair should be singed, their clothes ashes, and their skin charred away.

But Ciere and Alan walk away from the fire unharmed.

Ciere's hand is clasped in Alan's, guiding him through the fire. He walks gingerly; he didn't move fast enough to avoid the shot completely. While the illusion was meant to look like Alan took the full force of the bullet, the real Alan was grazed. Blood runs down his right arm, and Ciere knows they will need to bandage it. Her body is still jumpy with adrenaline, and her legs tremble slightly with each step. Her grip on Alan is as much to anchor herself as to steady him.

Guntram gapes at them both. His head twists from side to side, and he looks as if he would love to ask a question, but has forgotten all the necessary words. She and Alan should be dead, should at the very least be burned. But they walked through the flames like they didn't exist. Guntram opens his mouth, and then closes it wordlessly.

Ciere knows exactly what he wants to ask: *How?* She

doesn't need words to explain. She simply holds out her hand, palm up.

A flame blooms out from her fingers. Just like the flames currently engulfing the ship.

It takes a second, but Guntram understands. He lets out a startled laugh, and then pauses, as if unsure whether that is the right reaction. Then he is roaring with laughter, filled with so much mirth that he forgets to stanch the bleeding, and Ciere sees fresh droplets run down his neck.

"How..." Guntram says, finally finding his voice, "how the hell did you manage this?"

Ciere looks back at the ship. Her own mouth is pulled into a smile that is all teeth. "That man," she answers. "He ordered me to show him who I was." She holds up her hand and watches as the flame licks along her palm.

She doesn't explain how Aristeus's command freed her. It shattered the mantra she's lived by since she was eleven years old. She doesn't tell him about how hiding has inhibited her immunity, about how her guilt over her mother's death has plagued her for six years. She doesn't tell him that when Aristeus commanded her to reveal who she was, he wasn't anticipating her answer. She is an illusionist.

So the fire doesn't burn her. None of these flames do.

It's just an illusion.

38

CIERE

It turns out that arriving on Kit's doorstep with a dog and Devon Lyre was nothing. Arriving on Kit's doorstep with a bleeding Alan Fiacre, Brandt Guntram, and a cheery Conrad is much, much worse. So much worse that Kit doesn't bother with the screaming and the cursing; instead, he hugs Ciere so tightly that her ribs feel permanently mashed out of shape.

Guntram and Conrad are immediately offered every hospitality Kit has to offer, but they decline. Guntram says they are off to find a hotel and regroup with their team. They'll be back tomorrow, they add, to pick up Ciere. They'll give her a night with her handler so she can pack.

When the door shuts and all eyes turn to her, Ciere reddens. She hasn't been looking forward to this. But if she doesn't speak up, Magnus and Kit look ready to tie her down and interrogate her like they did Carson. Ciere negotiates for a cup of tea in exchange for information. With the warm cup held snugly between both her palms, she stares into the dark liquid and opens her mouth to explain.

She tells them everything—the wild flight back to Philadelphia, the meeting with Brandt Guntram, the deal she made, the feds following Carson's GPS to the docks, the resulting firefight, Guntram getting knocked out by Aristeus, Ciere and Alan trying to hide on the barge, Aristeus ordering Ciere to show him who she was, Ciere using her illusions to create a double of Alan while vanishing the real boy and Aristeus shooting the double, Ciere creating a fire, Aristeus flinging himself into the water to escape the nonexistent flames, finding Conrad lurking behind a crate, being whisked away by the Syndicate's reinforcements, and driving away in the chaos that Ciere's illusionary fire created. As she speaks, Magnus grows shades paler, and a thin smile stretches across Kit's mouth.

"But how...?" Magnus flounders.

Kit picks up where he leaves off. "How did you manage to thwart Aristeus's immunity?"

Alan and Ciere glance at each other. "It's simple," Alan says with a quiet note of satisfaction. "You may have noticed I'm not entirely comfortable with eye contact. He never got into my head."

Kit laughs out loud and asks for them to continue the story.

Ciere doesn't tell them about the formula or Alan being an eidos. She also doesn't mention Aristeus's job offer. She doesn't want to tell them how, for the briefest second, she actually thought about accepting it.

To her surprise, Kit has little to say on the subject of Ciere's deal. "It's not a bad trade-off," he admits. "From what I know of the Gyr Syndicate, they'll have to follow through on Guntram's word. Accountability and all."

Magnus speaks up. "What about Alan?" he asks. "Do you plan to take him with you?"

"I kind of have to," Ciere says. "With him being my bodyguard and all."

Two incredulous stares.

"I had to explain his presence somehow," Ciere says, scowling. "So if he suddenly backs out, it's going to look a little suspicious."

Alan wrings his hands. "There's no use in my going to TATE," he says. "If Aristeus was right about there being traitors in the organization, it's not safe."

"Besides, everyone thinks Alan's dead," Ciere adds. "What's the harm in letting him go along?" She directs her next question to Kit. "Speaking of Aristeus, do you think he survived? I mean, he did jump into the middle of a fast-moving river."

Kit touches a finger to his lips. "Oh," he says quietly, "I'm sure he survived. He'll be looking for you now that you've outwitted him." He narrows his eyes. "Keep your guard up."

"Always," Ciere agrees. She turns to her left, instinctively ready to flash a grin at someone who isn't sitting there. It's then that Ciere consciously realizes that something is wrong. There is a gaping hole in their circle, and she is struck by the empty seat.

"Wait," she says, panic climbing up her throat. "Where's Devon?"

Devon is gone.

Not *dead* gone, but simply *gone* gone. Devon already had his luggage, and he and Kit simply parted ways—Kit drove back to Philadelphia with Magnus, while Devon hitched a ride to a bus stop.

Ciere calls him. He doesn't pick up, and it makes her wonder if he hasn't smashed his own phone. A few hours later, when she is lying in bed and nearly asleep, a soft beep brings her back to wakefulness. She reaches out for her phone and sees an unknown number. The text reads, *Gone to Hemsedal to see if they actually have vodka. So you're alive?*

She smiles, but she feels a pang of worry. She texts, *Fine. Lured the bad guys into a trap. Everybody's good. You okay?*

Free mini-booze on international flights. The Bloody Marys are bloody delightful.

And that is the last she hears from him.

The next day, Ciere packs for her stay with Guntram. Before running off the barge, she remembered to snag her Hello Kitty backpack. It smells like gasoline, and there is an oil stain across the cat's left ear. But the bag is still functional. Ciere goes through the contents, packing and repacking what she thinks she might need. Her hand goes still when she finds the sprig of dried lavender. She holds it in her palm for a moment; it looks incredibly fragile, like it might crumble if she squeezes too hard.

"What's that?" Alan asks.

Ciere holds the sprig out to him. He sniffs. "Lavender," he says.

She holds the sprig up carefully. "When I was a kid," she says, "I cast an illusion over this plant. I was seen and the feds got called. They wanted to recruit me. I probably would've ended up like Aristeus if I'd gone with them."

Alan's eyes widen, and he stands a little straighter. "You could've, you know. I wouldn't have blamed you. If you joined up with Aristeus, you'd . . . well, you'd be free."

Ciere frowns. "The feds killed my mother."

"I'm sorry."

"I'm not looking for sympathy or anything." She carefully wraps the lavender sprig in a sandwich bag and tucks it into the backpack. It feels different to be carrying the lavender with her now. It's less of a burden and more of a reminder. Of who she is. Of what she is. And of the woman who died to keep her free. "It's just... my whole life, my immunity felt like it drew the feds to me. It's always been this thing I couldn't get rid of, almost a liability. If I hadn't been immune, my mom might still be alive."

"Yes," says Alan, "but I wouldn't be."

It's a startling thought. That her illusions managed to protect someone instead of endangering him.

"Thanks for not telling anyone about"—Alan waves vaguely at his head—"you know."

Ciere studies him—this boy holding the Praevenir formula in his head. She can't blame him for lying to her. With his knowledge, he could create armies. He could sell the formula for a fortune. He could bring about the rebirth of Fiacre Pharmaceuticals. He could change the course of history. But he's just standing there, smiling shyly, fidgeting and leaning against her dresser.

"It'd change everything, if people knew," she says. "I think it's better if we let everyone think you're either dead or just the last Fiacre."

As if, part of her can't help but think, *that wasn't dangerous enough.*

As Ciere walks down the stairs one last time, Tulip and Liz are waiting for her. Liz has a bundle in her hands, and she gives it to Ciere with a crooked smile. "Scones," she says. "For later." Then she gives Ciere a beady stare, and adds, "Make Copperfield proud." The way she says it, the words "or else" are all but tacked on to the end.

When Ciere goes into the foyer, she sees that Guntram is waiting and conversing with Kit. The two of them are clasping hands and nodding at each other, like they've come to some agreement. Guntram catches Ciere's eye and smiles. "You ready to go?"

She picks up Tulip and squeezes him for a second before setting him down on the ground. "Don't get rid of him," she tells Kit.

"I wouldn't dare," Kit replies. "I think Lizaveta's adopted him." Then he leans forward, and his lips press against her forehead. "Call me if these thugs aren't feeding you right."

Guntram's Honda is at the curb and Magnus stands next to it, talking to a taxicab driver. His duffel bag is being loaded into the cab's trunk.

"Hey," Ciere calls, trotting over to Magnus. "You headed out, too?"

"I have a job already," Magnus says briskly. "I don't need to join your crew to find work." To her surprise, he enfolds her in a brief, tight embrace. "You be careful," he says into her ear. "Both of you," he says, louder, when they break apart. Ciere notices that Alan and Kit have come up behind her.

Magnus gets into the cab and the door swings shut.

"Hey," Kit says, and it takes a second for Ciere to realize he isn't talking to her. Magnus rolls down his window and peers out, eyebrows raised. "Take care of yourself," Kit says.

Magnus gives him an unimpressed look. "You take off again," he says, "and I'll start leaving notes at your address in Kingston." The cab pulls away from the curb and vanishes around a corner.

"What's at Kingston?" Ciere asks. She knows all of Kit's bolt-holes and houses, but she hasn't heard of this one.

Kit shakes his head. "Nothing." He pats her on the shoulder one last time before trudging back up to the house.

"You all ready to go?" Alan asks. Ciere nods.

"We need to think of an alias for you," she replies, studying him. "Something good."

"Time to get going," Guntram calls. Ciere groans softly.

"Six months with the Syndicate," she says. "You think we can hack it?"

Alan doesn't answer, but his lips curl up at the corners and his hand slips into Ciere's. "It's what we do, right?" he says, smiling faintly.

For the first time, Ciere feels like she understands Alan's

odd serenity. She's spent so long running—not from the feds but from herself. From what she is. She's spent years fighting it, trying to hide her talents, and now she's standing with a boy whose life she saved with them. They'll never be normal or lead normal lives. For better or worse, they are immune. There's no changing that. And with that knowledge, a heavy weight is gone from her shoulders.

She feels free.

39

DANIEL

Daniel is seventeen years old when he trades away his freedom.

He sits in the waiting room of a hospital. There's a cloying sweetness to the air, as if someone is trying to cover more unpleasant smells. The chairs are worn and the floor smudged. A janitor is at work emptying trash cans.

Daniel spends the hours reading old magazines and contemplating if he could steal a cup of coffee from the nurse's station. He's just about to try it when a hand falls on his shoulder. He flinches and looks up. A woman stands over him. Curly hair, pretty features. And a brilliant black eye.

"Long time no see," says Morana. She eases herself into the adjacent seat. In addition to the eye, her left arm is in a sling.

"You missed all the action," says Daniel.

Morana's face sours. "So I've heard. You guys had quite the little adventure." She waves a hand at the swinging doors. "When's Aristeus due out?"

"No idea."

"I heard what happened. You couldn't fish him out of the river?" Morana says, chewing on a thumbnail.

The thing is, Daniel could have. He's been thinking about that river for the last six hours, but not for the reasons Morana thinks.

"If I'd gone in after him," Daniel says, very quietly, "I might have died."

What he doesn't say is how tempting that sounds. He's forbidden to hurt himself, forbidden to take his own life, but if he drowned while attempting to save Aristeus—

He wouldn't betray any more people.

—No rules would be broken.

For just a second, he'd considered it. Because the look on Ciere's face had been a knife through the ribs. It reminded him of how much he still had to lose. Of how many people he could still hurt.

But in the end, he hadn't done it. The moment slipped by, and Aristeus clawed his way to shore. Daniel found him on a dock, lying on his back and gagging on a mouthful of river water and bile.

Another hour passes, with Morana reading what looks

like a celebrity rag while Daniel stares at, but doesn't really see, an article on the upcoming election.

When Aristeus finally walks out of the ER, he looks bedraggled and exhausted.

"Still alive, then," Morana says dryly. But her eyes are shining.

"For now," he replies, and Daniel is disconcerted by the fondness in Aristeus's expression. "You okay to drive?"

Morana glares down at her sling. "Just fine. I'll bring the car around." When she walks past, her fingers brush Aristeus's forehead.

Aristeus carefully sits in the chair next to Daniel. He's carrying a paper bag, and when he opens it, Daniel realizes that the hospital must have taken Aristeus's possessions when he was brought in. Aristeus upends the bag into his own lap and begins sorting through the contents. He picks up a damp tie and begins rethreading it around his neck.

Among the items are a wallet, a suit jacket, a watch, and a bright pink Hello Kitty bobblehead.

"One of the FBI agents went back to the boat for the things I left behind," Aristeus says, touching the bobblehead. "I have no idea where this came from, though."

Daniel picks it up, quickly running a hand over it. Fingerprints are easily wiped away. He knows one thief with a fondness for the animated cat. "It's mine. Must have fallen out of my pocket."

Aristeus has to know he's lying, but he doesn't argue. He tucks his wallet back into his pocket and picks up the watch, rolling up his sleeve to slip it on.

That's when Daniel sees it—a series of roman numerals inked into Aristeus's inner wrist. A tattoo identical to the one on Kit's wrist.

"We need to talk," Aristeus says.

"Thank God," Daniel replies instead. "Every girl who's ever said that to me promptly ran for the hills. I'm hoping the same will hold true here."

Aristeus's mouth twitches. "Ah. Not exactly the conversation I had in mind." He picks up the last item from the paper bag—his small tablet. He flicks it on and opens a new file. After studying it for a moment, he hands it to Daniel. On the screen is what looks like a bank account. Daniel's eyes widen. It's a very full bank account. In the name of one Bethany Burkhart.

"This is an advance on your wages," Aristeus says. "I've arranged for it to be put into an account, and when your sister turns eighteen, she'll be informed that a private benefactor has offered her a scholarship. There will be no need for her to apply for federal scholarships."

"A bribe," says Daniel.

"A transaction." Aristeus crosses his arms and leans against the chair's armrest. Daniel suspects Aristeus needs the extra support to stay upright. One doesn't almost drown and then bounce back instantly. "Here's what I'm offering you: this money and my assurance that I will not try to recruit your sister. I will also keep any other federal programs from looking into your family. In return, you work for me. You don't try to run or betray me."

"My freedom for hers," Daniel says, just for clarification. Because that's what this money would mean—freedom. If not for himself, then for someone he loves.

"You're not going to be a slave." Aristeus sounds as if he's trying to come off as indignant, but all he can manage is tired and raspy. "I told you, I don't work that way. You'll have a place to live and an office to go to. You'll have a life. Think it over."

If Daniel takes the money, he'll be a collaborator. He knows he should resist—this is the lure that will draw him into the clutches of the UAI. He won't go from being a crook to a suit-wearing fed overnight, but he's not stupid. He'll end up in an office with nice clothes and nice food and a warm bed, and after a while he'll be comfortable there. He's only human. It might take months or even years, but he'll slowly come to accept his new life.

He lets out a shuddering breath. "All right," he says. "You keep my family safe. I work for you. Under one condition, though."

Aristeus raises an eyebrow.

Daniel holds up the tablet and uses it to punctuate his words. "You don't use me against my former crew, all right? You don't ask me for information about them, and you don't send me up against them."

Aristeus hesitates. "That illusionist—that girl—"

"Is off limits," Daniel growls. "You won't ask me how to find her."

For a second, Daniel is sure Aristeus will disagree. Illusionists are too valuable to be overlooked. He'll ask, and Daniel will have to answer.

"Fine." Aristeus rises to his feet. He crumples the paper bag and tosses it into a nearby trash can. "Your family is safe. I will leave your crew alone. Now, come along. We have work to do."

"Protecting the immune and saving the world?" Daniel says, but his sarcasm sounds hollow even to his own ears.

Aristeus smiles. "Something like that."

ACKNOWLEDGMENTS

Like they say, it takes a village. Or in my case, a large city. Here we go.

Brittney Vandervelden, for not drop-kicking me out the second-story window. Padraig Maloney, for letting me bounce ideas off him at one in the morning. Nikki Krueger, for all those walks and being my first shipper. Becky Gissel, for going with me to all those superhero movies. Katie Matlack, for believing in my stories waaaay back when. Kasey Jakien, for giving me that copy of Lloyd Alexander; Roman Jakien, for going along with all that make-believe. Bob, for the pen. My grandmother, Mary, for letting me crash at her place those two months. And to other various family/friends—thanks for all the support.

My family at Gallery Bookshop. I couldn't ask for a better group of people to work with: Christie, Sally, Terry, Katy, Johanna, Jane, Joan, Thelma, Mary, Alena, and Sichelle.

My agent, Quinlan Lee, for being a constant source of support and knowledge. To Josh and Tracey at Adams Literary, thank you so much.

Editor extraordinaire, Pam Gruber, for taking this story to the next level, for both reassuring and challenging me, and for believing in this book when I was ready to throw it against a wall. Working with you has been an absolute pleasure.

The Little, Brown crew, for all their amazing behind-the-scenes work: Joel Tippie, Tracy Shaw, Andy Ball, Frieda Duggan, and Jackie Hornberger. And to those who gave this book a chance: Andrew Smith, Alvina Ling, and Megan Tingley. I'm so grateful to all of you.

My mom. For being the Lorelai to my Rory.

Which brings me around to you—yeah, you. Writers can't exist without readers. Maybe you picked this book up at random, or maybe you follow me on Twitter, or maybe you're a distant relative and wondering what I get up to, or maybe you meant to grab the book a little to the left and ended up with this instead.

Thank you all the same.